Wet

PART TWO

S. Jackson Rivera

Sandy,
"Let's get Wet!"

S. Jackson
Rivera

Loreto, MX 2023

Chapter 1

The next morning, Rhees woke early and found herself on the mat, the memory of the night before gradually coming back to her. She reached behind her uncertainly, checking to see if Paul lay next to her, the way he had the last few nights. Her hand came up empty.

She hated how it all seemed to be unfolding. Were they still friends? Were they back to being enemies? And then she realized it didn't matter anymore, since she'd be leaving.

She sat up and noticed Paul's pillow next to hers. It hadn't been there when she'd fallen asleep—alone. It made her feel a little better for a second, but the senselessness of reading anything into it hit her again. He'd sent his message loud and clear and the wound seemed to be deepening by the minute.

She wanted her apartment, her bedroom. She needed a shower, a change of clothes, a change of scenery—she needed to get away. And then there were arrangements to be made—packing, a plane ticket to buy, goodbyes to be said—a sad fluttering battered her heart.

"Where're you going?" Paul called from the office as she walked past the door.

He didn't sound gruff and that felt better, but it didn't eliminate her need to escape. She told herself it was illogical, irrational. Running away from the pain of being sent away didn't make sense, but it didn't stop her.

"Home. I need to change."

"Wait just a sec, I'll come with you."

"You don't need to. I don't want to be a bother."

He rolled his eyes at her. "I'm coming. Just let me finish this email. I don't want you walking around alone."

"Okay," she answered, but she didn't stop. Overcome with dread at the thought of being near him, the desire to put as much distance between them as possible prevailed. She just kept walking and as soon as she made it around the corner, out of view from the office window, she ran.

When Rhees walked into the apartment, Regina confronted her.

"Paul called. He is very angry at you." Regina pulled her phone from her pocket and hit a button. One second later, she said, "She just only walked in . . . Yes . . . looks fine to me . . ." Regina handed the phone to Rhees, but Rhees refused to take it. Regina gave her a look of incredulity. "He would like to talk to you!"

Rhees shook her head again and gave Regina a wide-eyed, defiant look.

Regina put the phone to her ear again. "She does not want to talk to you . . . I assure you, I do not know why! . . . All right, I will tell her . . . yes, I will. You can count on me, Paul . . . I shall see you later." She hung up and stared at Rhees. "Paul wants Tracy and I should wait and walk back with you so you do not have to walk alone."

"For crying out loud! I've walked back and forth from the shop a million times, *alone*. You don't have to wait for me."

"I will not want to disobey that man. This is Paul I am talking about."

"Fine! I may be a while." Rhees realized how much Regina loved every minute of the situation. She and Paul were on the same side, some kind of secret partnership, making her feel closer to him. It annoyed Rhees and made her want to burst the bubble. "I hope you're prepared to face *Mr. Meanie-Head* when we all show up late."

Regina squirmed.

oOo

Rhees took her time. She wasn't purposely stalling . . . well, maybe a little. Mostly, she kept thinking of *one more thing* she just had to do before she could get back to the shop. The list of all she needed to get done before she left the island weighed on her. It overwhelmed her to a breaking point and she finally just lay down on her bed and tried to shut it out.

Regina eventually grew too nervous to wait any longer. She'd battled with her options, questioning which would displease Paul the most. The thought of seeing him sooner won over waiting for Rhees to *never* get back to the shop. She grabbed Tracy for moral support and left.

Rhees heard the screen door slam and knew they were gone. It felt good to finally be alone. She'd been worried she would break out crying again, and she didn't want them to hear her. But now that she was finally alone, she felt too numb to cry.

She wanted to sleep, forget everything and possibly dream about something better than what was happening in real life. She tried to drift off, hoping for a brief escape. Seconds later, she thought she heard a noise outside on the porch.

How did he not get the point when I refused to speak to him on the phone?

She jumped out of bed and put the lock on the screen door. She listened—waiting for whoever happened to be coming up the stairs outside—no one showed up.

"Paul?" She waited for an answer. Nothing. "Tracy? Regina?" She waited again, thinking they'd changed their minds and came back for her.

Still no answer. She laughed at herself and went to the kitchen and got a drink of water. She heard the floorboards creak in the other room. She froze.

She poked her head around the wall to double-check. The lock still hung on the door—it could only mean that someone had already stole into the house before she locked it.

"Paul, calm down. Don't hurt them. It's just a prank. Everyone knows you'd beat the heck out of anyone who broke in. Paul, please don't hurt them." She hoped her bluff would scare anyone out of hiding, but no one came out of the woodwork to confess they'd come to play a joke.

She ran back into her bedroom and slammed the door. She locked it too. She glanced around the room, searching to make sure the room was safe, no one crouching in the corners. Her heart pounded. She lunged onto her bed and clawed her way to the farthest corner. She sat waiting and listening. She didn't hear anything. She looked into the bathroom. The shower—the shower curtain—anyone could be hiding behind it. She slid quietly off the bed and tiptoed to the door.

She listened for a minute before opening it, unsure whether the biggest threat was ahead, outside her room, or locked inside with her. She took a deep breath and charged from her apartment, forcing herself to take the time to lock the doors behind her when all she really wanted was to bolt.

She felt better when she reached the bottom of the stairs. The pleasant little yard soothed and helped her clear her mind of all thoughts of strangers lurking in her house. She admitted her imagination had been working overtime, but it still left her feeling jittery. She headed toward the shop.

Oceanside stood at the end of the street, a side street no one traveled unless they lived on the road. There were a few houses along the way that always gave Rhees a creepy feeling but today, as she walked past the worst ones, she felt her hair stand on end. She quickened her step.

She neared the banana tree orchard, a long stretch of the road that had always intrigued her. The orchard appeared neglected and she often wondered if it had been abandoned and why. The trees grew thick and too close together, too dark to see much past the first few rows but someone had spent a lot of money to put up an ornate, wrought iron fence.

For some reason, the owners decorated the top of the fence with broken bottles and animal skulls. She once assumed it was to keep kids from sneaking in and stealing bananas, but today, visions of Voo doo warnings came to mind. From the shadows, she imagined eyes watching her, following her, waiting for a chance to grab her and drag her into the dark.

Her heart hammered harder. She could hear it pounding in her ears. She felt hot and cold at the same time, and her stomach rolled, doing somersaults. She ran, though she already struggled for breath, as fast as she could make her legs move.

She saw the main street up ahead, saw people walking by, and she thought if she could just make it to the main street she'd be safer—if she could just get past a few more creepy houses with dim doorways.

She rounded the corner and just when she finally felt she might be safe, someone grabbed her. He threw his arms around her and picked her up off the ground, refusing to let go. Her feet dangled, removing any chance she had at gaining enough leverage to break away, so she kicked. She screamed and writhed, looking around frantically, in a panic, for anyone who might help her.

"Hey! Hey, what's wrong?" Paul pulled her to him, even closer. He'd seen her come barreling around the corner, and grabbed her when he realized she hadn't noticed him coming for her. When Tracy and Regina showed up at the shop without her, he'd taken off. He needed to make sure she was all right. The thought of her walking around alone, unprotected, gave him what he knew to be irrational anxieties, but he couldn't turn them off.

"Rhees! Hey!"

She fought him like a mad woman and he struggled not to drop her.

"Shh! It's okay, it's me."

She finally looked at who had her and moaned with

exhausted relief. With a sob, she threw her arms around his neck and circled her legs around him, throwing him off balance. He hung on to her as best as he could while he steadied himself.

"What's wrong? Did more of Mario's friends turn up?" His muscles tensed and his nerves bristled, ready for a fight.

She whimpered, shaking her head. She buried her face against his neck. He felt her trembling.

"Only in my imagination," she sobbed. She didn't let go for another minute but finally peeled herself off him and climbed down. She covered her face with both hands, shamed and humiliated, and part of him wanted to smile. She looked so cute, squirming and floundering as though she didn't think she'd ever recover her dignity. But he worried too much about what had just happened.

"I told myself the whole time that it was just my imagination. I knew it wasn't real, but . . . I was so scared!"

Paul hugged her. "Rhees. You're trembling. Let's get you to the shop."

"No!" She didn't catch herself fast enough to conceal the alarm. "I can't face everyone like this."

"Okay, let's go back to your place."

"No!" Alarm again. She couldn't get the ghost lurkers at her apartment out of her head.

"Okay." The worried look on his face grew worse with every second. "What about my place?"

She couldn't believe how patient he seemed, considering she happened to be acting like a lunatic. She nodded and out of nowhere, hug bombed him again, even tighter than before.

He picked her up and held her, and never once tried to make her let go until she was ready. When she did climb down again, she took a deep breath while he took her hand and led her toward his apartment.

oOo

"Rhees, I'm worried about you." Paul handed her a small glass of wine. "This will help calm your nerves."

"I'm all right, really. I just freaked myself out." She tried to laugh off his concern.

"I think you should see a doctor." He started thinking out loud. "But the health care system here sucks. The doctors are all quacks. You might need anxiety meds or something to help you through this, but you'd need to get stateside, or you might just wind up getting your leg amputated, or worse." He shook his head in disgust. "The horror stories I've heard—"

"So, Saturday isn't soon enough?" She didn't hide her bewilderment. "Are you in such a hurry to get rid of me? Maybe I should just leave right now?"

"Saturday?" Paul stared at her, confused.

"I'm leaving Saturday."

"Why are you leaving Saturday?" It was his turn to sound incredulous.

She rattled her head, not understanding why he acted so surprised. "Because I want you to get out of here before I do something I might have to feel bad about," she paraphrased him in a mocking tone.

He looked down. A breathy laugh came out as he shook his head.

"You've already booked your flight?" He stared at the floor.

She shook her head. "But I'll get it. Don't worry!"

She hasn't booked a flight—yet. That was good, though getting a flight off the island wasn't hard. The airline had an office on the island, but most people didn't stop in to purchase their ticket until they were on their way to the airstrip.

His brows knit together, his head spinning from her announcement. "Since when do you do anything I say?" He couldn't figure out why she suddenly decided to jump so quickly on something he said at such an emotional moment. He had to think of something.

"Saturday is a busy day for the airlines. If you wait . . . if you left on a weekday, it might be cheaper." He grasped for any way to stall her—keep her—knowing how tight she was with money. It's all he had. "Do you *really* want to go home?"

"Yes," she whispered. "You're right. It's for the best."

He exhaled hard and ran his hand through his hair. "Can you wait until next week, at least?"

She didn't look up, wouldn't look at him, but she nodded.

oOo

That Saturday, Paul counted his blessings. Instead of standing hopelessly by as Rhees boarded a plane to leave, he was able to watch her board his boat. He designated himself her dive buddy that morning, something he hadn't done since her twenty-ninth dive—the one where he could tell she finally *got* what diving was all about. That dive, he'd been able to tell she'd finally relaxed and let herself enjoy it instead of watching her gauges the whole dive—as though she was just counting the minutes—waiting for it to be over.

In his experience, it seemed to take most divers between twenty and twenty-five dives to get there and he'd started to worry she'd never really like it. But when they came up her twenty-ninth time, she'd said, "Wow! I actually liked that dive."

He'd laughed and teased her about what she'd thought about the previous twenty-seven dives—he knew why she didn't enjoy the first one.

Rhees was leaving the following Thursday. She had four more days to dive and he wanted to spend as much time with her as possible. Everyone on the boat made their entrance into the water. Paul gave the bobbing heads one last inspection, gave them all the thumbs-down signal, tipped his chin to Randy, and did his characteristic flip into the water.

He made his way to Rhees on their way down and watched as Mitch took over the supervising of the dive before taking Rhees' hand and leading her away from the other divers. He had something he wanted to show her.

She seemed confused at first about leaving the group, but he gestured for her to follow him. She shrugged and so willingly obeyed, no reservations—so trusting—it made him uneasy all of a sudden. He didn't think she should put so much faith in him. He'd never let anything happen to her—while diving—but he'd been fighting demons since he'd been spending so much time with her on the surface.

They reached the site he wanted to show her. The area was comprised of a series of rocky pillars and underwater caves—rarely visited because so many of the divers on the island were beginners and not ready for diving the enclosed environment. Rhees had just finished the bookwork for cave diving so the timing was perfect as Paul gave her a personal tour of one of his favorite sites.

The coral, the majestic formations, and the way the light penetrated the caves through small crevices scattered throughout the site, were breathtaking. He excitedly watched her face—her eyes, since it was hard to see too many facial expressions with a mask on and a regulator in your mouth—but he could tell she thought it was as beautiful as he did.

Paul expertly navigated his way through the maze and she followed. At the last tunnel, he hurried ahead and turned to wait for her to come through—he wanted to see her expression when it happened, remembering the first time it'd happened to him.

She came through, her eyes on him at first, but when she looked down, he could see her whole body tense as though she thought she was about to plummet hundreds of feet—off the edge of the steep cliff she'd just unknowingly crossed over. He laughed into his regulator as she met his gaze and put her hand over her heart to tell him how relieved she was to remember she could float.

Paul finned to her side and got close to her ear.

"Magnificent, right?" he yelled through his reg.

She nodded but then removed the reg from her mouth and exaggerated a smile to make sure he knew how much she appreciated him showing her. He chose to take it as an invitation—he removed his own regulator, slipped his hand around her neck, and kissed her before she could do anything to stop him.

They put their regulators back in their mouths and hung suspended, over the deep, gauging each other—Paul looking for her to signal he'd made a mistake—slap him or something. He smirked, thinking about how ineffective a slap underwater would be. Rhees startled and broke eye contact to look past him, pointing at something behind him.

He hesitated to turn, thinking it a ploy to get back at him. She could use the distraction to steal his mask or something, but instead, he saw wonder reflected in her eyes. He turned to see two porpoises within feet of where they hovered.

The impressive creatures played together, tossing a stick back and forth between them, like playing catch. One of the dolphins had somehow figured out how to hold the stick with his fin and he carried it around that way. Paul held Rhees' hand as they floated there watching in awe until their air supply dictated it was time to head back to the boat.

"I've never seen anything like that," Paul said after he and Rhees excitedly recounted the experience to the other divers on the boat. Everyone listened and talked about it while they removed their gear.

oOo

Monday night, Annetta sat Rhees and Paul at a table inside Fratelli's. He pulled Rhees' chair out for her and then pulled one of the other chairs around so they could sit next to each other.

The waitress wasted no time bringing Paul his standard

two beers and one for Rhees before confirming they both wanted Paul's usual. He grabbed his napkin, set it on his lap, and then casually put his arm up over the back of Rhees' chair. He took a long drink of his first beer and exhaled loudly.

"Long day?" she asked.

He frowned and nodded before he looked at her, strangely.

"What's that look for?"

He just gave a nonchalant shrug, but she continued to watch him suspiciously.

"Aren't you going to put your napkin on your lap?" he asked.

"When dinner gets here."

He licked his lips and chewed on them for a minute. "Growing up in my house, with my mother, we learned to put our napkin on our laps, right away."

"Okay . . . keep your pants on."

He gave her a sidelong glance. "My pants are and have been on . . . you're welcome."

"Um . . . thank you." She blushed and chose not to point out the night on the deck, the reason she'd be on a plane, headed home, in just three more days.

"You've never acted like it bothered you before, the napkin on the lap, the second I sit down, thing." She wanted to clarify so there were no mixed messages. She reached for her napkin, but as soon as she picked it up, she noticed one of those velvety jewelry boxes sitting under it. Her mouth dropped open while she stared at the box. A million thoughts ran through her head—but the box was too large to be a ring.

Paul grew impatient and finally grabbed it, handing it to her.

"It's a going away present." He put it in her hand and cast his eyes down, suddenly nervous, and if she wasn't mistaken, a little sad.

She lifted the lid, and inside, a dainty silver necklace with a pendant of two intertwined dolphins lay against the black velvet background. Blue gemstones framed each side of the pendant, and one large blue gemstone lay between the two dolphins. Rhees stared at it, speechless.

"I thought the dolphins looked like the ones we saw on our dive the other day," he said as he reached over and lightly touched the pendant. "I didn't have a lot of time. I called my jeweler on the mainland Saturday when we got back to the shop. I gave him some ideas of what I wanted, asked him to rush it. Mitch and Shanni picked it up for me today."

"You have a jeweler? Is that like having your own doctor? Lawyer? Accountant?" She smirked. "I've seen you wear this shark tooth necklace occasionally—" She tugged on his necklace. "—Dog tags even less often, and various watches."

Paul looked like he'd been caught and had to think of a credible response. "It's a transient island. A lot of people come and go. Some make a bigger impression than others—going away presents—you know." His voice dropped low. "Though, I usually just get a cheap bracelet."

"I take it this isn't cheap, then," she said without thinking—a reflex response because she couldn't take her eyes off the necklace. She usually didn't like the idea of him spending his money on her, but in this case, she didn't mind—she wanted his gift—she'd keep it forever.

"It's not a big deal." He sighed, obviously thinking she was about to reject the necklace. She might have—under normal circumstances. "I wanted to get you something to remind you of your time here. The dolphins—that dive—one of our last dives together. I'll never forget it."

Once again, she noticed a hint of sadness in his eyes. He glanced down at the necklace, touched it again.

"The stones are the same color as the water around the island, don't you think?"

The color of your eyes, she thought, looking at him once more to confirm it. He looked so lost.

"I love it," she whispered. She couldn't stop staring at it. "Help me put it on."

He perked up, relieved. He slipped it around her neck and clasped it into place.

"How does it look?" she asked.

He shrugged, trying to make light of his gesture. "Like a necklace."

She exhaled loudly to show what she thought of his answer. She reached back to unclasp it from her neck. When she had it, she leaned toward him to put it around his neck.

"What're you doing? I got it for you. If you don't like it—"

She shushed him. "I said I love it! I just want to see what it looks like on. There're no mirrors in here. You're going to have to model it for me."

Annetta brought their food and wine. She gave them both a strange look as she watched Rhees put the necklace on Paul. He smiled bashfully and seemed embarrassed until the waitress walked off again.

"All right, how does it look?" He fluttered his eyelashes and tried to look girly, an impossible task. Even when he made silly faces, he still looked beautiful.

Rhees looked the necklace over, focusing on it to get past the touch of sorrow trying to squeeze her breath away from the inside. She'd come to appreciate spending time with him—they'd spent so much of her time on the island together. Even during the bad times, they were together the majority of it, but now it was coming to an end.

The color of the stones—it hit her again how they matched his eyes. She had to fight to avoid letting the gloom overwhelm her—in just a few days, she would never see him again.

"I'm going to have trouble looking at this without crying. I'm going to miss you." She pretended to laugh it off and bumped herself against him, playfully. "Thank you for the necklace. You're the best boyfriend I've ever pretended to have."

Paul mumbled something inaudible before reaching behind him to take the necklace off.

"No! Don't. Leave it on."

"You've seen what it looks like."

"I know, but . . . I want you to wear it for a while. Please? Give it a chance . . . to absorb your energy. It'll make me feel closer to you when I wear it, knowing you wore it first."

Paul's eyes looked a little shiny, but he grabbed his beer and gulped it down. "I should have gotten something for you to wear . . . oh wait, here." He reached back and removed his shark tooth necklace and put it on her.

"But this already means something to you."

"It's just a shark's tooth, makes me look badass." He grinned, but showed no sign of having any significant attachment to it. "Now it will."

He looked out the window, away from her, and they didn't say anything else for a while.

oOo

Paul, true to his word, never did let her out of his sight. Rhees' panic attacks kept them from spending much time in public. She did fine during the day with all the familiar people around, including Paul, so no one knew, but the girls on the island noticed Paul hadn't been hanging around his usual watering holes. A lot of speculation circulated about where he was spending his time. No one considered he could be with Rhees, day and night after night.

He'd started out sleeping on the couch, but her recurring nightmares and night terrors brought him running to her side several times a night, holding her until she fell back to sleep.

He'd moved to the twin bed, telling her he hoped the closeness would help—he really did hope that—but it didn't. He'd also wanted to prevent a repeat of Regina finding him asleep in her apartment. At one point, that was exactly what he'd wanted—rumors—about him being with Rhees. Now it didn't matter anymore. She was leaving and all he wanted was to get her through the panic attacks.

Mitch had warned him the girls on the island were asking where he disappeared to every night, especially Regina. She'd always used more stealth in her stalking of him, but according to Mitch, she seemed to be getting more open and determined to find where he'd been spending his time. The last thing Paul wanted was to wake up and find a naked Regina next to him, so he'd been careful. So far, she and Tracy had never come home early enough to find him there again. By three o'clock in the morning, their bedtime, Rhees had already wrapped herself around him, finding restful sleep, at last.

At night, Rhees felt better with Paul there than without him. He was her nightmare repellant. In his strong arms, resting her head on his chest, listening to his steady heartbeat as fleeting images flashed through her Swiss cheese of a memory—Paul saving her from Mario. When Paul held her, she dreamed of him saving her from *everything*.

In her mind, he'd proven he'd keep his promise and, surprisingly, she felt no fear about *that*. Sleeping with a man—yes, just sleeping—it was all so foreign to her, something she'd never spent much time imagining, but Paul was strength personified—safe. He exuded power and confidence, and apparently, that was exactly what she needed, even in her sleep—especially in her sleep.

He'd started out on the couch and then tried sleeping on the twin bed in her room a couple of times, but always, the nightmares made him end up next to her. Finally, one night, she climbed into her bed, slapped the spot beside her, and told him they might as well save themselves the trouble. He'd hesitated for a minute but decided she was right.

Chapter 2

"*N*ecklace looks good on you," Shanni said in her British accent.

Paul had forgotten he still wore Rhees' necklace. "It reflects the real me, don't you think?" he asked with a smirk.

"The shark tooth is a closer fit."

"You're probably right."

"What's up? Rhees didn't like it?"

"She did. Apparently she's into Chi—wanted it to absorb my energy to take with her, or something like that."

Shanni grinned, patted him on the back, and walked away.

Paul found Rhees and slipped the necklace around her neck from behind. "All energized and ready for its owner."

She closed her fingers around the pendant and imagined she could feel him in it. "Thank you." She took his shark tooth off and handed it back. He stared at it before he put it on, actually trying to sense any vibes that might be leeching from it.

"You know," he whispered in her ear, "a girlfriend would probably give her boyfriend a kiss in exchange for a piece of jewelry . . . in case anyone's looking."

"I'm leaving. Does it really matter what anyone thinks?"

"What about what I think?"

He'd won. She took a deep breath and seemed to have to brace herself to reach up and kiss him lightly on the cheek.

"That's the kind of kiss you'd give me if I'd given you a going-away pencil."

She jerked back to study his expression, see if he was serious, but then she smiled and leaned in again, kissing him on the lips, softly—tentatively.

He grinned wickedly, snatching her up and holding her against him. He smashed his mouth against hers and slipped his tongue inside, long enough for everyone on deck to notice.

"Mm! Now that's a kiss. If you keep that up, I'm going to have to run home and jack off." He'd thought to make her laugh, but she wrenched from his hold and the look on her face made him sorry he'd said it.

Shoot! He surprised himself when the word popped into his head. *She has no clue that a guy in my situation might need . . .* He hadn't been with anyone since the night she'd called him the epitome. He chuckled and nudged her with his arm.

"I'm kidding!" he lied.

oOo

The divers on the boat readied themselves. It would be Rhees' last dives, maybe ever.

"Are you sure you want to wear that in salt water?" Shanni asked, pointing out Rhees' new necklace.

"I'm never taking it off." Rhees fingered the pendant fondly.

"You know that's worth, like . . . a thousand dollars, right?"

"Really?" Rhees almost couldn't even respond. She knew Paul well enough to believe it could be true.

"I don't know how much Paul spent. It was already paid for when Mitch and I picked it up, but my dad owned a jewelry store in India, where I grew up. I know a nice piece when I see it."

Rhees slipped her fingers around the pendant again and gently stroked the dolphins but didn't say anything.

"I'd say that's white gold or even platinum, and those gems . . ." She nodded her head, impressed. "Definitely blue diamonds. Do you know how rare blue diamonds are?"

Rhees shook her head. She took the necklace off and slipped it into the dry bag she kept under the bench. "Don't tell anyone it's here, okay? I'd be sick if it got stolen."

"I won't tell anyone."

oOo

During the surface interval, Rhees pulled Paul aside.

"You know, I would have been just as happy if you did buy me a pencil."

Paul held his poker face, but silently cussed to himself. "Oh?"

"Shanni says her dad is a jeweler in India. She can spot an expensive piece of jewelry from a mile away. She said this is worth at least a thousand dollars." Rhees put the necklace in his hand. "Paul! Why would you spend so much of your money on me? You know how much I hate—"

"I didn't pay a thousand dollars." He put his finger over her lips so she'd stop scolding him.

She didn't appear to believe him.

He flashed a big cheesy smile, grabbed her and spun her around so he was standing behind her, and then held her with his arms wrapped lightly around her shoulders. Their cheeks rested against each other. He opened his hand so she could see the necklace again.

"I swear."

Luckily, she didn't seem to catch how he'd said swear and not promise. She finally relaxed in his arms and took the necklace from his hand. She leaned into him, and he returned the gesture with a swift kiss on her temple.

"Thank you. I do love it," she whispered, reassured. He let go of her and she walked away to prepare for the next dive.

"Damn." He hated lying to her. *Note to self.* "From now on, buy jewelry from India. It's cheaper. Damn, I paid three—even in this God-forsaken, Third World country," Paul said under his breath.

oOo

Rhees and Paul grew quiet the closer it got to the time of her flight. He insisted on taking her to the airport, using the ferry to the mainland and a cab to the international airport to buy more time.

He stood in line with her at the ticket counter, handling her check-in, taking advantage of her limited Spanish, and the poor, unsuspecting attendant. Using his charming smile and twinkling eyes, he upgraded Rhees to first class at a substantial discount. Small airports such as this one didn't tend to have first-class lounges so Rhees wouldn't realize what he'd done until it was too late. Getting chastised for spending money on her was a brutal experience to endure, but it never stopped him.

He followed her up the long, circular ramp to the second floor, carrying her backpack for her. He paid her exit taxes, ignoring her complaints about it as they made their way to the security entrance. He frowned at finding no one in line, no good excuse to keep her waiting outside with him a little longer, still befuddled at how they'd ended up here. He couldn't believe she'd be on a plane soon and he'd never see her again.

He held her hands. They alternated between looking at each other and the floor, trying to keep emotions under control. Rhees tried not to cry, her poor attempts becoming a little too obvious each time she choked up but then reeled it back with a sigh and a nervous giggle. Paul didn't say much at all, less than usual.

"No use prolonging the misery. Maybe it'd be best to just get this over with." She pulled away, one hand slipping apart from his.

"Yeah, I suppose." His grip tightened on the hand he still held. She paused, mercifully, he thought. "Please email me as soon as you can."

"Okay."

"I mean it. I won't be able to relax until I know you've found a place to live, not sleeping in a cardboard box on some riverbank."

"I will. I promise. Place to live—first thing on my agenda."

"Good." He pulled her chin up and gazed at her face, giving her a chance to prepare before he kissed her softly; a sweet, innocent kiss, but his lips lingered, unable to let go. He gratefully noticed she didn't pull away or cringe, not this time, the last time. "I'm going to miss you." *You have no idea how much.*

"I'll miss you."

He leaned his forehead against hers and took a deep breath, let it out.

"I should go." She didn't want him to remember her as a blubbering mess, but she didn't know how much longer she could hold it back.

She walked backward, still holding his hand until their arms stretched as far as they could. They let go and she turned her back to him when she reached the conveyor belt to work on getting through security. She couldn't bring herself to look back again until she'd walked through the metal detector and retrieved her backpack and shoes. He hadn't moved from where she'd left him. He watched her, his cheek and mouth twitching.

She waved and stood, trying to memorize his face until the tears started to fall. He nodded. She waved once more before she staggered around the corner, plopped down in a chair in the waiting area, folded over, and sobbed. It embarrassed her to break down that way in public. She wanted to stop, knowing people probably pointed and stared at the crazy woman, but she couldn't seem to control herself.

She asked herself over and over, "What am I doing?" Not one good answer came to mind, and yet she was only an hour from walking away from everything that mattered to her. She loved the island, the diving, and especially the shop. She loved working there, hanging out there, and Claire. She loved Claire. She would miss Dobbs too, but most of all, she would miss Paul. She had nothing—no one waiting for her in Utah.

She didn't know how long she'd been crying and saw no end to the misery until she sensed someone standing in front of her, closely—too close. She was sure that some compassionate soul in the airport had finally taken pity on her, had come to console her. She wasn't ready to be consoled. She didn't believe it possible, and didn't want to waste anyone's time. She especially didn't feel like talking to a stranger, forced to put on a happy face just to make someone she was never going to see again stop worrying about her. She pretended to not notice, hoping whoever it was would go away, but she wiped her eyes, just in case. Guilt stung at her conscience for resenting the poor, misguided good Samaritan.

With clear eyes, she opened them and got a look at the feet of the person standing in front of her, a man. A man wearing jeans and brown leather flip flops—the kind Paul always wore. She looked up, afraid to hope.

Her eyes slowly rose to see the angel standing over her—a beautiful angel named Paul.

"I started thinking. I don't travel enough anymore. There're so many places I've never been—like Utah. I've never been to Utah." He sounded so casual, as if everyone just hopped on a plane at a moment's notice.

She jumped up and threw her arms around his neck, wrapping her legs around his waist. He didn't hesitate to hold her to him until the new round of tears, the ones seeing him again had caused, finally stopped.

"The guys at security are getting suspicious. Are you in the mood for a good strip search?" he joked.

She finally let go and he put her down, but he left his hands on her waist.

"What are you doing here?"

"I told you. I'm headed to Utah, going to check it out."

She noticed a small suitcase next to him and eyed him carefully.

"After you left, I stood there like an idiot, forever, thinking about how worried I was going to be until I knew you'd made it safely, and you were all established." He grinned. "I know myself well enough. It'll drive me absolutely crazy with worry. So I went downstairs and booked a seat on your flight. This way, I can see for myself you're all settled in before I come back."

"And you just happened to have a Hello Kitty suitcase."

"Oh. Yeah." He blushed. "Taye and I learned a while ago you don't just buy a one-way ticket and try to hop on a plane without luggage to give you the appearance of an honest traveler. For some reason, TSA sees that as a red flag. They totally treat you like a bomber or something." He shook his head with a silly grin.

"How long will you stay? When's your flight back?"

He shrugged and looked like he'd just been caught doing something illegal. "I bought a one-way ticket."

"One-way ticket?"

"I don't know how long it'll take to get you settled. I'll buy a return ticket when I know you're all squared away."

She wondered how long he'd really stay—if she never got squared away. Could she pull that off? She smiled at the thought.

"So, I popped into one of the little kiosks downstairs, looking for something to give me the appearance of a real tourist." He looked at his bag and seemed embarrassed. "Hello Kitty's all they had."

"And I'm sure TSA didn't think it strange at all that a grown man put an empty, Hello Kitty suitcase through screening." She giggled.

"It's not empty." He gave her a mock, *how stupid do you think I am,* look and snorted. "I bought several souvenirs to remind me of my visit to this country."

She giggled, but then she threw her arms around him again. "I can't believe you're doing this."

"Neither can I."

oOo

Rhees sat, all curled up, her feet on the chair, her knees to her chest and her arms wrapped around her legs, relaxed. She faced Paul, smiling. He slouched, sprawled out on the chair next to her, his head resting against the back of his chair and turned so he could look at her.

"I knew you'd be crying, and I knew it would break my heart to see you like that—I really, *really* hate it when you cry."

She forced a grin. "*I* kept asking myself, 'Why am I going back to Utah? There's *nothing* there for me. *Everything* is here'."

"Then why *are* you going back?"

She shrugged and whispered, "You said I should go home."

He sighed and he looked angry with himself. "I know, but . . . since when do you listen to me?"

"Do I sense you don't really want to go to Utah with me?" She raised an eyebrow, questioning his sincerity with sarcastic humor.

"Of course I do." He winked at her. "If you're set on going back—I definitely want to go with you. At least until I'm sure you're going to be all right."

"But if I don't really want to go back?" She bit her lip, afraid of how he might answer.

His eyebrows knit together and his mouth twitched a few times. "Then . . . don't."

She thought about it for a minute but leaned her head against her hand in a defeated gesture and glanced away. "It's not really a choice. If I don't leave now, I'll just have to leave later—and not *much* later. My money isn't going to last forever, and the only jobs on the island pay a dollar and eighty cents an hour, I've checked. You know Frida, that blonde girl, from Denmark? She's the one who waits on us at just about every restaurant on the island. Working four jobs won't leave me any time to be at the shop. Maybe it's best to just get it over with."

"I've been thinking about that, actually." He sat up and leaned forward. He would have to discuss the money with her eventually anyway. He'd arranged to have ten thousand dollars put into her bank account to ensure she'd have money to pay deposits, rents, utilities and other things requiring money upfront. He'd about choked on his dinner the night she'd told him she only had four hundred dollars to her name. "I need to pay you for all the work you've done."

"No, you don't. I never once expected to be paid for any of it."

"You're the hardest worker I've ever had, the most trustworthy and dependable—Rhees, I honestly don't know how I'll manage without you. You are personally responsible for the biggest boost in business that I've had so far. Even Claire can't compete with that. Not only do I owe you for what you've done, but *if you stay*, I need to start paying you—to make sure you'll stay at the shop and not get scooped away from me by the competition."

Her mouth dropped open indignantly. "I would never go to the competition!"

"I know. That's why you're worth the salary I plan to pay you." He smiled big. "In fact, I'm making it a condition." He realized how risky it was to give her an ultimatum, but she was a creepazoid magnet—including himself. He had one more concern on his agenda that needed addressing. It was best to lump it in—lumping things together often worked as a distraction tool.

"If you stay, I pay you for all you do around the shop . . . and we still go ahead with my plan to convince everyone we're together."

She blushed, embarrassed that it hadn't even occurred to her they wouldn't still spend most of their time together. She'd totally taken it for granted. As far as getting paid to do it—she loved helping out around the shop. It seemed fair, but she never expected compensation for doing what she loved, though it would solve a lot of her problems. The logistics of staying on the island had always seemed like a vicious, unappealing cycle of working someplace to earn enough money so she could stay at the shop, where she wanted to be, but she wouldn't really be staying at the shop because she'd be working so many hours someplace else. It made her head spin just thinking about it.

"Give a guy a break. You're the first girlfriend I've ever pretended to have, but you're ending it before we even had a chance. Imagine the pretend scars you're going to leave on me." He tried to sound serious and dramatic. He didn't sound like he was kidding.

"We could just pretend to have a long-distance relationship."

He smiled his private joke smile. *Money argument avoided.*

"I've heard long-distance relationships never work—"

"It's just pretend." She giggled.

"I've heard long-distance relationships never work—especially pretend ones. I'll never be able to trust my heart to another pretend relationship again. Can your conscience live with that?" He looked at her with accusing eyes. "Huh?"

"I could probably pretend to manage," she mumbled, but then seemed concerned about something. "You know we never carried out that plan."

"What's your point? The most meaningful, pretend relationships take time."

"Have you been reading Cosmopolitan?" She smiled. "You sound pretty knowledgeable about this, Mr. *Never-Been-in-a-Relationship*, pretend or otherwise."

"Oh, *please*. The Internet is *so* much more reliable."

She rested her cheek against the palm of her hand, looking at him sideways, contemplating, considering . . .

Come on . . . He held his breath. *Almost there . . . nope.* She shook her head, and he sighed, waiting for another objection.

"What about our plane tickets? What do we do about those?"

"Screw the plane tickets." His eyes squeezed shut, realizing his mistake. She'd never be able to disregard that amount of money. "*Okaay!* I'll get them refunded," he lied, taking advantage of her lack of knowledge on the matter. "They'll charge a small cancellation fee."

"Okay," she whispered, nodding.

"Really?" Paul smiled as broad as his face. "Awesome! What're we doing here then? Let's go home." He didn't understand her fleeting expression, but it vanished as fast as it emerged, leaving her to smile her beautiful smile. Her eyes sparkled as she gazed at him.

He'd won.

oOo

Paul strolled into the office and set a phone in Rhees' hand.

"I have a new policy. All staff is now required to have a phone."

"I've told you, I don't want one." She handed it back to him.

"I've told you, you need one." He tried to refuse to accept it, but she would have let it drop to the floor. He had to catch it before it did.

"I had one before I came here and I almost never used it. I had to cancel my dad's plan after he died, and when I tried to get my own, they said it wouldn't work down here unless I paid a huge chunk of money for an international plan. I decided I'd deal with it when I went back."

"And now," he reasoned, "you're staying for a while."

"Yes, and I've been here a while *already*. I've been just fine without one."

"You need a phone," Paul said slowly, and in a monotone voice. "This phone has a local plan."

"It's a small island. I can walk anywhere in fifteen

minutes. If I need to talk to someone, I can do it in person, just like I have so far."

"There've been times I've needed to talk to you but couldn't."

"Only because I didn't want to talk to you—on the phone or otherwise."

She scowled. He deadpanned.

"No one's ever needed to talk to me so desperately they couldn't just come and find me—except you—Mr. *Impatient-Pants*. And now we're always together anyway. It's an unnecessary expense."

He'd expected her to say something like that. True, he never let her out of his sight, but when he thought of the few times he had—his frustration started to rise all over again. She had a habit of running away from him and he was tired of calling Regina every time he needed to track Rhees down.

"Office policy," he mouthed. His stern expression deepened and he turned on his scary eyes to try to intimidate her into submission, but she didn't back down. He didn't really think she would.

"You don't pay for Claire's phone."

"That's because Claire is *smart*, and *reasonable*, and she understands the value of having one. So she pays for it herself, and so do Dobbs, Mitch, and Randy. Unfortunately, I can't say the same for the *rest* of the staff." He smirked—a little too pleased with himself, as Rhees was the only staff member left.

"But, *Paul* . . ." Rhees whined.

He put his hands on his hips. She would argue about it until he grew old and gray if he didn't find a way to settle the matter once and for all.

"Did you hear Mr. *Meanie-Head* and Mr. *Grumpy-Pants* got married? They adopted a baby and named him *Pissed Offerson*. They're all headed this way and if you don't stop arguing about this, I'm sure they'll have a thing or two to say about it."

"You don't fight fair." The second she laughed, he knew

he'd won.

"Of course not, I fight to win."

"Okay, you *win*." She took the phone, walked to her backpack and put it inside, making a show of burying it as deep inside as possible before she turned back to him and said, "I have a phone, now. You happy?"

She smiled sweetly and walked out of the office, without her backpack or her new phone.

Chapter 3

Paul woke in Rhees' bed. She hadn't had a single nightmare all night, but she'd still snuggled up next to him. He snuggled back, nuzzled her hair, and inhaled before he realized his mistake. He wondered how much longer he'd be able to sleep next to her and still be a gentleman, and right then, he needed a good swim. He gently slid out from under her clinch. When he slipped free, he stretched.

Oh! He tilted his head from one side to the other and listened to his neck pop. *What a horrible bed.*

He quietly tiptoed to the bathroom, self-conscious about relieving himself—after he'd emptied his bladder. The bathroom had no door, and Rhees slept three feet away, in view of the toilet. She'd freak out if she woke while he was there, taking care of business.

Please. Don't. Wake. Up.

He gave up and crept back into the room. He slipped on his jeans but he didn't bother to button the fly, giving his morning glory a chance to fade. He unlocked the door, slinked out of the room, and made his way to the kitchen. He usually bought coffee at Miranda's store, next door to the shop, but he had an agenda this morning. For the first time since he'd bought the shop, he hadn't scheduled an early dive, so he wouldn't have to be there at the crack of dawn.

He *had* still scheduled Regina to be at the shop earlier than normal—making sure to talk to her personally about actually showing up—as a personal favor—he knew he could count on her for just about anything. She agreed before he'd had a chance to mention whether she should bring Tracy or not, and he had to endure the disappointed look she gave him when he told her he needed them both. He'd made it up to her by flashing one of the smiles he'd learned worked on women, and all was forgiven. He felt guilty about using her crush for his own purposes.

He looked around the kitchen for what he needed.

oOo

Ten minutes later, Regina walked into the kitchen in her T-shirt and panties.

"Oh, no!" She jumped, shocked to find her glorious Paul in her apartment.

"Good morning." Paul took a sip of his coffee.

Regina gulped air when she remembered to breathe. Adonis couldn't possibly have looked as beautiful sitting at her kitchen table, reading a magazine, her Popular Photography magazine.

"Morning," she squeaked. She backed out of the kitchen, not taking her eyes off him until she slithered into her bedroom, slowly closed her door, and acted out having a silent fit. She ran to Tracy's bed and shook her awake. "Paul's here again, he's here. Paul's here!"

Tracy and Regina dressed in record time and stumbled into the kitchen, trying, but failing, to act nonchalant. Paul still sipped on his coffee, working hard to make his cup last, but it had cooled to almost freezing a while ago.

"Good morning ladies. If you'll excuse me, I'd better get to the shop." He rose from the table, rinsed his cup, and walked into Rhees' bedroom. He left the door open and plopped himself onto her bed, waking her up by draping his body over her and running his tongue up her face from her jaw to her temple. Rhees squealed in protest—just the reaction he'd hoped for.

"You're very cooperative this morning," he grinned cheerfully.

"What?" She dried her cheek with the sheet.

"Nothing." He chuckled and then he began tickling her while she squealed vehemently for him to stop. He continued until Tracy and Regina crept to the door to sneak a peek at what was happening. He pretended not to notice them there.

"I'm heading to the shop now." He spoke loud enough to ensure the roommates heard, but then spoke quietly to Rhees. "Stay in bed. Get some rest. Come with Tracy and Regina, so you don't have to walk alone, okay?"

"I can come now. I only need a minute."

"No!" He made sure his voice projected the desired sternness. "Stay in bed." He got up and pulled his shirt on, slipped into his flip flops and finally buttoned his jeans. He walked to the door and paused, looking back at Rhees with a mischievous grin on his face.

His voice louder this time, he said, "Don't think just because you're sleeping with the boss, it means you can be late!"

He pulled her bedroom door closed, knowing Tracy and Regina had raced back into their bedroom, trying to avoid getting caught eavesdropping. They peeked out of their room as he hung the padlock in the hook, locking Rhees in her room.

"She's going to want to kill me. Don't let her out until I've had a good head start, okay?" He gave them a wink, letting them in on his prank, but then he hesitated as if asking them a very personal favor. "I'd appreciate it if you didn't tell anyone I spent the night—you understand, right?"

With that, he ran out the door and down the stairs. Tracy and Regina squealed at the thought of Paul spending the night at their apartment again, and not on the couch this time. Being in on his game with Rhees was just icing on the cake.

"Paul! Open this door!" Rhees pounded from inside her room, not knowing he'd already left. "Paul!"

The two friends looked at each other with wide eyes and burst into Rhees' room. "What's going on? Are you and Paul really . . .?" They squealed so excitedly, it almost scared Rhees.

"Tell us everything! Everyone's been wondering, but we didn't know for sure." Tracy prepared herself to hear the greatest gossip ever.

"I cannot believe I did not know. I am sure I looked like a complete idiot with my mouth all hanging open, staring at his gentles, while the most—"

"His gen-i-tals?" Tracy corrected, biting back a laugh. "You mean his crotch?"

"Yes. Staring at the most beautiful genitals, I mean crotch, I mean—" Regina slapped her forehead at how frustrated he'd left her. "—I could do nothing but gawk as the most beautiful man in the world sat, drinking his coffee in *my* kitchen. You should have told us he was here, that you two were—" Regina suddenly stopped and thought about it. Her excitement evaporated as she realized. She'd never have a chance.

Rhees stood, dumbfounded. She just now understood what Paul was up to and it amazed and annoyed her he hadn't given her warning . . . or instructions.

"Paul and I have spent every night together since you found him on the couch . . . you know, the night you were both getting picture-perfect proof." The words already out of her mouth, she realized they wouldn't take what she said as innocently as it really was. She groaned at being sabotaged. "I'm going to kill him."

"No way!" Regina shrieked. "He has been right next door—from where I sleep—and I did not know? How did I not know this thing?"

"You guys always come home so late and sleep late. Paul and I go to bed early and get up early." The truth worked for Rhees.

"So, it's official? He got you!" Tracy swooned. Regina looked shocked.

"Got me?" Rhees' mouth dropped open. She didn't like the sound of it. "Geeminy, that sounds so . . . *flattering.*"

"Is it not true?" Regina looked smug, letting her jealously show a little.

Rhees blushed. No, not true, but she knew they believed it. She resisted the urge to set them straight.

"I guess."

"He's been here the last few nights," Tracy said thoughtfully. "Will he be here again tonight?"

Rhees wasn't sure what she was supposed to say. Paul shouldn't have left her on her own. She shrugged and went with coy.

"I dunno. You'll have to ask him." Rhees shrugged again, proud of herself for putting the ball back in Paul's court. "I need to get dressed. You heard him. He said not to be late."

Their mouths dropped with envy when she took Paul's T-shirt off, the one she'd slept in. She stuffed it into her duffle bag, and ran into the bathroom to throw on her swimming suit and pull on some shorts. She decided she wouldn't bother with a T-shirt today. Her roommates stood in her doorway, gaping at her as she slipped into her sandals.

"You guys coming to the shop, or not?"

oOo

Paul saw Rhees from out of the office window. He could tell by the look on her face, she was coming for him. He smiled, and with playful anticipation, ran out of the office to the far edge of the dock, Rhees on his heels. He laughed readily, making everyone turn to look—just what he wanted. With excited, sparkling eyes, he held his hands up and turned sideways to her in mock defense, laughing.

She tried to push him into the water, but he'd expected it, and she didn't manage to even budge him. He grabbed her around the waist and picked her up, and when she tried to wrestle him off, he turned that into a playful bout of grappling until they both laughed and wound up holding each other, smiling.

He'd changed into his trunks, shirtless, and the body contact with her deck attire felt suddenly intimate. Without thinking, he kissed her, but she snapped back with a gasp. He winced, wishing he could take it back, and didn't know how to save it, with her or all the spectators.

"You locked me in my room!" She forced the shocked look off her face and feigned a childish pout. "I'm not a child. You cannot lock me in my room."

Fully aware how everyone's eyes feasted, watching the show, he smiled gratefully at her quick thinking. He let her down, breaking contact with her warm body in hopes of getting his brain back. She pulled him to the far side of the deck so they could speak privately.

"You planted a bunch of questions in Tracy and Regina's minds, and then left me on my own to answer them." She gave him a bug-eyed look. "Are you crazy?"

He smiled again. She'd figured out how he'd ambushed her into putting their plan into action.

"What?" His expression turned playfully indignant. "Did you expect me to stick around and talk to them about the birds and the bees?"

"And you thought *I* was the better candidate to give that talk?" She arched a brow, folded her arms, and waited for him to consider what she meant.

He suddenly felt worried about something. "You do know where babies come from, right? You said you never had sex education in school—I just realized you might not—"

"Yes, Paul." She seemed offended. "My mom explained it all to me."

"My mom's a doctor—you'd be amazed how ignorant people can be." His shoulders relaxed with relief, but then his mischievous grin slowly returned. He leaned in closer and used a deeper voice than usual. "I bet she didn't demonstrate. I know I promised, but I think people learn better when there's a demonstration—it'd be purely educational. The stories I've heard about misconceptions—"

His mom had told stories of the ridiculous things she and her colleagues needed to explain to their patients over the years. He was telling the truth—but it also made for a good tease. He'd never known anyone as sexually uptight as Rhees.

"—So I know how important it is to know this stuff. I could live with a broken promise if it was for the sake of your education."

"You know, there is one part of it I've been confused about. A demonstration *would* be helpful." The look on her face expressed pure bewilderment. The look on his suddenly became much too hopeful. "Doesn't it hurt—" She paused and looked directly into his eyes.

She was serious and he grew nervous. All humor dropped from his face—he'd never been with a virgin and didn't know the answer for sure. He'd heard it hurt, but how much, for how long? What could he say?

"I mean," she continued, "when the stork drops the baby down the chimney—how does the baby not get hurt?" A slow smile grew on her face and she was giggling by the time she finished. "Do you think the soot works like padding? Or maybe it's like Santa. *He* doesn't get hurt dropping down the chimney either."

Paul rubbed his chin and watched her laugh at his expense, full of admiration for this woman. She never ceased to amaze—or confuse—the hell out of him.

She rolled her eyes. "Next time you come up with a plan to get this pretend romance rolling, could you please give me a heads up?" He'd lowered his defenses and Rhees gave him another push, managing to knock him off the deck. He gave her a touché wink before plunging into the water.

Her hands flew to her mouth, shocked it'd worked. She stood frozen as satisfied surprise turned to horror . . . Paul swam toward the ladder faster than she thought humanly possible, sporting a, *you're going to be so sorry,* look. She screamed and ran toward the office, wondering why everyone just stood around, too stunned at the unusual familiarity between them to move out of her way.

She screamed again and shuddered giddily when she made it into the office and grabbed Claire, positioning her like a shield. Paul had unbelievably made it out of the water in record time and dogged her heels until she flew through the office door. He reached in after her, barely missed grabbing her arm, but he stopped short of following her inside. He didn't want to risk the water dripping from his sizeable frame, flying all over the office, damaging the computers or the paperwork.

She covered her mouth with her hands again and watched him, concerned about what he might do next.

"You're safe . . . for *now.*" He exaggerated his wink. "But I plan to take it out on you, *later.*" He bit his bottom lip and grinned salaciously before turning back toward the deck. Everyone stood watching, faces curious. "No one has anything better to do than stand around? We have a boat to load."

Claire turned to Rhees, aghast. "Are you—did you—are you and Paul?"

The humor of the situation evaporated immediately. Leading everyone on, in general, didn't seem so hard, but this was Claire. Rhees couldn't bring herself to lie. She shook her head, shamefacedly.

"Thank God! I knew you were smarter than that, but you had me worried for a second."

Chapter 4

"Rhees?" Paul stopped at the little window of her bedroom that faced the porch. He'd walked her home and left her to get ready for the deck party later that night while he ran back to his place to shower. "Are you decent?"

"I'm dressed. You can come in." He heard her unlock her bedroom door and reach over to take the lock off the screen door. He followed her inside and stopped to watch her. She reached for her shoes, the bronze sandals, but seemed preoccupied and didn't look up at him.

The brown dress didn't survive the Rohpynol, and he missed it. He'd asked his laundry lady to try, but the vomit stains wouldn't come out—no dry cleaners on the island. The sadness of the loss didn't last long though as he watched Rhees from the doorway.

She wore his second favorite outfit, the orange floral shirt and white shorts always looked great on her. He thought about it—everything she wore looked great on her. She had a unique sense of style, classic, crisp, clean . . . modest—he leaned against the doorjamb and admired the view as she put her foot up on the chair to fasten the strap on her sandal. She did the same on the other foot.

"Mm." He grunted to show his appreciation. "You look *very nice*. But I can't believe you're already dressed. I thought there was some universal rule. Girls are required to take hours getting ready." He thought of all the hours of his life he'd never get back, waiting for girls to get ready just to go out. It annoyed him. He just wanted to eat or go get a drink. In most cases, he'd already *had* them. He didn't care what they looked like anymore.

"It's easy to be fast here," she said. "I hate cold showers—no lingering there. I get clean. I get out. I don't have a hair dryer—so drip dry." She pointed to her still damp hair. "Also—no curling iron—this is as good as it gets. And even if I tried on everything I have, looking for the perfect outfit, it would take me all of one minute."

"If you miss them, why didn't you bring a curling iron and more clothes?"

"Kind of the same reason I don't have pajamas." She laughed.

"You wore panties and a sports bra to bed before I gave you some of my T-shirts." He snorted, remembering the first night they'd slept in her apartment after the Mario incident. He'd raced to her side during one of her nightmares, and when he climbed onto her bed to calm her, he'd found her sleeping in her clothes because she didn't want him to find her in her usual night attire.

"You packed minimalistic to meet the airline's weight limit."

"Exactly. My gear alone weighed thirty-four pounds. I had to make some sacrifices. No pajamas, bare minimum clothes, and no hair dryer or curling iron."

"You could have paid for an extra bag."

"Pfft. Fifty dollars? The sacrifices haven't been *that* bad." Her incredulous expression turned to disappointment. "Except in times like these."

She put her hands up, as if showcasing herself, but surrendering at the same time.

"Mm." He grunted again.

"Thanks," she said with a giggle. She finally got a look at *him*. He wore dark blue jeans—he always wore jeans in the evenings—a contrast after seeing him all day, every day in nothing but swim trunks or board shorts. Always the same fit, his Levis varied from faded with ripped knees, to brand new dark blue or black, but they always looked a little too good on him.

His slate blue button up shirt with collar was a soft, shiny, fabric. He'd rolled the sleeves up, as usual. His shirttails hung out, untucked—he never tucked his shirttails, but it suited him, accentuating the long outline of his form from his broad shoulders to his slim hips. He looked nice, almost dressed up, but still casual enough for the island. Rhees actually stared for a few seconds. He looked so good, she felt underdressed and out of his league.

"What time is it?" She wanted time to find something better to wear, but then she surrendered to the lost cause. She had nothing better since her brown dress had given up the ghost. She frowned.

"We have time." He walked into her bedroom and lounged on the twin bed. "Rhees? What's wrong?"

"I need new clothes." She shook her head. With the exception of a few shops that carried souvenir T-shirts, there were no clothing stores on the island. "I packed for three weeks. I've been wearing the same few things for months. Not only is my wardrobe lacking variety, things are wearing out."

"Did you hear me when I told you how nice you look? I could have easily said you look beautiful—I should have. It'd be more accurate."

"It's just . . . no one is going to believe we're really together." She sat on the edge of her bed.

"Don't say that." He sat up. "If anyone has trouble believing it, it'll be because they know you're too good to wind up with me."

"So, I know tonight's the night, but you haven't filled me in on how we're going to let everyone know we're . . . supposedly, together. I hope you're not planning to bushwhack me again, like you did with my roommates."

"Bushwhack?" He chuckled. "I was thinking more along the lines of just doing what comes naturally."

"Not instilling a lot of confidence in me—your natural or mine?" She cocked her head to the side and bugged her eyes at him. "Because my natural means we're staying home and eating quesadillas. Your natural means we have an appointment with Frock?" She shuddered at the idea.

"No Frock," he grimaced. He wanted her—*really* wanted her—and he wasn't used to not getting what—*who*—he wanted. The irony of the whole thing would have made him laugh if it wasn't so damned frustrating. His ability to win anyone else was the very reason he couldn't have her. So he'd taken a page from her book and set his own goal to get his life under control, if possible . . . so far, so good.

"You're right. Sorry." His face twisted up in thought. "First off, I should drink. People expect it." He hadn't been drinking his usual amount since the night he kissed her in her bedroom. He wanted to be careful, to ensure nothing like that happened again. He needed to stay clear to keep on track with his new goal.

"Then, when the sharks start to circle—" It embarrassed him to admit aloud how he knew the girls would compete for his attention, but they would. "—I'll look your way and pay no attention to any of them, at all. I'll only have eyes for you."

Rhees made a skeptical face, probably not meant for him to see, but he did.

She doesn't believe that's possible, he thought. He'd let the way he'd said he'd only have eyes for her, sound like a joke, but—Shelli knew it was true, several other girls too. They'd said as much. They wished he would just have Rhees so he could finally move on. In the back of his mind, he never allowed himself to dwell on the thought too long. He'd begun to enjoy *not moving on.*

"And at some point in the night, I just need to do what I usually do, make my move. We're talking blatant, over-the-top, gross, non-disputable PDA—typical Paul style, and then I'll drag you off with me, leaving everyone to gossip about what they're sure will happen when I get you home." He watched her eyes, waiting for her reaction, suspecting she'd be uncomfortable.

Right on cue, she grew anxious, wringing her hands, practically trembling, on the verge of hyperventilating. She jumped up and walked to the far corner of the room. He stood too and grabbed her, putting a stop to her pacing.

"Rhees." He kept his voice low and comforting, the tone he used during the night to calm her down when she woke crying and thrashing in the bed. "Tell me what's wrong. Please?"

"Paul." She scrunched her eyes closed and made a pained face. "There's something wrong with me. I get nervous . . . uptight—scared even—with intimacy . . . I freak out!"

"No shit!" He chuckled. He'd hoped for an explanation as to why, not an admission of what he already knew.

She just stared, shamefaced, not saying a word.

"Yeah! It's kind of hard to miss . . ." He watched her for a second then glanced down, bashfully. "But it's nice to hear it isn't just me."

"If you already know the way I am, what makes you think we can pull off what you've planned? It's not going to convince anyone if I panic and start screaming at you to get away from me." The volume of her voice steadily increased.

He pulled her chin up with his finger and tilted his head, studying her.

"Then don't."

"I can't. Help. It."

He stepped closer, reached for her hands and held them. "I know. But you're letting me touch you now."

"You can't tell how fast my heart is beating."

"You kissed me at Ray's, and it seemed quite convincing to me."

"I was just pretending to be grown up. I was making a point. You're the one who turned it into . . . *convincing.*"

"I wake up every morning with you *all* draped around me like your life depends on being close."

"I'm not conscious when I do that!" Her answers amused him.

"Don't you see?" Her voice raised a couple of octaves. "This isn't going to work! No one will believe you could possibly be happy with a frigid, uptight freak like me."

"I don't care what anyone thinks."

She took a step back, tried to put some space between them, but he stepped closer again.

"Paul! The point of this whole idea has everything to do with what everyone thinks."

"Oh, yeah." He pretended to scowl as if his plan had just collapsed. He feigned concern, but his eyes twinkled with mischief. "What shall we do?"

It was her turn to smirk. "You tell me, smarty pants. You obviously have an idea, or you wouldn't look so smug."

"I think we should *practice*." He drawled his sometimes accent on the last word and put his hand over her butt, pulling her sharply against him. He leaned to within an inch of her face and studied her, waiting to see what she'd do.

She tried to brave through it, closed her eyes. He squeezed, wrapped his other arm around her waist and stroked her back. She fidgeted for a second before she twisted sideways to him, as much as his strong hold allowed. He didn't allow her to turn too far. Using her elbows, her forearms braced along his chest, she set her hands firmly on his shoulders to maintain some space, unwilling or unable to look him in the eye.

"See? You can do this."

She stopped pressing away from him to laugh. "Yeah, looks like I can't keep my hands off you, I'm *wilting*, right in your arms."

"That reminds me—I have a questionnaire I need you to fill out."

They both laughed for a second, but as the merriment subsided, without thinking, one of his hands reached up and he tucked a strand of hair behind her ear before he leaned down and brushed her lips with his. She tensed and tried to duck away but seemed to regret it immediately.

"Sorry, reflex."

"Relax. Look at me." She finally met his gaze and he felt her ease in his arms, but the concern lingered in her eyes. "Remember your first dive? You practically tackled me on the shelf. I thought you were going to jump my bones, right there."

Her eyes grew wide, full of disbelief at his audacity. He used the distraction to bring her in even closer. ". . . And as we ascended, you clung to me so close—you couldn't keep your hands off me. Can't talk underwater . . . or I would've said, 'Rhees, not now, I'm too busy saving your life'!"

She didn't seem to notice how intimately he played with her backside. She just gaped at him, her mouth opening and closing again, several times before she finally found her tongue.

"It wasn't like that and you know it. I was more afraid of dying than getting ra—" She cut herself off abruptly and looked down.

"Than getting what?" he asked quietly.

She shook her head, refusing to look at him again. He made a thoughtful face and moved along.

"Rhees, I'm holding you *very* close . . . taking liberties with your ass. *He's* getting all hopeful and excited, but you haven't flinched. You're not tense, writhing, or screaming. You've even stopped pushing me away. Why is that?"

"I don't know. You—you're flustrating me." She shook her head again, still looking down.

"Flustrating." He narrowed his eyes to think before one of the corners of his mouth twitched up. "Let me guess. Flustered and frustrated. I like how you do that."

He gently weaved his fingers into her hair and pulled just enough to bring her face up to look at him so she couldn't get away. He kiss-bombed her mouth. His tongue pushed its way inside, eagerly. He continued mauling her mouth until she gagged. He threw his head back and laughed.

"What the crap was that?" She glared at him indignantly.

"*Practice.*" He tried to stop laughing, but it took him

a second. "You didn't push me away or crawl out of your skin."

Again, her mouth hung open, appalled.

"You did gag . . ." He feigned serious contemplation with a slow-forming grin. "But that may have had more to do with my germs than whatever it is you have going on about being touched. Did you gag because of my germs? Or something else?"

"You're not funny," she snapped. "None of this is funny."

"If you're having second thoughts—have you changed your mind?"

"No." She'd been a mess since the Mario incident. Panic attacks, anxiety, nightmares, paranoia. She couldn't be alone for very long without driving herself into a hysterical frenzy, but Paul was always there for her, always able to help her through it. He'd become her anchor.

"No, you haven't changed your mind, or no, you don't want to do this anymore?"

She shook her head, confused. "I haven't changed my mind, but you're—"

"Rhees, you're tough as nails. You can do this." He didn't seem to be going for the laugh anymore.

"You always say that, but I don't feel so tough."

"You *can* do this because you're—*we're* making a point, we're pretending, try not to be so conscious of everything all the time, and maybe think about how much worse it'll be if we don't pull this off." He used every one of her excuses. He still had a hold of her and she still didn't notice or mind. "You won't be alone. I'm in this too."

He tightened his hold around her waist and leaned in for another kiss, but she tensed, her hands squeezed his arms where she'd placed them, giving a push while she turned her head. He breathed a heavy sigh of defeat.

"See!" she cried when she realized what she'd done.

"Okay, plan B. We get you drunk."

"I don't like to drink. It tastes nasty and the last time,"

it made me sick."

"Don't drink because it tastes good. Drink to *relax*. And yeah, the last time, you overdid it. You really shouldn't have inhaled my drink the way you did. I'm talking drunk, not wasted. Do you remember what happened after the dance contest?" She shook her head, embarrassed about being too drunk to remember.

"I scraped you up off the dance floor and brought you home." He watched her carefully as he shared the information. "You were *awl* over me."

"I was not!"

"Oh, yeah. You *wawnted* me—jumping into my arms, hugging me, hanging on me—of course, you couldn't really walk . . . so maybe I read a little too much into that." A serious crease formed between his eyebrows. "But *awl* that kissing. Well, in retrospect, I might have been the one initiating the kissing, so . . . "

There were so many holes in her memory of that night, she couldn't be sure if he was teasing or not. In spite of the shock of hearing about it for the first time, she fought to suppress a smile . . . a laugh. She'd never seen this side of him, keyed up, energetic, animated even, funny and so cute.

His tone suddenly changed to sound almost fatherly. "I am *nawt* going to stand here and argue who was all over whom."

That tipped the scales and she covered her mouth with her knuckles to hide her smile.

"I was quite the gentleman. Well, *mostly*—but my point is, you didn't wither, cringe, or crawl out of your skin that night. Not once." He squinted, and his mouth twitched while he watched her process the information. An apparent afterthought made him grin and a look of awe entered his eyes along with a hint of mischief.

"Your breasts are real by the way," he said with complete seriousness.

"Of course they are," she huffed. "Why would someone

like me want to draw *that* sort of attention to myself?" Horror crossed her face again as she realized. "How do *you* know?"

"No scars."

"That's not what I meant and you know it. How would you know I don't have scars?"

"I couldn't let you sleep in that pretty dress." He seemed to get a kick out of the stupefied look on her face. "After very prudently removing said dress, I asked where your pajamas were. You told me you didn't have any on the island; that you slept in a bra and panties. I mentioned that didn't sound comfortable, and you launched into an explanation of how your mother had warned you, girls who are endowed as well as you and her needed to wear a bra to bed or your 'boobs' would hang down to your belly button by the time you were thirty." He couldn't fight his smirk anymore.

"So I left your bra on, but when I sat on the edge of your bed to reset your alarm clock—I figured you'd appreciate a little extra time to sleep it off—I saw your sports bra hanging in the bathroom. It looked like you'd washed it and left it there to dry. I thought it looked more comfortable than the underwire bra you were wearing at the time." He paused. "So I changed it for you and got you into bed."

He watched, waiting for what he knew was coming. She turned pale but stared at him with absolute incredulity.

"Oh, sure! You look at me like that now, but you thanked me that night, said I was very *helpful*. You told me you were surprised I could be so nice. I can be nice . . . if I want to."

She stood frozen, like a wax museum statue, just staring at him.

"I swear, I didn't even look," he insisted innocently, snapping her out of it.

"Liar! You looked for scars!"

"Oops. Okay, I looked . . . a little, but I didn't see anything." He held his hands up in mock surrender, loving the look on her face. "Nothing I haven't seen before, except the. Most awesome. Beautiful. *Real* breasts I've e-ver seen in *my life*. And in my defense, I didn't know you were keeping them private at that point. Okay, since you won't let it go, I admit it. Maybe it *was* a little revenge thing . . . for lying to me, because I still thought you lied to me at that point. If I had to do it again, now that I know you didn't lie, I would never have taken that revenge look—it was just a revenge *glimpse*, really. But now, knowing you didn't lie, it would have totally been all about lust—I would have *so* taken a lust look, totally. So aren't you glad I thought you lied to me?"

She covered her face with her hands in utter embarrassment, and he laughed again.

"I was drunk," he exclaimed. "But you were even drunker than I was." He closed his eyes, but then opened one of them, looking at her warily. "Want me to shut up now?"

She giggled, too amused by his performance to be angry. "Case in point. You said you have to drink tonight because everyone expects it. If I'm drinking too—"

"Oh please. I can look like I'm drinking everyone under the table." He let go of her and leaned against the small desk attached to the wall, next to the bathroom. "I've worked very hard for years to reach this level of alcohol tolerance. I only get sloppy drunk if I mean to. Trust me."

She nodded. She did trust him. She trusted him more before he'd confessed to his unappreciated peep show. He'd meant trusting him to know his alcohol tolerance, but he didn't have to stop the night on the deck, the night she'd asked him to deflower her and he . . . didn't. She trusted him with more.

"And in spite of your incapacitation, you handled yourself, and me, cussed me out, slapped me around." He snickered. "You're tough as nails, you know that, right?" She rolled her eyes.

"I've never known anyone like you, you're so sweet and nice, and vulnerable—defenseless almost, as if you couldn't hurt a fly, but man, push you into a corner, you come out slugging. And girl, you pack one hell of a punch!"

"My mom used to say something like that." She half smiled. He took her hands in his.

"I know I've been kidding around about all this stuff, but I wanted to cheer you up, make you laugh, because Rhees, I *know* tonight is going to tax your limits and you're worried, scared, but we make a good team. You didn't die at the bottom of the ocean. And you breathed new life into my dive shop with your new marketing strategies. You called me the epitome of everything you don't want, which really hurt until I realized it was true, and I didn't want to be the epitome anymore. And the night that creepazoid— we've been through some pretty taxing situations, but we made it through, together. I'll help you through this. *We* can get through this night, together."

She opened her mouth to say something, but he pulled her close again and put his finger to her lips.

"But just to tip the odds in our favor, I have a present." He walked out to the porch where he'd left a bottle of wine and two glasses. He carried it back in and proceeded to open the bottle. He winked at her, first a half wink with his right eye, and then a full on wink with his left.

"Let's get you drunk, not wasted, just relaxed. This will get us started, anyway."

"Paul? Are you sure you want to do this? You're giving up so much."

He stared at her. Her eyes, her beautiful, honey brown eyes, shined. He turned his attention back to the bottle and concentrated on opening and pouring the wine. He had to clear his throat before he could answer.

"I'm not giving up anything I care about."

Chapter 5

Paul and Rhees showed up at the shop together but were separated as soon as people started to arrive, demanding Paul's attention to get the party underway.

"Have a drink," he said, pointing to a cooler. He turned to follow Mitch and Eddie, off to help carry tables to the deck.

She grabbed a beer. She could finally tolerate those after spending time with Paul. She pulled a chair over to her favorite spot on the edge of the deck while she waited for things to get started. She found it fascinating, and lost track of time watching people show up and transform from socially awkward sober to loud, life of the party a few drinks later.

The deck party had been dubbed in honor of Peder and Assif, who planned to leave the dive shop and the island. They'd heard the next diving destination calling to their vagabond souls and decided to heed the call and move on. Also, the shop's most recent guests, a group of college students who'd rewarded themselves for their recent graduation by coming to Paradise Divers, would be leaving the next morning.

Claire and Dobbs rarely attended deck parties, but showed up shortly after nine. Rhees heard them tell Mitch about the electricity outage on the rest of the island, a common occurrence. The outage interrupted the movie they were watching at home. They didn't want to go to bed early, and thanks to Paul's investment in solar panels at the shop, they decided to join the party for a change, instead of sitting at home in a dark apartment.

Paul drank as he circulated through the crowd, joking and talking. He seemed so relaxed and happy, though Rhees knew he'd prefer a quieter setting. Shy at heart, he did great in social settings, so few people ever figured out his true nature. Rhees happened to be one of the few. His eyes sparkled when he smiled and carried on conversations with everyone he talked to. She thought of her initial impression of him. She liked this Paul better, so much better.

Rhees enjoyed watching Paul through the night but, as expected, several other girls couldn't take their eyes—and sometimes their hands—off of him. She couldn't help but notice how many girls *hovered*, as he had once described. True to his word, he gave no hint of interest in any of them.

Eventually, most of the snubbed girls turned their icy glances to Rhees after realizing how often Paul looked over to watch her. Then there were the few diehards, who just refused to take the hint. Especially a girl named Nicole, one of the guests. She followed him around, flaunted her skimpy outfit in his face, and touched him as often as possible.

Rhees forgot she was supposed to be working on her buzz. The wine and the beer had given her a good start, but her high had faded a bit from neglect. She'd been too interested in her study of human behavior.

Christian finally showed up and Paul seemed excited to see him. He made his way over to greet him, with Nicole still on his heels. The two men engaged in what appeared to be a lively discussion with a lot of hand and body gestures. Nicole tried to participate, never taking her eyes off Paul.

Rhees watched, enjoying how expressive Paul's face could get when he got excited. Once again, he reminded her of a little boy. Her mother used to say all men were little boys. She'd never understood until she met Paul.

Every now and then, he'd have a quick look her direction and smile warmly, with glistening eyes, before turning back to Christian. It did warm her, made her stomach flutter. It felt good, but scary at the same time. She cursed herself, but refused to ask herself why.

She looked away to clear her mind. When she looked back, her heart sank, and it felt like her lungs closed off. Paul held Nicole in his arms as they drifted gracefully across the dance floor together. Her face beamed, never looking away from his as he whirled her around.

Rhees should have known. The real Paul danced before her eyes with another woman. She'd fooled herself again. She'd been a fool her whole life, refusing to face reality, living in fear of her own shadow, life itself. She laughed, no surprise there, so why was she surprised? And why did she feel the need to cry? She'd known all along their little ruse wouldn't last long. It wasn't in his nature. He'd told her as much.

She took a deep breath and wanted nothing more than to just get the night over with, follow through with the plan—make everyone believe that Paul had won. It stung her pride, but that was exactly what she needed.

Yes, she'd never pretended to imagine their fake relationship would last long. It only needed to last long enough to help her appear to be a real grown-up. Once they established that, she needed Paul's help to at least get the sleaziest creeps off her scent, it wouldn't matter anymore what he did.

If she didn't believe so strongly in the plan, she'd go home right then—but it was dark now, and it was a long walk back. She actually began to tremble as she remembered the neglected banana plantation and all the dark, shadowy corners along the way. *Oh, my gosh. I'm never going to be a real grown-up.* She looked for Paul again, her safe harbor. It'd become a reflex. He was still dancing with Nicole.

"He's already changed his mind," she whispered, as the light of understanding hit her.

He didn't want to go home with her and do . . . *nothing*. He wanted Nicole. She obviously had sights on him, hoping to do more than just nothing. He'd forgotten all about their plan. *All about me.*

She shoved up from her chair and headed toward the temporary bar, needing help.

"What are you having, Rhees? Coke Light?" Eddie took his turn that night as the designated bartender for the party.

"No. I need a real drink."

"What do you need?"

"I don't know. I had tequila and beer at the dance contest, and bourbon. That worked." Getting wasted sounded pretty good, after all.

"Um . . ." Eddie looked at her skeptically.

"She wants a gin and tonic, extra lime, make it a double. Triple the lime." Paul slipped in behind her, set his hands on her waist, and whispered in her ear, "They don't taste too bad. Ta-kill-ya's not a good idea tonight."

"Ta-kill-ya?" She looked up and behind at him, surprised, not only because she didn't understand what he'd said, but that, out of the blue, he stood behind her, touching her.

"Tequila. Remember what it did to you last time? We want you relaxed, not plastered." He still hadn't let go of her waist, but turned back to Eddie. "Give me another bourbon, the secret bottle behind the cooler, two fingers."

Rhees took her drink back to her spot, leaving Paul at the bar waiting for his. He met her at the chair in the darkest corner of the deck before she sat down, and he looked back at the party to see what she'd been seeing all night from her vantage point.

"You can see almost everything from here."

He didn't understand the dirty look she gave him.

"How're you holding up?"

"Fine!" she snipped.

"Are you having second thoughts? I need to know." He

eyed her, trying to figure out what brought on the sudden bad mood.

"No. I'm ready to get this over with. I know *you're* ready to be done with it too."

"What the fuc—" He reeled in his too-quick temper, not wanting to be irritated with her tonight. "What does that mean?"

"You're going to make me say it? I saw you dancing with Nicole. You're stuck with me when you'd have more fun going home with her."

He eyeballed her, suddenly very interested. He tilted his head.

"Are you jealous?"

"No," she gaped. She did absurd quite convincingly.

"Take a drink of your G and T—a big one." He tightened his lips so they couldn't break into a grin, but his eyes gave him away. They too often did.

"Why?"

"Because you need to chill out. The stress of all this is getting to you, more than I realized."

She took a gulp, cringed when she swallowed. "I thought you said these tasted good."

"I didn't say it would taste good. I said they don't taste too bad." He watched her with his lopsided grin. "Take another drink."

She let out a breath, closed her eyes, and gulped down another big swallow and then another. They both watched each other as they continued to take drinks from their plastic cups.

"Okay, now tell me why you think I'd rather go home with Nicole?"

"No."

He shook his head and gestured for her to take yet another drink. She did. He licked his lips and pressed them together in a thin line before running through several more of his facial motions.

"You're a very oral guy, did you know that?"

He worried, sure she'd changed her mind.

"You're always doing things with your mouth. It's like a nervous tick or something. Are you even aware you're doing it?"

"It's been pointed out to me once or twice." He relaxed. He thought she'd meant something entirely different. Only four people besides his family had ever noticed his nervous habit. His brow furrowed. "But no, I don't usually realize I'm doing it."

"You use your tongue a lot too. Are you aware of that?"

"Yeah, I know." Now she was closer to what he thought she meant the first time.

Her brooding made him grin, wondering where she was going with this, and thinking the alcohol must already be working. She never finished explaining what she meant by bringing up Nicole, but he didn't want to remind her at the moment, just in case she hadn't cooled off yet. He'd learned long ago, addressing one woman's accusations about another rarely ended well.

"It might help . . . when you kiss me, if you'd not assault me with your tongue, right off the bat."

"Assault you." His eyes widened. He waited, amused.

"Yeah, it's a little shocking. Maybe if you'd start out with your mouth closed. You know, just a soft, chaste kiss . . . but lingering, and then work up to a little open mouth, for a bit. And when you do finally—maybe just introduce your tongue first. You know, like knock on the door for a second, don't just barge in."

"Are *you* giving *me* kissing lessons?" He bit his lip, not sure if he should laugh or be embarrassed.

She took another big drink. She shrugged. "I don't know how all the *other* girls like it, but I guess I am telling you how *I* would like it to be done."

They stared at each other again, his tick doing its thing, but then he put his arm around the small of her back and pulled her to him somewhat forcefully.

She tensed. "And another thing, do you have to always surprise bomb me with your moves? I don't do physical contact well, especially by surprise. I need a second to prepare myself for it." He pursed his lips into a frown. He let out a loud breath.

"I'd like to put my arm around you now. Is that okay with you?"

She closed her eyes, but grinned and nodded. He reenacted what he'd just done previously, only in slow motion. She smiled, big and genuinely, blushed a little.

"May I?" His eyebrows flashed up, questioning as he drew closer, and it became clear he intended to kiss her. She didn't answer, but let him, very carefully, position his mouth gently on hers, chastely. He lingered for a second and then gently caressed her lips with his. She didn't tense up. Instead, she put her free hand on the back of his neck.

"Mmm. . ." he moaned, and put the arm with the drink in his hand around her shoulders, careful not to spill it on her. She returned the motion with her other hand, wrapping it around his back. As unobtrusively as possible, he ran the tip of his tongue lightly over her lips before pausing. He opened one eye to check on her. Her eyes were already open and she giggled.

"Am I still doing it wrong?" he asked, without removing his lips from hers.

"No, but you seem so uncertain, like *I* usually am." She didn't pull her lips away either.

He smiled and tugged gently on her bottom lip with his teeth. They broke into laughter. "Finish your drink, then come dance with me," he said. "People are starting to notice us over here. I'd say that's our cue."

Her nerves knocked again, knowing the time had come. The show was about to begin. She finished off her drink.

"I should have gone for the Ta-kill-ya. I'm so nervous."

"Want the rest of mine?" He lifted his glass, offering the one big swallow of bourbon he had left.

She looked at it, looked up at him with an arched brow.

"Oh, yeah. Backwash." He raised the glass to finish it off, but she reconsidered, snatched it from him, and recoiled as she gulped it down.

"You're such a lush." He laughed and sneaked in a

quick kiss. He set their cups down on the rail of the gazebo. "Come on." He took her hand, towed her onto the dance floor where he pulled her into his arms and started dancing a simple slow dance.

"I told Christian I wanted to dance with you the way he did at the dance contest. Nicole happened to be making herself obnoxiously handy, so I used her to help with the lesson. That's all it was."

"Oh." Rhees looked up at him, wondering how she'd read more into it. "I'm sorry."

"You *are* my pretend girl, right? I need to know, because, I'm about to pretend to let everyone know."

"Yes. Let's do this." The song ended, and a livelier one came across the speakers, motivating her to move.

"I want to see the backbend again."

"Backbend?"

"Yeah, the night of the contest, you did the sexiest backbend."

She groaned. "Gads! That night is going to haunt me for the rest of my life."

"And I'd kill to see you shimmy those hips again, up close." He moved his hands down to her hips and swished them for her, back and forth. "I've had dreams about it."

She covered her face with the palms of her hands. "Oh my gosh!"

"Pleeease!" His head dropped back like a small child ready to throw a tantrum, as if he'd die if she refused.

She nervously looked around, trying to make a decision, but her eyes landed on his, the extraordinary blue.

"All right, but support me with your arm. I haven't done a lot of backbends since college. The last one made me so sore I could barely walk for a week."

He smiled, and decided not to bring up the other things she'd done that night that may have contributed to her soreness.

"You didn't say anything about being sore."

"Making a point. The last thing I needed that day was you, grouching at me about slacking off."

"Tough as nails," he mouthed.

"Not stiff!" she mouthed back. "I remember that much."

"Me too, but remind me again."

She yielded with a grin and folded herself backward, giving him his wish. He slipped his arm around her waist and pulled her to him, touching, hip to hip. He grinned wickedly as she righted herself, finishing face-to-face.

"That doesn't feel like pretending." No humor showed on her face.

"Girls pretend that better than boys."

She tried to put some space between them, but he held her without breaking eye contact.

"I thought we were dancing. I can't shimmy if you won't let go."

"You have a point." He still didn't let her move away. "I know how to dance, but you're the best dancer I've ever seen. I just hope I don't kill us trying to keep up with you."

"I'll hold back."

"No, don't. Well, maybe a little, unless you want to humiliate me, and I'm sorry, but I won't be throwing in all the hip wiggles and wrist flicks that make Christian a better dancer than I."

"Spoil-sport." He released her hips and she started moving to the song. "Ready?"

"Oh yeah." He twirled her and the music carried her away.

By the time the song ended, they'd attracted the attention of almost everyone at the party, but they kept on dancing through several calmer songs.

"Where did you learn to dance?" Paul pulled her in to dance the way you would for a slow song, even though it wasn't.

"I just always knew how. As a kid, a bunch of us, other little girls in the neighborhood, we spent our time on each other's front lawns running through the sprinklers, learning how to do cartwheels and worked up from there. We used to pretend we were competing at the Olympics and we danced." She giggled. "In high school, I joined a dance club. We met in the choir room after school, a couple of times a week, making up dance routines and teaching each other moves we learned somewhere else.

"Occasionally we performed at school assemblies, or at halftime, but I'd get so nervous, performances made me sick. I didn't know alcohol cured stage fright." She laughed. "It would have helped in college too. I took some belly dancing classes. That was fun, but quite intimidating. Our finals—the teacher made us perform a recital—solo, and in a Bedleh, those skimpy Aladdin-ish costumes."

"Mm!" he grunted and flashed his eyebrows up with approval. "Still have one?"

"A Bedleh?"

"Uh-huh."

"No, thank goodness. I see the look on your face." He seemed more than pleased with the way she danced with him at the moment. Noticing only made her self-conscious, and she took it down a notch.

He pulled her closer and rubbed noses briefly, gazing at her. His eyes reminded her of the night he kissed her in her bedroom, making her nervous again. She glanced down.

"Don't," he whispered, but she couldn't look back up. "Look at me. It'll be okay."

He hugged her so her cheek pressed against his chest and she could hear his heart beating, slow and steady. It always made her feel better for some reason. At night, when she had nightmares, his heartbeat, as she rested her head on his chest, helped her relax. He kissed the top of her head.

"Do you realize how much that helps, or is it just a lucky coincidence?"

"What helps?"

"You resting my head against your chest when I'm nervous or upset."

"I've picked up on a few things." He squeezed her tighter.

The next song played slow and beautiful. *"Everything"*

by Lifehouse. Mitch dragged Shanni onto the dance floor and began dancing amorously next to them. Rhees squeezed her eyes shut, knowing the time had come to get serious. Paul pulled her chin up and gave her a reassuring smile. His right eye winked and his mouth twitched a few times, surprising her to think he could possibly be nervous too.

"Put your arms around my neck," he coached.

She took a deep breath, let it out, and snaked her arms up over his shoulders, around his neck. Both of his hands moved around her waist, and they swayed together, smoothly, back and forth. He kissed her, quick and easy, once, and then proceeded to kiss her the way she'd coached him. It made them both laugh for a second, but then it wasn't funny anymore.

Paul stared into her eyes, the intense blue kept her focused, and she actually didn't mind—knowing the goal—until she realized he was only getting started.

He kissed her again, but no longer took his time. He pulled on her, caressed her, and worked his way up to pawing. Every time, just before she reached her limit, tensed and squirmed, he slowed down, reminded her to look into his eyes. He talked to her, soothed her, giving her a chance to recover before he resumed, but there was no mistaking, she felt his growing desire pressing against her—he took pleasure in the performance.

"This is going to be *our* song," he whispered, and kissed her again, tongue first.

"You really know how to pretend to be romantic." She felt jittery.

"Mechanics," Paul corrected. "It's not romantic, *He's* just turned on. *He* knows what he wants and I know how to get it for him."

"Oh." How could she fault him for his honesty? "Well, sorry, but it helps me to think in terms of romance."

"Pfft!" He paused to look at her, concern in his expression. "It's time to make our exit, but Rhees . . ." He hesitated. "You need to be extra careful tonight once we leave here." He kissed her again, very passionately, and he sighed. "I'm sorry, but I'm—I'm worried that when we no longer have witnesses—I've never practiced a lot of restraint. Do you understand?"

She nodded, but she wished he hadn't said anything. It only made her worry more. He tightened his hold on her and buried his nose in her hair. He inhaled, kissed her again, mercilessly. He grabbed her butt with both hands and rubbed himself against her with a gratified groan.

She gave him a bug-eyed look, letting him know she knew he was taking advantage of the situation.

"I doubt I'll ever get another chance to get away with anything like this again." He bit his bottom lip and pressed against her once more before giving her a wanton wink. She gasped quietly at his shameless groping.

"Sorry, I'm a better actor than *He* is. *He* believes in me, so when he figures out this is just pretend, he's going to throw a tantrum."

It was only fair to pay him back. She rolled up on her toes, and skimmed his Adam's apple with her teeth.

"Mm!" she grunted, imitating what he always did when he kissed her. She watched his eyes grow wide and his mouth break into a wide, brilliant smile.

"Don't forget what I said." He rested his hand on her cheek, letting it sink in before taking her hand. "Let's go."

He turned to leave, but a fist to his face stopped him cold. Rhees screamed as Paul dropped to the floor. Her hands flew to her mouth in alarm and she looked to see who'd punched him. The other people on the dance floor had scattered in shock, giving Paul, Rhees, and the culprit a wide berth.

"Dobbs!" she yelled.

Dobbs stood over Paul, his hands fisted. "Get up! Get up now, so I can hit you again!" A scene flashed through Rhees' frenzied mind—Paul got up, and Dobbs wound up in the hospital. She couldn't let that happen.

She slammed Dobbs with both hands against his chest. "What. The. Fuck. Dobbs?" Her shrill voice enunciated each word for emphasis.

Dobbs gawked at her for a second, clearly confused. He finally pointed a finger at Paul, who still sat sprawled on the floor.

"Why? You selfish bastard! Why couldn't you just leave her alone—you don't have to sleep with every woman on the planet. Not her."

Paul rose up on an elbow, rubbing the jaw on his left side, staring at Rhees. Her reaction appeared to have shocked him. He finally managed to stagger to his feet, about to retaliate, but he had to pull his punch when Rhees frantically threw herself between them. Taylor's story of Paul almost killing the hobo with his bare hands, Paul telling Mitch he'd killed someone, and flashes of Paul beating Mario—it terrified her, sure that Dobbs, Paul's friend and hers, was about to receive the beating of his life and all because Dobbs wanted to protect her.

"Stop it!" she screamed. She turned and tried to bury herself into Paul's arms, trying to remind him what they were doing. "Let's go, let's just go," she begged.

"I'm not letting you leave with him," Dobbs yelled. "I thought you were smarter than that—better than that. You're too good for him. Don't be stupid, Rhees."

Paul tried to twist away from Rhees and lunge at Dobbs, but she shouted for him to stop again and managed to wrangle herself between them once more. Paul finally took a step back, not wanting to chance hurting her. She turned to Paul and grabbed his shoulders, pleading with him to let it go. She wasn't sure he was listening, but she didn't give up. He wouldn't take his furious eyes off of Dobbs. Dobbs returned the glare, not backing down.

She didn't dare let go of Paul, but she turned enough to look at Dobbs. "It's too late Dobbs. I'm going home with Paul tonight, but it won't be the first time."

There was a collective gasp from the circle of spectators who were inching their way closer, tightening the circle they'd formed around the entertainment.

Dobbs looked like someone had hit him in the stomach.

His surprise quickly changed to rage and he lunged toward Paul again. Paul tried to move Rhees out of the way in an effort to protect her from Dobbs' attack, but she fought him. It was all he could do to throw his arms around her and turn, hoping to absorb the blow with his shoulder.

"Stop it!" she screamed again. She started to cry. "It's not his fault. It was me—he tried to turn me down, but I—"

"Rhees, don't," Paul hissed, knowing what she was trying to do.

"After Mario tried—" She gulped quick breaths between her sobs. "I didn't want to be a target anymore. I asked Paul to help me—I begged him."

"And he was all too eager to oblige! Rhees, you played right into the bastard's selfish, conniving hands." Dobbs pressed his finger into Paul's chest.

"No! He said he wouldn't do it. He said I was just in shock and I should wait a few days, that I'd realize I didn't really want that. He said he couldn't take advantage of me that way."

Dobbs shook his head. He didn't believe it.

"It's true." It really was—most of it. "He told me to wait, that I'd change my mind, but I didn't want to wait. I didn't want to change my mind."

"Enough Rhees," Paul growled.

"I took advantage of him. You know he hasn't let me out of his sight since it happened. He's been staying at my place, but he's been a perfect gentleman."

"I don't believe it," Dobbs said.

"It's true," Tracy blurted. "We saw Paul sleeping on the couch. Then another night, he wasn't on the couch when Regina and I got home, but the next morning, he was there. He sat in the kitchen and had coffee—half naked—his pants were undone." For once, Tracy's big mouth had come in handy.

"That's right. He started out on the couch. I waited until he fell asleep." Rhees reclaimed her story before Tracy hijacked the show completely. "By the time he woke up and realized what I was doing—I don't think even Christian would have been able to stop."

Paul closed his eyes and pursed his lips, not sure if he was angrier with Dobbs or Rhees at the moment.

"We've been sleeping together ever since." Rhees' voice faded, knowing that in telling the truth, she'd just deliberately lied. They had been sleeping together, but not in the way she implied. Not in the way she needed everyone standing around—gawking at them—to believe.

"The morning we found him in our kitchen," Tracy added, excited to have even more information to share, "he asked Regina and I not to tell anyone. When he left, he told Rhees, 'Just because you're sleeping with the boss, don't think you can be late'." Tracy must have thought she was still helping, but Regina watched Paul's furious expression. She nudged Tracy with her elbow and gave her a dirty look, insinuating she should shut up.

"Stop it Regina. Dobbs needs to know. Paul and Rhees have been sleeping together." She faced Dobbs again. "See? It's not the way you're saying. When have you ever known Paul to spend so much time with the same girl? Rhees must really mean something to him."

Gossip began circulating as the people at the party discussed the new revelation. Paul rolled his eyes when Dobbs' anger with Paul transformed to disappointment in Rhees. Dobbs looked away from her, disgusted.

"Come on, Baby," Paul said, offering Rhees his hand. "Let's go home."

"Baby?" Rhees asked, surprised. Paul didn't know what her deal was about nicknames.

"You're my *girlfriend*." He threw his hands up in exasperation. "*Remember?*"

Dorene, Krista, Regina, and even Shanni gasped.

"It's just a nickname—a term of endearment," he said with gritted teeth, glaring at Rhees. "I think guys call their *girlfriend*s, Baby. So get over it."

"Okay," Rhees said quietly, blinking back.

"Let's get out of here." Paul grabbed Rhees' hand with exaggerated insistence, not waiting for her to decide whether to take it or not this time. He pulled her along behind him to the corner of the building where he stopped and turned back to Dobbs. He paused, wavering on whether he would say it or not, and decided he would.

"Do you think Claire knows why you're so invested in Rhees' virginity . . . and who you thought deserved to have it?"

Everyone looked Claire's direction. She flushed pale and stood frozen in place, staring at Dobbs before she stormed away. Paul tugged on Rhees and had to practically drag her out of there. She wasn't sure she wanted to go with him, but she didn't want to stay at the shop either. She couldn't stay, not with the way everyone stood around, glaring and shooting accusing looks her direction.

oOo

Paul walked so fast she had to run every few steps to keep up, and she got the feeling he preferred her behind him so he wouldn't have to look at her.

"You're angry with me."

"No shit!" He didn't break his pace.

"Why? I'm the one who should be angry."

He finally stopped, but he didn't turn around, still avoiding having to look at her. She moved in front of him, forcing him to.

"You shouldn't have said that—about Claire. You shouldn't have interfered with their marriage like that. It was cruel."

"You shouldn't have risked yourself by jumping into the middle of a fight, and you sure as hell shouldn't have made up that cockamamie story—I don't need you to fight my fucking battles for me!"

He really was angry. She took a step toward him.

"I didn't see it as fighting *your* battle. I thought the

whole point of all this . . . it's because you're helping me fight mine." She folded her arms and looked down. "If I, for one second, thought this plan would come between you and your friends—Dobbs is your friend, Paul."

"He attacked me, remember?"

"But *he* would never have killed *you*." Their eyes locked.

"I don't start anything I'm not willing to finish." Her observation surprised him.

"Dobbs is your friend! And he's my friend. He's just looking out for me because he cares . . . and poor Claire. Why would you hurt her like that?"

"Pfft!" Paul rolled his eyes. "I'm not a *kind*, bleeding heart type of soul. I don't have empathy for everyone and everything." He made it sound like the traits were offensive.

"Don't. Don't run yourself down like that," she said quietly.

He rolled his eyes. "There you go again. You're hurt right now because Claire is hurt, and maybe Dobbs too. They're hurt because of me," he laughed unconvincingly. "But you still stand there and tell me not to say anything mean about *myself*—that doesn't sound crazy to you?"

In his irritation, he leaned in at her when he spoke, maybe to intimidate her a little. He felt bad about it as soon as he did, but found it easier to lead her to believe his anger pointed at her, not himself. She shouldn't have taken the blame for something he wanted the blame for. Tracy's observation wore on him as well.

"You know what? Dobbs was right. You're too gullible. We *all* thought you were smarter."

The look on her face made him wince. She turned and started to walk away, but he grabbed her arm. By reflex, she turned and slapped him, catching the same side of his face that Dobbs had hit. Her hands flew to her mouth in horror at what she'd done.

"I'm sorry. I didn't mean—"

"Of course not." His smirk reflected the angry edge in his voice. "That's probably the first *honest* thing you've ever done, but you still won't own it."

She scowled at him and walked off again.

"You're not walking home by yourself."

"Leave me alone! I don't want you anywhere near me," she yelled. "Just leave me the hell alone!"

"Watch your mouth, young lady," he mocked her. She didn't stop. He half grimaced, half smirked and then followed her, keeping his distance until she made it to the yard at Oceanside. He stood by the path entrance and watched until she reached the top of the stairs, and he saw her get safely inside. He exhaled his frustration and finally left to go find a bar where no one from the party would find him.

Chapter 6

*T*racy and Regina walked in ten minutes after Rhees. She ran to the door to greet them.

"Paul?" She wilted with disappointment. "Did you see Paul? Do you know where he is?"

"How should we know?" Regina sounded cold. "He left with you."

"We had a fight." Rhees ran to the kitchen window and tried to look out at the road again, hoping to see him, but the view didn't face directly to the street. In the dark, she couldn't see anything.

"I never would fight with Paul. He can do whatever the hell he wanted, and I would not never care as long as he found his way back to my bed at night. That man should realize what he is missing out on me."

Rhees heard Regina ranting to Tracy about Rhees' intelligence or lack of, and her inability to appreciate what she'd let slip through her fingers.

oOo

Rhees heard scuffling on the porch. In her half-sleep state, she panicked and reached for Paul, wanting to snuggle up to him, trusting he would calm her. Her hand came up empty, and it stirred her back to reality, as did the loud bang on the door. She checked her clock, two thirty in the morning. She'd only been asleep for a little while.

"Damn it Danarya! Open this . . . fucking door!" Paul stood outside on the porch, drunk. Not just normal Paul drunk, but sloppy, word-slurring, falling down drunk, and he still sounded angry, so she didn't move, and planned to ignore him, though she found herself relieved to finally know where he was.

She heard the girls in the next room moving about. She jumped out of bed and raced to her bedroom door, threw off the lock and opened it just as Regina reached to unlock the front door.

"Don't open it!" Rhees pushed Regina out of the way and checked to make sure the lock still hung secure.

"It's Paul. He would like to come in." Regina sounded incredulous.

Rhees glared at her. "Paul is *my* problem, not yours. *I* get to decide how to handle this, and right now, I don't want to talk to him." Regina ignored her and reached for the lock on the door again. "Regina, I swear, if you open this door . . ."

Rhees glared, teeth bared, daring Regina to see what would happen if she didn't walk away.

Regina looked torn, but finally gave in and went back into her room. She slammed her door. Rhees shuddered, knowing Paul had probably heard them. She laughed to herself, realizing he had to know she was home. Where else would she be? She went back into her bedroom and plopped herself down on her bed. She worried what he would do when he realized she didn't plan to let him in.

"Open this door, wo-man!" She heard him snicker to himself. He pounded again.

She tried to ignore him as he made one attempt after another to talk her into letting him in, like, "Honey, I'm . . . home. Never fear, Paul . . . is here. Home is where your Paul is." After a while, he stopped banging on the door and called to her through the small, open window facing the porch. She knew he couldn't see her with the curtain closed.

"Danarya. Let me . . . in, pleeease."

"Go home Paul. Leave me alone." She finally gave up trying to ignore him. "Someone is going to call the police if you don't go home and stop making so much noise."

"I can't go home . . . I can bare-ly walk." He laughed. "Let me in, I just want to sleeep."

His tone sounded calmer and it grew harder to ignore him, but she reminded herself how mean he'd been.

"Little pig, little pig, let me come in," he sang quietly through the window. He began amusing himself with his inebriated cleverness. "Not by the hair of my chinny-chin-chin," he sang in a false, high voice and then he laughed, still amused at his personal joke. His voice dropped to a low growl. "Then I'll hufff, and I'll pufff . . . and I'll ba-looow your house in."

He fell silent for a minute, and Rhees wondered if he'd fallen asleep leaning against the wall on the porch or something. She didn't have to wonder long before she heard him mumbling, but it sounded like he was talking to himself now.

"But the big baaad wolf couldn't blow the house in . . . he hufffed, and he pufffed, but *Rhees* lived in a house . . . *nawt* a house made of bricks . . . oh, no, no. She lived in fucking Fort *Knawx*! . . . with a mm-moat." He clicked the T sound with emphasis. He paused. "Filled with hungry alligators . . . and pi-rrraw-nhas . . . and *zommbbies*. I hate fucking zombies." He paused again. "A category five hurricane . . . couldn't blow herr house down."

She threw her pillow to her mouth to stifle the giggles. He might be acting funny and cute, but she still didn't think the situation was humorous.

"Dani Girrrl," he cooed. It shocked Rhees to hear him call her Dani Girl. Of all the stupid nicknames he had tried to give her, he finally found one she didn't mind. "Pleease let me in. I don't l-like to sleep alone. I've never liked sleeping alone." He sounded so sad, even through his slurs. "I used to sneak into my little sister's room. I always told my mom that Mary was the one who was afraid, but it was really me." He paused.

"She wet the bed sometimes. It was *sooo* gross." He sighed loudly. "But . . . I still . . . I still preferred getting

Wet

peed on than sleeping in my big ol' room . . . all by my—s-
self. I'd wake up awll wet, clean both of us up, and I'd carry
her to Pete's rooom so we could all sleep together—just
like old times—before things went to shit. But then Pete
started to *ne-ver* be in his rooom anymore." He paused
again. "When I got older, I found out why." Silence again.

"That's when I figured out that *I* could get girrls to sneak
me into their rooms, too." He laughed at his cleverness.
"My parents ne-ver knew I wasn't home . . . or they just
didn't fucking care.

"I'd spend the night with the girls. A few times . . .
parents walked in on us . . . just sleeping—well one time,
we weren't *sleee-ping . . . yet.*" He laughed quietly. "After
getting the *shhi-it* beat out of me by an angry father—I
didn't fight back. I could have, but . . ." He stopped to
think. "If I found some dickwad like me in Mary's bed, I'd
beat the shiiit out of him too."

Rhees listened to his story. He so rarely shared his past
and he'd never opened up this much before.

"I got pa-ritty fast at grabbing my stufff and getting out.
I'd go home and crawl into my own bed, all by myself—and
nawt sleep. But you see . . ." His voice got louder, trying
to make sure Rhees heard him. "Sleeping with you is like
sleeping with my siss-ter. Or the *just* sleeping with girls—
aff-ter the sex. *It-snot* so much the sssex—the sex isn't bad,
don't get me *wrawng.* I like it—a *lawt!* Just not as much as
I like the company. *Pleease,* don't make me sleep alone."

Rhees pressed her hands to her face. She felt almost
guilty knowing so much about him, understanding that if
he wasn't so drunk, he would've never made such a detailed
confession. She couldn't stay mad at him, and decided to
let him in. She unlocked the doors, but by the time she got
outside, she found him asleep in one of the Adirondack
chairs.

She worried about the way he sprawled out. His head
hung over the side of the chair to his left, his mouth open
and his jaw cocked to one side. His right leg propped over
the opposite arm of the chair. He'd wake up sore in the

morning.

She returned to her room and grabbed two sheets and all three pillows. She tucked one under his ribs so the wooden chair wouldn't dig into him, trying to fix the pillow to give his head some support too. She tucked another under the leg draped over the arm of the chair. She covered him with one of the sheets and watched him for a minute.

"He's sleeping off a drunken stupor for crying out loud! How can he still look so beautiful?" She put the last pillow on the floor in front of his chair and sat down. She wrapped the other sheet around herself and rested her head against his left leg.

oOo

Paul woke and it took a while to figure out where he was, but he couldn't remember how he got there, or why he felt anchored to the chair. Rhees had wrapped her arms around his leg, her head rested against his thigh.

"Rhees?" Paul's voice came out deep and hoarse. "Rhees." He leaned forward in the chair and rubbed her back with his hand. He nuzzled her hair with his nose, inhaling, feasting on her scent.

He tried again to remember how they got there. *This isn't right.*

"You don't have to sleep alone," she murmured.

"Rhees? Hey, wake up." He wondered what she meant.

"Ow. I have a kink in my neck." She stirred.

"Why are you sleeping like that? Why am I?" A few memories started coming back to him. "Aw shit!"

"Hmm? What time is it?"

He checked his watch. "Damn, I should have been at the shop half an hour ago." He wanted to jump up and get going, but she hung on to his leg, still groggy. "Come on Rhees, wake up. You've got me pinned down. We need to get to the shop."

"I'm sorry. Oh . . . my neck hurts." She put her hand to

her neck and tried to rub the kink out. He reached down and helped her, massaging her neck and shoulders before taking her face in both hands and studying her.

"Is that better?" He kissed her on the temple.

Her memory of the early morning events returned and she sat up straighter, releasing his leg. She looked at him, afraid of what mood he would be in this morning.

"What's wrong?"

She stood up, avoiding meeting his eyes. "Nothing. I'll get ready." She headed toward the screen door, but before she made it into the house, he asked again, right on her heels.

"What did I do last night? Did I do something—anything I shouldn't have?"

"Not after you finally came home. I need to change."

He rubbed the stubble along his tensed jaw and felt the leftover soreness from Dobbs' punch. More and more of the events of the night before were coming back to him. He remembered everything, up until he followed Rhees, making sure she got home safely.

He remembered going to an obscure bar north of his shop, one, no one he knew well, ever frequented. He remembered Nicole. She showed up right after he did. He remembered realizing she'd followed him. He remembered buying her a few drinks, thinking she looked better than he'd originally thought . . . he hated himself. The thing is, he couldn't remember if he needed to or not.

"Rhees! I need to go. I need to get to the shop." He looked visibly harrowed about something. "Make sure you walk with Tracy and Regina. I'll see you later." He took off down the stairs.

"Paul? Wait for me! I'm almost ready. I only need a second." She'd already changed into her swimming suit. She rushed out of the bathroom, threw on a T-shirt, grabbed her pack, and ran into the living room, ready to lock her bedroom door, but he'd already left.

She walked out onto the porch, looked down at the street and caught a glimpse of him running away. Turning to the chair where he'd slept, Rhees sighed, wondering if now that the alcohol had worn off, he was still mad at her. She sighed before gathering up the pillows and sheets and taking them to her room. She threw everything on the floor and sat down on the bed. She didn't really cry, but she could have.

oOo

Dobbs and Claire didn't show up for work, giving Paul even more to do after racing around all morning, playing catch-up for being late. Rhees showed up, not too long after him, and did all she could to help. With the work done, she stood on the boat as it pulled away from the dock without him, watching him wave. He never told her he'd opted not to dive, leading her to believe he still planned to. The look on her face made him feel even worse.

Paul had told Randy he had some urgent business to attend to. As soon as the boat headed off, he ran. He'd arranged to have Ignacio's taxi waiting for him, out of view on the street, so Rhees wouldn't see it. He hopped in, knowing he'd just left his shop unattended, but the odds that no one would show up before the boat returned were in his favor.

"Get me to the landing strip, and hurry."

"You picking up guests?" Ignacio asked.

"Seeing one off."

"I don't think you'll make it."

"That's why I said to hurry."

Paul stared out the side window to let the driver know he wasn't in the mood for conversation. Ignacio knew how to get through the pedestrian crowded streets fast, and luckily, the plane was late. Paul jumped out of the van before Ignacio had come to a full stop.

"Wait for me," Paul yelled as he ran to the crude lean-to covered waiting bench that the islanders called an airport.

The college students waited for their flight, surprised to see him, but no one seemed more surprised than Nicole.

"Can I talk to you, please?" he asked. Nicole gave him a dirty look, but she agreed. Paul took her aside. "Did we . . . um, my memory of last night is a little fuzzy. Can you remind me what happened?"

"What, it wasn't enough to put me through that once? You want me to relive it again?" Nicole huffed, angrily.

"That bad, huh?" He drooped.

"Yes, it was."

"I'm so sorry. It shouldn't have happened."

"Right, you son-of-a-bitch."

"I know," he agreed. "But please. It's important." He did his best to smile the way that seemed to warm most women's hearts. He wasn't in the mood so it was hard to do.

"Don't look at me like that. That's how it all started."

He almost panicked that she was on to him, but he turned up the eye power instead of turning it down as she'd requested. He had to know. He wasn't above fighting dirty to get what he wanted.

"All right," she agreed. He wanted to sigh in relief but didn't give himself away. "I was tired . . . and a little depressed, so I decided to go back to my room and pack. Those guys—" she pointed at her friends, "—wanted to party up to the very last minute, so I headed back to the hotel on my own. That's when I saw you wandering around by yourself."

He must have appeared impatient because she smirked and started filling him in on every single minute detail. He wanted to scream at her to just get to the important part but she was already unhappy with him about something. He had no choice but to count his blessings she hadn't started the story from the day she'd been born.

"It confused me to see you alone because of that whole violent scene at the party—I saw you leave with your *girlfriend*—you know, after three days of diving with you guys, I didn't even know you and Rhees were an item, but there you were, all alone."

"I remember this part," he said, hoping to get her to move it along but she ignored him.

"You looked upset, angry even. I got my hopes up as I thought, hmm, maybe he could use a shoulder to cry on. I followed you to that bar in the middle of nowhere and when I walked in and saw the look on your face, I knew I'd made the right choice."

"Maybe you misread the situation?" Paul's cheek twitched, knowing what she meant.

"Hell no! My wishful thinking may have misled me at the party. I guess I read more into our dance than there was, but . . . I *know* when a man is undressing me with his eyes!"

He winced. "So what happened?"

"We had a few drinks. Well, I had a few drinks. You drank the bar dry. Then you asked me to dance. I had to practically hold you up by then, but things got cozy. I thought we were hitting it off." Nicole frowned.

"What did I do?" Paul was sure she'd *finally* made it to the part he needed to hear.

"When a man leaves a party with one girl, and then shows up angry and alone at a remote bar—the way you looked at me—" Her eyes glazed over at the memory, but then she snapped out of it. "You were . . . *friendly,* and very attentive as you proceeded to get plastered, taking me along for the ride. Naturally, I thought you were out for some good old revenge sex.

"A fast song came on and you started twirling me around but then you said, very rudely, I might add, 'You don't dance like Rhees'. I said, 'No one dances like Rhees, but I'm a better lover than a dancer.' I asked if you wanted to go back to my place. I thought that's what we both wanted."

Paul closed his eyes and pursed his lips. He knew how the story ended. It just irritated him to have to hear her tell it.

"I'm sorry. It should never have happened."

"You're damn right. After being all, 'I don't like to be alone. I would rather hang out with you all night and drool all over you', Mr. *Dreamy-Eyes* suddenly looked at me like I'd grown a second head or something. You can be a scary guy, do you know that?"

"Yeah, I know—so I didn't . . ." He barely noticed her question. He finally felt hope that he hadn't betrayed Rhees. He'd tried to dismiss Rhees' concern about that, but from the beginning, he secretly worried he couldn't be loyal. He'd never tried. He just never imagined it would be so soon.

"Yes! You did." Nicole's voice went up an octave.

He ran his hand through his hair, hating himself, knowing he would never change.

"You bought me drinks, danced with me—you told me I was pretty—with your eyes when I first showed up, but it's the same thing. You led me on." She pouted. "But then you leaned down and told me, right in my ear—I thought you were going to kiss me, but instead, you told me I wasn't your type—*anymore*. You really hurt my feelings."

His expression went blank. "That's it? I hurt your *feelings*?"

"I told you. You led me on, made me think something was going to happen, and then you just stumbled out of the bar, leaving me there to lick my wounded pride."

It took all of his restraint not to smile. They heard the approaching plane and watched it land on the dirt strip.

"Look, I'm sorry. I never meant to hurt your feelings." He hoped she wouldn't catch the mockery in his voice. "But you just made my day."

"You really are a son-of-a-bitch."

"Yeah, I said, I know." He winked before he grabbed her shoulders and gave her a kiss on both cheeks. He felt almost giddy with joy. "Thank you."

She looked up at his smile, hopeful and dazed, as if he'd just professed his undying love.

"For calling you an SOB?" she asked in a breathless voice.

"Yep. Thank you. Don't miss your plane." He didn't want to hang around another second, explaining something so important to someone so unimportant to him. He ran back to the taxi.

"You're a good-looking SOB!" Nicole called out after him. "I'll come back next year. Maybe we can hook up then."

Paul didn't bother to respond.

Chapter 7

*M*itch and Randy were still out with the divers, and with Rhees diving too, Paul was on his own at the shop and didn't have a second to breathe. Dobbs and Claire still hadn't shown up, and Paul knew he'd have to do something about that, but at the moment, he couldn't take the time to figure out what.

The office phone rang and he cursed under his breath as Emil, the ferry operations manager, informed Paul he had a package. For important, *hard to find in this country* items, Paul just asked his buddies in the States to pick them up for him and bring it on their next visit, but if Paul needed something readily available from the mainland, he'd either pick it up himself, send someone he trusted, and occasionally, he could convince the vendor to deliver the package to Emil personally and Emil would bring it across on the ferry—for a price.

"I don't need this right now," Paul grumbled. He said the next sentence in Spanish. "I'll pick it up later this afternoon."

"Not possible, my friend," Emil answered back in his native tongue. "It's my wife's birthday. This is my last run today. Hector is taking over the ferry until tomorrow, so if you want this package, you'll have to come before we head out in thirty minutes."

"Thirty minutes," Paul grumbled again. He told Emil he'd be there and slammed the phone down on the receiver. He ran out of the office to the end of the deck and looked out over the bay, hoping to see the boat headed back—it should be back any minute. He glanced around to see who'd trickled in. A handful of students were huddled under the gazebo, talking, and obviously absorbed in their conversation. He decided to take his chances and took off toward the ferry at a run.

To his dismay, he'd not been able to find the ferry manager right away and it had taken him forty-five minutes to get his package, a small envelope filled with new O rings—hardly worth the trouble it'd caused him, he thought. The shop needed to supplement their supply of the emergency item on a regular basis but he wondered why they had to arrive on this day of all days.

oOo

Rhees wondered all morning about where their fake relationship stood. The dives relaxed her, but the boat ride and the surface interval were miserable. Dorene and Krista talked endlessly about the previous night, not caring she might hear, but she tried to pretend she didn't. Mitch and Randy gave her sympathetic glances every now and then, but she couldn't wait to get back. She needed to talk to Paul, or more, she needed him to talk to her.

The boat docked, and Rhees jumped off to look for him before putting her gear away but discovered he'd left the shop, though no one knew why or when he'd left. She despaired, worried about Claire and Dobbs, about Paul—it became all she could do to rinse her gear and put it away before she ran back to her apartment. She needed to cry, really cry this time.

oOo

Paul finally made it back to the shop to find the boat docked in its spot, equipment all put away, and everyone settling in for a routine day—everyone except Rhees. He walked all around the shop, but still didn't find her. He tapped on the locked bathroom door but the new guy,

Adrian, answered back.

Paul asked around, asked if anyone had seen her, but no one admitted to it, and that pissed him off. He was already in a bad mood, angry with himself, but knowing how too many of them treated her—the girls still resented her and the guys still drooled and shared fantasies about her—right on his deck.

With him, Dobbs, and Christian around, none of them dared say anything as offensive as he'd heard away from the shop, around town, but he didn't know how much longer he'd be able to keep himself from just kicking every single student, man and woman, off his property and start over with a new clientele.

He hoped the performance-gone-very-wrong shock of the night before would finally put an end to the stupid high school behavior, but at the moment, he needed to find Rhees and figure out where they stood. He worried, sure the reason he couldn't find her was because she'd heard what he almost did—what he was sure people thought he did—what he'd thought he did with Nicole—before he'd asked her.

He knew people talked about him, too often, and too many would love to make sure Rhees found out about his activities, and if history was any indication, they'd exaggerate—fill in the blanks with their imaginations— imaginations based on real memories of his past.

He feared his temper had guaranteed their pretend relationship was over before it'd even started, and that made him sick to his stomach—but for some reason—he didn't understand it—he felt the ache of it higher up in his chest.

He pulled his cell phone from his pocket, dialed her number and walked around, listening for her phone to ring. He perked up when he heard the ringtone she'd assigned him, Darth Vader's theme song from Star Wars, and he followed the sound to her backpack, in the office. That idea was a bust, and he let out a stream of cuss words because of her stubborn, irritating, *cute as hell*, little hide.

He might have smiled if he wasn't so distressed.

He didn't care about respecting her privacy at the moment, he had to know. He checked the backpack and found her clothes neatly folded inside, her shoes sat on the floor next to the pack. She'd never wander around the island without first getting dressed—

Suddenly it felt like a vise had seized his heart and started squeezing. He tried to dismiss his worst fear and stay calm as he walked to the end of the deck again. He looked out over the ocean, hoping she'd gone snorkeling. No sign of her. He exhaled roughly, stood frozen for a second, but then bolted, headed next door to Miranda's store, where she lived with her son, Randy.

"You called roll after the last dive, right?" Paul yelled as he barged through the door, uninvited. "Tell me you called the fucking roll!"

"Yes. I called roll." Randy jumped up from his kitchen table, knocking his lunch to the floor. His wife and Miranda looked up at Paul like a crazy man had just broken into their home.

"Everyone was accounted for then?" Paul asked desperately.

"Yes."

"What about Rhees? Tell me you didn't leave Rhees stranded out in the middle of the ocean!" Paul knew he was still yelling, but he couldn't help it.

"I called roll. Everyone's back on the boat. Specially cousin Rhees. She's fam'ly. I'd never leave Rhees. I'd never leave anyone. You know that, mon."

Paul ran his hand through his hair and bit his lip before his nervous tick took control of his mouth. He ran back to the shop and frantically threw the closet door open to check for himself. Her wet gear hung inside and he dropped forward with relief. He leaned his hands on his knees as he reeled in his breathing and tried not to faint.

"Thank you, God," he whispered over and over.

When his heart recovered and his mind cleared, he remembered their conversation about her having a phone.

There've been times I've needed to talk to you but couldn't, he'd said.

Only because I didn't want to talk to you, she'd answered. *—on the phone or otherwise.*

He sighed, knowing this was one of those times, and he wished he could take it all back, do last night over again. He took care of a few things before he ran across the street to check his apartment, the closest possibility first. As expected, the lock hung on the door, a sign she wasn't inside.

He broke into a run and didn't stop until he'd reached Oceanside. He flew up the stairs two at a time and bent forward to rest his hands on his thighs, taking a moment to catch his breath, when he saw the door open.

Relief—he finally felt optimistic. All the thoughts running through his head since he woke up that morning, fears he'd betrayed Rhees, fears she'd been left stranded in the ocean, fears she'd figured him out and wanted nothing more to do with him—he wouldn't blame her, but the thought bothered him and he wasn't used to feeling that way. He needed to breathe. He didn't call out. If she was inside, he wouldn't find her happy.

He pulled the screen door handle. The door opened.

Why didn't she lock the damn door? He shook his head and tried not to be too upset about her careless disregard for her own safety. Not today, anyway. He tiptoed in, quietly, looking to the right to find her bedroom open as well. He almost sobbed, overcome with relief when he finally saw her. She lay safely on the bed, her back turned to the door. He didn't hear crying, but his pillow displayed a telltale wet spot and he felt like such an ass.

"Rhees?" he said softly, in case she was asleep. She didn't answer. He crept in, delicately crawled onto the bed, and snuggled up next to her. "Hey." He couldn't think of anything else to say.

She stared at the wall, sniffed, grabbed a tissue from the box she had on the bed, and wiped her eyes.

"You've always known I'm an ass. Last night shouldn't

have come as a shock."

She laughed and rolled onto her back to look at him. "You called me Dani Girl."

He huffed out a quiet laugh. "Of all the horrific things I need to apologize for, you're starting the list off with a new nickname? I knew you hated them, but I guess I never realized how much."

"I liked it." She laughed again.

"Oh. So we're starting with the only thing I did *right*." He furrowed his brows, confused and cautious.

"My grandpa called me Dani Girl when I was little. I haven't heard it since he passed away."

Paul studied her for a few seconds, but then rolled onto his back and rubbed his face. His breathing sounded harsh and he moaned. He was drained.

"Aw, Rhees."

With a warm smile, she leaned up on her elbow to look down at him, pulling his hands away from his face so she could see him. His eyes felt tired and bloodshot. After all he drank the night before, yes surely, they were bloodshot. He probably looked pale too. He only hoped he didn't look as miserable as he felt.

He did have the hangover from hell, but his misery didn't have as much to do with the hangover as the reason for it and the things he, thankfully, hadn't done, but could have.

"You don't deserve this. You're too good to have to put up with me. You need someone who can treat you right."

"Stop it." Her smile dropped as fast as it had formed. "Wait . . . are you breaking up—I mean pretending to break—breaking up, pretending to be my . . . What am I trying to ask? You're bored, *already*?"

"I'm not bored! But maybe it would be for the best." He sighed loudly. "I should—if I was a better man, but when I die, the last thing I'll be remembered for is my altruism." He looked at her, sadly. "If you knew what was good for you, you'd run."

She smiled again and gave him a wide-eyed expression,

nodding her head slowly as if wholeheartedly agreeing with him. He finally smiled back, happy to see her happy and teasing him, but she shouldn't be—she *didn't* know what was good for her. She didn't because she was too nice, and sweet, and naïve. He considered himself lucky for that and then felt bad for it too.

"I need to tell you something, but I know you're not going to like it." Her features drew down as she spoke, making him uneasy.

"Then can it wait until this hangover stops kicking my ass?" He closed his eyes and pinched the bridge of his nose.

"You mean your head."

He opened one eye to look at her and smiled. "Yeah, my head hurts so bad, I confused it with the beautiful pain in the ass I've been sleeping with, but can't actually sleep with."

"No." She didn't even pretend to acknowledge what he'd said. "It can't wait. I'm going to tell Claire and Dobbs that I lied. I'm telling them the truth about us."

"No, you're not." It came out, not angry, not surprised, just matter-of-fact.

"I'm not asking your permission. I only wanted to tell you first, as a courtesy. My mind is made up."

He rolled back onto his side to face her. "Why would you undo everything?"

"They're our friends. They don't deserve to be lied to. This whole thing isn't worth sacrificing the people we love."

"Pfft! Love. You've known them since March. I've known them for years, and I wouldn't say I love them."

"*Whatever.*" She dropped onto her back and stared up at the ceiling, looking saddened to hear him deny having feelings for them. "*I* love them, and I hate that I lied to them—that I thought I could—that I planned to keep lying."

"That's why you should have left the lying up to me. I'm good at it." The scowl on his face, the angry look in his eyes, must have been what made her sigh. He didn't say it to brag, it just happened to be another demonstration of his self-loathing. "That whole speech last night—you shouldn't have . . ."

He couldn't finish. He sighed too and tenderly pulled her so they faced each other on the bed. "I don't want to go there again. Last night was . . . I don't want to be angry with you, and I sure as hell don't like it when you're angry with me."

"Me too."

He stroked the side of her face while they both took time to think.

"I think it's a bad idea. We don't need any weak links in this chain. Have you forgotten how your secret got out in the first place? You told Tracy, and now the whole island knows. Telling even one person is one step closer to danger. Rhees, you can't walk down the street without drawing catcalls."

"That happened one time."

"One fucking time too many!" He licked his lips a few times while he calmed down. "And the only reason it hasn't happened again is because I tried to knock the dirt bag's nose to the back of his head—you shouldn't have stopped me. You're making it a habit of stepping into my fights."

There was a hint of satisfaction in her expression. He assumed it had to do with keeping him out of jail for assault. "I won't discount the possibility there're more creeps like Mario out there. We *have* to lie."

"*I* love them. Apologizing and telling them is the only way I'm going to fix how awful I feel. They didn't show up at the shop today. You know that right?"

"I noticed." He scowled again. She suddenly sucked in a loud wheeze of air.

"Who's watching the shop? You and I are here, Claire and Dobbs didn't show up."

Paul's face twisted, understanding her concern. He answered tentatively. "Mitch."

Her mouth dropped open in disbelief.

"I see by your expression that doesn't put your mind at ease."

Mitch happened to be a very nice guy, very likable, had

a great sense of humor, but he wasn't the responsible type. She rolled off the bed and Paul watched her scurry around the room, frantically.

"I hope I can get back before he decides it would be a great idea to build a bon fire on the deck, you know, on the deck made of old, wooden planks? . . . Or some other equally brilliant plan."

Paul pressed his fingers over his eyes. He knew she was right, but for the first time since he'd bought the shop, he didn't want to go back. He didn't move.

"Shoot!"

Paul looked to see the problem. Her shoulders dropped and she hung her head, like she just remembered she'd forgotten something important. "I can't believe I left the shop wearing nothing but my swimming suit. I don't even have my shoes."

He understood why. "You ran. You were upset. You don't think rationally when you're upset. You run first, think later. Like now." He watched her pull on one of his T-shirts over her suit and bend over to pick up her bronze sandals. "You're running now."

"No, I'm not. I need to make sure the shop is still standing." She glanced down at herself. "This looks stupid. Baggy men's shirt with nothing but heels." He listened to her grumble as she moved around, getting ready to leave.

"Dani Girl?" Paul said quietly.

She stood up straight and looked off blankly into the corner of the room. He could tell she was trying to fight his persistent attempts to call her back to the crucial topic they still needed to address. He watched her warily.

"About last night," he pushed.

"Water under the bridge." She bent over to put on the first sandal, dismissing his lead-in.

"I want you to know, I wasn't really angry with you."

She exhaled, a little too forcefully. "Bullcrap!" She stood up straight again. "You just said you were, not five minutes ago. 'I don't like being angry with you'."

"*Bullcrap*," he repeated under his breath. She actually

made him grin, even with everything from the night before still hanging between them, nearly sucking the air out of the room. He sat up and stared at her, wondering how she could be so . . . like she was.

"I said I don't *want to be* angry with you . . . and I'm not, wasn't—maybe I thought I was for a second, but I'm really just angry at myself."

She closed her eyes, and her bottom lip quivered. He stood and made it to her side in one giant step.

"Aw, Rhees. Don't. Pleease."

"You were—*are* mad at me! The things you said, those things have obviously bothered you for a while. You don't respect me. You can't respect me for caring about what others think or feel and for being scared all the time, about everything, but I don't know how to change it." Her voice dropped to almost a whisper as she repeated what he'd said. "I sure as hell don't like it when you're angry with me."

"God, Rhees. Is that what you think? I don't respect you?"

She didn't answer, she didn't look up, and she didn't do a very good job holding back the tears. He put his arms around her, held her tight, heaving harsh breaths into her hair, mustering the courage to tell her the truth.

"I've watched you all this time, wondering, 'How is it possible? No one can be so naïve, and so sweet, and so—good'. I told myself you can't keep up this game forever. I've been watching, waiting for you to slip up and finally reveal that chink in your armor."

"That's what you think of me—" She couldn't have looked more hurt.

He put his finger over her lips and shushed her. "I was sure it was just an act, because you are just *too good* to be true, but the better I get to know you, the more I realize how genuine you are.

"So, no, I don't think that about you anymore. It's just me—it's all me. It'd be so much easier for me to believe you were just like me, well, maybe like everyone else—no one's as bad as I am. I thought you weren't being honest with yourself or anyone, putting on a facade . . . Because if I admitted that you really were different, then I could have been different too, but I'm not. I've spent the last few years convincing myself that everyone has a dark side. Some people just hide it better than others. I got tired of hiding it."

"I don't understand."

Of course she didn't. Her genuine innocence made it impossible.

"You've been an unwelcome reminder that I've just been fooling myself and making excuses for my really shitty behavior. So no, I'm not angry with you. I respect you, I admire you . . . I am in awe of you!"

"I'm not that good, Paul. I don't know what you see, but—"

He kissed her to shush her instead of placing his finger over her lips. It was a chaste kiss; no tongue, no grabbing, just a kiss of admiration . . . and emotion. She didn't fight him, but it left her with a confused look on her face, as though she didn't understand why she'd let him.

"I need to apologize to Dobbs," she finally said, moving the awkward moment along.

"And Claire too, right?" He sighed loudly. "All right. We'll go together."

oOo

"I still think this is a bad idea," Paul said. "It's not too late to change your mind."

Rhees glanced at him once and knocked on the door with a look on her face to suggest he should stop wasting his breath. She knew what she had to do and he couldn't talk her out of it.

"I said I have to do this!" No one answered so she knocked again.

"Their place is exactly like mine, it's small. It's not like they didn't hear you knock the first time."

Rhees slumped, looking defeated, and then her eyes rolled to the side like she was about to cry, but trying not to. Paul stepped closer and put his arms around her waist, rested his forehead on hers.

"Please don't cry. I'll help you find them. We won't give up until we do. I'm sure they're just out." He didn't recognize himself by the words coming from his mouth. He didn't want her to find them, blow their cover story, and put herself in jeopardy again. "I know how important it is for you to apologize."

The door suddenly flew open. "Not only is the apartment small, but the windows are open and we can hear everything people right outside are saying." Claire stood at the door with her arms crossed, glaring accusingly at Paul. "What the hell does *Rhees* have to apologize for?"

oOo

"Rhees, are you sure this isn't just part of his plan? Maybe he's just playing along to—" Dobbs let Claire do all the talking, afraid Paul might make anything he said sound perverted, again.

"I'm sure. I told you what happened." Rhees glanced at Paul. He sat staring out the window, detached from the discussion. "He's been the perfect gentleman and I don't know how I would have gotten through all that mess with Mario, without him."

"Dobbs and I've been talking." It wasn't hard to imagine Dobbs and Claire spending hours talking about the recent events, and it made Rhees feel bad they'd found it necessary to hash out that sort of conversation because of her. "Dobbs may have been harboring a bit of resentment toward Paul for buying the shop out from under us. Hell, *I'm* still pissed about it! Dodger really screwed us over."

Paul suddenly decided to lend the conversation his full attention. He looked at Dobbs, shell-shocked to learn the new information.

"Who's Dodger?" Rhees asked, taking advantage of the silence.

"The previous owner," Paul answered quietly as Claire and Dobbs communicated some private message between them. "He's dodged his own grave so many times with all his crazy, reckless stunts, people call him Dodger." His eyes darted back to Claire and then Dobbs. "He never told me he'd agreed to sell you the shop."

"The man's a certified lunatic," Claire said with disgust.

"We had an offer on the table, but Dodger wouldn't sign it—said his word was gold." Dobbs tried to laugh. "So I couldn't understand how you just swooped in and took away our dream."

"It would have taken us another year to come up with the down payment," Claire said. "But Dodger said we could manage the shop like it was our own until we came up with the money."

"I appreciate that you kept us on," Dobbs continued. "You treat us well—almost like partners. You pay us more than a fair salary, so it isn't justified I'd harbor resentment. It wasn't a conscious effort." Dobbs ran a hand over his smooth, bald head.

"I'm sorry. I didn't mean to bite the hand that's been feeding me, but I've sat back the last three years and watched you get everything you want, like a spoiled kid. Everything comes so easy for you, and I didn't think it was fair." Dobbs gave Rhees a glance, but quickly looked away, like he was afraid someone would read more into it.

Too late, Paul did. He worked his mouth a few times, assessing the situation. He caught Rhees watching him and he wondered if she could see the storm brewing inside. Knowing that she probably did helped him calm down enough to hold his tongue. He wondered how she knew him so well already.

"And then, here comes little Rhees." Apparently, Dobbs didn't know when to shut up, Paul thought. "She's so sweet, and she doesn't want anything to do with you, in spite of how much you—"

"It gave Dobbs a sense of satisfaction to see you finally want something so badly, and for once, you couldn't have it." Claire looked at Rhees as she finished the story for her husband. "Last night had more to do with losing the shop than what Dobbs thought you'd done to Rhees."

Paul stared at them, stunned. He wondered if Claire really believed what she'd just said. He thought he saw a flash of doubt—but she wanted to. Normally, he'd argue with them about things being easy for him, defend himself. Normally, he'd lose his temper and start voicing his rage. Normally, he'd fire their asses—

Rhees jumped up and slid into his lap. She took his face between her hands and forced him to look at her, making a gentle shushing sound.

Claire watched Paul's eyes immediately melt from black ice to warm Caribbean blue as he consented to Rhees' attempt to soothe him.

"I'm sorry," he said, still locked on Rhees' expression. He finally glanced down at the floor, resigned. "You're right. I always get everything I want. I am a spoi—"

"Don't," Rhees said, still comforting him. "Nothing just falls into your lap. You get what you want because you work for it. You're intelligent, and you're a hard, determined worker. You go after what you want and you don't give up until you succeed. You don't start what you're not willing to finish—I heard someone say that once." She smiled.

They gazed at each other, and Claire watched as a million words passed between them, unspoken . . . and suddenly, she understood.

"We'll be back to work tomorrow," she said to Paul. "That is, if you'll take us back."

Dobbs shot Claire a surprised glance. She knew he'd be relieved. They'd spent too much time the last few hours discussing their options. They were leaning toward Malaysia or the Maldives, but she could tell, in spite of everything, he didn't want to leave.

Paul looked at Rhees one more time and sighed,

resigning to the new and improved man Claire had noticed him trying to become.

"The shop doesn't run itself. I learned that this morning," Paul said with a reserved chuckle, but then he nodded his head and seemed to genuinely speak the truth. "I appreciate all you do for the shop—for me."

Rhees leaped off Paul's lap to give Claire a hug. "Thank goodness. I'm so sorry I've caused all this trouble, but I'm happy we're going to be all right. I love you guys."

"Thank you," Claire said to Paul while Rhees squeezed the life out of her.

"I appreciate Dobbs' help," Paul said, locking eyes with Claire as an evil grin curved on his lips. "I guess I'm still stuck tolerating yours."

Claire considered the prospect of their ongoing feud, which reminded her of the reason Paul and Rhees had shown up in the first place. Her eyes narrowed as she and Paul held a staring contest.

"You'd bloody well better take care of her," Claire mouthed, pointing to Rhees, who still hadn't let go.

Paul returned a wide-eyed look, conveying to her he intended to try, but she couldn't help but think he suddenly looked like a deer caught in headlights. She wasn't sure if she wanted to worry for Rhees or laugh at what Paul had gotten himself into.

Chapter 8

Paul woke to find Rhees nestled up to him with her back to his front. He carefully rolled to snuggle a little closer. He softly kissed her shoulder and she moaned pleasurably. This was his absolute, favorite time of each day.

There were ten to fifteen seconds every morning when he was awake—mostly—and she was asleep—mostly—where he could be affectionate, and she actually seemed to enjoy it without the cringe factor.

Sometimes the guilt of taking advantage of her while she slept stung a little, and it usually made things *uncomfortable* for him for the few minutes following, but he loved the way she responded—before she had the chance to overthink, the way she had to overthink everything.

"Paul?" she mumbled quietly.

"Hmm?" He didn't stop nuzzling her.

"Did you just . . . *lick* my shoulder?"

"Uh-hmm . . ." he murmured.

She rolled over to look at him, now wide awake. Her expression surprised him. "That's gross! You don't think that's gross?"

He bit his grinning lip. His eyes narrowed and he moved in closer. "I would have no problem licking even grosser things than your shoulder." He held her down and licked her face from her chin to her forehead while she squealed, horrified, and yet, she should have come to expect that type of thing from him by now.

"One of these days, I might surprise you and return the favor. Then we'll see just how funny you think it is."

"Don't make promises you can't keep, Dani Girl." He licked her again, but he couldn't stop laughing, knowing how she thought licking her face was what he meant by licking grosser things than her shoulder. She was such a lovely, innocent, pure being, and reminding himself how much he liked her that way kept her safe—he hoped it would stay that way.

He finally jumped out of bed. He'd learned his limits.

"You don't crawl out of your skin when I get all snuggly in the mornings."

She sat up on the bed, suddenly quiet. She watched him getting dressed with his back turned to her. "I'm sorry. You know that I wish I wasn't like that. I think you handle my psychosis pretty well, though."

He grinned. He was trying, he really was. "I'm just saying there are those few seconds every morning when you don't mind, no cringing, no recoiling, no shrinking away from me. I just wish you could do that when you're awake. You know, let yourself go—relax and just enjoy . . . *just once!*" He turned around to face her, and she noticed his morning glory poking through his jeans. The look on her face registered shock for a split-second, but she fell back on the bed in a fit of laughter that caught him off guard.

"What?" He looked down at himself. "I'm sorry. You know *He* has a mind of his own." Paul chuckled. "But surprisingly, I'm keeping him in check. Can you give me a little credit here?"

She shook her head as she continued to laugh hysterically. She finally got it under control and sat up again. "Did you just hear yourself?" She arched a brow and looked at him mockingly. "*Just once?*"

He looked confused, and she giggled again.

"I'm a virgin, Paul." She could barely keep from bursting into another laughing fit. "Just once? The way *I* understand how it works, that's all it takes." That was it.

She fell back and laughed again.

He sat on the twin bed and chuckled too, but mostly because he loved hearing her laugh. He rarely got to see her this way, letting go, carefree.

oOo

The new boat finally arrived almost a week late due to bad weather, at least that's the story the delivery crew gave. Paul threw a deck party that night to celebrate, the first since the most notorious party Paradise was now known for. He christened the boat, "Swell Dancer", ignoring Rhees' suggestions they find a different name.

The next morning, the new boat set out on its maiden voyage. The bigger vessel accommodated more than twice the number of divers than the Porgy, so nearly every student at the shop sat in their respective spots, next to their gear, ready and excited to dive.

Everyone loved the ease of getting in and out of the water on the roomier boat with two ladders, but when the time came to head back to the shop, the engine refused to start. Paul and Randy tinkered with the motor, but they finally had to radio for a tow.

Two more emergency tows back to the shop and two more attempted fixes, they'd confirmed the new dive boat was a lemon. Paul had been on the phone for days, trying to contact the company where he purchased it, but got nothing but a runaround.

"The biggest group we've ever had booked is coming in less than two weeks. Until then, we'll manage with the Porgy as usual, but if we don't get this *piece of shit* running—" Paul worked, hard, to control the storm brewing inside over being sold a boat with a faulty engine.

"*Piece of Ship*. I like that name better," Rhees said. For some reason, the new name made her uncomfortable. He supposed she didn't like the idea he'd name his boat after her, which he had, but he wouldn't admit it. It couldn't have been too hard to figure out however, since he told her over and over how much he loved the way she danced.

He also supposed she didn't want him naming his boat after her because she expected their pretend relationship to fall apart someday, sooner rather than later. Who wouldn't? All four people involved in the ruse, including himself, knew if it blew up, it'd be his fault. So far, he hadn't even been tempted, but that didn't mean he wouldn't screw up. The Nicole scare was proof enough of that.

"I like that. It fits, anyway," Paul said to Rhees as they, along with Claire and Dobbs, stood on the deck, watching the mechanic not really working on the boat. "I should take it back. Think the Porgy could tow it all the way back to Corpus Christi?" He laughed, though they could all tell he didn't really think it was funny. He sighed irritably.

"It could take months to get it replaced. We don't have time." Claire had been the one who'd so insistently nagged Paul to finally invest in a bigger boat. Everyone knew he wanted to eventually, but a large singles club from the States had inquired about reserving a dive trip with them, and Claire really wanted to book that group. The possibility of repeat and word-of-mouth business if they pulled it off was too great an opportunity to pass up. "You have to get it fixed. We can't cancel on this group."

"What am I supposed to do?" Paul stood, glaring at the mechanic, his arms crossed, his cheek twitching along with his mouth, a sure sign of irritation, which meant looming anger—possible temper—outburst. "The laws in this stupid country require me to use local labor. I can't drive my own boats or bring in a fu—a real mechanic. As the only native mechanic on the island, Fred actually makes more money if he doesn't get it running again. My boat has just become his steady day job." Paul raised his voice. "Fred, you suck."

Rhees gasped and tried to throw her hand over his mouth. "You'll hurt his feelings."

Fred didn't seem to hear them with his earphones on and his music playing too loud. The four of them had watched anxiously for days as Fred came late, took longer breaks than the time he actually worked on the engine, and left for lunch. When he returned, the afternoon followed the same pattern until he finally left for the day around three o'clock.

"Hurt his feelings?" Paul asked incredulously. "Broken arms and legs hurt a whole lot more. He'd better get my boat running and soon."

Rhees locked arms with Paul and rested her head against his shoulder and immediately, it calmed him. He glanced down at her, wondering if she meant to do that, and figured she did. It had only been a little over three weeks since the start of their fake relationship, but he noticed more and more how she seemed to be tuning in to his moods—and managing to control them.

It felt good to have her touch him. He wanted to touch back, but he didn't want to spoil the moment. He'd learned it didn't bother her to touch him, to initiate physical contact, but when he took it as a sign to push for more, she pulled away and he ended up back in the, look, but don't touch, zone. He wanted a more physical relationship, but he settled for what she willingly gave. For now, he thought.

"Some people do their own work, at night—when no one's watching." Dobbs let the suggestion sink in.

Paul rubbed his forehead, understanding what Dobbs implied. "I've tinkered with engines, but I'm not a competent mechanic, not good enough for—"

"Could be our only hope."

Paul nodded and then smiled. "This boat really does need a new name. *Swell Dancer* is too pretty for this clunker. It doesn't fit anymore. She's given me nothing but trouble since she got here." He sounded so serious and everyone nodded in agreement. "I should have just named her *Danarya*."

Rhees only managed a pouty smile while the others broke into loud laughter at her expense.

"Fitting," Dobbs said to Paul with a wicked grin. "Since neither one of them are ever going to let you take her for a ride."

Claire slugged Dobbs' arm, but it didn't make him stop

laughing. Paul glanced awkwardly at Rhees. She blushed, betraying her effort to act like a good sport.

"So, life has given you *two* lemons. Too bad you don't like lemonade," Rhees said as she followed Claire to the office and Dobbs headed toward the deck.

"On the contrary, I've acquired quite a taste for it, I'm afraid," Paul said once he was alone.

oOo

Claire and Rhees watched Paul horsing around with some of the other guys on the deck. He stuck out his tongue in a nasty gesture and Claire noticed Rhees grimace before she slinked back to the office.

"Let me see your tongue," Rhees said when Paul walked into the office later in the day.

"What?" He chuckled. "I'll show it to you for a kiss."

"Just let me see it." She wasn't in the mood to joke around.

He stuck it out and wiggled it around, curious. She grimaced again, before running to the fridge to grab a bottle of water. She twisted the lid off and poured a mouthful, swished it around and ran out of the office to spit it out into the water off the deck.

"Rhees, what's wrong?" Paul sounded concerned.

"Nothing," she said. She hung, bent over the edge of the deck, looking sick.

Paul put his hand on her back and rubbed soothingly. "Are you sure? Are you ill? You don't look so well." She stiffened, and he removed his hand like he'd been bitten.

"I'm fine," she barked as she moved away from him.

He held his hands up in surrender. "All right, just let me know when you're, *more fine*, okay?"

He finally walked off, obviously confused and worried about her, and Rhees walked back into the office looking upset.

"Rhees, what's wrong?" Claire asked after watching the whole thing. "And don't try to convince *me* that you're fine."

"Oh, Claire!" Rhees sighed. "I watched Paul wave his tongue around. It's huge! I'm surprised it fits in his mouth." She shook her head. "I never thought about it before. He likes to use that thing, but—blech!" She stuck her own tongue out and made a face.

"He kisses me with that, and he licks me. I just realized— I'm not the only . . . oh my gosh!" She'd worked herself up to near hysteria. "All I can think about is where that thing has been. Blech! I can't handle it. It grosses me out!"

"Rhees!" Claire took her turn to be incredulous. "I know you *care*." She tried to be discriminating in her choice of words. She knew Rhees was in love with Paul, but she didn't want to listen to her argue that she wasn't. "You're going to have to get over this, this *thing* you have about sharing . . . *those things*. I wouldn't share Dobbs either, if he was inclined to cheat on me. I'm not sure you'd even know what to look for. So I've been keeping my eye on Paul for you, but he hasn't done anything to make me suspect he's screwing around on you.

"If you're hell-bent on keeping up this game you two are playing—" Claire shook her head. She couldn't figure out a good way to break it to her. "Rhees. You may be a virgin, but Paul is not!" It came out louder and with more vehemence than she'd intended.

"You knew that when you signed up for this. You can't go back on it now and renegotiate that part of the contract. It's kind of a done deal. You've got to get over it, Sweet. Get over it!"

oOo

Paul and Rhees sat at the table in the gazebo eating lunch together. Paul ordered a plate of chicken and rice from Aunt Miranda. Randy lived next door to the shop with his mother, his wife, and four kids. His mother, Miranda, earned a little extra money by frying up her special donuts in the mornings, selling candy, soda, and beer from the window of her home facing the street, and taking orders for lunch from people at Paul's shop.

Randy's daughter, Olivia, brought the plate over for her grandmother, and Paul insisted Rhees share it, saying it was too much food for just him. He'd noticed her concern about spending money got in the way of her eating properly, even though he paid her American wages in a Third World economy. He wondered how long it would take her to realize she no longer needed to pinch her pennies.

He also wondered how much longer it would take her to notice the money he'd deposited into her bank account when he thought she was leaving for home. It drove him crazy that after nearly a month, she still hadn't checked her account, but he knew the second she did, he would be in trouble for giving her the ten thousand dollars.

He thought it would be easier to just take it back, and almost wished he could, rather than deal with her imminent reaction, but putting money in someone else's account was easy—getting it out would be criminal—not that it had ever been an obstacle before. He had to shake his head that she didn't pay closer attention to her bank statements, but he couldn't be too critical since he'd left his own financial management on auto-pilot for far too long.

His were more complicated, and he didn't quite realize how someone like Rhees, who had a small amount in one account, didn't need to check it too often. Four hundred dollars wasn't going to earn enough interest to be concerned about. The interest he earned was better invested someplace other than a simple savings account.

Paul didn't know how hard Rhees had been working to overcome her fear of his germs, even after her epiphany of where his tongue had been. Reminding herself that enough time had passed for none of *those* germs to still be in his mouth, helped. Paul also helped by being considerate about the way he ate, making sure not to touch food with his utensil unless he planned to eat it. It all amused him, and he made a game of it.

He thought it comical she struggled to eat a piece of rice

that may have touched his fork, but it grew increasingly easier for her to accept his tongue in her mouth when they kissed for show—sometimes. She'd even started reciprocating once in a while.

They finished their meal and sat watching as Mitch and two new students, Rafael and Barret, flexed their muscles, trying to prove to each other which one of them had the biggest.

"Why do guys do that?" Rhees asked, bemused.

"I don't know. Men are just stupid little boys sometimes," Paul said, disgusted. "Guys refuse to grow up."

He leaned over and gave her a swift kiss before getting up. He headed over to talk to the guys and their muscles, and a few seconds later, Paul joined them, flexing his own. He looked over at her and winked.

Chapter 9

"Tell me something about yourself."

Rhees noticed Paul sitting, staring thoughtfully up at the ceiling, sadness in his eyes. She closed the cover of the extra e-reader Paul just happened to own and insisted she "borrow" so they could read together at night without having to turn on all the lights. She'd whipped up an easy meal and they'd enjoyed a quiet dinner, alone in her apartment. Now they lie in bed for the night, but not ready to fall asleep.

"I'm not quite six-three. I have blue eyes. I own a dive shop—"

She playfully smacked his arm.

"You *said—*"

"I know you prefer to listen, but I'm tired of reading and I do most of the talking. You're probably tired of hearing me ramble on."

"I never get tired of listening to you."

She made a face that meant the same thing as rolling her eyes.

"I don't like to talk about my past. The last time you *forced* me, you didn't like what you heard, remember?"

She looked appalled. "I *forced* you?"

"Yeah!" he teased, putting his hand over the arm she'd just slapped in a defensive move.

"You promised you would tell me, and then you tried to get out of it."

"I never promised. I may lie, but I don't break promises."

"I know." She smiled, admiring him for his commitment to keep his word. "It's just, I do all the talking. Tonight I'm in the mood to hear you carry your share of the conversation for a change. She had a specific topic in mind, hoping to get him to clarify what Shanni had said when she shared her bit of gossip with the Coitus Club.

"Have you ever been in jail?"

His eyes shot to her in surprise at the question. "Yes," he answered somewhat reluctantly. "Several times."

"For what?" She braced herself for a confession about killing someone.

"Well, they put us in a jail cell for hopping trains. Remember Taye's story? They took Bryce to the hospital for observation but the rest of us spent the night locked up, waiting for our parents to come and get us." He checked her expression, looking like he hoped he could be done.

"And the other times?" She wasn't going to let him be finished. He looked at the ceiling again and acted tentative about admitting more.

"That was the first time. There're things I did in between that *could* have landed me in jail, but I was too good at talking my way out of trouble. Sometimes, all it took was a smile or a wink."

"I think I'm the only one who's had to deal with Mr. *Meanie-Head-Grumpy-Pants*. You turn on the charm for everyone else."

"I showed you charm. Was I not charming just before you told me you were a lesbian?" He smirked. "Hey, I just realized. You can't say you don't sleep with men anymore." He laughed at his own joke and she smiled.

"So how did you fail to charm your way out of jail the next time?"

"The next time—few times, were in Asia. In Thailand, I was arrested for beating a man."

She hoped he'd missed her silent gasp. He must have because he didn't stop.

"We were at a bar. A friend told me to meet her out back and when I showed up, she wasn't there, but another man was. He started coming on to me. I told him, very politely, that I wasn't interested, but he wouldn't take no for an answer. He tried to rough me up. I don't usually sit by and let anyone rough me up, but then you know that already, somehow. So anyway, I ended up in jail."

"Why didn't he end up in jail, too?" she pumped for clarification. If the guy went to jail with him, Paul couldn't have killed him.

"The guy was some important dignitary. His bodyguard jumped in when his boss didn't fare so well against me. When that didn't help, another one showed up with the police. They whisked the guy off, out of the public eye, and hauled me to jail."

"So, he isn't dead," she said quietly, thinking aloud before she realized it.

"No. He's still breathing." Paul gave her a funny look. "I found out later that my *friend* had pimped me out for a hundred dollars. She took the guy's money, lured me into that alley, and ran."

Rhees' mouth hung open in shock.

"When I got out a few days later and caught up to her, she gave me some lame excuse about needing the money, and how she knew I could take care of myself."

"Some friend."

"That's Ginger for you."

Rhees had heard the name, a lot.

"Ginger was your girlfriend?"

"No." He didn't hesitate to set that record straight. He exhaled loudly and narrowed his eyes. The crease between his brows grew deep as he thought for a minute, acting anxious. "Look, that's just one more story about my past you'd have been better off not knowing. It only gets worse. Can we drop this—me doing the talking? I don't like polluting your beautiful mind with my trash."

"Have you ever been to prison?"

"Rhees," he warned, and she backed down, but she hoped that someday, he'd trust her enough to tell her.

"Okay, but you're not off the hook. Tell me something

that isn't bad or hard to talk about, or just make something up. I don't care. I want to hear you talk."

"All right, all right." He rolled his eyes and exhaled again. "I got one."

Rhees snuggled up next to him, making herself comfortable.

"My mom was always trying out the latest trends in nutrition. She got on this kick once about eating raw. For the duration, we couldn't eat anything except raw fruits and veggies. For dinner, we'd have these elaborate salads with every vegetable you can imagine, but after the first eight days, I refused to eat anything but nectarines. I'd lost my taste for anything else. I started losing weight and it frustrated my mom, the doctor, to hell." He laughed.

"Mom tried everything, bribing, threats, blackmail . . . she finally gave up and told Carmen to serve me whatever I wanted." He laughed wickedly. "I didn't *wawnt* to eat anything else. It had to be nectarines or nothing. I held out for days—then Carmen brought home a cheeseburger from my favorite drive-through, the one mom had banned the year before." His laughter quieted.

"To this day, if I had to choose one thing to eat for the rest of my life, it would have to be nectarines."

They lay on their sides, looking at each other, smiling. Paul leaned over and kissed Rhees a little too passionately, a little too suddenly. She whimpered and put her hand on his cheek to gently hold him back.

"Wait," she breathed.

He looked disappointed, and collapsed back on his pillow while she took a deep breath.

"Okay. Let's try that again. I'm ready this time."

He stared at the ceiling and didn't move.

"Paul, please, you can kiss me now. I'm all right. You just took me by surprise, that's all."

"Naw, it's okay."

She sighed with frustration. "I'm so sorry. You'd think I could get over that by now."

"Naw . . . your hymen just has good self-preservation

instincts—a strong will to survive." He suddenly grinned. He lifted the sheet and glanced down at himself with a raised brow. "It simply sensed the appropriate danger."

She sighed again and flopped back onto her own pillow. "What are you doing here, still? Why do you put up with all my crappy issues?"

"Because you put up with all of mine."

"Well, I think I got the better deal." She giggled.

He hopped out of bed and started hopping up and down like he needed to burn off energy. "I've got it extra bad tonight. How about we head down to the shop? Let's sleep there tonight. I could use a swim. I'll jog circles around you on the way, and then I'll do a few push-ups."

oOo

Rhees overheard a few of the girls planning a trip to the mainland. Paul, as usual, made them promise to arrange to go as a group.

"Safety in numbers," he said. They wandered around the shop asking everyone if they wanted to go.

"Rhees, do you need anything you can't get on the island? You could come with us." Dorene surprised everyone by inviting her.

"No," Paul answered for her.

"Actually, Paul, I've been making due for quite a while. I really could use a few things. I tried to order them online, but they never showed up. I'm getting desperate."

He shook his head in disgust. "Yeah, the mail in this country is unreliable, and that's putting it kindly. Order what you need but have it sent to Taye. He or one of my other buddies will bring it with them the next time they visit. We came up with that system a while ago. It's worked pretty well."

"I would never send what I need to Taylor!" She needed new panties and a couple of new bras. It horrified her to think of Taylor anywhere near those items meant for her.

"Okay, but I can't go this time. We have the singles

group coming in a few days. I don't like the idea of you being over there without me."

"Okay, I guess I can wait a little longer."

"Is that how you keep him?" Dorene asked later in the day.

Rhees had no idea what she meant.

"Paul's found his own personal lap dog. You do everything he says. It's like he owns you."

"He doesn't own me. He's just concerned about my safety."

"You don't even realize, do you?" Dorene smirked. "I personally know he likes to be in control. You just make it all too easy. No wonder he's still into you after all this time."

Rhees went searching for him.

"Paul, I don't want to put it off. I really do need to buy some things."

"Okay. How about we take a trip to the capital as soon as our group leaves? Just you and I?"

That sounded really fun, but it felt good to be included for a change, and she couldn't get what Dorene had said, off her mind. "No. I want to go with the girls. They rarely invite me to do anything with them and the things I need are personal."

He sighed. He realized he was in for a battle he didn't want and decided to handle it the way he knew best. He moved in close, slowly, so she knew he was coming. He held her hips with his hands and her attention with his eyes.

"I've got so much on my mind with this singles group coming. I need you. Here, with me. How am I supposed to manage without my right hand girl, hmm?" He rubbed her nose with his, still hypnotizing her with his twinkling eyes. "I can't do it without you. You know that." His eyes sparkled gloriously. His right eye twitched, doing the half wink thing.

"Okay," she breathed as she gazed back as intensely as

he gazed at her.

He closed his eyes for a second and let out a quick smirky breath. "I promise. I'll make sure we get what you need." He opened his eyes and resumed with his strategy. "After this group has come and gone, okay?"

"Okay." It was all she could manage to say.

Chapter 10

*I*t was after seven o'clock and Paul stood on a crate in the water so that it reached just below his chest. He focused, concentrated, holding the propeller parts together, looking at them like a puzzle to be solved. He'd been online all afternoon, researching the problem, and once Fred went home for the day, Paul had decided to check out the propeller. With no one left at the shop except Rhees, he went to work, hoping he'd found something in his research that would help him get the still unnamed boat running again. In the meantime, he'd been calling it *The Piece of Shit* until he could come up with the right name.

"Are you hungry?" Rhees asked.

Paul didn't answer and she asked again.

"Just order something. Whatever you want."

She sighed. "Miranda is the only one on this island who delivers, and that's only at lunchtime. She doesn't do dinner, and even lunch is only because she lives right next door . . . *and* because she has a crush on you. Naughty Aunt Miranda." Rhees giggled. "I can run home and make something quick. I'll be back before you even notice I'm gone."

He glanced up at her and she knew he didn't like her suggestion. "I don't want you running around by yourself." He turned his attention back to the boat. "Just call Fratelli's. Call whomever you want. They'll all deliver if you pay them enough."

She sighed again. "I know I had trouble walking alone for a while, but I can do it now. I'm fine. I just want to go home and make something quick and easy—and cheap."

He didn't answer. She'd lost him to the problem with the boat. She frowned as she watched him, water dripped from his skin, making him shine. The muscles in his arms bulged as he manipulated the parts in his hands, his expression serious, but he looked . . . so cute.

His tongue stuck out slightly and he mindlessly manipulated it, rolling and flexing it between his lips. His brow furrowed as he thought about what he was doing, recalling images he'd seen online. He stared intently at the pieces, his cheek twitched, and the muscles in his neck were taut.

Paul had the sexiest neck she had ever seen. She'd never noticed or paid attention to men's necks before, but as she watched him—she wanted to kiss his neck—no, she wanted to take a bite of that Adam's apple of his. She closed her eyes and tried to banish the thought, but she couldn't completely get the idea out of her mind, especially when it would still be there, the second she opened her eyes again.

"Paul!"

"Hmm?" She wasn't convinced he grasped how she really wanted his attention.

"I don't want to order delivery. I'm going home to make us something to eat."

"If I don't get this fixed by Sunday, we're screwed." He obviously hadn't heard her.

"I'll be fine. I'll hurry. Don't worry about me, okay?" He didn't respond. Entrenched in the problem, he wasn't about to slip out of mechanic mode anytime soon. "Okay, I'm leaving, but I'll be right back."

Still nothing, and she didn't want to press her luck. She stood and pulled her shorts from her backpack and slipped them on over her swimming suit bottoms, but didn't bother to put the T-shirt over her tankini top. She'd be back to get it in less than an hour.

"I'll see you later. Please don't worry."

She started to walk off but stopped, knowing he would normally have a fit about what she planned to do. The fact that he didn't say anything made her worry. She hated seeing him so stressed out and wished she could help. She really wanted to just burn that darned boat. It'd been nothing but trouble since it arrived.

She made it to her apartment in record time and decided not to shower. She went straight to the kitchen and set about making a tuna salad. She decided to eat before heading back, knowing Paul was too preoccupied to have any hopes of having anything that resembled a dinner date. She put the rest of the salad in a bowl with a lid, and grabbed two beers from the fridge before heading back to the shop.

oOo

Paul still stood in the water as she'd left him, holding pieces of the boat, looking perplexed that he couldn't get it to work in spite of what he'd learned on the Internet.

"Why don't we just burn it?" Rhees asked with a playful grin. "I'll get the match."

He didn't look up, but at least he acknowledged her with a, "Hmm?"

"I have some dinner for you," she said. She looked down at him from the deck but he just grunted again. She sat down on the floor, put the food next to her, and watched him for about a half an hour until she started to worry about all the bacteria growing in the unrefrigerated salad.

"Paul. You need to eat before this goes bad. I know you don't care about germs like I do, but you'll never convince me that food poisoning is a figment of my imagination."

"Okay, Babe. Just a minute."

Hmm . . . Babe. At least he knows it isn't Dobbs keeping him company.

He pulled the mask from around his neck, up over his eyes and slipped under the water to fiddle with putting the parts back. She sighed. Two minutes later, he resurfaced.

"Paul?"

"Hmm?" He still hadn't looked at her.

She rolled onto her stomach, and with the salad in one hand, the spoon in the other, she leaned as far over the edge of the dock as she could while still balancing herself. She spooned a bit of salad and held it out to him.

"Paul, eat!" The stern, motherly tone in her voice was odd enough to make him break away from his engine troubles. As soon as he saw her, he did a double take. The way she hung over the edge of the deck, her swimming suit top—the way her breasts dangled in her suit as she leaned . . . over—it caught his attention.

He hardly noticed the spoon she held for him, and didn't really care about it until she gestured that she wanted him to eat. He opened his mouth. She put the spoon in, and he closed his mouth around it but didn't let go. He didn't take his eyes off . . . her. He raised his eyebrows in approval.

"You like it." She smiled, pleased with herself and relieved he didn't seem to be upset about her walk home and back, alone, against his wishes. His eyes gleamed, and he nodded, slowly.

"Let go of the spoon, and I'll get you some more."

He released the spoon, but before she could scoop up another bite, he reached up and grabbed her, pulling her down into the water with him. She squealed in protest, and it was all she could do to hang on to the bowl and spoon and not drop them into the water.

"What are you doing? I almost spilled your dinner."

"Mm," he grunted, drawing her to him and holding her close. "I'm going to kiss you now, so get ready." He leaned in and gave her a gentle kiss on the lips. "Mm!"

"I thought you liked my salad." Ending up in the water had thrown her off. She didn't think about the closeness or react in her usual uptight way. She crooked her elbow around his neck to hang on, trying not to spill the salad.

"I like the way you're feeding me. I like it a little too much." He opened his mouth again to suggest that he was ready for more, and she fed him another spoonful. He chewed but didn't stop studying her. He mused at how the island had turned her whole body his new favorite color. Her skin had tanned to a beautiful golden brown, matching her hair, which had lightened after spending months in the sun. He'd always thought it the color of honey, but now it nearly glowed, just like her golden amber eyes. After he swallowed, he pressed his lips against hers again, more passionately than before. She returned his kiss but not very enthusiastically.

"You have fish breath," she said, her lips still against his mouth.

He smirked and gazed at her. "I would love to have fish breath."

"Oh, you have it, all right. Trust me." She made a face.

"I mean a different kind of fish breath." His eyes sparkled with wicked humor.

"You don't like tuna? Do you like crab? I almost made crab salad instead."

He broke into laughter and squeezed her tighter. "Oh, Dani Girl!" *You have no idea what I'm talking about.* "Mm. I think your salad is delicious. Just like you." He gave her another quick kiss and helped her out of the water.

oOo

"How about naming it, *The Tow'd*?" Rhees walked up behind him as Paul finished tying the new boat off to the dock.

His research had paid off. He and Randy had just taken it out and back with no problems. Paul hoped the fix would last, at least until the singles group came and went.

"*The Toad*? I like it." He smiled and put his arm around her. Her whole body stiffened, and he promptly removed his arm.

She closed her eyes and took a deep breath. When she opened them again, she smiled up at him and snuggled against him to assure him that she was ready this time.

He glanced sideways at her but tentatively wrapped

his arm around her again. He pulled her close enough to rest her ear against his chest. That always helped. She took another breath, not as deep, and didn't flinch.

"*The Toad*, fits. Toads are as disgusting as this darned boat!" He tried to suppress a secretive smile.

"I meant Tow'd, as in needing a tow." It relieved her he no longer wanted to name it *Swell Dancer*, and she'd been trying to help him come up with a new name—that didn't reference her in any way. "You know, since you've had to tow her so many times."

"Oh, I thought you meant toads—because you hate those ugly, disgusting creatures."

She stared at him with a strange look on her face. "How do you know that?"

He grinned and shrugged his shoulders with a little too much emphasis. "Lucky guess."

The night after the dance contest, when he'd helped her home, they'd come across a knot of toads in the road along the way. She'd jumped into his arms, screaming hysterically about how she hated toads and calling them, "Ugly, disgusting creatures."

"*The Tow'd* it is." He kissed the top of her head and let her have it her way. The boat, in his mind, would be named after her, or because of her, without making her uncomfortable the way *Swell Dancer* had.

Later that day, the painter arrived. Ninety minutes later, the boat officially had its name.

He'd made Rhees promise to stay in the office until the painter finished. Paul led her around from the other side of the shop and stopped so they were across the deck from the boat, looking at it from a distance. He removed the hand he had over her eyes.

"What do you think?" Paul asked. He stood behind her, his hands resting on her shoulders, as he pointed her toward the boat to inspect the new name.

"It looks good," she answered.

"Why don't you get a closer look—just to make sure."

She moved closer, but he stayed where he was and

braced himself.

"The" and "Tow'd" were painted in large gold letters with a black outline. The other words were painted in a small gold font, without the outline. From a distance the smaller words weren't noticeable, but up close, the boat's title read:

The Gosh Darn Freakin' Tow'd

Rhees spun around to let him have it, but he had disappeared.

Chapter 11

Claire couldn't contain her excitement—they'd pulled it off. The singles group came and went, and miraculously, *The Tow'd* didn't break down once. The group loved how Paradise treated them and had already booked a repeat trip for the following year.

The day after the singles group left, a new girl showed up in the office.

"I want to sign up for diving lessons."

Paul sat at his computer, but he didn't even glance up. "Claire, can you get that?"

"Um, actually, Paul, you're the one I was hoping to talk to. A couple of friends and I came to dive, but my friends preferred to go to Island Divers. I insisted on diving here though, because . . . I wanted to meet you."

Paul looked up, and Claire noticed a quick look of surprise shoot through his eyes. The girl was a knockout. American, blonde, hot! Paul turned back to his computer. "Claire, could you get her started on the paperwork? I need to finish this."

Claire was impressed.

Ten minutes later, Paul finally stood to greet the girl while she filled out the last few items on the forms. He offered to shake her hand, but she didn't let go when he tried to pull away. She smiled at him.

"Just a sec." He picked up the microphone. "Rhees, Baby. Could you come to the office, Honey?"

Paul noticed Rhees' flushed cheeks as she walked cautiously into the office, not knowing what to expect. He'd never been so lovey-dovey over the microphone before.

"Hey Dani Girl! This is . . ." Even though he remembered the girl's name, he made it a point to look down to get it off of the paperwork, just to make sure Rhees, the new girl, and even Claire, knew he hadn't paid attention, or cared. "Sarah, our newest student. Sarah, this is my *girlfriend*, Rhees."

"Hi, Sarah," Rhees said with uncertainty. Paul hurried around the counter. He grabbed Rhees and gave her a big, hard, passionate kiss, catching her off-guard. Rhees gasped and tensed up, and he let her go before she had a chance to push him away too forcibly. His eyes pleaded with desperation, hoping she'd notice.

"Where've you been? I haven't seen you for a whole ten minutes. I've missed you." He put his arm around Rhees, possessively.

"Um . . . on the deck, reading." Rhees looked at the new girl and smiled. Sarah's face registered confusion, and then Rhees looked at Claire. Claire appeared to be trying to warn her without being obvious. "Um . . . I missed you too, *Babe!*"

"Sarah, let me show you around," Claire said. "It's my job to initiate the newbies." She didn't give Sarah a chance to argue. Claire grabbed her by the arm and pulled her through the tunnel and into the equipment room.

"What was that?" Rhees whispered to Paul.

He seemed embarrassed and didn't answer. All he could do was shrug.

"Do you want to be with her? Is that it?" Rhees finally had to ask. "You know we've made our point. We can end this any time."

Rhees felt herself start to grow shaky at the thought of what might be happening—that he might be ready to end it.

"No!" The look on his face seemed very convincing.

He sighed. "Let's just say . . . having a girlfriend comes in handy." He still had a strange expression, but after a few seconds, a sly smile broke across his face. "Bet you never thought you'd hear me say *that*, did you?"

oOo

"Rhees," Claire said thoughtfully that afternoon when they were alone in the office. "What will you do when Paul screws up?"

Rhees scowled and then shrugged. She didn't answer.

"Because, you know he's bound to at some point, right? He can't go on living like a monk for the rest of his life."

Rhees didn't like hearing it. "Everyone thinks I'm *broken in* now. Paul knows he can move on whenever he's ready." She tried to sound convincing.

"But you don't want him to."

"What makes you say that?"

"Don't give me that. I see what's going on between . . . It's not only you. It's Paul too." She let out one loud, ironic breath of air. "Who would have thought? Rhees, darling, I know he's trying. I'm amazed at how well he's doing—I never, in a million years, would have believed he could do this, but while he's acting like your boyfriend, you need to act more like a girlfriend."

Rhees' face flushed pale. She thought she knew what Claire meant and it made her sick inside, knowing she just couldn't. "I can't. You know I can't."

"No. Not that. It's girls like Sarah. If a girl even looked at Dobbs the way Sarah looks at Paul, I'd scratch her eyes out. It's sickening, the way she goes after him, right in front of you."

"I told you. Paul's a grown man. If he'd rather move on . . ." It was harder to say than she realized. "He can just break up with me or pretend to."

"Rhees." Claire wheeled her computer chair closer to her and turned Rhees' chair so they were face-to-face. "If Paul were *my* boyfriend—if this was Dobbs we're talking about—Dobbs understands. He may think about other women. I can't control his thoughts, and sometimes letting him have a fantasy or two actually works to my favor." Rhees didn't understand—especially the sad look that flashed across Claire's eyes as she'd said it. "But he wouldn't dare sleep with anyone else because he values his life."

"But we're just pretending to be in a sexual relationship," Rhees said. "He really is my friend though, and friends don't put demands on each other like that."

"Rhees, honey. Listen to me, okay?" Claire looked into her eyes. "I don't know how much longer Paul can keep up this thing you two have going, but he's not ready to stop. I don't understand what's going on with him, but he needs this, at least, for the time being. I see it every day. But a little territorial behavior will go a long way in making sure a man like Paul remembers that."

"Okay," Rhees grumbled. "I'll try."

"Don't try. Do!" Claire seemed desperate to get it through to her friend. "And while you're at it, you need to be more convincing in the, *I'm his girlfriend* department. I actually think Paul would appreciate a little help with the skanks. Sarah's not the only one throwing herself at him."

"What does that mean?"

"I've overheard things. Sarah isn't the only cheap trollop sniffing around your man. The other girls are complaining, wondering how a man like Paul wants to have a girlfriend who is so cold—physically. People are noticing how hard it is for you to let him touch you."

Rhees threw her hands over her face. It was difficult to hear someone tell her the same thing that had been going through her mind for weeks.

"Listen Sweet. Just try, okay?"

Rhees took a deep breath and nodded.

oOo

Rhees tried for the next few days to act more girlfriend-like, but she felt too inadequate to pull it off. At least Sarah, the new girl, didn't appear to get the message. She constantly hounded Paul, acting, Rhees thought, obnoxiously slutty. Even Paul rolled his eyes at Sarah, walked away from her in the middle of her sentences, and tried ignoring her completely, but she didn't give up.

Rhees' attempts to initiate affectionate behavior led Paul to falsely get his hopes up. When he reciprocated the affection, she tensed up, writhed away, and downright scorned him.

"Trouble in paradise?" Sarah asked Paul after watching Rhees suffer through one of his surprise affection bombs, aimed at getting Sarah off his back.

"Never," Paul answered tersely.

"That's interesting, because I really get the vibe Rhees just isn't that into you. She's crazy. Who couldn't be into you?" She tried to make eye contact, but he wouldn't look her way.

He gritted his teeth and regretted what he believed he needed to do.

"I guess she's just so *into* me in private, she's too worn out for a lot of PDA, she needs to save her strength— or should I say—I'm so *in* her?" He arched his brow suggestively, but on the inside, he felt sleazy for making such a dirty slur against the girl who was his beautiful, virtuous princess. Sometimes the stakes in this game got a little high, even for him.

"*I* am into *her*, so until she kicks my sorry ass to the curb, I'm in it—*with her!*" He hoped that settled it once and for all, but it didn't.

oOo

That afternoon, Rhees was surprised to find Paul at his computer, in the middle of the day.

"What are you doing in here on this lovely afternoon?"

Paul didn't want to tell her how he'd grown tired of Sarah's constant flirting, and the office sounded like a good excuse to be out of her reach. Looking for things to do in the office made him think about the business he'd neglected for so long.

"Rhees." He reached for her and pulled her onto his lap. "There are some things I should work on. I've been ignoring it for years, but this new, "*it's time to grow up*", plan you have me on is making me feel like I should, at least, take a look at it. I may seem a little preoccupied for the next few days. Okay?"

"I don't have you on a plan. Is that what you think? Paul?" She didn't like what he'd said.

"It's a good thing, Dani Girl. I like that plan."

"No." She put her hand on his cheek, but he quickly shushed her with a kiss. "What is it you'll be working on?"

He shrugged. "Just business. Old investments, unrelated to the shop. I've left it all on auto-pilot for too long. I think, maybe I'm finally ready to take a look at it, make sure it's all still doing what it's supposed to be doing. I'm sure after all this time, there will be things that need to be rearranged, restructured, that sort of thing." He forced a smile, knowing how he could get when he was in businessman mode—the man he'd been trying to run away from the past five years.

Rhees had to be the only reason he'd been thinking about that part of his old life again. The new self-awareness program he had himself on, because of her, had him thinking about a lot of things besides being a man-whore, a tyrant, and an overall asshole.

oOo

Rhees sat across from Paul, reading. He sat at a table on the deck at Tanked with his laptop, absorbed in his recent business project. He said he preferred they hang out where she wouldn't get lonely while he engrossed himself in his work.

He didn't talk much about it, and Rhees didn't understand it when he did, but while he worked, the rest of the world ceased to exist, even her. She understood why he'd apologized for it up front. She missed him.

"I'm thirsty. Would you like a beer?"

He grunted but didn't seem to notice when she got up. She wandered around the bar, saying hello to everyone who'd come into the bar since she'd arrived and then ordered a soda for herself, a beer for Paul.

She knew, based on the past few nights, that they'd be there a while. He'd lose track of time, and when she grew tired, she'd tell him. He'd say, "Just a minute", and another thirty minutes would go by before she'd tell him again and eventually, she'd have to literally pull him away from his work so they could get some sleep.

She didn't mind. It was just another demonstration of his inability to do anything halfway. She wished he'd find a better balance between his obsession to get this project done and taking care of himself. If it weren't for her, she thought for sure he wouldn't have eaten, or slept for days.

She headed back toward his table with their drinks but stopped dead in her tracks.

"How about a beer, Babe?" Paul didn't look up from his computer.

"Sure, *Babe*. Anything for you, what kind would you like?"

The strange voice made him look up, but seeing for himself didn't lessen his confusion. He hadn't noticed Rhees leave or Sarah sit down in Rhees' stead. Sarah smiled, and shamelessly undid one more button, exposing even more of her cleavage than before.

"Where's Rhees?" He glanced toward the bar, searching for her. Sarah shrugged, but didn't drop the annoying smile on her face.

He finally caught a glimpse of Rhees laughing with the bartender before she turned and headed back to their table with a soda in one hand and a beer in the other, his favorite brand. Such a little thing, but—he faced Sarah again and smiled, thinking this flirtatious, forward woman didn't stand a chance against his Dani Girl. He found it surprisingly nice how comfortable he'd become with Rhees and the way she seemed to read his mind, anticipating when he'd want a beer and she knew what kind he drank.

Rhees made her way slowly, cautiously, to Paul's table, watching him smile at Sarah. The warmth in his eyes for the new girl troubled her. *Scratch her eyes out.* Claire's words ran through her mind. What a stupid saying, she wasn't exactly sure how to do that, but it sounded pretty good at the moment. She walked up right behind Sarah and stood for a second, trying to decide what to do. Paul looked from Sarah to her.

"Hey." He smiled up at her, so genuinely, all relaxed, as though he hadn't just been caught flirting with another woman. Rhees waited for him to vault into a lame excuse about what the two of them had been doing, but he didn't say anything else. His right eye did its adorable winky thing instead.

Rhees glanced away for a second, took an extra deep breath, and moved to his side of the table where she set his beer down in front of him. She finally dared to look at Sarah, who now watched, with what Rhees imagined, an arrogant air on her heavily made-up, slutty face.

"Hey," Rhees replied back. She still hadn't taken her eyes off Sarah. "I brought you a beer. How's the *work* coming?"

She set her own drink on the table and slid her hands around Paul's neck and down his chest from behind, pretending to look at his computer screen as if she understood what it was he was doing. She leaned into him so their cheeks touched, and then, so out of character, she turned and feathered his jaw with her lips, nipping at him sensually. She reached his mouth and tenderly gave him a long, but soft, kiss. His lips parted and she felt his surprised intake of breath.

"I'm going home...to bed." She used the most seductive voice she could manage, and didn't break contact with his eyes as she slowly pulled away, begging him with her eyes to leave with her . . . If he knew what was best for him. She finally broke contact and moved so she stood behind Sarah again. She mimed the actions of pulling a pistol from a holster at her hip, and she shaped her hand to resemble one. She pointed it at the back of Sarah's head.

Sarah didn't take her eyes off of Paul, surely hoping she'd finally have a chance with him if Rhees left him there on his own, but Paul didn't take his puzzled eyes off of Rhees. Rhees made a jerking motion with her hand, still pointed at Sarah's head, blew a puff of air at her extended fingers as if blowing the smoking end of a gun. She holstered her pretend pistol and walked off, leaving Paul with his mouth agape.

"Excuse me. I need to go!"

"But Paul, this will be the first chance we've had to really get to know each other," Sarah whined.

He didn't miss a beat, as if he hadn't even heard her. He smiled giddily like a kid as he stuffed his things into a nylon briefcase and took off after Rhees, leaving Sarah still sitting at the table, looking disappointed.

Rhees walked faster than normal, and it took Paul a minute to catch up.

"Rhees? Hey, Rhees!" He finally reached her, but she still didn't stop. He grabbed her arm, making her swing around to face him. "What was that all about?"

"Nothing." She glanced away. She looked angry.

"Are you jealous?" He finally had to ask, but knew he sounded much too amused.

"Should I be?" Rhees finally dared to look at him.

She *was* jealous and Paul couldn't help the silly grin on his face.

"What!" She impatiently folded her arms.

Rhees didn't understand the look on his face.

"I don't know." He grinned his goofy grin again, as if he could ever look goofy.

She didn't soften her scowl. She even felt a strange urge to smack him, sure he was making fun of her.

Still smiling, he shrugged again. "It's just . . . I always thought how dreadful it would be to have a girlfriend, you know?" He seemed to have a hard time containing his glee. "Dreadful to put up with things like being told it's time to go home, like a little kid being sent to his room. And things like, let's say . . . *jealousy*." He smirked and looked down like it embarrassed him to admit it, but he also looked a little smug and much too flattered to think that maybe she was.

"But damn girl! That. Was. So. *Haaawt!*" He looked at her like an excited little boy on Christmas morning. His eyes sparkled more than usual.

"You're happy I'm jealous?"

He nodded enthusiastically, eyes wide and ridiculous grin still intact.

"Well don't think it's ever going to happen again. Do you hear me? If you think I'm going to put up with you running around, blatantly and grossly flirting—flashing those—those beautiful blues of yours to all the girls—"

He put his arms around her and picked her up so he could look her in the eyes. She had no choice but to put her arms around his neck for support and then she couldn't help it, she wrapped her legs around his waist. She'd become comfortable with the position. It made her feel safe and she needed to feel safe.

"Did I do that?" he asked, still a little too amused. "Because I don't think I did anything like that."

They eyed each other for an extended time and all the silliness died away, no longer anything silly about the way he looked at her.

"You have nothing to be jealous of, Dani Girl." He studied her a second longer before dropping his head, glancing down. His brow furrowed and his lips twitched a few times. With his head still bent forward, his eyes slowly rolled back up to meet hers. It gave him a devilish appearance that made her nervous. He made a quick, growling sound.

"I'm going to kiss you now, Dani Girl." He gave her a second to prepare and then he did, long and wet, and she didn't mind.

"Haaaawt!" He growled and kissed her again.

Chapter 12

"What do you guys do?" Claire asked. They sat at their chairs, each working on their computers. "In all the time you two spend together, if you're not—you know?"

Rhees giggled, nervously. "Claire!"

Claire shrugged. "I know it's not *that*. Why do you think I'm asking?" They turned their chairs to face each other.

"We talk. We read, work on computers together, cook. Well, I cook. Paul watches and tries to help, but he's pretty hopeless in the kitchen." She smiled at the thought of him lurking in the background, unsure of what to do with himself, but never abandoning her to cook and clean alone. At least he kept her company.

"Sometimes we dance. He's always asking me to teach him. He says he wants to look like he can keep up when we dance in public. I'm not sure why he thinks he can't. His mother insisted her kids take dance lessons for a couple of years, so he knows all the traditional ballroom—" She suddenly worried she'd breached his trust. He never spoke of his family, except to her, and even that was a recent and rare development. She made a mental note to be careful. She didn't want to share personal information he wouldn't share himself.

"He's probably using it as an excuse to watch you at your sexiest. You're pretty sexy when you dance. Have you ever noticed any drool during these *lessons*?" Claire fought back a smirk.

"Claire!" Rhees blushed and got all giddy. "How do you know I don't enjoy watching *him*? The man's got moves—my pretend boyfriend is really *hawt*—in case you haven't noticed."

"I've noticed." Claire didn't try to hide her shock. "I'm just surprised to hear you have."

Rhees felt her face grow warm again, embarrassed, but not as much as she would have been a few weeks before. "He also tries to teach me self-defense. After—" Her breath caught. She wondered if she'd ever be able to think about what Mario tried to do to her without the threat of a panic attack.

"He worries I can't defend myself, so he shows me things to do under various situations. We always end up fighting though—not self-defense fighting, real fighting. He gets so mad that I won't try to hurt him. He tells me, '*Okay, now kick me as hard as you can*'. But I can't do that and things escalate, and the next thing I know, he's all angry and bothered."

Claire watched her, fascinated.

"I'm a hopeless cause. We go through that over and over. You'd think he'd drop it and save his angry energy for something else."

"I think you kind of like angry Paul," Claire teased. Rhees bit her lip and raised a guilty brow, but didn't admit it with a vocal response. They both laughed.

"Sometimes I wonder how he got so aggressive. He's so tough, inside and out. Is it just a man thing? Are all men like that? My dad was tough, but not like Paul—Paul is so *high-strung*."

"Dobbs wouldn't hurt a fly—" Claire made a strange face and glanced at Rhees. The memory of Dobbs slugging Paul came to mind. "That's why I fell in love with the big lug. He's so mild-mannered—at least he *was*. He's going through a mid-life crisis or something." She made the face again.

"Well it's no wonder Paul's in such good shape. You'd

think that with all the physical activity he does during the day, all his sports, the diving, and adrenaline-filled activities he's always up to, he'd be too tired to swim so much in the middle of the night. I can't believe how much energy that man has. He's practically hyper sometimes."

"He swims? In the middle of the night?" It took Claire a minute, but she burst into riotous laughter.

"What?" Rhees asked innocently.

"Oh Rhees, baby." Claire had never called her that, but somehow Rhees knew it was about to fit the situation. "Hun, does he tend to swim when—have you noticed him—does he have a *bulge*?" Claire practically stuttered, appearing to have trouble spitting it out.

Rhees understood, at least that part of her question. "Yes. It does indeed coincide. I'm not *that* stupid. He's open about that with me. Swimming makes it go away, burns off that energy."

"Oh Sweet." Claire laughed again, even louder. "I'd bet money it's not the swimming that makes it go away. It just gets him away from you so he can—you know."

Rhees didn't know.

Claire made a gesture by forming an O with her hand and she shook it a couple of times. She laughed again when Rhees drew a blank.

"Well good for him." Claire moved along. "I'm glad that *swimming* is working for him . . . and keeping you safe. What do you talk about?"

"Everything," Rhees said quietly, knowing she should know what Claire meant, but she didn't really want to figure it out. She brushed it off and brightened again.

"I do most of the talking, most of the time. I have to practically threaten him to get him to open up to me, but he's always a good listener. He says he appreciates that we don't have to talk sometimes, that he feels comfortable with me because I'm not all uptight like other girls, when we go, sometimes hours, without speaking at all."

Rhees knew Paul, she believed, better than most people. She remembered the pictures Regina kept of him, sitting on the deck, watching the sunset. A quiet, private, even shy, man, Paul needed his time to reflect on whatever he spent so much time reflecting on. She liked knowing he felt comfortable doing it with her around.

"I see how happy you are." Claire looked envious. "Both of you."

Rhees smiled. "I am happy."

"I'm happy for you then. I never would have thought. Paul!"

"I know," Rhees said dreamily. "Who would have thought, right? Paul is . . . he's always been great. It's just . . . he doesn't often show this side of himself—the side I get to see."

"All right, but don't stop being *careful*, okay?"

"Claire!" Rhees grew defensive. "That's not fair. He's done nothing to make you say that."

"It bloody surprises me, that's all. When you two started this weird relationship, I thought *you'd* be the one changing." Claire had a concerned look on her face. "I knew the old Paul too well. I'm not sure what it'll take to stop worrying about my friend."

"Me, your friend, or Paul, your friend?"

Claire's head dropped back and she laughed.

"Paul and I are not friends."

oOo

Rhees sat in Claire's chair, watching Paul at his computer. He concentrated on his work and didn't notice how she stared. In his focus, not only did his mouth move through its usual motions, but his tongue had jumped into the act. It poked out, and he'd lick his lips, hold it in the corner of his lips, bite it, roll it, lick again. She finally laughed, and he turned to see what she was up to.

"What?" He seemed cautious, his face still held the serious expression.

"Nothing." Rhees giggled at getting caught watching him. "Just that mouth of yours, and your tongue." She giggled again. "Always busy doing something."

"You mention it a lot." He rolled his chair closer to her and her eyes grew wide in anticipation of what she imagined was coming. He leaned into her face, just barely, not touching her, and watched her, curiously.

"I can think of a few other things I'd like to do with my mouth . . . my *tongue*," he teased.

Her smile dropped along with the humor he'd aimed for.

"After all this time, I wish you—" he rasped out just above a whisper. "Is it my germs, or is it just me?" Their eyes locked in serious consideration. His expression slowly twisted into remorse, then confusion as hers changed to mischief.

"Do it. I dare ya."

His eyes grew wide at her challenge. "Oh, Dani Girl, you do *nawt* want to be daring me to do anything."

"I double dog dare you."

Paul studied her eyes to be sure, but he wasn't about to argue. He leaned in and kissed her softly, holding the kiss for a moment, tenderly, but timidly outlining her lips with his tongue, careful to not impose himself on her more than she could handle. He leaned back just enough to look at her, gauge her reaction. She hadn't flinched, cringed, or shied away. He moaned pleasurably and licked his lips, savoring what little of her still lingered there.

Rhees felt no fear and hoped she'd shown him she didn't mind anymore. She must have, because he grinned, looking very satisfied, before he leaned in to do it again.

Chapter 13

*R*hees stepped into her shower, yanked the curtain closed, stepped as far to the side as possible, and turned on the water so she wouldn't get wet right away. Routinely, she took a deep breath, taking a second to brace herself before stepping into the shocking coldness. She was just about to take the plunge.

"Rhees!" Paul said.

A chill ran down her spine, colder than the shower water she hated so much. Paul stood right there, in her bathroom, nothing but a thin shower curtain between her naked body and him.

"You know the rules!" she yelled. "You're not even supposed to be in the bedroom while I'm in the bathroom."

"I know. I'm only here to tell you about your birthday present."

"My birthday isn't for two days. Get out!"

"Rhees." His tone sounded stern, and it surprised her. She mentally ran through her day, wondering what she'd done. They'd been getting along so well, very well.

She poked her head around the curtain, careful not to expose herself to him. She gave him a bug-eyed look to get across how much she disapproved. He wore a brilliant smile, which confused her even more.

"Before you step into the water and groan miserably because of the cold, I wanted to tell you that for your birthday, I'm giving you a warm shower."

"How are you going to do that?" Her mind ran through

possibilities, but she couldn't come up with a logical plan that wasn't a little creepy.

"Well, if I tell you that, it'll ruin the surprise. Duh."

"You just told me what my present is. How is it a surprise?"

"You'll have to wait and see." He beamed as he leaned toward her and stole a quick kiss.

She yelped at the closeness. She felt so naked and exposed. She *was* naked!

oOo

"You'll find the arrangements have been made, Sir," the bellboy said as he opened the door to the hotel room

"Fine," Paul said. "Thank you. We'll manage without the orientation." Paul slipped the man a generous tip and ushered Rhees inside the room. They had no luggage, only their backpacks, so the bellboy nodded and winked as Paul closed the door. *He thinks I'm in a hurry to get her into bed.* Paul almost laughed.

His body verged on calling a truce with abstinence, finally! It had been hard in the beginning, damn hard, but he'd made a decision, a promise to Rhees—a promise to himself. He wanted—needed—to change, and after almost six weeks, the fight had become easier—easier, not easy. He couldn't afford to fool himself. She couldn't afford for him to fool himself.

Sure, he liked teasing her, licking her because she hated it, sneaking in a kiss now and then, pushing her beyond her comfort zone, the way she pushed him. But he respected her, admired her goodness. There was more to it than just virtue, everything about her, her entire being screamed decency and innocence. He'd never known anyone like her.

Her temperament fascinated him. Her big heart forgave any offense. He'd witnessed her in situations where anyone else would walk away permanently offended—and justly so—but not Rhees. She held no grudges toward the other students at the shop who'd shunned her and treated her so harshly in the beginning. She'd forgiven *him*, the worst offender.

He didn't think she even noticed their efforts to hurt her most of the time. He could only guess it had to do with the fact that her mind didn't work that way, so she didn't comprehend how theirs could.

On the other hand, he knew, even she had limits. Rhees was no pushover. She saw herself as one, but he knew better. She had teeth. Push her far enough and she knew how to bite.

The room looked like no hotel room Rhees had ever stayed in, all three times. A four-foot long counter with a sink took up the corner to the left of the entrance with a small fridge and a microwave. A round table sat nearby with a silver cloche on top. The sitting area spread straight ahead, with two red couches placed at an angle to each other, a red armchair in the right corner, with a black leather ottoman in the middle of the red furniture.

A large desk sat in front of two windows, set at an angle to each other and looking out over the city. To the right, French doors lay open, showing off the bed with a dark wooden headboard and a white comforter.

"This is not the average hotel room." She looked accusingly at Paul.

"Looks pretty average to me." He feigned sudden enlightenment. "Are you trying to tell me they have rooms more average than this?"

She didn't dignify his response with an answer.

"What's the point of staying at a luxury hotel if we just wanted the same room we could get at any budget motel, a bed, maybe two, and a dinky bathroom?"

He added as an afterthought, "I'd go crazy in a room like that."

She didn't stop glaring and he pretended to be affronted. "Hey, I'm already slumming it for you here. This hotel is missing a star. I grew up believing anything less than five meant you'd go home with cockroaches, lice or bedbugs."

"Seriously?" She believed it could be true.

"Almost." He grinned and kissed the top of her head. "I have issues with confinement—I need room to breathe. Come on. Let's explore the other rooms."

The bed she'd seen through the door turned out to be king-sized. To the right of the bedroom lay a large closet that lighted when the doors opened, and a bathroom.

"Darn. I'd hoped for a little nicer shower than this." Paul opened the frosted door and looked inside.

"If the water heater works, this is the most luxurious shower I've seen in months."

"You're so easy to please." He leaned over and kissed the top of her head again.

The walls were done in creamy colors while rich dark wood and red accents decorated the entire suite, giving it a clean, sleek and refined look, but the comforter looked irresistible. As they strolled from the bathroom, at the end of their expedition, Rhees couldn't help herself. She kicked her shoes off and took a flying leap onto the bed.

"Yep," she said with a happy giggle. "Sumptuously soft and squishy." Paul beamed at her delight. He followed her to the bed and offered his hand to help her up.

"You can sink into the downy quicksand later. I have a birthday present for you in the kitchen."

"The kitchen?" she sounded confused. "I thought we were here so I could have a warm shower for my birthday?"

"That too, but I have something else for you." He pulled her back on her feet and toward the kitchen.

"Something else? Besides the shower and the plane tickets, and the hotel room that is average for you, but not for people like me?"

"You promised." He exaggerated an annoyed glance.

"Don't look at me like that. I'm trying to be grateful and appreciative here. I really am, but since I can't say you've spent *way* too much money on me for my birthday, because you made me *promise* not to say that again . . ." Her lips pressed together to hide her grin at sneaking in a way to say it again without saying it, but her curiosity got the better of her when he moved to the large silver cloche and pulled out an ice bucket with a bottle of something chilling from behind. She only then realized the cloche didn't come standard with the rooms.

"You know how you always say you wish you could order dessert first, because you're always too full after dinner to enjoy it as much as you want to?" He lifted the cloche, revealing a plate full of desserts. "We have crème brulee, tiramisu, chocolate covered strawberries, and an incredibly, *ooey, gooey, caramelly goodness*, turtle cheesecake." He pointed to each one in order, repeating her own words from an earlier conversation when he described the cheesecake. He often quoted her, word for word.

Rhees stood speechless, but he waited.

"This is *sooo* . . ." She stared at the plate, forever. Her eyes rose to meet his with awe. *"Romantic!"*

Paul practically staggered, taken aback. In all his planning, he'd never once thought of it that way.

"Word of advice to my pretend boyfriend." She gave him a sideways glance with a smirkish, but understanding, smile. "If you ever have a *real* girlfriend, and she tells you you've done something romantic, just roll with it, or at least, pretend to. You'll score points." She giggled.

He tried to smile, but his discomfort ruled. He didn't know what to say. He'd only wanted to make her birthday special. He dodged his unease by rounding up plates, spoons, and wine glasses from the cupboards. He held the bottle up.

"Champagne." He opened it and poured.

They ended up eating on one of the couches, each with their own plates. Rhees sat next to him, close, facing him, her legs draped over his lap, as her side leaned against the back of the sofa. He sat, turned slightly, facing her. She took a bite of a strawberry and swooned with delight.

"If this really was *romantic* . . ." He glanced at her to

make sure she knew it was her word, not his. "I'd be feeding you the strawberries, but I know you wouldn't really enjoy that—after I touched it." He raised a mocking eyebrow at her.

"Ah." She groaned, accepting her faults. "I know. I'm sorry. You're really great at putting up with all my quirks. But, actually, I've kind of gotten used to your germs." She lowered her eyes, embarrassed. "I might even *like* them now, maybe."

He didn't believe her. He smiled skeptically as he looked at his plate to scoop up another bite. She set her plate down on the ottoman and took his face in her hands, gazing at him. He'd just filled his mouth, and he looked comical as he tried to keep his lips from gaping open and revealing the food inside while being completely caught off guard.

She kissed him, which surprised him even more. He couldn't tell her to stop as he struggled to keep his mouth closed and the dessert inside. He tried to swallow and get rid of it, afraid he'd gross her out. He wondered how she didn't understand that was about to happen if she kept up what she was doing.

Her tongue pushed past his lips and he almost gasped as she heartily explored the inside of his entire mouth. She pulled back and licked her lips with pleasure.

"Mmmm . . . delicious. You taste just like crème brulee." She looked funny, as if holding a straight face for as long as she could. "You should see the look on your face," she said, and then her head fell back in a burst of laughter.

He sat stunned, just staring, trying to understand what just happened. She finally recovered from her laughing fit. Her brow furrowed with concern.

"Are you mad at me?"

"No." He glanced off toward the windows.

"Then, what's wrong?"

He shook his head, staring just off to the side of her, still not giving anything away. She'd confused him. He choked the next words out, barely. "Have you . . . changed your mind?"

"Yes." Her smile lit her face.

His eyes grew wide, and he gulped in a breath, realizing he'd missed a few. He pursed his lips and nodded slightly, still thinking it over.

"I just showed you. Your germs don't bother me anymore."

He closed his eyes, kneading his lips against each other. "Okay," he said slowly, understanding that she had no idea what he meant or what he thought she'd meant. A few seconds and a few more labored breaths later, he said, "Why don't you go take your first hot shower? The goal is to try and squeeze in as many as you can before we have to go back."

"What are you going to do while I'm in heaven?" she asked, smiling.

"Oh . . ." It came out breathy. He pursed his lips again and ran through a few more distortions. "I'll find *something* to do. Take your time."

She watched him for a few seconds.

"Paul?"

He took a deep breath. "Hmm?"

"Are you trying to get rid of me?"

"Rhees, I brought you all the way to Utah because I promised I'd arrange for you to go shopping, and I thought you'd appreciate taking warm showers while we're here."

"I thought we were here because you need fresh gear for the shop so you can rotate out some of the worn-out stuff."

"That too." He smiled. "I originally thought if I ever met the person who sold you your gear, I'd give him an earful about upselling to newbies, taking advantage of their excitement about the sport, but after seeing how you swim, I want to thank him for making sure you have, possibly, the best fins ever made. And since your overly expensive gear may have saved your life, I've decided to reward him by spending a fortune on his merchandise and taking it back to the island."

"You used my birthday as an excuse. You really just needed me to help you pack all that gear back home."

Paul did a double take at her calling the island home. He watched her pretending to pout, and chuckled. He'd already explained the dual purpose for the trip. It would have been easier to buy everything in Texas, but Paul wanted an excuse to see where Rhees came from.

"We're here for your birthday—number one reason. I swear." He motioned a cross over his heart. "So go take advantage of my gift of a warm shower."

"It is the sweetest birthday present anyone's ever given me." She looked up at him and sighed. "But Paul?"

She paused, staring at him with those warm brown eyes. "Remember when you said there were things we could do . . . that wouldn't disrupt my relationship with my hymen?"

He closed his eyes tightly, wondering how they'd wound up going down this road. It made him uncomfortable. He needed time to think, change the topic. He reached for his glass and took a long drink.

"Would any of those things . . . help *you*? Right now? Because I can feel you against my leg. You're always doing things for me. I—I want to do something for you."

He had his glass to his mouth, but he suddenly shot forward. Champagne spurted from his mouth and nose. He choked on the portion that went down the wrong tube. Reflexively, he reached for his napkin and started wiping the wasted champagne off his face and clothes as best as he could, still coughing and gasping for air.

"Are you all right?" she asked.

"Rhees!" He almost knocked her to the floor when he jumped up off the couch. He darted to the kitchen to get more napkins—and to put some distance between them. "You can't say things like that to me! It's bad enough you just shared my crème brulee—from my mouth. *Gawd!* Dani Girl, you have no idea what you're doing to me."

"I'm a slow learner, I know, but I've picked up on a few things." She bit her lower lip and watched him. "I'm just trying to say, I'm willing to help you with . . . *that.* I feel it's the least I can do after everything you do for me."

"Shit! Rhees. S*tawp* it!"

She flopped back down on the couch and stared at the ceiling. He took his shirt off and grabbed a clean one from the other room. When he came back into the living room, Rhees still lay on her back. She looked sad and it broke his heart.

"Hey," he said lightly. "Don't worry about me. This is all my choice." She wouldn't look at him. He moved to the couch and kneeled so he could lean over her. She turned her head away, but he pulled her back and got in her face with a silly grin. She had no choice but to finally look at him.

"You don't fight fair." She smiled, a little.

He nuzzled her nose with his. "I told you, I fight to win." He sighed and stroked the side of her cheek as the seriousness of the moment returned. "Don't worry about me, Dani Girl. I would give up *all* the sex in the world to be right here, with you."

She closed her eyes and turned her face into his touch, wondering how she wound up the luckiest girl in the world to be his friend. She opened her eyes to tell him, but a playful, mischievous grin played on his face, his eyes sparkled magnificently. He leaned in closer.

"You know what? I *did* give up all the sex in the world and here I am, right here, with you." His grin broke into a dazzling smile, and she couldn't help herself. She put her hands on both sides of his face, pulled him down to her, and kissed him, but not for long. Paul was the one to pull away.

"You *really* should go have your shower," he said quietly, with another heavy puff of air.

"Okay." She gazed a second longer, thinking what a beautiful man he was, her friend, and then she got up and headed for the bathroom.

"Rhees," he called after her. She turned back,

expectantly. The look on his face worried her a little. "Lock the door."

oOo

"I meant to ask, how was your *swim*?" Rhees climbed into bed with a knowing smirk on her face. Paul rested against the headboard, propped with pillows, reading.

"Hm?" The book must have been interesting. He didn't seem to hear what she'd said.

"Just curious how you're holding up in the desert."

"It's cold," he said without looking up, but after a beat, he did. "Desert? We're right below the most majestic mountains I've ever seen."

"It's a *high* desert." She let out a little laugh. "The Wasatch Front has great mountains. The La Sal Mountains are beautiful too, but most of the state is pretty desert-like, unique, and magnificent, but Utah is hot and dry in the summer." She giggled. "It's July, Paul—*not* cold."

"But the air conditioner hasn't shut off once since we got here."

"That's because it's July in the desert. It's hot." She reached for the sheet and pushed it up to his chin, making a production of tucking him in. "Is that better?"

He smiled back and was about to sneak a kiss, but she hopped off the bed and over to adjust the thermostat.

"There. That should be better."

"Thanks." He watched her climb into bed this time. "What was that about a swim?"

"I, uh . . ." She blushed, regretting bringing it up, pretending to be so bold. "I was curious about how you plan to deal with your need to go for a swim, when there's no ocean around here. Utah Lake is down the road, but I wouldn't recommend swimming in it."

"Oh." His gaze shot back to his e-reader, a little too quickly. He pursed his lips. "There're other ways of working off that energy."

"Oh." She sat quietly, thinking. "And those, 'other ways',

would include what I offered today, but you refused?"

"Rhees," he said with a heavy breath. "Let's not go there again. *Please*?"

"Okay." She conceded more readily this time. "Good night."

She lay down and rolled onto her side, facing away from him.

"But thanks for the offer."

oOo

"It's freakin' freezing in here." Paul reached for Rhees and pulled her into him to spoon. "Can we snuggle? I dreamed I was cold, and I couldn't find you. I prefer our little bed at home. King-sized beds are overrated."

"What time is it?" Rhees asked, groggy after only a few hours of sleep. She reached back and patted him on the cheek before entwining her arms and feet with his to help warm him up.

"Two fifteen. Sorry to wake you, but the air conditioning is still on hyper-drive."

"Want me to turn it down some more?"

"No. Don't get up. I'll be okay if you'll keep me warm."

"Sure. How many times have you snuggled with me through my nightmares? But just a sec." She broke free from his hold.

"Brrr . . . don't leave me." His arms stretched out after her.

She reached down to the bottom of the bed and grabbed the corner of the comforter, pulling it up over them before settling back down into their spooning position.

"Better?"

"Yeah, it's nice, but not as nice as you." He kissed her ear and they were both asleep again within seconds.

A couple of hours later, Paul stirred, his body clock held true, not needing to adjust to time zone changes. Since the island didn't observe daylight savings time, Utah's time happened to be the same as what he was used to. Like most mornings, when he stirred, so did Rhees. This morning, however, every muscle in her body went rigid, waking with a small jolt.

He did a quick mental check to determine the problem. His morning-ness knocked against her soft behind, a problem, but it had happened many mornings when she was the one who'd initiated the snuggling. She'd grown used to it as long as he didn't make the mistake of trying to grind on her, even a little. Another assessment later, he detected the real problem.

His right arm remained draped across her body, the palm of his hand splayed out affectionately over her belly. Still shouldn't have been a problem, except her T-shirt had somehow drawn up during the night. His hand had found its way to exposed skin, his pinky and ring finger rested low, below her panty line, under the elastic, against, not only her bare skin, but tangled in her pubic hair.

He immediately yanked his hand away and smoothed her T-shirt down, but she didn't relax.

"You okay? You know I didn't mean it, right? I was asleep. I'm sorry."

She didn't respond so he pulled on her, rolling her toward him. She fought his attempt but he persisted and won. She squeezed her eyes shut, but nodded, a little too jerkily, as if over-compensating assurance, or lying.

"There's your answer about giving me a hand with—" He pressed his own eyes shut at his unintentional pun.

He'd hoped to make light of the situation, but he didn't think the circumstances very comical. It actually worried him, and reminded him of thoughts, concerns, he'd entertained before. He'd never asked about it, thinking a woman's reasons for this sort of thing would be very personal. If Rhees wanted to talk about it, she would. At least that's what he'd always told himself, until now.

"There's another reason you're still a virgin, isn't there . . . besides wanting to wait until you're married?"

Her eyes burst open, and he would have burned from the intense glare if she didn't look away even faster than she'd looked his way. She threw the covers off and got out of bed.

"I need the bathroom." She sounded alarmed, almost panicked.

"Rhees?" Paul sat up, ready to take after her, his anxiety worse than before.

"Yeah?" she asked calmly, turning. She smiled the warmest, most relaxed smile, as if she'd just swallowed a ray of sunshine, no trace of the terrified panic she'd exhibited only seconds ago. He hated the possibilities that had crossed his mind about what could have caused her to be this way, but he decided it best to return to the, *wait until she's ready,* approach.

oOo

Over the next two days, Paul played tourist, with Rhees as his tour guide. They got up early and hiked Y Mountain to watch the sun rise and light up the valley where Rhees had grown up. They sat on Brigham Young University's symbol and ate take-out Kneader's French toast with buttermilk syrup, a local favorite. Paul claimed the treat was now his favorite breakfast too. They drove around town in their rented Jeep while Rhees showed Paul her history. He insisted on seeing every school she'd ever attended and every house she'd ever lived in. She showed him all but the one she lived in before starting kindergarten. She said she didn't remember where it was.

At the last house, they dropped in next door to say hello to Mrs. Michaels, but she kept them much longer than they'd expected, insisting they stay for dinner. Rhees tried to make excuses, thinking Paul would be bored out of his mind spending the evening with the old woman.

"I'm sorry," she'd said. "But Paul's made reservations—"

"We'd love to, Mrs. Michaels," he contradicted Rhees. "I'll call and reschedule our reservations for tomorrow."

"Please," the woman said. "Call me Karla."

Rhees could hardly hide her bewilderment at Paul's

enthusiasm about staying, and knowing that, in all the years she'd known her, Mrs. Michaels had never asked her to call her by her first name.

"Mrs. Michaels," Rhees teased during dessert, as Paul pumped Karla for information about young Rhees—she'd figured out why he'd accepted the invitation. "Are you flirting with my boyfriend?"

"Of course," Karla answered. "A widowed woman can get away with shamelessly flirting with a man this handsome if the age difference spans more than forty years."

Paul didn't help matters, as he'd been giving her the unabridged version of his Paul, *the seasoned lady killer*, experience since they'd shown up at her door.

Paul watched Rhees pull her family album from one of the boxes of personal belongings Mrs. Michaels had been storing for her. He sat on the bed with her and they thumbed through the pages.

"I'd like to take this back with me. Do you think it would be safe? I mean, I'd hate it if the humidity on the island ruined the pictures. This is all I have left of my family."

Paul put a comforting arm around her and kissed the top of her head.

"I wouldn't risk it, but we could go to one of those copy places and have it scanned so you can keep it online. A digital copy will last forever and you can look at the pictures anytime you're at a computer."

She nodded, and then laughed at herself for choking up. Paul squeezed her to him tighter. He pulled her chin up with his finger and kissed the tears from each eye before they had the chance to fall down her cheeks. After they'd looked through the album a couple of times, they resumed going through the boxes, looking for more items she might want to take with her.

"My hair dryer!" she exclaimed excitedly as she pulled it from the box. She reached back in. "And my curling iron."

"You don't need those," Paul said, amused. "You wear

dive hair better than anyone I've ever known."

She snorted in disbelief.

"The humidity will just undo any effort you waste trying to style your hair, and *I like* it the way you've been wearing it." He found himself running his fingers down the length of her hair, adoringly. He loved her hair. He loved—he suddenly felt uncomfortable with his feelings. "Add that to how much I *really* like how speedy my pretend girlfriend can get ready—"

"There's the truth. Speedy and simple—the island way," Rhees mumbled as she put the hair styling tools back into the box, oblivious to the real reason he'd played it off. "You're probably right."

She resumed digging through one of the boxes while Paul snooped through her things in another. He held up a short, spaghetti strap nightie and glanced over at her. She was too busy looking through her own box to notice, but he tried to imagine her wearing it to bed. He quickly wadded it up and stuffed it to the bottom of the box he'd been working his way through—she'd be safer sleeping in his baggy T-shirts.

oOo

"I'll make her call you once in a while, I promise," Paul told Karla as they walked out the door. "I'm sorry you've been so worried about her. If I'd known she hadn't contacted you since she left, I would have made her." Paul gave Rhees a bug-eyed look about never using her phone.

"I'm sorry. I didn't think." Rhees blushed with remorse and Paul put a comforting arm around her.

"Thank you. I won't need to worry so much anymore now that I know she's got you, but it would be nice to hear from her once in a while—both of you." Karla winked, keeping up the act that she and Paul had something going on between them.

"You take care of this boy, Rhees," Mrs. Michaels warned. "If you don't treat him right, I may forget how much I love you and steal him away." That made them all laugh and they said their good-byes.

oOo

The next day, they visited Thanksgiving Point to see the dinosaur museum, and later, ice blocked down the slopes of Rock Canyon Park. Rhees had watched people doing it, but never dared try it herself. Paul had never heard of ice blocking before, but she told him it was another fear she'd vowed to overcome, so he patiently helped her cross it off her list.

"Is there anything you're afraid of?" Rhees asked after he'd flown down the slope without a moment's hesitation, to show her how easy it was.

He helped her onto her chunk of ice as he appeared to ponder the question, but shook his head.

"Nope." Once he'd said it, he seemed to think better of his answer. "Only you."

"You're not afraid of me." She snorted.

He raised his eyebrows high at her statement and gave her a push, sending her on her way down the hill. She screamed bloody murder, and a few obscenities directed at him, which surprised him.

That afternoon, they hiked the steep trail of Bridal Veil Falls in Provo Canyon, and afterwards, they walked around Robert Redford's resort, Sundance, before having dinner at the Tree Room.

"Robert Redford and Paul Newman are better looking than you," she said, trying to hold back a grin. They stood on the bridge and watched the water flow beneath them. He gave her a sideways glance and smirked. "But that's about it. I can't think of anyone else who even comes close."

"They're ancient."

"I've only watched cartoons and old, classic movies, remember? I'll always remember them the way they looked as Butch Cassidy and the Sundance Kid. I was sad when Mr. Newman passed away, but Mr. Redford lives here. People I know have run into him when they've come up to ski."

"We could go look for ole' Bob if you want." Paul pretended to be looking for Mr. Redford. "I'm sure we can find him, no reason to settle for *number three*."

He seemed a little too serious. She watched him warily—worried he hadn't taken it as the compliment she'd intended. Who would get offended at being compared to two of the greatest looking men to have ever lived? "No. That's all right. He had his chance for twenty-four years and totally snubbed me. I can pretend to settle for third best."

Paul was too quiet for the next few minutes.

"Are you jealous . . . of *Robert Redford*?"

"No." He sounded pouty. "I can still turn a few heads, you know. I'd be willing to bet, in a contest, I'd turn more heads than even Bob—the old *pud*!"

"I meant it as a compliment!" She giggled, realizing how her comment really bothered him. "Don't you worry about coming across as conceited?"

"What am I supposed to do? Deny it? 'Aw shucks. That's only the third time I've been told how handsome I am, *today*, but I'm not good looking. Everyone must be wrong'. Rhees, there's hardly been a day of my life that my looks haven't come up, so, am I supposed to pretend like I don't believe what thousands of people say is true? My whole life, everywhere I go, no matter what I do, it's just my life. Personally, it's meaningless to me. Yes, I have a pretty face—" He deadpanned. "I can't believe I just called myself pretty. Please, don't ever call me pretty. It's bad enough to be called beautiful all the time, because I'm not. I'm an ugly person."

"No, you're not. Looks aside, you're—"

"Stop," he said in a no-nonsense tone. "*You* are true beauty."

"Ha!" She scoffed. "You are the only person on the planet who has ever said that. Well, my parents too, but parents have to say that about their kids. It's a rule or something."

"Rhees." His disposition had turned so solemn. "I was born looking this way. I had nothing to do with it. Everything about me that I *could* control, I've screwed it up. *You* are *so* beautiful! You are absolutely exquisite, inside and out. You inspire me. I'm trying to be more like you." He tried to laugh it off, not liking how vulnerable he suddenly felt. "But dang. It's hard, and I'm not doing a very good job."

"You're wrong. You are not ugly, not on the outside, obviously, but not on the inside either. If I'm really as good as you say, and you're as bad as you—"

"Don't even." He put his lips over hers to shush her. It had become his favorite method. "I know where you're going with this. Don't feel sorry for me for being even better looking than Robert Redford *and* Paul Newman." He smirked, but then was serious again. "Don't feel sorry for me."

She hugged him and didn't let go.

"I can't help that I was born so damned, incredibly good-looking, or that I know it . . . or that I learned to use it to my advantage whenever possible."

oOo

Their last day in Utah, they arrived at University Mall at lunch time. They ate Chinese, something they'd both longed for since there were no Chinese restaurants on the island. After lunch, they began exploring the mall in order for Rhees to refresh her wardrobe. She dragged Paul from one store to the next, and he decided he'd finally discovered a flaw. Her method of shopping drove him absolutely crazy.

She had to see every item of clothing in every store, try each item on, and if she liked something, she couldn't decide if she wanted to buy it until she checked to see what the next store had first. If she didn't find something better, they had to go back to the first store again.

"I need a drink," he said. "How about I go find a bar

and wait for you there."

"Good luck with that," she answered. "I'm sure there are others in the valley, but I only know of one bar, and it's in Provo, not far from our hotel. Even people I know who drink say they wouldn't recommend it."

"Where do people get a drink?"

"They don't." She giggled. "Paul, this is Happy Valley, Utah. The majority of the people here don't believe in drinking."

"I had a beer at the restaurant. I'll go back there."

"You'll have to order food again. They can't serve you a drink unless you eat, first."

"You've got to be kidding me!"

"Nope." She held a skirt up to herself and looked in a mirror on the wall, trying to decide if she wanted to try it on. He had to smile at her.

"Meet me in front of the restaurant in, what, an hour and a half? Two?" He got a better look at the skirt she held. "I like that one."

"Really? You don't think it's a little too colorful and short?"

"No. I like it. You should get it."

"I'll have to try it on first, but I *could* buy it and half the clothes in this mall—now that I'm so rich."

He grinned at how she thought ten thousand dollars made her rich. The tone of her voice still sounded a little irritated, making him recall her reaction when she finally did find the money in her account. They'd fought, and she insisted on giving it back, but he, using all the charm and powers in his arsenal, finally convinced her it was honest wages for the work she'd done the first few weeks at the shop and a well-earned bonus for putting up with Mr. *Meanie-Head* as a boss.

"Are you really going to leave me on my own?" she mocked him. "You never let me out of your sight."

"This is probably the only place I would dare leave you alone. You've been safe here the first twenty-four years of your life." He noticed something flash across her expression. He suddenly worried she'd have a panic attack if he left her.

"Do you want me to stay? I'll stay if you need me. I just figured—"

She smiled and shushed him by putting her finger over his lips. "I'll be fine. Go get a drink—with your appetizers." She giggled, understanding what visitors from the rest of the world had to put up with in her home state due to the unusual laws regarding alcohol. He moved closer and put his hands on her hips, resting his forehead on hers.

"It's not *you* I want to get away from, you know that, right?" He kissed the tip of her nose and then grinned. "It's your shopping habits that make me want to kill myself." He snickered and moved to avoid her playful slap across his arm.

"Well, my methods are better than yours," she said. "'You like it? Buy it. Just buy the whole darn store'!" She imitated him with some exaggeration.

He smiled and gave her a soft, but quick, kiss on the lips. "See you later. Take your time and have fun. Remember, this is all about your birthday."

"The best one I've ever had. Thank you." She kissed him back.

Rhees headed back to the dressing rooms and Paul headed toward the store's entrance. On his way out, he noticed a display of board shorts that caught his attention. He realized his wardrobe could use a little refreshing as well. He'd been so focused on Rhees getting her shopping done that he didn't think about buying anything for himself. He changed his mind about going for that drink and decided to just do some shopping himself—he wouldn't have to leave Rhees on her own after all.

He glanced back to tell Rhees of his change of plans, but she'd disappeared into the dressing room. He grabbed a few things and headed toward the back of the store.

He walked to the dressing rooms and stood, trying to figure out which stall Rhees could be in so he could let her know he'd stuck around after all. The only attendant he could see busied herself by opening the door for another customer, so he waited.

"You want to try those on?" Another attendant returned from putting unwanted items back on the store floor, and when she got a look at him, her mouth dropped open and she seemed to lose her train of thought.

"Yes, please."

The woman led him to a stall and unlocked the door. She kept turning back to look at him, and it made him want to roll his eyes. He scowled instead and stepped inside. A few minutes later, he heard someone call Rhees' name.

"Rhees! Is that you?" he heard a female voice ask. "Oh my gosh!"

"Kylee?" he heard Rhees respond. He remembered the name from Rhees' story about her *pud* boyfriend who hurt her by sleeping with her best friend, *Kylee.*

He scowled again.

"Oh my gosh! Rhees. It's been such a long time. What've you been up to? I heard you left the country and never came back." It came out as if Kylee thought the idea contemptuous. "That surprised me *so* much. You were always so darn chicken. When I heard that, I thought, shoot, how did Rhees manage to do something so freakin' adventurous? But that obviously wasn't true because here you are."

"Yeah. It's been a while. Um, yeah, it *is* true, actually. I have been in the Caribbean. I'm just visiting for a couple of days. I'm going back."

"Oh my *gosh*," Kylee said. "I could never do that. Gads."

Paul almost laughed out loud as he strained to listen. Kylee sounded so much like Rhees. It helped him understand her a little better.

"No. Really. It's absolutely the best thing I've ever done. I'm working as a dive master, and I'm planning to become an instructor. I love it there. This is probably the last time I'll ever come back to Utah. I see no reason to ever come back again."

Paul frowned at that.

"Seriously?" Kylee almost shrieked the word. "I might get brave enough to leave Orem someday, but never Utah. Gosh, you never know what kind of thing you'll run into out there. I could never live away from my family. Well, you've always been more, *worldly,* than the rest of us. I guess it makes sense, *for you.*"

That made Paul angry. Kylee was the one who banged Rhees' boyfriend. He didn't like the snide undertone he felt from her comment.

"What are *you* doing now?" Rhees asked.

"I work here. Gotta support my little girl . . . after the divorce and all."

"You're divorced?"

"Yeah."

"Oh, I'm sorry."

"No, it's a good thing. Now I can find someone who will take me to the temple. I should have known Brady would never go to church."

"Brady Bird? Yeah, I wouldn't imagine."

"Yeah, I thought after we got married he'd change, but he wasn't interested in even pretending to get religious. How about you? Did you ever get married?"

Paul imagined Rhees didn't want to talk about marriage and relationships with this particular girl. He didn't hear her answer and assumed she'd just nodded.

"Of course not, I can just imagine the kind of guys you'd meet out in the world. Brady's a good guy. We just want different things. You and him would have been a better match, you know, since you're not worried about going to the temple either."

Paul grew livid with this girl and her stupid mouth.

"Um . . . there are some really good people outside of Utah, too," Rhees said. "Well, I need to finish shopping. I'm supposed to meet someone." She sounded anxious to get away from the girl.

"Yeah. Gosh. It was so nice to see you." The pleasantry in Kylee's voice sounded fake to Paul. "Don't get eaten by a shark! Imagine that. Rhees, of all people, in the Caribbean."

"Yeah, I know. I won't get eaten, I promise." The conversation was over.

Paul finished trying on the clothes and walked out of his stall. He took a minute to figure out which girl had spoken to Rhees. He heard her voice talking to another customer and zeroed in on her.

"Oh my gosh. Isn't that shirt just so stinkin' cute? We just got those in this morning."

Kylee was the same obnoxious dressing room attendant who couldn't take her eyes off him earlier. He waited for her to return from letting her customer into a dressing room.

"How did those work for you?" she asked, a little too enthusiastically at seeing him waiting for her.

"I'll take these," he answered, holding up the items he wanted. He returned her annoying gaze with a smile, letting his eyes twinkle. It had the effect he'd hoped it would. She seemed flustered and dropped the clothes as he passed them to her.

He reached down to pick them up at the same time she did. He smiled at her again, letting his eyes twinkle some more.

"Can you ring me up or do I have to have one of the other clerks do it?" He hoped his right eye would twitch as it often did when he smiled the way he smiled at Kylee. It did. He'd learned, for some reason, the twitch, more than a real wink, endeared flirty women to him.

"Sure." Kylee practically salivated. She led him out to the storefront, turning back to look at him several times as she walked. She checked out his ring finger while she folded and bagged his purchases. "Not married? How is a good looking man like you not married?" she flirted when he shook his head in answer to her question.

He smiled with a shrug and took a quick glance around the store, looking for Rhees. She must have gone back into the dressing room—another thing he didn't understand. You go through a store, find what you want, try on a few things if you absolutely need to, pay for them and get out.

The thought of her made him smile again, genuinely.

He turned his attention back to Kylee and handed her his credit card. She appeared to assume he smiled because of her and he did nothing to dissuade her assumption. She smiled back and didn't take her flattered and hopeful eyes off of him until the card was in her hand, but then she froze, staring at it like her eyes were about to pop out.

"You can't have one of these without an invitation. They're rare."

"That's right. So rare, I'm surprised you know what it is."

"The last time—*only* time—I've ever seen one, the uppity woman using it bragged nonstop to make sure I knew how important she thought she was." Kylee blathered away as she swiped the card. "She was demanding and threw a tantrum over every little thing. She went on and on about how rich—" Kylee stopped as if her voice caught on something in her throat, and then she looked back up at Paul, her mouth hanging open. She started gushing over him, even more obviously than before.

"I've never seen you in the store before." She actually batted her eyes.

"My first time in Orem," he said. "It's a nice place."

"Oh my gosh." Her eyes brightened as if she'd just hit the jackpot. "You need a tour guide. There're so many cool things to see that you wouldn't know about unless you have a native Oremite to show you around. I could show you, after work." Kylee's gaze moved to something behind him and the expression on her face cooled. Paul turned to see why.

Rhees slowly inched her way to the counter. Her eyes shifted uncertainly between Kylee and Paul. She appeared hesitant as she set her own purchases on the counter. Paul noticed the skirt he'd said he liked and it made him smile again.

"Did you really like that or are you buying it because I did?"

"I don't think it'll fit you," she said dryly. Rhees' gaze

moved back and forth between him and Kylee again.

"You know Rhees?" Kylee asked, looking at Paul as if she didn't understand how that could be possible.

"Danarya?" He turned what he knew were his most twinkling eyes to Rhees. "Rhees is my girl. Isn't she beautiful?" Paul leaned over and gave Rhees a quick, feathery kiss. He thought she looked like she'd slap him—he took her hands in his to make sure she couldn't.

"Hey Baby," he said in a seductive voice. "Just put her things on my card, too." He tipped his chin to Rhees' pile and gave Kylee a, *you never stood a chance,* look.

"No," Rhees snapped. "Don't put it on his card."

"She hates it when I spend money on her," Paul told Kylee, to let her know how familiar he was with Rhees.

Rhees turned on him in a huff. "I don't need you to pay for my things—especially when you insist on running around, dropping absurd amounts of money into my bank account."

Paul chuckled at how Rhees had played into his game and didn't know it. He snaked his arms around her and lifted her off the ground, planting a passionate kiss on her before she had a chance to say something to ruin the moment.

"Mm!" he grunted. He knew he needed to carefully navigate the very thin line between using physical affection to keep Rhees from scolding him in front of Kylee, and freaking her out with all the touching.

"Gads, Rhees. You didn't tell me you had a boyfriend." Kylee put on a friendly face again and tried, but failed, to hide her discomfort, disbelief . . . and disappointment. She flashed Paul another questioning glance, hoping she'd read the situation wrong.

"Um, yeah." Rhees pushed on him to gain a little distance. He put her back down, but then he pulled her in front of him and lovingly wrapped his arms around her shoulders from behind. Rhees couldn't see his face but he could watch Kylee's. "Paul, this is *Kylee*. Kylee, Paul, my *boyfriend*." Rhees sounded monotone.

"I'm her boyfriend," Paul repeated. He rested his chin on the top of Rhees' head but gave her hair a kiss every few seconds.

"So how do you and Rhees know each other?" he asked. He felt Rhees tense in his arms and figured she didn't realize Paul remembered.

"Rhees and I go *way* back. We've been friends forever."

"We kind of drifted apart toward the end of high school," Rhees added, making Paul want to laugh, but he didn't.

"Yeah, I know," Kylee said in a sing-song tone, apparently struggling to keep putting a positive spin on their, no longer existent, friendship. "We've had our ups and downs, but that happens, even with the tightest of friends, right?"

Rhees forced a polite smile at Kylee and turned her head to make the same attempt at being pleasant to Paul. He gave her another loving smooch on the temple.

"Tight." Paul made a sound of skepticism. "Rhees, Baby, why haven't you mentioned your *tight* friend here to me?" He glared at Kylee now, knowing Rhees couldn't see the coldness in his eyes for the slut.

He would have preferred to drop the act and just ask Rhees, right in front of Kylee, 'Is this the skanky whore who fucked your pud boyfriend?', but he didn't. Rhees had been making such an attempt to be civil and nice to the skanky whore, he didn't understand why, but he decided to respect her effort. "Did you find everything you need, Baby? I'm ready to get you back to our hotel room and do *worldly* things to you." He loved the shocked look on Kylee's face—Rhees' face—not so much. He may have crossed the line with that one.

"Yeah, I have what I need." Rhees looked like she didn't recognize him.

"All right, *Kylee?* . . . Was it?" Paul played dumb very well. He'd been doing it his whole life. "It's been nice to meet you. You should come and visit us sometime, *in the Caribbean.*" He said it in the same manner you'd tell a scary ghost story. "We can get you a good deal on a dive package. *We* own the shop."

Rhees shot him another surprised glare. "*We* do?"

"Yes. Rhees and I . . . *you know.*" He winked at Kylee and flashed his, *melt any girl's panties,* smile. "If you ever want to learn to dive, get in touch. We'll hook you up. Rhees is the best dive master on the seven seas." He looked into Rhees' disorientated, and a little angry, eyes. "I don't know what I'd do without her—professionally or *otherwise.*"

"Nice seeing you again, um, Rhees. Nice to meet you." Kylee eyed Paul, handing them their sacks with the new clothes, never once breaking eye contact with him.

He followed Rhees toward the store's entrance. "Oh, no. I forgot my credit card." He kissed her on the forehead. "I'm right behind you." She stomped off and he reached to feel the wallet in his pocket—the wallet he knew he'd already slipped his credit card into. He sauntered back toward the register where Kylee stood in a daze, probably still wondering what had just happened to the connection she thought she'd made with the handsome, rich dude—he hoped.

"You came back." She looked much too hopeful at seeing him again.

He smiled, one more beautiful smile, just for her. "You're nothing but a fucking skanky whore," he said.

He'd decided to say it after all. He turned and headed toward the entrance but turned back once again to see Kylee gaping in shock. He raised his hand to his lips and blew Kylee a kiss, but as he pulled his hand away, his fingers formed into an obscene gesture.

"Thank you," he mouthed, and he winked once more before exiting.

"Hey," he said, catching up to Rhees. She kept walking, ignoring him. He had a good idea why.

"Is something wrong?" He sounded too innocent.

"You're attracted to her!" she sobbed, without turning to face him. People bumped into them because of their abrupt stop in the middle of the mallway.

"No, I'm not."

"I saw you when you didn't think I was around to see you, but I saw you trying to *hypnotize* her with your *magical gaze*. You use your eyes like Kaa, from *The Jungle Book*. If you're ready to end this stupid, pretend relationship . . ." She appeared to be trying not to cry, but failing. "Then just do it. But please." Rhees blubbered a little. "End it for any reason except—except her," she sobbed, but then her voice dropped to a whisper as she sucked in a shaky breath of air. "You don't realize who that was."

His shoulders fell as he sighed—sickened with himself, seeing how badly it had all backfired. He didn't mean to hurt Rhees. He just wanted to—he was selfish. He swept her into his arms and held her, rocking gently from side to side until she stopped trying to push him away.

"I'm sorry," he said humbly. "I am not attracted to her. I swear—promise—I promise I do *nawt* find that cunt attractive. I couldn't help myself. I had to mess with her." He pulled back so he could see Rhees' face, keeping a tight hold on her shoulders in case she tried to get away. "I *do* know who that was. I remembered the name and I—" He shrugged, embarrassed. "I'm sorry. It was stupid. I wanted her to notice me."

Rhees gasped and turned red with anger. He thanked his intuition about holding on to her because she did try to get away from him. He wrangled her back and forced her to look at him.

"Yes. I wanted her to find me attractive. I used what I know. Yeah, I used my *'Kaa'* eyes." He swooped in close to her face and made googly eyes, trying to make her smile. She didn't, and he glanced down at his feet to gather the courage to admit the rest.

"I used what I know. I turned on the charm and made her notice me—which was all too easy—it's always too easy, but then I showed her how *you* are the one I have eyes for—at least, that's what I was going for. I haven't had a lot of practice at staking my claim—you know that." He was thoughtful for a second as regret ran through his mind. "Maybe I should have just stuck to the other thing I understand and just slugged her."

That did make one side of Rhees' mouth twist up a little.

"I wanted her to know she might have won the pud, but you won the *third* best-looking man on the planet." He closed his eyes, but then he opened one to peek at her, acting cautious. He grinned when he saw the smile she'd been fighting finally steal the show on her beautiful lips.

"I'm sorry, Rhees. I didn't consider how it would hurt you if you misunderstood my intention. It was petty, and it was mean, and truth be told, I should have thanked her instead." He deemed it wisest to omit he had.

"Why would you thank her for hurting me the way she did?" Her smile had jumped ship and he knew he'd made the right choice in not telling her he did go back to thank Kylee. She blinked a few tears away from her shiny eyes.

"Because, Rhees. I'm sorry she hurt you—I am. I get the strongest urge to hurt anyone who's ever caused you pain, even if it was only a broken fingernail. But that girl is the best thing that ever happened to me." He gently dried the tears on her cheeks with his thumbs and then he kissed each of her eyes.

"Dear, sweet Dani Girl." He put his arms around her in a tight hug. "That dumb girl, Ky-leech, is part of your past, and your past makes you who you are today. Who you are today is the reason *I've* changed. I will be forever grateful to her for what she's done . . . *for me*." He leaned back to watch her expression as a slow smirkish grin broke on his face. "The bitch!"

Chapter 14

*P*rivate time had become precious to Rhees and Paul. Their days were filled with work, surrounded by students and guests. Paul still couldn't eat at a restaurant, hang at a bar, or walk down the street, without girls trying to talk to him, flirt with him, or flat-out proposition him. Even as Rhees stood at his side, her hand in his, or his arms around her waist—his tongue down her throat. All for display, and yet it rarely made a difference. Sometimes they needed a break from being on show all the time.

Except for one abandoned, dilapidated building thirty yards north, Randy's house and then Paul's shop were the last buildings on the ocean side of the street at the north end of town. A house and then Paul's apartment building were kitty-corner to the shop and a few more homes were across the street. One lone bar sat a hundred yards farther north on the public beach, but never drew more than an intimate crowd after sunset.

The topography of the island went on another five miles, but remained uninhabited, except for a small development of summer homes on the north tip, accessible only by private boat or water taxi. Paradise Divers was perfectly situated for the privacy Rhees and Paul preferred some nights.

Oceanside didn't always feel as comfortable since Regina and Tracy had suddenly developed a rare case of homebody-ness, once Paul started spending more time there. The deck had become Rhees and Paul's refuge. In the beginning, Regina and Tracy would show up at the shop after hours as well, looking for the new couple, using lame excuses, hoping to hang out, but it was easier for Paul to scare them off from his property than it was to run them out of their own home.

Regina, for as well as she knew him, didn't know Paul was only pretending to be foul-tempered to get rid of them—at least, Rhees believed he was only pretending. The shop not only afforded them the privacy they desired, it was also practical for so many of the things they liked to do.

The deck was great for dancing, the ocean was great for swimming, and the mat was great for reading. They could talk for hours without interruption. They kept sheets and pillows in the extra room, and they'd decided the deck was the best place for a good night's sleep without having to worry about roommates eavesdropping, listening through walls for squeaky beds that never squeaked.

oOo

Rhees screamed, waking with a start. A flash lighted the sky, bright as day, and shortly after, another deafening bang, the loudest thunder Rhees had ever heard cracked around them. Lately, she and Paul had slept on the deck more nights than they'd spent at her apartment.

"We need to move." Paul was up and had the mat and all the bedding in his arms faster than she thought possible. "It's going to rain. We need to find cover."

Rhees ran under the gazebo thinking that's what he meant. Paul made it to the covered walkway before he realized Rhees wasn't behind him.

"Rhees? Come on. I said we need cover."

"I have cover." Just then, the sky opened up and dumped water—it was nothing like rain. It was more like a bucket brigade had formed above her and started dumping buckets of water over the deck. The gazebo roof gave her no shelter whatsoever. The water gushed sideways, drenching her in two seconds. She screamed at the shock of the first assault.

She ran to Paul, where he stood pressed against the wall, laughing very non-gallantly. "Sorry. I didn't think. You couldn't possibly have known. We've officially started the rainy season."

"It's August," she yelled over the loud downpour. Another crack of lightning lit the sky. Paul threw his arms around her, bracing her just as the thunder shook them both to the core. She screamed anyway. The water leeched from her clothes to his and they were both drenched.

"Welcome to the tropics." He laughed some more. Her life experience had been so encapsulated, limited. "It'll rain a lot. Mostly during the night, like this, until about December. We can't stand here all night."

"My apartment is so far away. We'll need our scuba gear to get there."

"Yeah," he yelled back, smiling at her sense of humor.

"Your apartment is closer."

He shook his head, adamantly, suddenly bothered about something. "I don't want you in my bed." Even though he held her close to keep their soaked bodies warm, they had to talk loudly to be heard over the storm.

"You always say that. Why not?"

He shrugged and acted uneasy.

"Paul. What's wrong?" she demanded.

"Too many memories. I'm not mixing you in with those."

She nodded her understanding. "My apartment it is, then. I really *will* need my fins." She laughed while he considered for a moment.

"In here." He reached into his pocket for his keys and opened the door to The Room That Had No Purpose. He'd officially named the extra room after hearing her call it that several times. Once inside, both of them dropped their shoulders at the same time when they realized their mat was wet.

"Luckily, I have some extra sheets right here." Sure enough, a pile of folded sheets lay on the table. She gave him a questioning look. He offered the only explanation he could, "I like clean sheets."

She laughed at his response. "I know that, but it doesn't explain why there're three sets sitting in a room no one uses."

"We sleep on the deck all the time." He shrugged. "I started keeping a few sets on hand."

They dried off with towels from the office and settled in, using every set of the sheets, folded over several times to make a passable mat on top of the table. It was narrower than the mat, but Paul didn't mind the excuse to be extra cozy with her. She didn't complain either.

oOo

Brita sounded obnoxious and Rhees braced herself. She thought the old Coitus Club would have disbanded by now, but it continued to hang on.

"I just saw Paul at the ferry. He met a gorgeous woman when she disembarked and he kissed her cheek. They headed toward Rhees' apartment." Brita faked sounding secretive, but Rhees heard every word, and Brita obviously knew it.

"She was beautiful, like she stepped out of a fashion magazine. Skinny! Long, shiny black hair, swept to one side, white see-through blouse with a black bra, skinny jeans, red high, high heels, and red lips to match," Brita recounted. "You'd think he'd have the respect to take her someplace other than Rhees' own apartment."

"But Rhees would probably see him if he tried to sneak a woman to his own apartment. He's safer cheating on her at Oceanside. It's not like Rhees is going to go all the way there by herself. Rhees never goes anywhere without him," Dorene said.

Rhees' heart skipped a few beats. Was it true? Or was this just another jab at her from Paul's old, jealous girlfriends?

She tried to ignore it. She trusted him—he'd never given her cause to be jealous—except for the Kylee incident over a month ago, and that turned out to be innocent.

She couldn't help herself. She headed toward her apartment. She reached the top of the stairs as Paul and the beautiful stranger were coming out. He was about to lock the door behind them, but stopped when he saw her.

"Rhees!" He sounded much too guilty. "I didn't expect you."

"Obviously."

"Um . . ." He glanced at the stunning woman, looking for help, but she gave him nothing. "This is Fahtima."

Rhees glared. She felt weak in the knees and nauseated.

"Um, Faht's been giving me a hand."

Rhees increased the intensity of her glare, but then she had to sit down at the top of the stairs before she fainted.

Paul hurried over to her. "Are you all right? You look ill."

Rhees tried to brush him away. She didn't want him touching her. He sighed with understanding and walked back to Fahtima.

"Faht," he said, "thanks for your help. Once again, you've done a great job."

"It's my pleasure, Paul. I'm always available to help you, my favorite customer." She kissed him on both cheeks and turned to leave. She didn't say anything as she walked past Rhees and headed down the stairs, but Rhees could see cold resentment in her glare.

"Pfft!" Rhees rolled her eyes and looked out over the treetops, trying to let herself go numb so she'd stop hurting so much.

Paul moved to the stairs and sat down next to her. "Rhees?" he asked tentatively. She refused to look at him. "It's not what you think."

"You're saying you didn't sleep with her?"

He glanced down, looking guilty.

"I knew it!" She tried to keep her voice level, but failed. "It's over. You're tired of me—I get it. But couldn't you at least have had the decency to *do it* someplace other than *our* bed?"

"Rhees! I *did*—Yes, I've been with her before—before you. It isn't what you think, *today*. I know how you'd think that, but—"

"Don't! I knew this day would come. I'm surprised we lasted this long."

"Rhees, come inside and take a look."

"What do you want me to see? The red lipstick stains all over *my* pillow, like the *redonkulous* stains on your face? Do you need me to change the sheets for you? Make the bed?"

Paul looked up at the sky with a deadpan face and twitched his mouth.

"Just go take a fucking look! . . . Please?"

"No! I never want to go in my bedroom again. I thought that's why we never sleep at your apartment, in your bed. You didn't want me sleeping in your old memories."

He dropped his head and pursed his lips while they sat in silence. Finally, his eyes rose to look at her while his head still hung down, a wicked grin on his face. He stood and scooped her up, throwing her over his shoulder.

"Put me down!" she snarled vehemently, but he swatted her butt for it.

He carried her into the apartment, unlocked her bedroom door, carried her into the room, and threw her onto the bed.

"Faht was here *today*, purely for professional purposes."

Rhees' scowl intensified.

"Not *that* kind of professional. She's an interior decorator. She decorated my apartment years ago—it's been years since we—I've never, in my entire life, needed to pay for sex. It's always been too readily available to me." They locked into a staring contest, he waiting for her to believe him, her refusing to. "Though, people have offered to pay *me*."

She tried not to laugh, but lost the battle. Rhees looked around the room, taking in the differences. In the corner where her bag once stored her clothes, a free-standing closet rod stood with a shelf across the top for smaller items. All of her clothes were neatly hung. The simple twin bed had been replaced with a more couch-like, daybed. The double bed now faced the other direction so the view from the pillows no longer looked directly on the toilet.

The walls were now decorated with art and new curtains hung on the windows. It looked very nice compared to the barely functional, sterile room it was before.

Paul sat quietly on the daybed and watched Rhees take it all in.

"I'm sorry." Rhees felt terrible. "I should have trusted you. You've never given me a reason to be worried about . . . what I thought. I should have given you the benefit of the doubt."

"Nawt! I understand exactly why you would think what you did. I do. I can't expect to change opinions about me overnight, opinions I worked *extremely* hard to form, by the way, for years." He tried to laugh it all off, but Rhees knew she'd really hurt him. "I'm a pig, Rhees, and I know it."

She sat quietly for a minute. "It's not my opinion that matters. I wish *you* would change your opinion of yourself."

He didn't have a response.

"You got me a new mattress?" She bounced to check it out, trying to change the subject.

"Us. Yeah, I got us a new mattress." He grinned as if he had a private joke. "Your old mattress was a torture contraption. Now that we're into the rainy season, we're sleeping here more. I felt a mattress would be a good investment."

"Nice sheets. You got new sheets too?"

"Yeah, I have a thing, it's kind of a big—" She remembered him saying he had a thing about nice sheets before, but that isn't the image that popped into her mind.

"I've seen your *thing*, remember?"

He snorted incredulously. "I cannot believe you just said that to me."

She shrugged mischievously, surprised at how much easier that subject matter seemed to be getting with him. She looked down—maybe not as easy as it felt a second ago.

"Well, you saw *my thing* when *He* was on vacation. *He's* even more glorious when it's time to go to work—" Paul appeared to be in thought. "Or maybe it's the other way around—*He's* working when I'm going to the bathroom, but it's a vacation when *He*—" Paul suddenly looked like he remembered something important. His voice went up an octave. "Aw . . . *maaan!* You and I should never have this conversation again, understand?"

Rhees didn't know if she felt more relieved or disappointed.

"Rhees, did I jump the gun here, or am I not going to be around to enjoy the new, comfortable and luxurious bed?"

"I thought *I* was the pig."

Paul looked at her, confused.

"You said I was the little pig, and *you* were the big bad wolf."

He practically flew to the bed and pounced on her. He lay on top of her, his lower body to the side to avoid a problem, but he had her pinned.

"Whoa!" she said, still shocked by his fast and unexpected movement.

"Just don't ever forget that." He held his face close to hers, gazing into her eyes as if looking for something, she didn't know what, but all the hurt and anxiety was gone. He finally rolled so that he lay to her side with his arm around her. They both looked around the room again.

"What do you think? Do you like it? Everything looks nice, don't you think? You hate it, don't you?"

She giggled at his attempts to validate his latest project. He could be such an insecure baby sometimes. He startled her when he slapped the mattress.

"What about the mattress? Do you think you could stand to sleep on this baby for the rest of your li—" He stopped midsentence, and she looked to see why. He had a frown on his face. He returned her gaze, still a serious look on his face, before he forced a smile and recalculated the way to pose his question.

"Is this better than before, or should I call Faht, have her bring the old mattress back?"

Rhees took her turn to frown, as she reached up to wipe the lipstick off of his face. "I think I can manage to suffer with this one. If that's the price I have to pay for sharing my bed with such a rickety old man."

"Watch it!" he growled. "I may be trying to grow up, but I'm never going to get old!"

"I think it goes the other way around." She giggled. "You can choose to not grow up, but there's no controlling the getting old part."

"You're the one who just had another birthday. You're going to catch up to me if you're not careful."

"But I get to be twenty-nine for a while, remember?"

He smirked. "I remember too much." He had a devilish look on his face again. "Only four more." He rolled to hover over her again.

"Who's counting?" she asked.

He raised a brow, but then feigned confusion. "Let's see, twenty-nine comes after twenty-five?"

"I thought you remembered everything," she teased.

"Unfortunately." He lay back down and looked around the room again. "But it's better to play dumb sometimes. It's easier to do when I'm thinking with my *other* head."

"What?"

He jumped off the bed. "I keep going down the wrong path. It's time to go."

"But I want to stay a little longer and enjoy this new surprise."

"No." He sounded too serious.

She didn't move, hoping he would change his mind.

"Hey. Little pig," Paul barked. "The wolf is hungry. It's time to go!"

oOo

They were on their way back to the shop and Paul laughed, unexpectedly.

"Redonkulous?"

"That was forever ago."

"What the heck is redonkulous?"

She shrugged. "It's like a cross between ridiculous and asinine. Ridiculous didn't sound strong enough to fit the way I felt at that moment."

"Like flustrated, and where did you get creepazoid?"

"I don't know. I don't think I'm the only one who says that." She turned to face him. "What about you? What's with you calling every single person in the world by something other than their name?"

"What do you mean?" He played dumb.

"You refused to call me Rhees for weeks. You call Mitchell, Mitch, Shannon, Shanni, Shelli, Shell, Taylor, Taye . . . I actually thought Dobbs' name was really Dobbs! I just found out, like two days ago, that his name is Bartholomew Dobbson . . . until you came to the island."

"Dobbs is so much cooler, don't you think? Bartholomew! Really? Who names their kid Bartholomew, for crying out loud?"

"Okay, I'll give you that one." She couldn't help her giggle. "How about the way you say certain words sometimes? Nawt! Hawt! Whawt?" she mocked.

He feigned hurt feelings. "You don't like my accent?"

"I love your accent, but you don't say it like that every time."

He looked like he had to decide whether he wanted to explain it or not.

"My dad's from LA, the stereotypical surf bum, before he got all executive on us. My mom is from *Bawston*. As kids, Pete, Mare, and I noticed that even though they were from opposite ends of the country, they both said certain words the same. We started out just poking fun at them, but I guess it became a habit."

"Wait. Your brother is Peter, you're Paul, and your sister is Mary?" She sounded skeptical. "Are you kidding me? And you're ridiculing Dobbs' parents for their choice of baby names?"

Paul looked taken aback, thoughtful. "No one's picked up on that for a long time." It dawned on him why. He hadn't talked about his family for such a long time. "What can I say? I was a little young to be offering my expert advice on the matter. How do you even know about them? Peter, Paul, and Mary were more our parents' generation."

"Exactly. My parents listened to them all the time. We need a new law requiring parents to check with you before they can officially name their kids. It could be the, *Don't Name Your Kids Stupid Names Bureau*, or something." She giggled. "My parents could have used some help with that, too. Danarya. Blech!"

He rattled his head. "I love Danarya!"

"Watch it there, buddy." She stopped walking and tilted her head at him with a mocking smirk. "You wouldn't want anyone to hear you say that out of context."

It took him a second. "Oh." It sunk in a little more. "Oh!" They both laughed and then they were quiet for a second.

"I know you're so much more intelligent than I am, but sometimes it's too easy to mess you up."

"Don't say that." He frowned. "Let's not talk about messing each other up."

"What's wrong?"

He cocked his head to the side and looked away. "Because my buddies and I say that—it means something different to me. I don't want to be reminded of that around you." His expression brightened. "And yeah, I turn into a complete imbecile around you, because you're such a ball-buster." He started laughing and put his hands up, pretending to defend himself against an anticipated attack. She obliged by swatting his arm before they resumed walking.

"Claire is just about the only one you haven't found a pet name for." Rhees started the conversation where they'd left off.

"Claire is *nawt* my pet!"

His pronunciation choice made her giggle again. "Oh, you love Claire. I know you act like you don't, but you do."

"Nope." He drawled on the word and let the P pop on his lips.

"I know I can be gullible, but that's one I'll never believe." She raised her brow at him, skeptically.

oOo

"You're in for a surprise." Tracy waggled her eyebrows, suggestively, at Paul, making him feel a little uncomfortable.

"Dare I ask why?"

"Some of the girls convinced Rhees to wax, Brazilian." She smiled, too excitedly, and waggled her eyebrows again. Tracy's absence of an information filter left him aghast. "You'll be surprised tonight."

"Uh . . ." He didn't know what to say. "It would have been a better surprise if you hadn't said anything."

Tracy just smiled, completely oblivious, and walked off. Paul saw Rhees come around the corner, surrounded by Regina and a group of his old standbys, and he about died.

"Shit."

When the girls made their way to the deck, Paul slipped an arm around Rhees' waist and kissed her more passionately than he usually did, even in public.

"Hey, *Baby*." He smiled at Rhees and then at the other girls. "I need to borrow my girl. I didn't know she'd left, and now I have to make up for the time I've missed with her." He dragged her off to the bathroom.

"Paul?" Rhees' voice sounded shaky and nervous. "What are you doing?"

He closed the door and stared at her for a minute. "Can you please tell me why you left the shop without saying anything to me?" He finally found his voice, the one that wouldn't sound as frustrated as he felt. She went a little pale.

"I couldn't tell you. I was too embarrassed about where we were headed."

He huffed out a humorless laugh. "And why would you be headed to embarrass yourself?"

"I don't want to tell you. It's kind of personal. I'd hoped I could be back before you noticed and I'd never have to explain."

Another breathy laugh. "Word of advice? If you don't want me to know something, don't take Tracy along."

"Oh, crap." Rhees paled even more and dived into an explanation. "I didn't want to do it! I stupidly mentioned I never have and the girls were shocked. They were all talking about how much you liked it—I didn't know what to say when they asked why I didn't wax for you."

"Rhees, Baby." He let out a long and quiet growl, venting his frustration. "The last thing I need is to be thinking about what you got going on down there." He scrubbed his face, hoping to wipe away some of the tension, before he noticed her eyes welling up. "Aw!" he groaned. "I'm sorry. This is my fault." He pulled her to his chest and hugged her sympathetically. "I'll fix it. Nothing like this will happen again . . . And for the record, I've never been picky about that."

oOo

Once Rhees assured him she was okay and she'd settled at the computer to work on Dailies, Paul headed out in search of the Coitus Club girls. He couldn't believe he'd started calling them that in his head. He thought "the club" would have disbanded by now. Dorene and Krista were the only ones left from the native group, but there were still other past partners from around the island who continued to hang out at Paradise.

He didn't mind people from the island hanging out at his shop, people tended to do that, but he didn't understand why this particular group of girls couldn't seem to find another topic of discussion—one that didn't include him and his sex life—past sex life.

"Hi Paul," Maya said with a wink as he approached.

The girls sat in the shade of the gazebo. They all watched him expectantly, and he understood they thought he'd just discovered Rhees' surprise.

"Hey." He tipped his chin in greeting, but looked them over. "I have a question for you," he said to no one in particular.

"Sure," a couple of them answered as they perked up with anticipation.

"How many of you have I had a monogamous relationship with?" His question let the wind out of their sails. They sat, silently watching him, waiting for what else he'd have to say. "That's right. I'd say Rhees is the only one qualified to be handing out advice about what I like and don't like. And me, of course—I know what I like better than anyone." He paused for effect. "I like Rhees." He paused again, taking the time to look each and every one of them in the eye.

"I like everything about her—just the way she is. You girls have a nice day," he said as he walked off.

oOo

"Paul, Paul!" Claire came running from the office, toward Paul and Rhees, as they sat in the gazebo sharing lunch. Paul braced himself for bad news. "We need to find a Japanese instructor, fast."

"Why?"

"A cruise company based in Japan just contacted me and said they saw our website. They're thinking about adding the island to the itinerary of their Caribbean liner."

"Really?" Rhees asked. "I can't believe the reach we've been getting lately."

Paul kissed her temple. "It's all you, Babe."

"No." Rhees denied it could be her marketing strategy.

"Yes," Claire said. "They'd be sending a luxury cruise ship with about fifty people every three months. They're looking for a dive shop to accommodate their guests. Their only requirement is that we provide instruction in their own language."

Paul rattled off several sentences in Japanese, the first thing that came to mind, the words he'd used the most during his travels to Japan. Claire and Rhees stared at him.

"You speak Japanese." Claire sounded annoyed. "Why didn't you tell me? Do you know how many small groups we could have booked?"

"You never asked."

"What did you just say?" Rhees asked excitedly, watching him in awe.

He looked down, wishing he could kick himself for opening up his past in front of her. He'd only thought of answering to Claire, but now . . . he didn't want to answer, but refusing would only make it worse.

"Listen up. I'm the new owner of this company. These men are here to liquidate the assets." He waved his right hand in the air and then his left. ". . . And these men are here to break the arms and legs of any man who tries to interfere."

He looked at Rhees warily, wondering what she would think of him. He'd had to make a choice. Tell her the truth or endure her constant efforts to get it out of him.

"You like to say that. Remember Fred?"

He nodded.

"Have you ever really done that—broken any arms, and, or, legs?"

"Only my own. My leg, when I was seven. I jumped off the balcony of my second story bedroom."

She finally smiled, assuming he was only joking around. Paul counted his blessings she'd accepted his explanation without more details. He turned his gaze back to Claire.

"For future reference, I also speak Italian, Irish, thanks to Mitch and Ginger, Cantonese, Malay, Kadazan—several of those dialects, and Arabic. I'm fluent in Spanish. Growing up in Florida with a Cuban nanny made that a given. I can get by in Portuguese, and French too, but I haven't heard those enough to say I'm fluent."

Rhees put her arms around him and gave him a hug.

"You are an amazing man, Paul Weaver. And I thought I was doing well, finally learning a little Spanish and getting the hang of the island's version of English." She giggled. He kissed her on the nose, noticing how she didn't mind the way he was slowly working his way toward her lips with his little innocent kisses.

"Get a hold of the manuals and the video in Japanese. If I read it once and listen to it, I'll be able to teach it." He grew wary again at the way Claire watched him. "What? I'm a fast learner."

Chapter 15

Late October meant business slowed down because of hurricane season, school schedules, and whatever else made tourists not want to travel to the island that time of year. Except for *The Tow'd* breaking down four more times since July, life had been pretty uneventful, even peaceful, at the shop.

"Things will have to be different," Paul told Taylor over the phone. "If I decide to come, I'm bringing Rhees, and there will be no sharing. Do you hear me? No sharing. I swear. She's mine and only mine." His memories of their past Testosterfest activities made his stomach churn.

"All right, Paul, I get it," Taylor yelled, seasoning every sentence he spoke with tasteless words. "I don't understand why—I thought you'd be the last man standing, but I get it. No sharing. Just come. We don't want to do Testosterfest without you—not again. I'll pass it along to the guys."

"You'd better understand. I mean it. No one touches her. Do you hear me?"

"Yes!" Taylor yelled. "Fuck. Paul. I fucking hear you."

oOo

Paul and Rhees met Taylor, David, and Bryce in the baggage claim area of the San Jose airport in Costa Rica, and their *dates*. They made the customary introductions, stowed their luggage in the van, and climbed in. The driver pulled from the curb and headed to the beach house.

Just as the van pulled into the large gravel driveway,

Angel, the property manager, flew from the house to greet them, excited to see them again. Paul and his friends knew the property well. They came to the beach house every year, Paul had missed a few, but neither Rhees nor the other girls had ever been there.

Angel waved for them to follow him inside. They walked into a very large living area with a high, vaulted ceiling. A dining table, big enough to seat twelve people, a conversation area with several couches set in a square, and a pool table, weren't enough to fill the room. Several enclosed rooms lined both sides of the gigantic space.

To the left, a long breakfast bar lined with eight stools, divided the living area from the kitchen, and beyond that, a well-stocked bar with more stools, hugged the wall.

On the right, double glass doors revealed a media room complete with an oversized flat screen television hanging on the wall between four smaller versions, two on each side of the larger one. A long set of shelves under the televisions contained various game consoles with an array of games and movies on DVD. A large overstuffed sectional couch wrapped the remaining walls, offering maximum comfort while using the room.

Large floor to ceiling windows lined the next room on the right, displaying an office filled with computers, printers, and any gadget a guest might need to conduct business, long distance. A wide set of stairs, also to the right, led up to a railed wrap-around walkway, which connected four master suites, two on each side of the living area below. The rustic décor gave the impression of a log cabin but with luxurious amenities.

Glass windows and doors filled the entire back wall, showcasing the magnificent view of the ocean. Angel pushed a button and the glass doors began sliding themselves to the sides and into a pocket in the wall. The room opened out, first into a spacious screened room, and then to a giant outdoor deck with Cabanas lining both sides. At the end, in the middle, a sparkling pool gave the illusion it spilled over the edge, into the ocean.

A beautiful property, built with basic and simple materials, but luxurious at the same time, the house sat in a secluded section of beach with no visible neighbors and surrounded by jungle.

"Like it? Think you'll be happy here the next few days?" Paul sounded concerned about Rhees.

"Lo siento!" Angel said in Spanish. "My wife's sister is ill. Loretta can't cook for you. She had to go to Puntarenas to take care of her dying sister. I'm afraid I haven't found a new cook. The pantry is full, but I have no one to cook for you. My daughters will clean, but they don't know how to cook."

The only ones in the group who didn't speak Spanish happened to be Rhees and Liz, so Paul and Taylor translated for their dates in hushed tones as Angel explained the problem.

Paul stood behind Rhees, holding her protectively, as if needing to make a statement, or a claim. She pulled out of his arms and he watched as she wandered into the kitchen. She opened the fridge. Stocked for an army, her facial expression demonstrated how the contents impressed her. She opened the pantry and again made the same face. The kitchen was laid out like a commercial restaurant, a large gas range with double ovens, a large industrial sink, two bread makers, two microwaves . . . who couldn't make due in this kitchen?

"I can cook," she announced.

Paul shot her a killer glance.

"Don't look at me like that. There's plenty of food. I can do this, piece of cake."

David's date, Ashley, balked. "I didn't come a thousand miles to eat macaroni and cheese."

"Mac and cheese is Rhees' specialty." The defensive tone in Paul's voice was as impossible to miss as Ashley's insult.

"I knew it." Ashley rolled her eyes with a groan. "This was supposed to be a luxury getaway, but of course, it's turned into a disaster!" She slapped David's arm, as if it was her date's fault.

"I can't promise gourmet," Rhees said, "I'm not a trained chef, but I know how to cook—I like to cook. I can, at least, make sure no one starves."

Ashley turned to David. "This is not what you promised. You said we'd have a professional cook."

"Who knew this would come up?" David looked helpless. "Come on, Ash."

"I would rather eat out."

Paul rolled his eyes.

"How many restaurants did you see on the way here?" David asked. "This is a remote area. We'd be in the car all day if we tried to eat out, and delivery isn't an option."

Ashley folded her arms and pouted an obvious, obnoxious pout. David tried to put his arms around her, but she brushed him away, giving him a dirty, *don't even think about it,* look.

"Okay then. It looks like I'm cooking," Rhees said.

"Rhees, this is supposed to be your vacation," Paul objected.

"My life is a vacation nowadays. I can do this." She snuggled back into his arms, and looked up at him, gratefully.

"I know you can, but I don't want you to."

"What other choice do we have?" She rolled her eyes at him and turned to the others. "Okay then, I can keep your bellies full. You'll have to be the judges as to whether or not you'd rather they weren't."

oOo

When Paul invited Rhees to be his date at Testosterfest, he filled her in on what to expect and apologized ahead of time. It embarrassed him to even consider bringing her, but he loved his friends and couldn't imagine not coming, missing out on seeing them again. He also couldn't imagine not bringing Rhees. He knew his friends too well. He needed her to keep him on track. He feared he could, too easily, fall back into his old habits without her to remind him of his new life changes.

Paul failed—purposely—to give Rhees one bit of information about one past Testosterfest tradition. The guys had always made a game of trying to seduce each other's dates. The ongoing challenge stood to see who could score with the most girls over the event. All four of the men were above average in looks, but Taylor usually went away the winner because he cared more about winning than Paul. Bryce and David had stopped trying to compete with the two of them by high school. This year would be different—Paul had *promised* his friends.

He'd made his decree clear—no more sharing. They'd all been duly informed—touch Rhees and die. David jumped on board without hesitation, as he and Ashley had been together for over two months. His friends had already started ridiculing him about biting the dust. Taylor and Bryce didn't like the new rule, but they went along— they were stuck with the girls they'd brought for the week.

"Macaroni and cheese," Rhees answered, when Bryce asked what smelled so good. Paul insisted she make it for dinner the first night, leading her to believe he wanted to let his friends know how good it could be, but it turned out to be a passive-aggressive attempt to get back at Ashley for insulting Rhees.

A tense moment passed between David and Bryce as they feared Ashley's reaction. It had already become clear Paul and Ashley would never be great friends.

They all sat at the spacious dining table and enjoyed Rhees' meaty version of the all-American pasta dish, salad, garlic toast, and lemon bars for dessert, except Ashley. She picked at her food and pretended not to like it with a scowl on her face, but she ate plenty. After dinner, Rhees started cleaning up—alone.

"You know, the maids will come in the morning. We could leave this for them." Paul knew he fought a hopeless battle, but he needed to try.

"Do you know how many germs there will be by morning

if we leave these food encrusted dishes all night? I'm not making breakfast in a bacteria-infested kitchen."

After all the time he'd spent with her, Paul had learned enough about clean up that he could pitch in, and he did. Once the kitchen sparkled, clean and disinfected, he took Rhees in his arms and thanked her for saving the vacation.

"But you look tired," he said. "Jet lag?"

She smiled and nodded. "Maybe, or it might be that we've been up since early this morning to catch our flight."

"Go get ready for bed. I'll be up soon."

"Take your time, be with your friends. I noticed while cooking dinner, there is most definitely a water heater somewhere in this great house, *so* . . . I want to shower first, before bed."

"The sacrifices you make for me." He only half joked. She did put his needs first, too often. "I'm going to kiss you now, okay?"

She made sure he knew she didn't object by reaching up on tiptoes to kiss him first, twisting her fingers into his long hair. He'd stopped getting haircuts after their Utah trip, and stopped shaving three weeks before, in preparation for Testosterfest. For some reason, the guys felt the need to look like cavemen, but she liked his beard. Her tongue also introduced itself before his had the chance to do so. The kiss drew out, longer than normal.

"Mmm," he moaned, and reluctantly pulled away. "I'm going to stop kissing you now, okay," he said teasingly, and they both smiled about the progress she'd made concerning physical touch.

"I should be done in twenty minutes," she said.

"Enjoy your shower."

As soon as Rhees climbed the stairs and shut their bedroom door behind her, he marched over to the conversation area where everyone else lounged lazily, drinking wine.

"Consider tonight our turn for clean-up duty. There're four days here at the beach house, four couples. Don't think that Rhees is going to cook *and* clean every night.

You're all taking a turn."

"I knew it!" Ashley whined. "This is supposed to be my vacation. It's bad enough to have to eat _homemade_ food, but I am _not_ doing dishes!"

"Ashley's right. We were promised a nice vacation." Jeannie pressed Ashley's position. "I don't cook or do dishes at home."

Paul leaned against his hands on the back of the couch, pursed his lips, and tried to keep his temper in check, but his protective instincts had already slipped into overdrive. His friends could see it, and they knew better, but the girls didn't know Paul well enough to understand what was happening.

"I have never washed a dish in my life. We have _people_ to do that for us," Ashley added snidely. "Rhees volunteered, remember? She's obviously more cut out for this sort of thing than the rest of us."

Ashley threw her nose in the air and glanced at the others with a smug grin on her face, as if they all would understand she'd just included them in her, _I grew up rich and spoiled club_, maliciously at Rhees' expense.

No one responded with the acceptance she was looking for. Paul's friends all sat with their mouths hanging open, ready to spring into action. Even Jeannie, who'd backed her up only seconds before, looked horrified at what Ashley had just said. Ashley just shrugged and seemed to use that information to categorize them all at a level beneath her and began studying her nails.

Paul's eyes narrowed. His mouth pinched shut, making the muscle in his jaw twitch as he leaned into the conversation area, but mostly toward Ashley.

"Rhees is _not_ the hired help," he hissed. "This is _her_ vacation too. _Everyone._ Takes. A night." He glared at Ashley.

"We'll all pitch in," David rushed to answer, and the men all agreed, watching to see if it was enough to pacify Paul. David patted Ashley on the thigh to conciliate her. "I'll do it our night, Honey. You don't have to help."

"And just what am *I* supposed to do while you're stuck in the kitchen all night?" Ashley whined like a spoiled brat, and David moaned, knowing Paul's patience had reached its end. His friends all read the signs.

"How about a game of pool?" Bryce jumped up and slapped Paul on the back, trying to distract him.

Paul glared at Ashley, and she glared back. Taylor and David both leaped off the couches and took Paul by the arm.

"What do you say the boys have a real drink out by the pool? We have some catching up to do."

Taylor and Bryce's dates started to get up, intending to follow them outside, but Ashley stopped them. "Believe me girls. We don't want to be around them when they start drinking and reminiscing."

Paul shook his head as Bryce and David prodded him toward the door. Taylor grabbed two bottles of Irish whiskey and four glasses from the bar before he followed them.

"Where'd you find this bitch, Davey? She can't sit on her lazy ass by herself and watch you do dishes, but she doesn't want to be near you while you sit by the pool and look out at the ocean on a beautiful tropical night?" Paul asked. After some coaxing, he finally gave in to his friends' rather forceful invitation to take the party outside.

oOo

Rhees stepped out of the shower and poked her head out the door of the bathroom, expecting to see Paul. She'd forgotten to bring one of his T-shirts into the bathroom with her and had only a towel wrapped around her.

"Paul? Could you hand me a T-shirt?" No response. She heard men's voices outside the open French doors and she stepped out onto the balcony to see. Paul and his friends sat in the whirlpool, twenty feet below, talking boisterously and having a good time.

Paul laughed and talked animatedly, the way he had

at Fratelli's when Taylor visited the island. She didn't get to see him so carefree very often and she couldn't help but smile. She leaned against the doorjamb to enjoy the opportunity to watch him without his knowledge. Paul and his friends could be such little boys, even though they'd each had their thirty-first birthday that year, she loved seeing this side of him.

Paul noticed movement and looked up at the second story balcony to see what it was. It caught him off guard and his breath hitched slightly at the sight of her. The soft flickering light radiating from the pool and patio made her just-showered skin glisten, her bare shoulders and legs. She looked beautiful, standing in the glow with nothing but a towel wrapped around her body.

He noticed he'd made her feel self-conscious when their eyes met, but she didn't attempt to run inside. They gazed at each other, lost in their own world.

"Now that's an eye fuck if I've ever seen one." Taylor broke the spell. He slapped Paul on the arm with the back of his hand and licked his lips to see if he could rile Paul. "That's the first glimpse I've caught of that girl that might help me understand what you see in her."

David and Bryce looked up to see what they were looking at, but Rhees had slipped inside as soon as Taylor so crudely ruined the moment.

oOo

One and a half bottles of whiskey later, the men were still in the whirlpool and the decibel level of their conversation had risen considerably.

The girls had all given up on their dates and gone to bed, including Rhees.

"I'm glad to see Rhees didn't hold out on you forever. I honestly didn't think she'd ever let you have her cherry."

Once again, Taylor's bluntness and crudity knew no bounds, and Paul couldn't really say anything in her defense. He chose to nod slightly and pretend it was no big deal.

"Virgins must really be as tight as they say. It's all I can come up with—why you're still with her. You have all those cute, worldly girls on the island, a fresh supply showing up every few weeks—"

"What's going on with you and Ash-witch?" Paul gave Taylor a dirty look, drawing the attention away from his relationship with Rhees by putting it on David.

"Her dad's a Senator."

"Oh! I get it," Taylor piped in, as though a light bulb had just lit up inside his head. "You're using Ashley to make her dad jealous."

"No, you." David wiped away a fake tear. "You know you are my first and only true love. I want you back. Why aren't you jealous?"

The guys all laughed.

"Dickwad!" David slugged Taylor's arm. "Her dad likes me, and that can't hurt my career, but you've seen her. She's the most beautiful woman I've ever been with."

Taylor and Bryce nodded in agreement, but Paul seemed confused. He hadn't given Ashley or the other girls a second notice, and it surprised him to realize it.

"You're a damned good attorney . . . slash, future politician—if that's still the course you're foolish enough to want to be on, but my point is—" Paul held up his finger to drive home said point. "—There are more important attributes to look for in a woman than her appearance," Paul said casually and took a drink.

Paul's friends all silently stared at him in disbelief before they all broke out into wild laughter.

"I think hell is going to freeze over while we sleep, and we'll wake up to see pigs flying in the morning. Did you guys think you'd ever hear those words come out of Paul's mouth?" Taylor threw his head back and laughed some more.

"The only thing that would surprise me more is if I heard Taylor say that." Bryce kept them on a roll. Paul laughed too, but not as loudly. The change in his attitude about women had sneaked up on him, and left him a little dazed as he only now realized how much.

"I mean it though," Paul finally said when they calmed down. "If Ash-witch doesn't stop being so offensive to Rhees, I'll have to bitch-slap you, Davey." Paul glared at David.

"Paul, seriously? You'd choose Rhees over David?"

Paul jerked around to look at Taylor for asking the question. "Not Davey. But I sure as hell would choose Rhees over his current fuck."

"Guys, we need to do an intervention for Paul. We have to save our buddy. He's fallen in love," Taylor mocked, feigning grave concern.

"Love?" Paul almost choked at the idea. "Rhees is just—" He suddenly felt agitated—he didn't know how to finish the sentence. He'd never allowed himself to think too much about it. It made him too uncomfortable.

"What's she got that I don't?" Taylor cried, throwing his arms around Paul and burying his face into his shoulder like a discarded girlfriend, stirring the others up into another round of laughter. Paul knew it was best to just let it play out. If he tried to stop Taylor during one of his drama queen rants, it would only make it worse. "Don't leave me for her. I'm better for you than she is."

At two thirty in the morning, Paul convinced the guys they should all sleep on the pool chairs so they wouldn't wake the girls. Taylor, the only one who didn't care, went upstairs to Liz anyway while the others passed out around the pool. Paul was too drunk to trust himself . . . but drunk or not, he was confused as to whether he even wanted to be near Rhees. The guys' ridiculing had really bothered him. He lay awake another hour, thinking about what Taylor had said, and it put him in a bad mood.

oOo

The next morning, Rhees not only prepared breakfast,

but made sack lunches for the guys to take with them on their testosterone-filled activity for the day. Paul stocked the cooler as she generously piled meat and cheese on the leftover bread she'd baked the night before.

The dates, in return for a free vacation, were expected not to complain as the men ran off every day on their adventures. The men had made it unquestionably clear. No girls were allowed during the day activities.

This first day, the plan entailed making their way to Pavone for a day of surfing. The logistics of getting there made it an all day trip and they were happy for Rhees' thoughtful sack lunches and her idea to take a cooler filled with drinks. She'd meant bottled water and soda, but the guys insisted the cooler be stocked with nothing but beer.

Rhees had to snag Paul to give him a hug as he and his friends tried to get out the door. He glanced around, nervously checking to see if the other guys noticed. He couldn't get Taylor's comment about being in love off his mind.

"I didn't sleep well last night," she confessed quietly. "You didn't come to bed."

"I didn't want to wake you, and honestly, I was too drunk to be a good citizen."

"I'm sorry." She sighed. "I wish it didn't matter. I wish I could just, you know . . . it would make things so much easier."

He did a double take. She must have understood the look on his face.

"Yes, I mean *that*. I'm tired of being so uptight about it. I wish I could—"

"Don't say that. It doesn't help. I should go."

She rose up on her toes to kiss him, but he only offered his cheek.

"My, you're grumpy this morning. Hungover?"

He nodded at the good excuse she'd given him. The headache didn't help, but it wasn't last night's alcohol that had him uptight and uncomfortable.

"Tonight, don't get drunk. I miss my snuggle buddy,"

Rhees said.

"I'll try, but it's hard." He hemmed and hawed, feeling uneasy about their relationship all of a sudden.

"Hey, Pussy-Whipped! Come on, we're going to miss the chopper," Taylor yelled on his way to the van.

Paul looked Taylor's direction, embarrassed. He lost his place. "Um . . . it's hard with the guys around. We'll see."

"I know." She gave him a warm, understanding smile. "Don't worry about me, I'll be fine. Enjoy your time with your friends."

"Why do you have to be so perfect?" His brows knit together. He felt bad for the doubts running through his mind.

"Mangina!" All three of his friends joined in the heckling.

Paul looked at them and hesitated before giving Rhees a quick kiss and running to the van.

Chapter 16

The girls sat around the pool, working on their tans, and getting to know each other. Rhees made a big salad after breakfast and left it in the crisper of the commercial fridge so they could piece on it as they got hungry.

Angel's daughters arrived and cleaned up the breakfast mess before they started on the rest of the house, but Rhees almost wished they hadn't. She knew how to clean and didn't mind doing it, and hanging out with the other women, all day, the next few days, caused her some anxiety.

"What's Paul's problem?" Ashley asked that afternoon. "He acts like a big spoiled brat. How do you stand to put up with him?"

"Paul?" Rhees' voice went high with disbelief.

"Yes, Paul. He's a bully."

"Come on," Liz said. "You only have to take one look at him to know why she puts up with him."

"David is good looking too, but I'd never put up with that kind of shit."

"Paul is not a bully." Rhees slipped in to defensive mode. "Paul might come across like that once in a while, but it's only because he takes things a little too seriously sometimes. When he cares about someone, he gets protective. He's really quite generous and thoughtful."

"I don't believe it," Ashley said with a humph.

Rhees shrugged, thoughtfully. "It's not just me. You know, he's still friends with almost all the girls he's been with. Even though he isn't with them anymore . . . never really was . . . actually." She reflected on that idea. In all the time she'd known him, Shelli was the closest he came to having a disgruntled girlfriend.

She smiled to herself, knowing he would deny Shelli was ever a girlfriend. But even after the way they'd parted company, Shelli had called him when she regained consciousness, to apologize for the way she'd acted. She told him she blamed herself for what Mario tried to do to Rhees.

After Shelli had left the shop, she'd met Mario and they hooked up quickly. Still upset with the way things had turned out, she said she'd talked too much about Paul the man-whore and Rhees' virginal status. She said it hadn't taken Mario long to start saying strange, inappropriate things like, he wanted to teach Paul a lesson, show him who the big bull really was, and how it would show Paul if he got to Rhees first.

Shelli told Paul that when Mario confessed what he planned to do, she tried to stop him, but he beat her for it, raped her, and left her for dead. Paul had told her not to blame herself and bought her a plane ticket home so her family could watch over her while she recovered from her injuries. The kind of person Ashley described wouldn't have cared enough to do that.

"But they all *still* consider him a friend," Rhees continued. "There has to be something to that. Like I said, he's generous, thoughtful, and protective."

"Bryce loves him," Jeannie said. "He said Paul would do anything for him."

"Taylor feels the same way," Liz added, and then she repeated, "and he's so pretty." Jeannie nodded in agreement.

"Don't let him hear you call him pretty," Rhees warned. "He tolerates good-looking, handsome, and even beautiful, but he hates being called pretty."

"See? Bully." Ashley had heard David say the same nice things about Paul, but she wasn't about to add that to his cause.

Rhees hated how Ashley ignored every nice thing everyone said about Paul and focused only on the one thing she'd said that made him look bad. She wished she could take it back and hoped to fix her blunder.

"Paul is more than just a pretty face. He's the smartest man I've ever known. He's a hard worker, he's fun, funny," Rhees continued. "So many of the things I admire. He's a man of his word. He keeps his promises—almost to a fault—it's annoying at times. Maybe what you're picking up on is his honesty. When he's angry, you know it. When he's happy, you know it. There's no guessing. He's so honest . . . except when he lies." She giggled, and the other girls giggled at that too.

"Isn't that the way they all are?" Liz said.

oOo

The next day included shark diving in the morning, and a round of golf that afternoon. Once again, he'd had too much to drink the night before and didn't come to bed. He'd made excuses to linger downstairs until all the other men went up to their dates before slipping into the media room to sleep on the couch. Rhees woke from a nightmare, found him missing again, and went searching for him. She roused him up and got him upstairs before anyone could find him and ask him hard-to-answer questions.

"Sharks?" She followed him around the bedroom as he got ready for the activity. "Why can't you use a cage?"

Paul was still confused about his feelings, and acted too invested in getting ready to answer.

"Paul, I'm so scared. Please, don't go."

"I have to go."

"Then promise me you won't get eaten." That made him laugh in spite of his attempt to stay aloof, and she was finally able to catch him, throwing her arms around his waist. She'd chased him around the room as he wandered, gathering his things and packing them into his duffle bag.

He liked the contact and that only confused him more.

"If a shark did take a bite, I'm so *nasty*, he'd spit me right out. Besides, I can't get eaten. If I weren't around, who'd take care of your beautiful ass?"

"That's right. Without you, I'd wither and die." She scowled at him and he sneaked in a quick squeeze of her butt.

That day, four massage therapists showed up after lunch and gave each of the girls a two-hour massage by the pool.

"These guys know how to take care of a girl," Jeannie said.

"Only when they want something in return," Ashley clarified.

oOo

At dinner that night, the guys went over their scheduled activities for the rest of the week. In the morning, they planned to do one of the longest and best zip lines in the world. The day after, their last day at the beach house, they'd scheduled kite surfing before they headed back to town for their last night together.

"A zip line?" Rhees' attention piqued. "I need to do a zip line. It's one of those things on my list of fears to overcome, like diving and ice blocking and . . . life itself."

The guys stared at her, alarmed at her comment. Paul looked at her, distress written all over his face.

"Paul . . ." Bryce and Taylor both said at the same time.

"Rhees, I'll take you sometime." Paul tried to save the awkward moment, and his man card. "Not this trip, okay, Babe?"

"I know you don't want me tagging along with you and the guys, but what if I went alone, or with the girls?" She turned to the girls. "How about it? Who else wants to do the zip line with me?"

"No way. I'd rather shop at Wal-Mart," Ashley said. The other girls weren't as vocal as Ashley, but it became clear they weren't interested.

"Okay, looks like I'm on my own. I'll go at a different time than you. I promise not to encroach on your, *Brotherhood of Testosterone,* time."

"No!" Paul snapped out.

Rhees glared at him, and he found himself taken aback by her wounded expression. *Shit! She's serious.* He suddenly felt torn between her happiness and appeasing his friends—his friends would be more vocal. Sure, Rhees would back down—she always gave in to him—he thought it would be a good opportunity to let the guys know he hadn't turned soft on a girl—even if he had—he hadn't figured that out yet, before this trip.

"I *said* I'll take you, *another time.*" He gave her a, *can we discuss this later,* look.

"Don't be ridiculous. Why would we spend all that money to come again when we're here now, and I can just check it off my list?"

"No. You're not running around in a foreign country by yourself." She rolled her eyes at him. "Rhees, I've made up my mind about this, you're not going alone. I said I'll bring you back, and we can do it then." She didn't look happy, but she dropped the subject like he expected she would.

That night, they all decided to watch a movie in the media room. The remote beach house didn't have cable, so they voted on which movie to watch from the large collection on the shelves. They decided on *The Patriot.*

Taylor and Liz didn't make it fifteen minutes into the movie before they sneaked out and to their room. Bryce and Jeannie started making out on the couch as soon as Taylor left, and eventually slinked off to their bedroom as well, leaving Paul, Rhees, David, and Ashley to watch the movie. David kept trying to get Ashley to make out too, but she acted more interested in Heath Ledger and Mel Gibson than David.

With the extra space made available by the exiting couples, Paul and Rhees stretched out on the couch, lying next to each other, Paul behind her. When the movie reached the scene where Anne's parents sewed Gabriel into a bundling bag, Rhees turned to face Paul with a questioning look on her face.

"I didn't know they did that back in those days."

Paul shrugged. He'd never heard of it before the movie. Rhees continued to stare at him, inquiring.

"No," he said. She raised a brow. She didn't look like she agreed. "No! We'll talk later." He tipped his head at David and Ashley to alert Rhees of Ashley's sudden interest in them, so Rhees turned her attention back to the movie.

Neither of them had slept well without each other the past two nights, and Paul and Rhees wound up falling asleep on the couch in their cuddly position.

David watched his friend, snuggled up to Rhees, wondering what was going on with Paul. He'd been acting different, strange all week.

"I saw Paul on the couch last night when I came down to get something for my headache. This is the first time they've slept together since they got here," Ashley said. She and David both laughed that Paul and Rhees were literally sleeping. "I'd say the magic in that relationship is long over. They're like an old married couple. I don't know why she puts up with him."

"You didn't know Paul, pre-Rhees. I can't figure out what he's still doing with *her*!"

"It's obvious. She worships him, and he's clearly into being worshipped."

David looked surprised at Ashley's conclusion. "No. That's not it at all. Paul's always been low-key, quiet, kind of shy. He listens and pays attention, to *everything,* and then he's just there when you need him."

"He is not shy. He's mean and grumpy and—"

"That's because you've been pushing his buttons. Ash, you don't want to push Paul's buttons."

"I'm not afraid of Paul. The rest of you can be if you want, but I'm not letting him push me around."

"He doesn't push anyone around. We respect him, and

he's usually right." David chuckled.

"You're saying I'm wrong? I am not wrong! How dare you say—"

David shushed her, turned the TV off, and they walked upstairs to their room.

"Paul's a watcher. He sits quietly and watches, listens, and learns. Maybe that's why he's a good judge of character, and I guess the reason he's so hung up on Rhees—I don't think he even realizes it though." David laughed at the thought of his long-time friend being blindsided by an emotion Paul always claimed to be incapable of feeling. "But she's good people. She's good for him. I'm just surprised."

"Rhees is a wimp. That's what he sees in her. She worships him and when he says jump, she asks, how high. If he were my boyfriend, he'd learn a thing or two real fast."

Again, Ashley's take on the matter surprised him. David thought the role was *reversed*, that Paul was the one doing all the jumping and worshipping. David didn't want to argue with Ashley about it. "It's like I don't even recognize him anymore. He disappeared, just took off when his brother died five years ago. His dad hired an army of private investigators to find him and sent Taylor to check up on him, bring him back, but Paul refuses to go home. He's changed—changes every time I see him."

"How'd his brother die?"

"No one knows the details. The police never solved the case. He was mixed up with some drug ring, I don't know, but they were very close."

"Was Paul involved too?" Ashley grasped for juicy information.

David ignored her question. "The Paul I knew would never fall for *anyone*, let alone someone as tame as Rhees. Taylor mentioned she was a virgin when they met."

"Are you kidding?" Ashley seemed too amused by the revelation.

"And have you noticed how territorial he is with her? He's always been more like Taylor."

"Taylor is so crude and horny. Poor Liz. They aren't going to last, I just know it."

David shot her a look. It wasn't news to him. Liz was just a pretty lay for the trip and David knew how hard it was on Taylor to stick to the same girl all week. He'd rarely seen him with the same girl twice. "Honestly David, this trip hasn't instilled a lot of confidence in me about your choice of friends. We're going to have to work on that, find you more suitable people to hang out with."

David's heart sank. He wished Ashley would stop trying to change him and he wondered again why they were still together if she didn't like anything about him.

"Well, the Paul I remember was more like Taylor, only stealthier. Taylor sees what he wants and goes for it, bold and loud, no holds barred. The girls either fall for him or they run like hell. Paul's always liked his girls to take the initiative. He sits, quietly watching as they start to circle. Like a predator being preyed upon, he waits in the grass, not moving a muscle, only his eyes . . ." David huffed a laugh.

"His eyes just kind of drew them in like moths to the flame, but he *never* fell for any of them." David paused, thoughtful for a minute.

Ashley slugged his arm. "You sound like you admire that piece of shit."

David regretted saying anything. He slid his arm around her waist and tried to kiss her, but she pulled away, slapping his arm again.

"Come on, Ash. Let's sleep together, and I'm not talking the Paul and Rhees kind of sleep." He waggled his eyebrows up and down suggestively.

"It's late, David. Their kind of sleeping together sounds better to me."

oOo

Rhees woke with a sore neck and had to reposition herself. She turned to face Paul. He didn't stir, worn out from all the physical activity. She watched him for a while, unable to get back to sleep.

She finally slid out from under his arm and held her breath, waiting, hoping her escape didn't wake him. She carefully crept out of the media room and went to the breakfast bar to look at the reservation confirmation for the zip line. She found the name of the company the guys had booked their excursion with and walked into the office. She sat down at the computer, took a deep breath, and started typing.

Chapter 17

Thursday morning, Rhees didn't need to prepare breakfast or lunch. The zip line company offered a package deal, which included meals, and the men had already paid for both. Rhees ate an apple and left the fruit out for the girls, knowing they only ate real food when their dates were around.

The zip line company provided a shuttle and the guys played Cutthroat while they waited for it to pick them up. Paul had a glass of juice while he waited for his turn at pool.

Bryce hollered a string of cuss words when he missed his shot.

"Get your ass out of my way, and I'll show you how a real man plays pool." Always so full of himself, Taylor pushed Bryce out of the way.

Ashley had been on a mission to annoy Paul as much as possible since the first day. She felt the need to prove him the bully whenever possible. She walked past him just as he lifted his glass to his mouth, and she bumped into him, pretending it was an accident. Orange juice spilled down his shirt.

"Dang it!" he yelled, brushing himself off, evaluating the damage, and didn't notice the stares being shot his way from his friends.

"Dang it?" Taylor asked. "What the fuck is this? Kindergarten?"

"God, Paul. You had the nerve to accuse me of being

henpecked," David said.

Paul finally realized what he'd said and it bothered him. He knew it shouldn't, but he felt conflicted between his old Taylor, Bryce, and David self and his new Rhees-inspired self-project. He wished he'd kept the two separate. He should never have come. He laughed it off, but he couldn't get it off of his mind and he grew irritable.

The van showed up and Rhees practically had to tackle him for a good-bye kiss, the only girl who bothered to give her man one. She'd made Paul feel even more self-conscious as his friends so obviously noticed and gave him taunting looks of disappointment. Rhees stood on the porch and waved as the men loaded the van and then she strode back into the house. She headed up the stairs to get ready.

Rhees had just made it to the landing at the top when she heard the door slam so forcefully, the whole house shook.

"Danarya!"

She dropped her head back and looked up at the ceiling. "Shoot." She turned slowly to see Paul standing in front of the door, his feet spread apart, his hands fisted, and his murderous glare, the one she hadn't seen for months, fixed on her.

"The driver wanted me to let you know that you're welcome to come with us *now*. The zip line company noticed the same address and thought you might be more comfortable coming with a familiar party than by yourself . . . *later*." He strained to sound pleasant and calm.

The other guys made it back into the house to offer Paul moral support while he laid down the law to his woman. Rhees had to think about her next move and decided to play it with the same calm, cool, and collected tone he'd used.

"Please thank the driver for his consideration, but I will be keeping my original appointment." It came out as steadily as she could manage.

"Like hell you will!" Paul yelled, dropping all attempts to sound reasonable. "You're cancelling. I told you I didn't want you going alone."

"I'm not cancelling," she tried to say, but it came out as a hoarse rasp.

"God damn it, Rhees. I'll cancel for you then." Paul didn't stop swearing as he stomped off toward the office, intending to go online and do just that.

"Paul, no. You have no right to do this." She leaned over the rail so she could still see him as he moved toward the room behind the stairs.

He stopped, looked up, and raised an eyebrow at her, challenging her to stop him.

She pinched her lips together in anger and ran into her bedroom. She grabbed her wallet, a jacket, and her backpack, and ran down the stairs and out the door as fast as she could. She jumped into the front seat of the van and slammed the door. She even locked it for good measure, although the sliding door behind her was still open.

"Thank you. I will be going now instead of later," she said to the driver.

Paul wasn't far behind her and he actually tried to open her door. He jumped in the back of the van. "Rhees! Stop acting like a baby. Get out of the van and we'll talk about this later."

She ignored him, staring rigidly out the front window. He growled and slugged his own backpack on the seat, already in the van. She shuddered at his display of anger but held her ground, refusing to look at him. The other guys made it back and each of them gave her a dirty look as they loaded the van.

"This is fucked up, man," Taylor said to Paul. "I never would have guessed *you'd* be the first one to fuck up Testosterfest."

Ashley suddenly showed up at the van before Taylor could get the sliding door closed.

"Why does she get to go? David! If she gets to go, why don't I get to go too?"

Rhees jerked around in her seat to glare at Ashley. "I asked if you wanted to come. You said you'd rather go shopping at Wal-Mart. I, personally, don't mind shopping at Wal-Mart, but you made it quite clear that you meant no."

"I did not. I've wanted to come all along," she whined.

"We don't want to be stuck here by ourselves." Liz and Jeannie showed up.

Everyone already in the van rolled their eyes and groaned, except the driver, who watched with fascination.

"Get in!" David yelled to Ashley, flashing Paul another dirty look.

Taylor punched Paul's arm while slinging a string of offensive words.

Paul would normally have fought back, but he was so incensed, he couldn't bring himself to do anything except stare angrily at Rhees. She looked straight ahead again, pretending not to notice.

oOo

They arrived at the facility and unloaded from the van. Rhees didn't make a move to get out until the others had moved inside the building, except Paul, who stood at the entrance, holding the door for her, glaring off into the distance with an impatient look on his face. His lips didn't move, he clenched them so tight, but the muscle in his cheek twitched furiously. She tentatively climbed out of the van and brushed by without looking at him. He didn't look at her either, but the scowl didn't appear to be leaving anytime soon.

They checked in, paid for the unanticipated guests and got in line at the buffet-style cafeteria to get breakfast. Rhees didn't get in line. Paul watched her vigilantly while she found a table and sat down before he finally got in line. He made a face and gestured at the food, telling her she should eat, without having to break his silence. She shook her head and looked away.

The minute Rhees realized Paul's attention had finally turned to the buffet instead of her, she bolted and headed toward the zip line orientation.

Paul didn't notice Rhees had taken off until he had his food and headed toward the table where the others had started on their breakfast.

"Where's Rhees?" he asked. The guys ignored him, confirming the tension hadn't eased.

"I think she's in the bathroom," Liz finally answered, trying to be helpful. She seemed the most uncomfortable with the strain in the air between Paul and his friends.

He sat and had only taken a few bites when he figured out Rhees hadn't just gone to the nearby restroom.

He swore. He'd been swearing under his breath since they'd left the beach house, but this time, he didn't care who heard him. He rose from his chair so fast, the legs squawked piercingly against the hard floor in protest. He took one quick glance around, determined which direction to go, and shot off after her.

oOo

It seemed to take forever for the attendants to strap Paul into his harness, find him gloves big enough to fit, and a helmet. He tried to rush them, repeating over and over that he needed to find his girlfriend.

"I'm sorry sir. We won't be able to let you ride if you don't listen to the orientation, and give us time to suit you up."

"Paul Weaver." He heard his name called with a thick accent.

"Soy Paul." He raised his hand to flag down the girl calling his name.

She told him, in Spanish, that a woman had asked her to get a message to him.

"Donde esta?" he snapped at the girl, and she told him Rhees was already on the gondola, headed up to the start of the zip line.

He took the note and unfolded the paper.

I'M GOING HOME. I'M DONE. RHEES

"What is it?" Bryce asked. The others had caught up to him; however, Bryce and Jeannie were the only other ones already in their harnesses. The other girls were driving Taylor and David crazy. Liz was having second thoughts, unable to make up her mind, while Ashley complained about how ugly the harness looked on everyone else and how it would wrinkle her outfit. Taylor cursed every few words and ranted.

"This is the reason we don't bring girls to do Testosterfest activities."

Paul stared at the note for a full minute, ignoring Bryce's question. He just took off at a dead run toward the loading dock.

He made it to find thirty other people in line ahead of him, waiting to board the gondola to the top of the jungle canopy. He cussed when he didn't see Rhees in the line, which meant she'd already boarded one of the cars, on her way up. He pushed his way ahead, ignoring the complaints from the other patrons until he reached the platform.

"Excuse me. I need to get on now. My party is ahead," he told the attendant loading the gondola, pointing to the cars already filled with people and climbing their way up the jungle. He strained to see which car Rhees was in so he would have an idea how far ahead of him she'd managed to get.

"Your party will wait for you at the top. Stand over there. I'll call you when I need a single rider."

Paul knew Rhees had no intention of waiting for him and he was ready to pull his hair out by the time they finally called him. He wasted no time jumping in so the gondola could be on its way.

"Sir! You must sit. No standing in the car."

Paul sat to appease the man, but stood again as soon as they were on their way and the attendant turned his attention back to the next load. He continued to look for

Rhees to no avail. The gondola climbed through the jungle, rising higher and higher from the ground below. In places, they floated two hundred feet above the ground while they skimmed along the treetops. His car finally reached the point where they broke above the trees and the view opened up, when he spotted Rhees, at last, nine cars ahead of him.

"Rhees!" He cupped his hands around his mouth and yelled.

He saw her look up to see who'd called. He waved. She folded her arms and made no attempt to return his greeting. He could feel the heat of her glare despite the distance the nine cars put between them.

"Wait for me when you get to the top!" he yelled again.

Rhees shook her head with enough exaggeration to make sure he saw it across the long gap. He was too far away for her to see his expression, but she knew a Paul-Storm was brewing, and she didn't want to be anywhere near it when it broke. She looked away to make her point.

She refused to look his direction again until she heard several people scream, sending her heartbeat on a race. The distraction with Paul had kept her mind off of the heights and the nervous anticipation of the impending zip line ride—fear of what she was about to do. But the screams brought it all back. She looked around to see what caused the commotion—sure someone had fallen to their death and sure she would be next.

She looked up and found the reason for the screams. She watched in horror as Paul flew from his gondola car to the one ahead of him. Again, there were screams, and she realized he'd jumped twice. He caught the rail, and as he pulled himself up and into the car, the gondola jerked and he fell back. He dangled from the car with only one hand. Rhees screamed and raced to the back of her car to get a better look, causing her car to sway and the people in it to yell at her.

The people in Paul's newly acquired car scrambled to

help, pulling him inside. She watched as he shook them off, apparently trying to convince him not to jump again.

"Stop, Paul!" Rhees shrieked. "You're crazy! Just stop it, right now!"

He jumped again and caught the rail with his hand. Swinging his leg up, he wedged his foot between the rungs on the rail and used it as leverage to pull the rest of his body into the car. Rhees watched in horror, hopeful, but concerned for the people in the car as they attempted to keep him from jumping again.

She knew him too well and worried about anyone who stood in his way. He managed to stand, wrestling with them as he forced his way over the rail again, but thankfully, they'd succeeded in pulling him back inside with each of his attempts, so far.

"Paul! Stop! Please!" Rhees begged hysterically. He didn't listen. She watched him struggling to free himself from the grip of the people trying to hold him in the car, determined to jump again. He was coming for her, and he would kill himself trying.

"Paul! I swear, if you jump again, I will too!"

That got his attention, but he didn't believe her. He pulled himself free and climbed over the rail again. Someone regained a hold of his leg so he couldn't leap. Rhees stood, taking advantage of his distraction. The people in her car didn't notice her climb onto the bench and she grabbed the rail that encircled the car. She looked down. The tops of the trees were so far down, and the ground, she couldn't see it through the high canopy. It made her dizzy, and it took a second to regain her equilibrium.

The car ahead was about eight feet away. She wasn't sure she could make it, and wished she could get a running start. She would have one chance to grab hold of the bar, and she reminded herself how her body's weight would work against her own hands. She would have to not only catch it, but hang on for dear life.

She turned back to look at Paul. He stood, poised to jump, so she pulled herself up and threw her leg over the rail. She was too short and lost her balance trying to hoist the rest of her body over. She wobbled and her hands slipped just as someone in the car grabbed her, giving her the brace she needed to right herself on the outside of the rail.

"No! Rhees! Please don't. I'll stop," he begged. "I'm stopping. See? I'm climbing back into the car." He did, and he raised his hands to show surrender. "Get down from there. Please?"

She looked down, and back up at the car ahead again.

"Please don't let her jump," Paul called to the other people in her car, and more of them grabbed her, trying to talk her out of it. She closed her eyes, took a deep breath, and let it out before climbing back inside.

"Are we on some kind of hidden camera show or something?" someone in the car asked. Rhees' body trembled violently. She covered her face with her hands and broke into sobs.

Her gondola finally reached the disembarking station. The attendant opened the door, and Rhees nearly bowled him over when she jumped out. She made a dash for the first zip line platform, running and passing people on the narrow trail. She could hear them grumbling about her cutting in line, but she didn't care. She wasn't ready to face Paul and couldn't afford to give him the chance to catch up.

She reached the first station and ran to the front of the line despite the complaints from the other patrons. The station attendants concentrated so hard on making sure the riders were hooked up properly and thankfully didn't notice. She watched as they hooked up the man they were working on and sent him on his way.

The attendants gestured for her to step up. Still shaky, she hesitated, wanting to turn back, but the idea of meeting Paul on the trail at the moment sounded worse than what she was about to do. She almost laughed. Jumping off from the safety of the station to careen along miles of metal cable—tiny little cables—at a hundred miles an hour sounded better than facing him.

She thought about it some more. She'd be suspended two hundred feet above the ground, in the middle of the rain forest, by nothing but a harness and a couple of metal clips—yep, still better than facing Paul.

She stepped up and numbly watched as the attendants connected her to the line. She screamed bloody murder, a reflex she couldn't help, when they pushed her off the platform and she dropped.

oOo

Paul ran his fingers through his hair and rubbed the back of his neck while he waited for his car to stop. A long and colorful stream of cuss words flowed from his mouth by the time the attendant finally opened the door and he jumped from the gondola. He sprinted along the trail, trying to catch Rhees, but he stopped cold when he recognized her scream, sending chills down his spine. He'd watched her run from the gondola, knowing she ran from him, and it wrenched his heart. The words of her note flashed through his mind, again. "I'm going home. I'm done."

He hunched forward and rested his hands on his knees, trying to catch his breath—he felt out of breath, helpless and weak. He didn't know what to do, how to fix it. Memories from his past blasted his head. The memory of the last time he'd tried to fix it, but failed—the events that made him need to run away. He wasn't supposed to let himself feel for anyone again. It'd all sneaked up on him. He mindlessly pulled his phone from his pocket and punched a few buttons.

"Claire," he whispered. His voice failed him. Silence hung between them for several seconds.

"Paul?" Claire finally responded, warily. "What's wrong?" She couldn't manage more than a whisper either. Paul would never call her from Testosterfest unless something was very wrong.

"It's Rhees." He broke. It came out a bleak sob.

"Oh my God," Claire wailed. "What happened? Not Rhees! Tell me she's all right?" Claire imagined all sorts of horrible accidents Rhees could have been involved in.

"She's leaving me. She's going home—back to Utah. She said she's done—I knew she'd get tired of me. She's leaving." He choked the words out and moaned miserably. Silence strangled the line again. "Claire! Help me. I don't know what to do."

"What did you do to her?" It came out accusing and harsh.

"I don't know!" he snapped. It took him a second to continue. "You know me . . . I told her she couldn't do the zip line . . . you know her, too. It didn't go over so hot."

"That's it?" Claire was confused. It didn't sound as critical as she'd originally thought. Not bad enough to send Rhees back to Utah.

"She said she's done. She's going home." He almost sobbed again. "I don't want her to leave."

Claire didn't speak again for a moment, shocked to be having this discussion with Paul, of all people. "None of this makes sense. She told me the island was her home now. She said she never wants to go back to Utah. Did she actually say Utah?"

Paul shoved his hand through his hair. He knew that. He dared to feel a little hope. "You think she meant the shop?" He almost laughed as relief set in.

"Paul!" Claire yelled over the phone, so loud he had to move the receiver from his ear. "You do not want to screw this up. This *thing* you two have going."

"I *know*." It came out exasperated.

"I mean it. Whatever you did this time—you'd better fix it."

His breath caught at how Claire used the same words that had run through his mind only seconds before, what he wanted, but didn't know how to do.

"Fix it," he mumbled.

"In the beginning, the night you two kicked off this farce, I was so angry, thought she was an idiot, that I'd misjudged her brain power, you know, for getting mixed up with you. But when you came to our apartment the next day, I saw something—I've been seeing it since. She's even smarter than I ever imagined. Rhees is . . . the first girl who's ever been smart enough to get under your skin. Do you understand what I'm saying?"

He didn't answer.

"Paul, she's the best thing that's ever happened to you. I hope you realize that. I think you do, or you wouldn't have called me. If you let her get away . . ." Claire paused for an uncomfortable amount of time. When she spoke again, she sounded like she actually cared, something he'd never heard directed at him. "I could tell you were trying to pick up the pieces of your life when you showed up on the island. You were still missing some, and you had a few pieces in the wrong places, but I've seen it getting better since Rhees has been around. I'm not sure I could handle watching you fall apart again." Another stretch of silence. "You don't want to let her get away."

"It might not be my choice. It may be too late." His voice came out low and hoarse. He cleared his throat.

Claire laughed. "Am I not talking to Paul? Mr. *I-Get-Everything-I-Want*?"

He shook his head. "I don't know, Claire. She really is too smart to put up with me."

"I'm going to tell you something. Don't you dare tell her that I told you. I would never betray her trust under normal circumstances, but this is an emer—Oh God, I can't believe I'm doing this. Rhees told me that when you use your magic, *hypnotic* eyes—for the record, those are *her* words—there are times she thinks that if you would hold out a little longer—if you didn't take pity on her and let her go from your spell, she wouldn't . . . be a virgin anymore." Claire waited for his response.

It took him a second, but he laughed. "You *do* understand

she probably means that literally." He laughed again at the thought of Rhees. "It wouldn't surprise me to discover she believes I really could take that from her with *just my eyes*."

"Yes, I understand that." They both laughed for at least a whole minute.

"She's like, from a different planet."

"I know, Paul, but the two of you—"

"To be honest," he interrupted, "the reason I look away—she's the one with magic eyes. When I try using my eye *powers*, she gazes right back. It scares the hell out of me. It's like she can see right into my soul, and—" He paused, surprised at his confession. "I'll lose her if she sees too much."

"She doesn't see things the way we do." Claire sounded motherly and serious again. "Rhees has a real problem with her eyesight. What you think she's going to see—the side of you that you think is ugly—Paul . . . she only sees butterflies and rainbows. She's helped you find some of those missing pieces and get a few of those wrong ones back into the right places. Now go get her. Apologize. Flash those magic eyes. Change her mind. You *will* change her mind! Do you hear me?" Claire sounded so confident in his abilities.

"She's not tired of you. She's just . . . making a point. Remember her stupid, stubborn objectives. What point is she trying to make? Think Paul. Think!"

Paul squeezed his eyes shut. "I have to go. I need to catch her before she reaches the bottom." He paused, thoughtfully. "I still don't know how it's going to work out, but I'm glad she has you. Thank you, Claire."

"Paul, I'd do anything for her, but she doesn't need me. She has you."

oOo

Paul caught his first glimpse of Rhees when he landed at the fifth station, one station ahead of him. He suddenly felt nervous. He'd been so preoccupied with catching up to her—he didn't have a chance to think about what he would do when he did.

It hadn't been easy to gain on her. The zip line was strung from one tiny platform, built high in the treetops, to another. You left one, landed on another, and waited your turn with your harness tethered to the lifeline designed to save you from falling to your death if you lost your balance or got knocked off by the other patrons crammed onto the platform. The footings were so narrow, there wasn't much room to maneuver around the other people in line, but Paul had managed so far, in spite of the attendants' harsh reprimands.

As usual, he found it easy to convince the women to let him shimmy around them, but the men were a different story. Fortunately, there were more women on the line that day than he'd noticed in previous years. He used the truth, his most brilliant smile, his eye power, and an occasional wink as he divulged his sob story over and over until he'd finally worked his way to within one station from Rhees.

"I simply forgot, for a moment, to treat my girl the way she deserves to be treated. I have to catch her—I don't know what I'll do—*I'll die* if she won't take me back."

They were eager to help a man in the name of romance, at least a man who looked like Paul, even in the face of danger, knowing he could knock them all off the platform. Maneuvering tightly, he had to unclip himself from the safety line and re-clip it on the other side of each person after sliding by. The closeness made it necessary to make intimate body contact and some of the older women took advantage of the situation by *helping* him—holding his body to theirs as he slipped past on the narrow planks. He grinned, playing the good sport. "Girlfriend," he would say. "Remember?"

There were a few men who weren't so eager to let him pass, but even most of the men were with women who nagged their husbands or boyfriends to let him by.

The seventh station landed on the hillside instead of

another tree platform. A narrow trail to the next station required a half-mile hike. He landed, helped the attendants unhook him so he could be free faster, and took off.

Rhees walked slowly just ahead, her head down, but he didn't call after her. The last thing he wanted was for her to run again. He quietly loped until he could maneuver around her, and stand to block her path.

"I'm sorry," he blurted, wrapping his hands around her arms to have a grip, in case she tried to get away.

She stopped just before running into his solid chest and tossed her head back as if asking why the heavens were against her.

"No." She sighed. "I'm the one who's sorry. You have to believe me. I never intended to ruin your vacation with your friends." She stopped talking and they both positioned their bodies on the path to let people on the trail pass. They winked at Paul and patted him on the back. When they were by, she continued. "I didn't know the zip company would ruin everything. I purposely picked a different time slot than you when I booked this last night. This is exactly what I was trying to avoid."

"Don't be too hard on him, Sweetie," an older woman said as she walked by. Rhees gave Paul the bug-eyed look, bewildered by the way every woman on the line seemed to be so invested in him. She shook her head, remembering how, back on the island, he used to get this kind of female attention everywhere he went. The other girls, most of them, eventually began to understand he truly wasn't interested anymore. They finally stopped acting so obnoxiously flirtatious, at least while she was in his company.

"If it weren't for the driver's big mouth, you wouldn't be angry with me. I could have come, checked this off my list, and made it back to the beach house before you ever knew. I would be happy, and you would be blissfully ignorant."

Paul stood stunned, his plan to smooth things over derailed by the new revelation. "That's your defense?" He returned the bug eye back to her. "Do you sneak around behind my back *often*?" His voice went up a few octaves, infuriated.

"No—and I don't need a fucking defense!" She folded her arms and they glared at each other. Her choice of words surprised him, and then she surprised him again when she didn't stop there. "You don't control me. I know you're protective—and most of the time, I appreciate that you care, but you don't *own* me—I don't *have* to *obey* you. *If . . .*"

She pinched her lips together and paused while another group of girls passed. Paul and Rhees overheard the girls commenting how Rhees wasn't pretty enough to be with a man who looked like Paul. Rhees looked away, staring at nothing in particular. She exhaled loudly.

Paul glanced down, irritated at how annoying all the interruptions were. His own lips narrowed, and when he looked up at her again, he didn't raise his head, emphasizing how unhappy he was with her at the moment.

Once the girls were by, she resumed, "If it looks like I'm obeying you, it's because I *want* to. Do you hear me? Not because I have to. It's *my choice*. I'm a big girl. You. Are. Not. My. Da . . . d." The last word caught in her throat. She glanced down and threw her hand over her mouth. Tears filled her eyes. She closed them quickly but it only squeezed the tears out and they rolled down her face.

"*Oh my God!*" she whispered. Her breathing became unsteady as she looked around, desperately searching for a place to run. Paul's anger visibly fell from his face, replaced instantly with alarm.

"*Aw shit!*" He didn't know why she'd switched so suddenly from fierce temper tantrum to, *the world is falling apart*, but he immediately picked her up. "Let's get off the trail."

She didn't stop sobbing and barely noticed how he carried her down the slope to a level spot twenty feet off the public path. He leaned against a tree with her still in his arms and tried to soothe her.

"What's wrong, Baby?" He braced his leg against the tree to help hold her while he brushed the hair away from her face, but his question made her wail even louder and wriggle for him to put her down. He tightened his grip and refused to release her. She used both hands to cover her face, and he realized she felt the need to escape.

"Listen to me. I'll put you down if you promise not to run away from me again." She didn't respond. "Rhees, Baby? Please, tell me what's wrong."

"Stop calling me *Baby*!" she blubbered. "Don't you see? That's the problem. Put me down."

He complied, but he hooked two of his fingers in the waistband of her shorts. As soon as her feet were on the ground, she turned and tried to put some distance between them, but he pulled her back. He considered himself lucky she didn't fight him. She wiped her face, but continued to snivel, unladylike for Rhees.

"No . . . *Rhees*." He sighed. He had to think, hoping he wouldn't choose the wrong name to call her again, not understanding why she suddenly hated him calling her Baby. He felt helpless, almost panicked because he had no idea what bothered her.

"I don't *see* anything. I'm trying—I'm really trying, but I don't know what's wrong. I thought you were upset with me for trying to protect you—this isn't about the zip line, right?"

She shook her head and then covered her face with her hands. She sniffed again.

"I'm so stupid—all this time." She dropped her hands to her side, dejectedly. "I seriously thought I was growing up. I've been *so* proud of myself. I thought, 'Look at me. I'm all grown up, overcoming fears—taking care of myself'. Ha!" She raised her hands in the air and made a *duh* face. Her tone changed to scorn herself. "But I'm right back where I started. No, wait! I never left. Different country, same big baby—I'm still just the stupid, helpless idiot I ever was. I have nothing to be proud about.

"I didn't grow up. I'm not taking care of myself, you are—I just found myself a *new daddy*!" Tears spilled from her eyes again and she looked at him with a haunting expression before she sank to the ground to weep.

"Don't say that." Paul covered his own eyes as he squatted down next to her. He outlined his eyebrows with his thumb and index finger and massaged his temples.

"Why not," she shrieked, snapping her head around to look at him. "It's true."

"No. Calm down, *please*? Let's just think this through, okay?" he begged as he sat next to her. She wept quietly while he took a minute to collect his thoughts. "I only call you Baby—it's not a description. It's a term of . . . *affection*."

"Pretend affection. Don't forget that," she sobbed. "I know I embarrass you."

"What?"

"The other guys, your friends, they all brought beautiful girls. I don't compare. You're embarrassed, ashamed to be stuck with me. You could have brought anyone else, someone beautiful like Liz, Jeannie, and Ashley, but you're stuck with me because you can't let me out of your sight for five minutes, because I'm a baby who can't take care of herself."

"No."

"Yes. Since we arrived here, you've been trying to distance yourself from me. When you're with the guys, you're happy and carefree, but you get in the same room with me, and suddenly you're sullen, standoffish—grouchy even. You cringe or recoil every time I try to touch you."

"Shit." Paul massaged the back of his own neck. "That's not it. I'm not embarrassed or ashamed, not by you."

"It's all right, I understand. This whole thing that we have—it's just pretend." She sounded so practical, spitting the words out in spite of how hard she was actually crying, talking over his attempt to explain what had been going on with him all week. "We decided to pretend to be together because you knew a long time ago that I'm not capable of taking care of myself. Taylor said you were protective. You felt the need to protect me, and I, apparently, will always need a babysitter." She tried to wipe the tears from her face with her arm.

"I'm never going to grow up. I'm always going to be a big, fat, hopeless baby, and you're nothing but my new daddy."

"Not only no," he finally yelled, "but *hell* no! That is *nawt* what I am." He looked out over the jungle, shaking his head at how she could say such a thing. He took a few deep breaths, trying to calm himself so he could bring the tension down to a normal level. "Rhees." He shook his head again.

"Somewhere along the line . . . I stopped pretending. I know we started out that way, but maybe—" He paused, struggling to say what he needed to say—he'd never said anything like it before. "Maybe I never was pretending. I don't know." He licked his lips and ran his mouth through a few of its nervous contortions. "I only know that *now*, I'm not pretending anything when it comes to you."

She stopped crying and held perfectly still, but didn't turn to look at him yet.

"I don't want to be your babysitter—and I sure as hell don't think of you as a daughter." He rolled his eyes. "Pfft! I have thoughts about you. I assure you, they are *nawt* the kind of thoughts a dad should have about his—that's just—really sick." She finally turned to see him, trying not to smile.

"And it really bothers me to think—shit, Rhees, I'm *nawt that old*." She laughed a quick breathy laugh and followed with a smile as she let the humor begin to heal her. It was all he needed to know they'd made it through the worst, but he didn't want to take any chances. He kept her smiling by launching into one of his quick-witted rants about being only six years older than she was, and how, even though he'd started young, the math didn't add up.

"You look *nothing* like me, and I'm pretty sure I never even met your mother. Yeah, I'm sure of it, at least, reasonably sure."

They both laughed quietly for a few seconds.

"Rhees?" He leaned over and rested his chin on her shoulder, serious again. "You're a lot stronger than you give yourself credit for."

"I don't know about that," she said softly, dropping her head.

"I do." He leaned even farther so that his face was right in front of hers. "There's got to be a way you can still by *my* baby, and not be *A* baby. Do you think we can work on that?"

She nodded, and then threw her arms around his neck. He welcomed the embrace with a relieved sigh.

"My feelings for you aren't pretend either," she said, and it surprised him how good it sounded to hear her say it.

oOo

They returned to the path and made their way to the next station.

"So, I need to be clear on something." Paul sounded cautious about bringing up the subject. "When you said you were going home, you meant the island, not Utah, right?"

"Of course. Why would I go back to Utah? There's nothing there for me anymore."

"Your note." He pulled it out of his pocket and unfolded it so she could see it.

I'M GOING HOME. I'M DONE. RHEES

"I worried you were done with me, and you were going back to Utah."

She stared at the note for a few seconds. "I knew that girl didn't understand what I said. There was a definite language barrier when I asked her if I could get a message to you. I wanted her to let me write it, but she didn't understand that either. It's supposed to say, 'I'm going home *when* I'm done'. And I meant the island. The island is my home now. How many times do I have to say that?"

"I've heard you. I just felt the need to make sure." He put his arm around her and kissed the top of her head.

oOo

They finished the last station, eighteen in all. They'd taken turns going first so they could get pictures of each other leaving and arriving. Paul wanted to make sure she had proof she'd crossed another goal off of her list. The attendants were surprised she'd never rode a zip line before, calling her a natural. She didn't brake until the last moment and gave a little bounce at the end to right herself, landing on her feet every time. Paul tried to copy her moves but never mastered it.

When they reached the bottom, they made their way to the cafeteria to wait for the others to finish. Paul had only eaten a couple bites of his breakfast and was starved. They were in line at the lunch buffet and didn't see their friends come in.

Taylor sneaked up behind them and enthusiastically threw his arms around Rhees, lifted her up, and planted a big kiss on her mouth, unleashing the mother of all panic attacks. She screamed and thrashed against him irrationally as if someone had grabbed her on a dark night and was attempting to drag her into the bushes.

Taken by surprise, Taylor froze, with her still in his arms, not knowing what to do.

"What the fuck, Taylor! Get your hands off her!" Paul yelled several other choice words as he pawed at Taylor, trying to get him to let go of her. Taylor finally regained enough of his senses to set her down and back away, while Paul stepped between them, his arms outstretched as if barricading everyone from her.

Taylor, as well as everyone in the cafeteria, stood and watched in shock as Rhees fell apart. She clutched at herself, and swatted the air, screaming and begging, "Don't touch me. Don't touch me."

"Rhees?" Paul whispered. He reached toward her but drew his hand back when she shied away. He turned on Taylor. "What the fuck were you thinking?"

"I wanted to thank her for making this the best zip line

trip we've ever made," Taylor said quietly. "What's wrong with her?"

"She doesn't like to be touched. Could you guys just get some lunch? Leave us alone for a minute. She needs some space."

"You touch her all the time—and since when do you call me *Taylor*?"

Paul gave him a dirty look, but ignored his questions, too worried about Rhees to argue.

"It's all right. No one's going to hurt you." Paul slowly moved a little closer. "It's me." He held his hands where Rhees could see them.

"I'm sorry. I—it—he just surprised me." She stepped back. Her voice sounded as shaky as her body. She turned away from him, not wanting him to see her that way.

"Rhees? I've never seen you react this severely before. I'm really worried. Have you ever seen anyone about this?" He stood behind her, not knowing what to do. He still didn't dare touch her.

She spun around and forced a smile, but her voice sounded a little too animated. "I'm fine. I told you, he just took me by surprise. It's just a reflex."

"A reflex reaction to being strangled by an axe murderer, maybe—not getting surprise hug bombed by a dopey friend."

She smiled and slid her arms around his waist, looking up at him. He watched her warily, but carefully returned her embrace. He felt her cringe, even though she tried so hard not to. Her body still trembled.

"Don't worry about me . . . *dad*."

He glared at her with a pretend stern expression for her comment, but he couldn't help his concern.

"Come on. You know I have issues with abrupt physical contact. Taylor just *really* surprised me. That's all."

oOo

They grabbed their food and sat down with the others

to eat.

"I'm sorry, Rhees. I didn't know," Taylor apologized.

"That I'd go bat-crap crazy on you?" Rhees laughed. "I'm the one who owes *you* an apology."

"Look, I just wanted to show my appreciation for making the zip line better. If it weren't for you, Liz wouldn't be here." No one could follow Taylor's logic so he continued. "Liz kept braking the whole way."

Liz interjected, "I didn't brake that much. They said I was too light."

"They *said* people who didn't weigh much didn't need to brake every three seconds. She stalled out mid-line and the attendant had to go get her, hand over hand. I was so embarrassed." Taylor rolled his eyes at Liz. "The second time it happened, I was next in line and already hooked up. They were just about to let me go when they realized she'd over-braked . . . again. They told me to hold up until they could get her, but I didn't wait. I jumped off the platform and went. When I reached her on the line, I did the hand over hand thing and got her to the next platform." He looked so proud of himself. "I've always wanted to do that.

"The attendants at the next station said they couldn't send her alone anymore." Taylor gave Liz a sideways glance. "They decided they'd have to get her down, tandem style, but they were short-handed and argued about how they were going to manage being down yet another man. I volunteered, and they actually agreed." His tone grew more and more excited, and he used more and more spicy words as he explained what happened. "Who would have thought that extra hundred and twenty pounds would make you go *so* much faster? We were *ska-ree-ming* down those lines, and I have Rheesy to thank for the most exciting zip line I've done since the first time."

"I do not weigh a hundred and twenty pounds." Liz sounded offended. "And I didn't brake every three seconds." She smiled sheepishly. "It was more like every five, at the most. And Taylor didn't brake, at all, *ever*! I was scared to death the whole time."

"You survived. I would never let anything happen to you." Taylor leaned over and gave her a big kiss. "I vote we bring the girls every year, from now on. Tandem's the way to go. WOO!" he howled like a banshee.

"No way, I'm never doing this again. This was the most miserable experience I've ever had in my life." Ashley crossed her arms and glared at David with a scowl on her face.

The three other men stared at him too, watching to see how he would handle his date. None of them ever brought the same girl to Testosterfest twice, but they'd started to suspect David and Ashley might be a real couple—to their dismay. They all hated her negativity.

"She's pretty loose with the way she categorizes her misery. Hasn't everything so far been the most miserable thing she's ever done . . . in her life?" Bryce whispered to Paul. Paul covered his mouth to hide his smirk.

"Okay, don't worry, Sweetheart. You'll never have to do this again. This was the worst experience *I've* ever had too. Next year, I'm bringing someone else," David said as he kissed Ashley's cheek, showing the guys he did have a spine. Ashley's mouth dropped open and she glared at him again. He ignored her as he and the guys all turned their attention to Paul and Rhees, wondering what Paul would have to say about bringing Rhees next year.

Paul grinned and glanced down, his shy, embarrassed look. He shrugged his shoulders before he stood. "I think we should go find our shuttle back to the beach house."

Chapter 18

That night, their last at the beach house, Rhees decided they'd roast hot dogs over a fire on the beach for dinner. Everyone except Ashley loved the idea, so David told her to stay inside, that he didn't need her to have fun. She joined them after all.

"Ash-bitch only wants more opportunity to give Davey the cold shoulder," Paul said in Rhees' ear with a chuckle.

After dinner, everyone sat on blankets around the fire, talking and drinking.

"I'm getting another beer. Do you want a refill? Bourbon, right?" Rhees asked as she stood, brushing any errant sand from her backside and reaching for Paul's glass.

"Yeah." He slipped her his glass. He looked up at her with a smile. He felt his right eye do its almost wink thing and it sounded like a good idea so he winked at her with his left. "I'll have my . . . I've lost track of which refill this will be." He chuckled.

He'd been drinking considerably less since he'd started sleeping in the same bed with Rhees, but he'd drunk more that week with his buddies than he had the past four and a half months combined.

When Rhees sat back down with their drinks, she surprised him by slipping between his legs with her back to him, cuddling up close and resting her head against his neck. He didn't expect the affection after the way she'd freaked out earlier.

"Are you all right?" he asked, wanting to make sure.

"Of course." She turned back to look up at him and smiled.

"Are you drunk?"

"I've had four beers since we came out to the beach. This is my fifth." She took a swig of the beer she just got. "Compared to the last time I got drunk, I hardly feel it at all."

"Compared to last time? You mean the dance contest? Rhees, that's not a good standard to be gauging by."

"I'm fine."

"Good." He enveloped her in his arms, careful not to spill his drink on her, wrapping them around her and giving her a squeeze. She didn't cringe or shy away, but he still wasn't convinced she hadn't been affected by Taylor's earlier stunt. He wished she'd stop pretending to be so resilient and finally confide in him why she kept it all locked up so tight, but then again, he'd never been gabby about his own past.

He nuzzled his nose through her hair, found her ear and nipped it with his teeth, his own intoxication making him bite harder than he'd intended.

"Ow." She turned to glare at him, not believing he would do it, but he grinned devilishly and tried to do it again. She turned far enough away to make him miss, but he snapped his teeth after her.

"Oh my gosh. What's wrong with you tonight?" She stared for a second. "I shouldn't have gotten you that refill after all, you're drunk enough."

"And you would be correct." His grin didn't change. He clicked his teeth together again a couple of times, making her giggle.

Taylor stood, pulling Liz up with him. "Excuse us, I'm ready to make out with my girl, but you're all a bunch of pervs, so we're heading over there." He pointed to a spot fifty feet away. "For a little *privacy*." He reached down, grabbed the blanket they'd been sitting on, shook the sand off and tossed Liz over his shoulder. He gave his friends an accentuated, suggestive wink and carried Liz, who didn't seem to mind, away.

"Taylor, you always have the best ideas." Bryce stood, and he and Jeannie followed their lead, scampering off to their own spot just beyond the light of the fire.

Paul and David watched each other across the fire while Paul sipped on his drink. The two men, who'd been friends most of their lives, stared each other down. Of the four, for the first time since they'd started the Testosterfest tradition their senior year of high school, they'd both brought girls they actually cared about. Based on what David had said to Ashley that day, and the cold shoulder she'd given him the rest of the afternoon, of the four, Paul assumed they were also the only two who weren't going to be getting *any* that night—but David didn't have to know that.

Paul roared out in laughter, and with a move designed to tell David that Ashley was the worst date ever; he fell onto his back, pulling Rhees down with him. She gasped at the unexpected movement and spilled some of her beer on his chest. He didn't care.

He rolled so he leaned over her, almost on top of her but, he hoped, not enough to scare her. He took the nearly full bottle from her hand and tossed it away from them.

"You ready?" he asked, answering her questioning expression, watching her through narrowed eyelids.

"Ready? For what?" Rhees studied him warily.

The tip of his tongue flicked out, wetting his entire top lip at once before he bit the one on the bottom. The salacious smile that creeped across his face made his right eye half-wink before he flashed his brows up and then down. He didn't break eye contact, fighting the urge to do so. He could only hope Claire was right, that Rhees couldn't really see his dark, sinful soul when she looked into his eyes the way she did at that moment.

He leaned in slowly, and softly brushed his lips over hers. She didn't close her eyes, neither did he.

"Mm," he grunted. She giggled, finally breaking the eye contact.

"Is it just you, or is it normal for people to grunt or

moan every time they kiss?"

"I don't grunt or moan every time."

"I'm sorry. I didn't mean to exaggerate." Her apology sounded sincere. "Let me try again. Is it just you, or is it normal for people to grunt or moan *almost* every time they kiss?" A coy grin formed on her face, and she started imitating his grunt in short staccato bursts. "Mm! Mm! Mm!"

He used his body to remind her how he had her pinned, and she pretended to try to get away, but he held her. When she stopped fighting him, he relaxed, but then she tried to wriggle away again. He wasn't about to let her go.

"I only make that sound when I kiss *you*." He kissed her all over her face and neck, purposely smacking his lips, grunting, and moaning as obnoxiously as he could while she squealed.

Somewhere along the line, his teasing kisses turned serious and without realizing the transition, *they* were making out—she kissed him back as passionately as he kissed her. He stopped, only briefly when she moaned, he had to see her, but it only incited him more.

"You're so beautiful," he whispered and moved a little farther on top of her, hooking his leg around hers to pull her closer. She still didn't protest.

Paul was getting close. It'd been a long time—a *very* long time. He wanted more. He ground himself against her and used his thigh to work his way between her legs. The warm pressure made him groan against her lips.

Rhees slipped back to reality. She didn't want to be in reality. For the first time in her life, she'd let go and she wanted to let go again, finish what they'd started. She tried. She focused on Paul's mouth. She loved his lips on her, his tongue, his velvety tongue felt like dessert or like she was dessert and he had a sweet tooth. She'd liked it, but nothing helped, she couldn't turn her head off and give in again. The grinding against her hips, while a moment ago felt so good, now felt like . . . a show.

She'd forgotten about being on the beach with everyone

else. She tried to look around between Paul's ongoing kisses. He skimmed his mouth from her lips to her jaw, neck and ears, back to her lips, kissing and licking while his warm hands caressed her and made her tingle. She gasped, remembering David and Ashley sitting next to the fire when Paul ambushed her, she looked back to where they'd been. Her body slacked with relief to see they'd slinked off, but she couldn't get her brain to shut off and just let herself enjoy Paul again.

Paul finally noticed Rhees wasn't actively participating anymore and rolled off of her, flopping onto his back in a barely disciplined resignation.

"God, woman! You're going to give me blue balls, *again*."

"Blue balls?"

His amorous advance had started as a means to poke fun at David, show him yet another reason Ashley wasn't someone he wanted to wind up with, but Paul never expected Rhees to let him take it so far. She should have objected, cringed, freaked out. He'd pushed her aggressively, farther and farther and she'd let him. He'd wanted her for so long—to finally feel her give in to him that way–he'd forgotten his promise.

"Never mind." He let out a long sigh, frustrated with his still raging body and with himself, thankful she did finally put on the brakes. He wouldn't have. He cursed at the reminder of what a selfish bastard he was. "You should go up to bed. I'm going to sleep on the beach tonight."

"But you haven't slept in the bed once."

"You're welcome!" He flashed her with wide, duh eyes. It came out a little more harshly than he wished, making the anger he felt with himself deepen. He shouldn't have let things go so far. Still surprised she'd let him, he hated himself for taking what she'd given. If she wasn't going to stop him, he should have been the one to do it, but he wasn't himself, or worse—he was more himself than he cared to be.

The week had been hard on him. He'd been torn, trying to find a balance between being the Paul his buddies knew and expected, and the Paul he'd become for Rhees—the two conflicted with each other. He scrubbed his hands over his face. He was tired, worried about her, drunk, and despite the guilt he felt about what had just happened, he still wanted her.

"I didn't say thank you." Her response sounded almost as harsh. She rolled, leaning over him. "Tell me, what are blue balls?"

He groaned out a curse. Usually her innocence made him smile, but she had no idea how hungry he was at the moment. He couldn't afford to keep looking into her beautiful, sweet-as-honey eyes—the ones making him wonder if she tasted as sweet as she looked. He shook his head to clear his thoughts. He needed to get rid of her.

"When a guy gets too aroused but doesn't get to go the distance, his balls get all—" He paused to think of the right word, "—congested. They hurt. There's your sex education lesson for the decade. Happy you asked?"

She frowned. "What about not coming to bed all week? I thought you didn't like to sleep alone. I thought you liked sleeping with me." He laughed because she didn't mean it the way it sounded.

"Why do you have to be so damned cute?" He reached up and pulled her face down to his for another quick kiss. "I *like* not ruining your life—any more than I already have. I've been too drunk to trust myself. If sleeping without you is the price I have to pay to nawt mess you up, then that's what I'm going to do. I willingly sacrifice my balls for you, to save your hymen . . . *so* you're welcome." If only he'd remembered that a few minutes before.

"You didn't mind messing me up a minute ago, and . . . I didn't mind letting you."

Damn if she couldn't read his mind—and what the— she didn't mind?

"Shit." He sighed and rubbed his temples. "Oh, Baby—" His voice caught, the memory of her berating herself earlier that day, having a breakdown, calling herself a big baby ran through his mind. She'd told him not to call her that. "Dani Gi . . . rrl." Another childish name. "I mean, *Rhees*? I don't even know what I'm supposed to call you anymore." He made several breathy, snorting noises, drunkenly laughing at his conundrum.

"Hey! *You!*" he barked. "There we go. Avoid all names completely. Go to bed!" he barked again. "Before I decide I'd rather find the cure for blue balls than not mess you up."

"Are you ordering me around again?" She seemed really mad. Of course she was angry again, she'd made it clear she didn't like to be bossed around, but it was for her own good. If only she'd understand that.

"How'd I end up with shit all over my face, again? Can I get a *little* credit?" Paul asked, confused. "I'm just trying to do the right thing here, *finally.*"

"I already apologized. You don't have to walk on eggshells with me. Baby is fine. I like the way you call me that, and I'm sorry about my meltdown today. I'm over it."

"Bullshit, *Danarya*. You aren't any more '*over it*' than you are over *other things*." He thought about how that came out. "*Aw shi-it.*"

"What does that mean?"

"You tell me. What do you need to *get over*?" He sat up on his elbows, waiting for her to admit the reason she hated being touched. Her reaction to Taylor's hug bomb was proof she wasn't over it, even if she did just let *him* maul her.

Rhees didn't give any indication she knew what he was talking about. She either had some serious memory repression—suppression thing going on, or she'd be the best fucking poker player in the world. That is, if she could just loosen up that beautiful but timid and uptight mind of hers and allow herself to learn how to play poker. He dropped back on the blanket.

She snuggled up next to him and mindlessly ran her fingers over his chest through his T-shirt. Her hand moved up to his neck and she softly traced his Adam's apple. He grabbed her hand in self-defense—he didn't need things getting any harder. He rolled to face her and brushed his lips, ever so softly, against hers and gazed into her eyes. He kissed her again with another moan before he stopped and rested his nose against hers.

"I'm sorry. I didn't mean to grouch. I don't care if you never get *over* it. Any of it. But I *neeed* you to go to bed."

"I'll sleep here on the beach with you."

"No." It came out a little too sharply and he saw how it hurt her feelings. She felt rejected. She clearly didn't understand what he was trying to do for her. He sat up. She did too.

"I'm pretty drunk, Rhees. When I get drunk—you just witnessed me getting carried away. You don't want to see me any more carried away than that."

"You don't know that."

"I do know."

"But I liked what we just did." Her eyes were hooded and lusty.

"You're *killing* me." He looked up at the night sky. "God, help me." He directed his gaze back to her. "I'm pretty sure what you think you want and what I want are two different things. I can't keep doing *just* what we were doing, it progresses, understand?"

"Yes. We've progressed. We're real now, right?" He knew she didn't understand. "We're not pretending anymore and real couples make out. You, more than anyone, know what a progression that was for me." Okay, she understood a little more than he originally thought.

"But there *is* a point of no return," he said. "I'm willing to bet your point of no return is different than mine. I love playing with fire, but in this case, I'm not the one who'll end up burned. Yeah, it's real now, and that makes it even harder."

"Makes it harder to want to kiss me?"

"No!" He made a snorting sound. "Shit."

He shook his head and sighed at how hard she made

things for him sometimes, without realizing it, and yet, her innocence was one of the things that kept drawing him to her. "It makes it harder to *stawp* kissing you. I don't know what I'd do if—" He growled, frustrated at the thought of the consequences.

"It would be really, really bad. I'd hate it if you—if the reason you freak out about being touched ended up having anything to do with me."

"But it doesn't. I don't freak out with *you* anymore."

"I *know*!" He raised his eyebrows, trying to convey how that fact was the root of his problem. "And I'd like to keep it that way."

She brought her knees up to her chest and rested her chin on the arms she folded over her knees.

"Rhees, what's wrong?"

"Nothing."

He rolled his eyes. "I either drank too much for this," he mumbled, "or not enough."

"What is angry sex?"

Paul swallowed wrong and coughed.

"Why are you asking about that?"

"Because you're angry, and it reminds me of what I've heard your groupies talking about. I've been curious for a while."

"I'm not angry."

"Yes you are, or maybe more like ornery."

"No, I'm not."

"Yes, you are."

"Am not."

"Are."

"Not."

"You big baby." She giggled.

He laughed. "I thought *you* were the big baby. I could have sworn that was you on that mountainside today, ripping my heart to shreds, making me about *die* inside because I didn't know what the hell to do or how to make it better."

"Yep." She leaned over and gave him a quick kiss.

"We're both big babies. I guess that means we deserve each other."

He chuckled but glanced down, knowing he'd never deserve her.

"So," she pushed. "What is angry sex?"

He sighed. "Angry sex is something you'll never have to know about." The last thing he needed right then was to sit next to the most beautiful, and yet, the most untouchable woman in the world, and talk about one of his favorite sports, at least it used to be. It'd been so long, he wasn't sure he remembered. He smirked.

"And I don't have groupies. Not anymore. You've disbanded the club."

"Oh, the club lives on, believe me. They're just waiting in the wings for you to—" She didn't finish the thought, but she knew what the other girls knew—he wouldn't be hers forever. "But what is it? How do you make love to someone if you're mad at them?"

"I've never made love in my life." He laughed, sardonically.

"But you—"

"Yeah, I've fucked every woman on the planet." He beat her to the punch. He thought it best to say it himself before he had to hear it from her lips, again. She'd said it before and even though she'd meant it as an exaggeration, the point of it rang true. It had stung coming from her. "But I've never *made love.*"

"Anger and sex don't go together."

"You'd be surprised."

"I don't get it."

"I've been angry at the world for a while. I've told you that." Against the better judgment he might have had if he hadn't had so much to drink, he started explaining, because the beautifully confused look on her face at that moment would have made him do just about anything.

"I like to mess girls up—actually, no. I've never *messed*

anyone up. The girls I've been with were already messed up before I got there. That's the problem with you and I. You're saving yourself for—" Paul sighed and looked down again with a frown on his face. "For someone who deserves you—Mr. Right—whoever the lucky *pud* turns out to be."

Paul hated the image of Rhees with any other man. In his book, any man she'd end up with would be a pud, better than he, but still a pud.

"Sometimes it can be fun to play. Yes, angry, rough play, instead of just straight up."

Rhees looked so innocent, so clueless, so shocked. He continued, like an idiot who should shut up, but he didn't.

"There's a reason I've always preferred wild girls, okay? If she's brazenly forward, she's more likely to want to play. If I'm drunk and in a bad mood—"

"You used to always be drunk and in a bad mood."

Paul didn't know if he should be happy, or scared to death at how well she knew him. Of course, his bar hopping had never been a secret, but no one ever really noticed— well, they noticed the way he looked—that was just the curse of his DNA, but they never did see him. Not the way Rhees saw him.

"So . . . what? It's like you pick a fight with some random girl, but instead of storming off, you take them home, yell at them, scare the crap out of them?" She seemed to be remembering something. Yes, she'd seem him scary and angry. "You fight, yell, and then, what? Bam! You just force—" She didn't finish her sentence.

"Yeah, you nailed it." He closed his eyes. His lips tightened into a thin line before he started running through his mouth exercises. "Actually, angry sex, for me, never had a whole lot to do with who I spent the night with. It was just for fun and more a product of my bad mood—my past . . ." His voice trailed off as he thought through the reasons he'd always been so angry. The last time he remembered *playing*, he'd actually been angry with Rhees—not a smart memory to have right then. "Damn it."

He looked over at Rhees and his desire smoldered. His hormones and his logic were in direct conflict. "*Pleeease*, go to bed!"

"I wanted us to progress, but this isn't the first time you've turned me down." She paused and sighed. "Never mind, I get it. You'd rather have blue balls."

She stood and wanted to storm off with nothing but her rejection, but he grabbed her arm and pulled her back down to him, cradling her on his lap. "When we're back home, things will return to normal, and we'll both feel better about this. Now, one more kiss."

He held her tighter and pressed his lips tenderly to hers, holding them there longer than usual for such a chaste kiss. He kissed her again, sweeping his tongue across her top lip.

"Oops. That was two more. I'm such a liar." He helped her to her feet.

"Yes, you are," she said, before stomping off toward the house.

oOo

The two men from the shuttle service carried the luggage from the porch to the van and loaded it into the back. Ashley followed them and climbed in, but Liz and Jeannie actually took the time to give an affectionate good-bye to their guys for the day. Rhees gave Paul a warm hug.

"I need you to promise me something," he said.

"Okay. What?"

He looked at her, surprised she would agree to a promise before she knew what he wanted, but her spirits were much higher than the night before.

"Promise me you'll spend the money I gave you."

"All of it?" She looked like he'd just asked her to cut off one of her arms.

He smiled. "Yes! And if you need more, use the credit card I gave you."

"Paul. You just gave me a thousand dollars."

Each girl had found an envelope with a thousand dollars cash, sitting on their breakfast plates that morning. The girls were to use the money to pamper themselves and buy an outfit for a night on the town. Paul had also slipped a credit card into Rhees' envelope, something none of the other guys would have ever dared to do.

"—On top of the ten thousand that you slipped into my account last time—at the wage you pay me—I've only had to spend a couple hundred dollars of that." She narrowed her eyes at him, baring her displeasure. "How can that not be enough?"

"You'd have to find an ATM to access that money. Good luck finding one. Please, Rhees, I'd normally never ask this, but please, just be like the other girls, and spend the cash."

"A thousand dollars," she muttered while rolling her eyes.

"I don't think any of these other girls are as reluctant to spend money as you are. A thousand dollars isn't going to last as long as you think it will."

"I can't waste money on things I don't need."

"See? That's exactly why I made you promise. You already agreed, so it's too late." He smiled again. "I want you to get some nice things for yourself. Promise me you'll buy anything—everything you like."

"What if I don't find anything I like? How can I spend that much money if I don't like anything enough to buy it?"

He sighed. "Promise me you'll *try* to like things, and then buy them—no matter how much they cost." She furrowed her eyebrows in protest but agreed with a nod. "Good." He kissed her forehead.

Liz and Jeannie finished with their own good-byes and headed toward the van where Ashley waited. Rhees started to pull away, but Paul didn't let go.

"Promise me something else." She wasn't as eager to agree again, and he grinned. "Buy a new dress, since the brown one got ruined."

"You really liked that dress, didn't you?" She smiled.

"I *loved* that freakin' dress!" He bared his teeth and snarled. His right eye did the involuntary wink thing.

"I do need something to wear tonight. I'll do my best."

"That's the spirit. Find something you can dance in—maybe something with fringe?" His eyebrows danced up and down.

"What if *you* don't like what I buy?"

"I'll like whatever you like."

"You sound like me, and you say it drives you crazy when I'm just being accommodating. What if you don't?"

"Then I'll rip it off of you, and you can go to the club nay-ked." He snarled again. She glared at him, blankly, and it made him chuckle. "If you like it, I'll *love* it."

"You should always be so easy to please."

"I'm always easy to please!" He really did wink.

She rolled her eyes, remembering the night before. "Except when you're drunk. You get ornery when you drink too much."

"Ornery, or brutally honest?" He hadn't been drunk enough to forget the night before. He picked her up, and she wrapped her arms and legs around him. "I already said I was sorry, and I came to bed the second I knew you'd be safe—as soon as the alcohol wore off."

"Thank you. I was in the middle of a terrible nightmare until you showed up. I don't think you understand how much having you there helps." Taylor's hug bomb really had upset her more than she let on. "I'm glad you've had fun this week, but I'm also happy we're going home tomorrow. Like you said, I can't wait to get back to normal. You're weird when you're around your friends."

"Weird?" He smirked.

"You drink more, swear more, get riled up faster . . . you're shaggier." She tugged a lock of his long hair.

"You said I was cute around my buddies."

She giggled. "I said that as we left the airport. You guys had been together a whole ten minutes. The cuteness wore off before we got to the house." She tried not to smile, but couldn't help it.

"Look at you. One day after upgrading this relationship and you're already trying to change me." He laughed, but she looked taken aback.

"I didn't mean to sound like I wanted to change you. I don't want you to change."

"Hey!" He squeezed her tighter. "You *have* changed me, profoundly, and I wouldn't have it any other way."

"I haven't done anything. You've done it all, unsolicited." He kissed her to shut her up.

"Shh . . . let's not waste time on that." He perked up. "Testosterfest is only once a year and it means a lot to me to know you'd come and put up with all our shenanigans. The hair and beard go tonight, deal? I know you like a clean cut man."

"How do you know that?"

"A little—a pretty big bird told me. Tracy mentioned it when you first showed up at the shop. I cut my hair and shaved before showing up at Ray's that night—I was out to get my trophy." The look in his eyes grew solemn. He squeezed her again.

"I do like you best with shorter hair, and a little less beard, but I think you'd be beautiful bald. I kind of like you like this, scruffy." She dragged a finger along his hairy jaw and winked at him. "Just don't take to one of those bizarre do's where you grow it all long and comb it over your face so you can hide behind it. I want to see your eyes. And, I know how hard you try to keep shaved, but your five o'clock shadow can't tell time. It shows up hours early."

Paul clicked his tongue with a tsk. "Yeah, sorry about that. Mom used to get flustrated with me. She expected her children to be more presentable than I could manage." He smirked. Little snippets about his family had started creeping into his conversations with her. He never liked to even think about his family before Rhees came along.

"One more promise," he said.

"Sorry. You've used up all your carte blanche promises for . . . at least a year."

"This one is the most important."

"I have to hear what it is before I'll agree this time." She narrowed her eyes at him.

He looked down and smiled the shy, little boy smile she loved. "Promise me you'll stay close to the drivers at all times."

She didn't understand the request and looked confused.

"Just promise me you won't let the other girls talk you into doing something stupid, like ditching the drivers. Stay within their range of vision no matter what the other girls do, all right?"

"Paul. Why?"

"Let's go. It's not like you guys aren't going to be *doing* each other tonight," Ashley called from the van. "You act like you're never going to see each other again. Let's go."

Paul gave Ashley a dirty look. "I hate that bitch."

Rhees put her hands on both sides of his face and drew him back. "Ignore her." She looked into his eyes. "Are the drivers bodyguards? Are we in danger?"

"We hired them to drive," he assured. "But I specifically asked for the biggest, most intimidating men the agency had." He chuckled and only partially lied. He'd hired a security agency to do the driving. Paul and his friends usually hired someone to look out for the girls on their shopping day. This trip, however, Paul had personally hired an extra man to watch out for Rhees, exclusively.

"You're worried." She didn't let up. "What's wrong, Paul?"

"Nothing. You know I always worry about you." He shook his head, she knew him too well. "Okay. A few years ago, one of the girls decided it would be funny to get flirty with a local. She thought she was being cute—making Taye jealous. The guy didn't know she was just fooling around. He called three of his buddies, and they followed the girls around the rest of the day. The girls panicked and did some stupid things." Paul grimaced.

"They should have just gone back to the hotel and security could have handled it, but instead, they worried about leading the men back to where they were staying.

It was a fiasco." Paul shook his head. "Ever since then, we've hired drivers to intimidate any sleazy *creepazoids*." He smiled, trying to assure her. "The drivers are just a *precaution*. Just don't—" He sighed. "Please, just don't try to ditch them. Okay?"

"I promise. Is that all?"

"Yep." He hugged her one last time and let her down. "Love you," he said, as she turned to head toward the van.

She stopped, turned her head back, and stared at him, in shock, not sure she'd heard him right.

"Be safe! I'll see you tonight." He slapped her butt to send her on her way. He didn't seem to realize what he'd said. She looked back several times on her way to the van, but he looked so casual, as if telling her he loved her was an everyday thing. She took one last glance at him before she climbed into the van. He blew her a kiss.

"What's wrong with him all of a sudden?"

oOo

After a hectic and stressful day, Rhees stared at herself in the mirror.

"Look at you," Jeannie said. The other girls seemed too excited about the way Rhees turned out.

"Does that mean you didn't believe it possible I could look this good?" Rhees turned to the other girls. "Who am I kidding? *I* didn't think I could look this good." They all laughed.

"Paul will love it," Liz told her. "You're a lucky girl. He's crazy about you."

After a day of what seemed like endless shopping, the spa—pedicure, manicure, and hair stylist, Rhees liked the way she looked. Her hair hung in loose curls, half up, half down. Her makeup—she usually only wore waterproof mascara—was perfect. Her dress was a bone-colored, slim-fit, spandex, retro Charleston-esque dress—complete with fringe and lacey detail. She'd fallen in love with it and hoped Paul would too.

"He's never seen me so put together."

Despite her nagging concerns she'd become too dependent on him, used him to replace her parents' role in her life, she missed him already. Even when they supposedly hated each other, they'd spent more time together each day than they'd spent together the past week. She couldn't wait to see him again.

Love you. His words stuck in her head. She told herself over and over again that he didn't realize what he'd said. He hadn't meant to say it. It was just a line like, good-bye, see you later, have fun . . . *love you*, but every time she thought about it, she couldn't keep her own feelings from popping to mind. *I love you too, Paul.*

oOo

The guys showed up at their respective hotel rooms after cleaning up at the beach house and stopping at a local barber on their way to the hotel. Paul knocked before he entered, cautiously. "Rhees? I'm here. You decent?"

She jumped up from the chair she'd been reading in and stood where he would see her the second he walked in. "Come in."

Paul froze when he saw her, his mouth gaped, stunned. "You look . . ." He appeared to be at a loss for words. It became awkward after the first minute of silent staring.

"I take that as approval?" Rhees asked. He swallowed, hard, and nodded.

"Approval granted," Paul finally said, practically drooling. "You look *exquisite*, as always, but . . . *oh my GAWD!*"

"You look quite exquisite yourself, Mister." Rhees couldn't stop staring at him either. She almost missed how he went on and on about the way she looked.

Paul wore his black jeans, and a fitted black dress shirt, tails un-tucked as usual, and unbuttoned to the small smattering of hair on his chest. His shark tooth necklace almost glowed against the dark color of his clothes. He

S. Jackson Rivera

wore his leather flip flops. They were brown . . . and they were flip flops, and wouldn't normally be considered the right shoes for the outfit, but it was . . . so very beautifully Paul.

Paul also wore a blazer, black with a subtle sheen. She'd never seen him wear one, and it took her breath away. Even with his un-tucked shirt and flip flops . . . the jacket, his new short hairstyle, and the cleanest shave she'd ever seen on him, she could have attacked him right then, but he'd left her too breathless to move.

Chapter 19

Rhees had never been to a club. Tanked was the closest she'd ever come, but this club was nothing like Tanked—*absolutely* nothing like it. The place intimidated her a little and she allowed Paul to lead her around like a puppy on a leash.

"You need a drink," he said, noticing her muddled nerves.

"Yes, please." The spa had provided champagne, but she no longer felt it. She welcomed alcohol's promise to relieve her anxiety. It had been a stressful day with the girls. Most women lived for days like she'd had, but Rhees wasn't used to the pressures of the female bonding rituals.

Her appearance also left her ill at ease. She liked the way she'd turned out. She liked the way Paul liked how she turned out, but she noticed more and more how much attention she drew from too many strangers, and it made her jittery. On the other hand, girls at the club weren't sneering at her quite as obviously as the girls on the island usually did. First they'd give Paul a thorough ogling, and then they'd look her over, judging as to whether she deserved to be on his arm or not—apparently, most seemed to accept that she did, for a change.

Paul, his friends, and their dates, spread out around the table and talked over the loud music. The first round of drinks went fast, and the guys all went to the bar to get more because the waitress took too long to come back around. She showed up right after the men left, so the girls ordered as well. Once the waitress realized what good tippers the guys were, she didn't make the mistake of neglecting them again. They were all feeling pretty good in no time, especially Rhees, who usually never had more than a glass of wine or a beer or two, if she drank at all.

Taylor, in one of his animated, drama queen rants, knocked over a drink, spilling it all over the table.

"I'll be right back." Paul leaned to speak in Rhees' ear before he stood. "I'll grab more napkins."

"Rhees," Ashley yelled from across the table. "Ask Paul to score us some coke while he's up. I heard he has connections." Ashley watched with a smug expression, waiting to see how Paul would react. He jerked around to face her, fury in his eyes, but the guys all jumped up, ready for some damage control—to make sure Ashley's face didn't get damaged. They'd never known him to hit a woman, but they also knew what a touchy subject Ashley had hit on.

"I don't want a Coke," Rhees yelled over the music, innocently. "Tonight, I'm having what all the big kids are drinking. I'm buzzed enough I don't mind the taste of alcohol anymore."

Paul's icy glare melted and evaporated immediately, and he couldn't help but smile at her. The guys all looked at him as if asking if she was for real.

"Where do I get me one of those?" David leaned in and asked.

"Well, I'm still trying to figure out how I got so lucky to have her land in my lap, but you have to wait for them to fall out of the sky."

"You're saying she's a fallen angel?"

"Hell no." Paul looked offended. "She was obviously pushed—all the other angels were jealous." Paul grinned triumphantly and reached for Rhees' hand.

"Let's dance, Princess Dani Girl." He towed Rhees out to the dance floor, the coke episode forgotten—well, maybe not completely, not until he pointed both hands at Ashley with a sneer, and one finger on each hand, the middle finger—after that, it was forgotten.

Later that night, after even more drinks, Rhees dragged Paul out onto the dance floor again. Rhees started out dancing with him the conventional way, but feeling the freedom too much alcohol grants those who indulge, she kicked off her shoes, flinging them from her feet, back to their table, and began to move as the music moved her.

The music inspired her into some kind of ballet, modern jazz dance routine and he lost her to another world. The way she moved captivated him, strangely fluid and graceful against the contradictory loud, thrumming drone of the club music. She twirled and melted to the floor, onto her stomach before arching her back, farther and farther, folding into a backbend before defying all natural human body movement by rolling onto the tops of her feet before popping to a standing position. Without missing a beat, she resumed her elegant, flowing dance.

"Ouch," someone watching from the side yelled. "That's gotta hurt."

A few people continued trying to dance on the fringes of the floor, but even they watched the girl whose body had become a work of art in motion. She exhibited no sign of clumsiness or inebriation through her movement but everyone knew she'd had too much to drink because a sober person just didn't dance like that at a club.

Paul stopped trying to keep up and moved to the side, blending in with the rest of the spectators and watched in awe. Taylor moved to stand at his side, and to admire the show.

She tired and finally slowed to a tranquil sway with the pounding rhythm. Taylor and Paul both took a step toward her before stopping to glare at each other. Paul smacked Taylor's chest with the back of his hand.

"I told you. No sharing." Paul glared at him.

"Just want one dance, bro," Taylor said. Paul's expression was lethal, inviting Taylor to rile him up even more.

Still lost in the world of music, a pair of hands slipped

around Rhees' waist from behind and swayed with her. She leaned back into the hard body behind her, and moaned. The hands ran up and down her torso, sensuously.

Paul and Taylor noticed at the same time. While they'd been posturing with each other, some creepazoid had moved in on Rhees and had his hands all over her. She swayed against him with her eyes closed and rolled her neck to the side, offering it to the mouth about to kiss it.

Paul and Taylor, together, flew across the dance floor. Paul peeled Rhees away from the man before the creep had a chance to register what happened, while Taylor's fist landed on the stranger's jaw, knocking him to the floor. Rhees' blurry mind scrambled to make sense of how Paul could be standing in front of her, his arms around her, protectively, when only a second before he had been caressing her from behind.

She stared, first at Paul, then to Taylor, then to the man on the floor, and back to Paul again, before the look on her face distorted to alarm, and panic, and then terror.

She struggled against Paul, screeching, but Paul had already anticipated her reaction. He picked her up in his arms and headed toward the entrance of the club.

Other men from the club noticed how Taylor had attacked their friend and began gathering to defend their buddy. Bryce hurried to usher the other girls toward the door, and David ran to get Taylor out of there. They all met on the street where Paul still held Rhees in his arms, cooing to her about how it was over and it would be all right, but she'd already calmed down.

She suddenly threw her arms around his neck and leaned against him. "I'm all right," she slurred and giggled. "I just found another thing alcohol is useful for. Wish I'd known that a looong . . . long time ago."

They flagged a taxi and jumped in, discussing how lucky they were to make it out alive.

"What now?" Bryce asked.

"How about another club?" David suggested.

"How about a nice, quiet bar? That was the worst

clubbing experience I've ever had in my life," Ashley said.

The guys all laughed at their private joke about her.

"I vote for quiet," Paul said. He frowned to realize he and the Ash-bitch were on the same page for once.

"I wanna dance!" Rhees yelled and gave Paul a kiss on his cheek.

oOo

"How are you feeling?" Paul hadn't given Rhees more than a half an inch of space since they left the club and found a decent bar.

"I need a drink."

Paul laughed as he watched her carefully. "You're pretty drunk. Can you handle another drink?"

"I have it in me for at least one more before I throw up." She laughed, thinking her comment funnier than he did.

Eventually, Rhees made her way to the jukebox, picked out a song and turned to Paul, who didn't take his eyes off of her. She called him over with her finger, seductively, and he didn't hesitate to heed her call.

"You ready for your public debut?" She giggled. *"There, There"* by Radiohead started to play.

"Baby, it doesn't matter how ready I am. You'll eclipse me no matter how I do."

Rhees, feeling the influence of what she called the cure for stage fright, let go and danced the way she did during the dance contest at the Emerald Starfish, only this time, Paul finally got to see it up close as her partner.

Her stilettos didn't slow her down and even made her look more like a real ballroom dancer. They matched her dress perfectly, but they'd been a peer pressure purchase. She knew she would never wear them again, as they were so wrong for the island, but the girls had insisted she couldn't go clubbing without them and her new dress.

The song ended, but Paul pulled her into his arms and they danced slowly, even though the next song was a fast one. He wanted an excuse to hold her.

"I never want to dance with anyone else," she said as she nestled her cheek into his shoulder. They danced to several more songs before making their way back to the table.

"You guys should audition for one of those dance shows on TV," Liz said and Jeannie agreed.

"Pfft!" Paul dismissed their compliments. He refused to accept any of the credit, insisting that Rhees just made him look good.

"Rhees didn't make his hips move like that," Liz said to Jeannie and they both laughed.

"I don't think they'd allow someone on the show who couldn't dance without getting smashed first." Rhees giggled and swayed in spite of Paul's arm around her.

Taylor kept ordering drinks, and Paul and Rhees both ended up drinking more than just one more. Later, every girl in the bar whooped and hollered when the Testosterfest guys took off their shirts, got up on the bar, and danced. They all had the moves, and their dates had to get territorial with some of the other girls in the joint.

They stood guard in front of the bar, rallying particularly with Liz since Taylor actually encouraged girls, other than his date, to slip dollar bills into his pants. He'd hold their hands *there* while Liz and her friends tore the other girls away. He'd pretend to feel sorry for the castoffs, crowing about what they'd miss out on.

"Try again next year," he yelled.

Paul didn't really want to do it. He'd tried to talk them out of it, but they insisted they couldn't pass up the opportunity to act as juvenile as possible their last night of Testosterfest. For someone usually the essence of alpha male, Paul had trouble saying no to his three friends.

Rhees laughed affectionately at his embarrassed discomfort when he started out, knowing his shy side didn't like being so openly on display, but he eventually got into it and had no trouble keeping up with the other three, confirming alcohol really was a miracle cure for stage fright.

"Wow. You really have the hots for him, don't you? How long have you two been together?" Jeannie asked, and Rhees blushed at getting caught staring at him. Jeannie smiled knowingly. "You look like you're in heat."

Rhees' gaze darted downward, ready to mask her reaction, to hide it from Jeannie because people tended to get weird when she freaked out about all things sexual . . . but to her astonishment, she didn't freak out. The only thing on her mind was the possibility Jeannie could be right. Rhees glanced back up and smiled guiltily.

"I don't blame you. Don't get me wrong, I really like Bryce, and all the guys are gorgeous, but I think Paul has something extra special about him."

Rhees glared.

"No. Don't get me wrong, I'm not after him. I'm trying to tell you, you're a lucky girl, that's all."

"Sorry, I just get so tired sometimes. He's constantly bombarded with unwanted advances from other women."

"I see why—but I would never try to steal him away from you—as if I could. And the fact other women's advances are unwanted only confirms what I'm saying. It's obvious he's really into you."

Rhees liked hearing it and turned to watch him again. She thought about what Jeannie had just said, about being in heat and believed she'd just experienced a miracle. She felt cured, cured by the miracle of alcohol and a perfect, beautiful man named Paul.

By two fifteen, everyone, except Taylor, agreed to call it a night. Taylor went along with the decision but relentlessly heckled his friends, calling them a bunch of pussies all the way back to the hotel.

Chapter 20

aul and Rhees leaned on each other as they walked—staggered—to their suite. They thought they were stifling their laughter as they traveled the long hallway, but they were much louder than they should have been at that hour. Paul opened their door, ushered Rhees in, took off his jacket, and went to the fridge. He pulled out a mini bottle of wine, opened it, and poured two glasses.

"Are you trrying to get me da-rrunk?" she asked with wide, accusing eyes. It made her laugh because she knew how intoxicated she already felt, almost.

"I think you're as drunk as I am!" He laughed, but stopped to brace himself against the counter. "Whoa. I want to make a toast." He handed her a glass and they clinked them together. "To the most beautiful, talented, perfect, non-pretend girlfriend a man could ask for."

"I can't drink to that." She giggled, shaking her head.

"Yes you can."

She shook her head and took a sip. He laughed hysterically, again using the counter to keep his balance. "You said you can't drink to that . . . then you took a drink." He downed his whole glass in one attempt. She smiled sheepishly and tried to follow his example but she couldn't do it.

"Here, let me help you." He took a large gulp from her glass and handed it back for her to finish off the last sip. She hesitated.

"Do *nawt* tell me you're afraid of my germs again." He held her face with both hands and rammed his tongue into her mouth, exploring every corner. It felt so good he didn't stop, and she didn't flinch. "If you can handle *that*, you can drink from the same glass." He laughed again for a minute but turned somber, almost sad, while staring at her. "You are *so* beautiful."

"Thank you. I couldn't have turned out without you." She thought he meant her outfit and professionally done make up. She lifted her hands in the air and twirled for him, but lost her balance. He caught her and didn't let go. "I spent all the money you gave me, and didn't have enough for the shoes. I put another hundred and seventeen dollars on your credit card." She looked as if she expected a scolding.

"Ashley called me brave for not being afraid of you. She said she'd be scared to spend so much if *she* were your girlfriend . . . but you *said* I should buy *anything*, and to use the credit card if I needed, and you were right about those girls. They kept pressuring me to buy more, and more, and more—"

He kissed her to make her stop talking and then he growled.

"Ash-bitch *should* be scared to be my girlfriend. It'd never happen." He stuck his tongue out, showing his disgust at even the thought. "She's just m-mocking you, Baby. You're worth ev-erry penny."

His eyelids grew heavy as he ogled her. He slipped his hands around her waist and moved in closer. He used his finger to pull her chin up and kissed her exposed neck. He worked his lips up to her chin and when he reached her mouth, he whispered, "I want you—I want you so bad."

"You have me."

"Mm . . ." His eyes burned into her. He tightened his hold and started driving her toward the bedroom while kissing her all over her neck and face, until they stumbled and fell. He turned so he landed first, breaking her fall.

"Are you hurt?"

"No, just clumsy." She burst out laughing.

"You have the most incredible laugh. I love that sound . . . when you laugh. It makes me happy."

"I'm happy to make you happy." She giggled again. She didn't even know why. "You said you love me."

"I said I love your laugh."

"You said you love me, this morning, when I climbed into the van."

"I did?" The look of surprise on his face disappointed her.

"I knew you didn't mean it," she whispered, suddenly heartbroken and it showed.

"I'm surprised I said it out loud. If I did, I didn't mean to say it out loud. I'm not sure I know what love feels like—*that* kind of love." His lips formed into a straight line as he considered the possibility that he'd really let slip the conflicting thoughts and feelings he'd been mulling over.

"I love *you*—" she whispered.

A loud burp erupted from Paul's throat.

"Aw dang! And you keep calling me *romantic*. I'll have to add that move to my reper-ta-wah!" They both broke into riotous laughter, the direction their conversation had taken, forgotten.

"Ooo, the room is spinning!" Rhees squeezed her eyes shut. "Make it *staawp*, pleease."

"Don't close your eyes. You gotta own it. Open your eyes and pretend you're a fighter pilot, flying a freakin' fast jet. It's fast, but you're flying it. You're in control and you can pull out of the spin. Pull it out and ride it out."

"Aaaah! I can't."

"Do it, Baby. You can do it. You're tough as nails."

She took a deep breath and stared at the ceiling. "I'm flying a jet, I'm flying a jet, and we're not spinning anymore . . . but we are. Aw shit."

"Pull your jet out of the spin, Dani Girrl!"

"I'm flying a jet, I'm at the controls, I'm flying a jet . . ." She gasped and then she giggled. "It works."

She looked at him and he looked back.

"Paul," she finally said. "We're on the floor."

"So?" He didn't want to stop taking her in.

"I think hotel room floors are probably dirty, all the people who've walked around in here, in the same shoes they wear when they walk into public bathrooms."

"Oh. Right. What was I thinking?" The next thing she knew, he'd jerked to his knees with her in his arms and set her on the bed. He kneeled in front of her, between her legs, with his hands on her hips, and resumed gazing again as though he'd never stopped.

He leaned in toward her and she backed away. He smirked his crooked grin with a wicked glint in his eyes and climbed onto the bed, crawling after her as she continued to scoot back, toward the middle of the bed. She stopped and he landed on top of her, staring longingly into her eyes.

"I want you."

"You have me."

"Do you have any idea how happy I've been the last few months, being celibate with you?" He huffed an ironic laugh, but didn't take his eyes off her. She shook her head, not understanding. "For the first time, since I was little, I feel like I'm doing the right thing. But right now, I don't want to do the right thing. I want you," he hissed.

His eyes narrowed and he shook his head. He collapsed to the side of her in frustration.

"You are so beautiful!" he shouted, as if trying to tell the whole world. He turned to face her. "And I'm sooo fucking horny right now. I want you. Do you understand? I *wawnt* you!"

"Oh." She didn't know what to say. Her naivety made him snicker.

"You said there're things we can do, and then you *lied* and said there aren't." She scowled at him for not being honest with her. "I *waawnt* to." She mimicked the drawl he sometimes put on his words and giggled again, watching him.

"Aw Dani Girl," he moaned, torn between his desire and what he knew was right. "It's too dangerous, Baby. I promised. What if I can't stop? I might not be able to stop. Do you understand?"

"I understand you get blue balls, because even the very thought of sex makes me want to rip my eyeballs out until you—"

"Yeah, that. You have no idea how much I suffer for you, beautiful girl, but I don't mind—not for you."

"I don't want you to suffer, and I know I couldn't do this with anyone but you, but Paul, tell me what to do. Please let me try." She looked so serious for a second, but the alcohol content in her blood shorted out the connection between her brain and giggle center. She had no control.

He leaned over her and she stopped laughing, immediately. He let his lips touch hers, barely, so softly, closing his eyes, savoring the feel. He opened his eyes again and took her bottom lip between his teeth, gently tugged before sucking on it, and then let it slip from his lips. He met her mouth again and outlined her lips with his tongue. Hers playfully invited his inside and he didn't refuse. They both moaned at the same time.

His hands wandered, but he used his eyes to keep her mind off of his exploration, ever mindful she could need him to stop any second. He gazed and kissed her softly while one hand held her to him, the other moved up and down her body, caressing every curve over her soft dress.

She watched his eyes and trusted him as he explored for the very first time. He didn't attempt to remove her dress, he didn't dare, but he let his hands roam across every square inch of her until he reached her lower stomach and moaned softly.

"I like bellies," he whispered. "Especially yours, I've wanted to spend some serious time here, just kissing it. I've wanted to lay my head on it, but I haven't dared get that personal." He paused, raising his brow, asking permission to continue.

She returned his question by flicking her tongue across his teeth. It incensed him and he began an oral assault on her mouth, his eyes open, watching her. He pressed the palm of his hand into her stomach again, lower, and he moaned again.

She gasped, a hint of panic appeared in her eyes. She had to look down to see what he was doing.

"Look at me," he breathed before he lost her. He waited for her to meet his gaze again. His eyes comforted her and she relaxed, but couldn't quite get a lungful of air. "Breathe, Baby."

He watched her with reservation as his fingers guardedly worked their way lower. He slowly hitched her dress up until he found access to her inner thighs and stroked the tender skin between her legs.

She squeezed her eyes shut and started breathing, squirming uncomfortably.

"Shhh. Look at me," he whispered. She opened them again and he smiled to reassure her. "Better?"

She nodded.

"Want to stop?"

She shook her head, awkwardly, and tried to smile. He met her uncertainty with another encouraging smile as he lightly stroked her face and peppered the skin around her lips with soft kisses.

"Don't close your beautiful eyes. I want to see them."

She nodded again.

He kissed her and pulled her dress up more, little by little . . . until nothing stood between his fingers and *her* except the new soft, silky panties she'd been pressured into buying that day. He glanced down to take a quick look.

"Mm," he grunted appreciatively and she smiled, almost forgetting how nervous she'd become. She took the faintest intake of breath when his fingers slipped into her panties and touched her, bare. She almost closed her eyes again, but he leaned more weight against her, making her need to see.

"You're beautiful," he mouthed.

He continued to watch her guardedly, with care, while his middle finger found its way into her folds. Her breathing quickened and became unsteady. She watched his face, faithfully trusting him. He swirled his finger ever so lightly, carefully gauging her cooperative response. She breathed out, soft and slow as her eyes closed again, her body giving in, and then he pressed the button.

She jerked, arching her back with a wispy, "Ah!"

He grinned, a little too pleased with himself that after so much time, he hadn't lost his touch. He tenderly kneaded and manipulated over and over until she tensed, a good tense, throwing her arms around his neck, letting out another forced, but quiet, breath of air.

He caressed her precisely where he solicited the greatest reaction, focused and intent on getting his way. Her hips alternated between trying to get away and pushing back against his fingers. With each spasm, her neck lengthened away from him and he had to pull her back so he could watch. He didn't want to miss a single second.

The mischievous look in his eyes was gone, no longer playful like before. His teeth clenched as he compelled her toward climax. He pressed himself into her side, fighting to stay focused only on her, but it wasn't easy. He wanted to witness her first orgasm, honored, grateful . . . privileged, to be the one to give it to her. He cherished the way she responded to him, the way she made him feel. He wanted to own her—body and soul.

She disintegrated and he absorbed her whimpering with his mouth as she melted in his arms. He smothered her face with soft kisses, reflecting on how he had never cared so much about his lover before. He had never wanted, been so concerned about anything, anyone before. It had always been about his own pleasure. He kissed her again, with affection that left him emotional.

Her breath came out sharp and irregular. "I never dreamed . . ." she tried to say.

"Shh . . . me too." He kissed her again, compassionately. He didn't need an orgasm. Showing her, giving to her and thinking only of her . . . it was . . . the most *beautiful* . . .

She took his face between her hands. "Ba-loo balls!"

He rolled, pulling her along with him so she landed on

top of him. He pulled her legs so that she knelt, her knees at his sides. She sat up to get a better look at him, but he pulled her back down for a kiss. The movement drew her along the fly on his jeans and he moaned—so much for it being all about her.

With his hands firmly on her hips, he rocked her back and forth against his hardness. "Okay, just a sec," he breathed. He reached down and hurriedly unbuttoned his pants as if he were participating in a race. "The buttons are digging into me."

She raised herself up and back as she helped him pull his pants down far enough to get them out of the way. His boxer briefs went with them, unintentionally, but still so, and he didn't have the restraint to pull them back into place.

She stared.

"I'm sorry." He smirked and waited for her to say something about his size. Girls always did. He wasn't thinking. Rhees didn't have anything to compare it to.

She giggled. "It looks different than last time . . . bigger."

"Listen to you, talking so dirty," he said humorously. She'd said the word, big. It would do.

"No I'm not." She sounded insulted, very insulted.

"Okay, you're not." He understood immediately she didn't like being called dirty. "You and your battle against germs, but your, *not* dirty talk, is turning me on so bad. I'm going to explode."

She giggled and he pulled her back down to his lips, attacking her mouth with his own, more fervently than before. With his arms around her, he guided her to slide back and forth against him, only the thin fabric of her panties between them. He reached down with his hand and pulled her panties to the side. She quietly gasped at the new level of intimacy, but he rushed to assure her. "I swear, I won't—I won't change you, I promise."

She nodded with complete faith in him. He hissed and mumbled a few praises to Rhees and to God, kissing and panting against her mouth.

"Sit up. I want to see you. I *need* to see you," he whispered, breathlessly. She sat up and braced her hands on his chest. "You are so beautiful."

"Stop saying that." She closed her eyes and continued to move back and forth. She moaned. "It feels . . . so warm and tickly."

"I'm not going to last. It's been too long. I'm going to come." And he did.

She dug at him even harder, biting her lower lip and scrunching her nose as she ground herself against him, taking unexpected pleasure in watching him lose himself. It made her feel so powerful to think she'd done that to him.

His head fell back, his chin jutted forward, and she stared at his long neck and Adam's apple. His glorious mouth gaped open, his lips forming a perfect O. He moaned, silently, his breathing forceful and erratic. Before he finished, he looked back at her again with awe.

He reached to pull her down to him, wanting to finish with her in his arms. He shivered as he crushed her to his chest.

"I love you," he said between breaths. He held her tight, too tight. She would have felt smothered by how tight he held her . . . except the alcohol had taken its toll. She'd fallen asleep. The second she felt safe in his arms and heard a few of his heartbeats, she'd given in. He held her a few seconds longer as he pulsed.

"I do love you, Danarya. I never want to let you go." His breath and heartbeat gradually slowed to normal and he drifted off to sleep, thinking about how beautiful the world had finally become.

oOo

Paul stirred just before dawn. He didn't think much about why Rhees still lay on top of him. He put his arms loosely around her and closed his eyes again, ready to get back to sleep. Two seconds later, his eyes popped open in horror.

"Shit." He felt her against his bareness. "Shit, shit, shit!"

He felt her dress under his hand and it gave him some relief—she wasn't naked. He slid his hand cautiously down her back.

"Shit." Her dress lay bunched up around her waist. "Oh, God! No, no . . . no, no, no." It all came out so fast. Her butt was covered, but with nothing more than a pair of thin, silky panties.

"Fuck." He exhaled hopelessly. "*Please . . .*"

He gently rolled, not wanting to wake her, but he had to see. He turned her over on her back and carefully peeled himself away from her hold, amazed he didn't wake her. She normally didn't sleep so soundly. He sat up, made a face, dreading what he knew he'd possibly discover, and finally checked. Remnants of him were all over the bed, him, and . . . his face fell into his hands and he begged one more time, "Please, no."

He needed to compose himself so he could continue his inspection. He looked Rhees over again, closer. Her panties were still in place, one consoling detail, a glimmer of hope, but he could see himself all over them as well. He knew how fast and easily he made it inside . . . panties were no obstacle for him. He felt sick.

Another test—he almost didn't dare.

Yes! Thank you, God! There were no bloodstains on the sheets, and to his relief, on her. It made him feel guilty, inspecting her so thoroughly, but he had to know. So far, the lack of blood gave him the courage to check himself. Paul moved his penis around, every direction, and finally looked up at the ceiling with a grateful groan.

He rubbed his eyes with both hands and massaged the muscles of his face. He let out another quiet moan. He stood and pulled his boxer briefs up, and then his jeans, and walked into the bathroom.

He leaned both hands on the counter and stared at himself in the mirror. He saw the hickey on his Adam's apple and groaned. *Look what you've done. You should have let her leave—she was going home. She could have been safe . . . from you, but you couldn't let her go. Look what you've done.*

oOo

A couple hours later, seven o'clock in the morning, Paul woke again. Rhees leaned over the toilet, throwing up. All the things he might have done—*did* do to her, flashed through his mind and revolted him again.

"Blech!" He had to shut out the sounds she made as she convulsed and the contents of her guts splashed into the water.

"You all right?" His voice came out lower than usual.

It appeared she'd emptied her stomach and had nothing left to heave. She finally noticed him sprawled out in the bathtub, fully dressed, with a pillow and blanket.

"Why are you sleeping in the tub?"

"I love sleeping in bathtubs. I can't help myself." His head cocked to one side and he studied the faucet in the tub, not really, but it looked that way.

She groaned. "How much did I drink?"

"Too much!" he snapped, angrier than he meant to be, but then his tone softened as he absorbed the blame. "Me too."

She sat on the floor and leaned against the wall, staring at him, looking concerned.

"Rhees, do you remember last night?"

She thought for a moment. "I'm drawing a blank on pretty much everything after we danced."

"Which time?"

She laughed but then groaned. "Oh, my head hurts too much to laugh." She closed her eyes and thought about it some more. "Okay, I remember showing the gang our dance." She smiled. "Mm, it was nice." She quieted for a second and then laughed again, quieter to keep the throbbing to a minimum.

"I remember you and the guys dancing on the bar. You were so . . . mmm, yummy." She opened one eye and glanced at him to see how he'd react to her description, testing their new, not-pretend boundaries—they'd yet to define what the boundaries were. He closed his eyes as if he didn't like hearing it, and she wished she hadn't said it. "Then Taylor ordered everyone some iced tea. It's all a blur after that."

"It wasn't iced tea, Rhees. A Long Island Iced Tea is a cocktail made with just about every kind of alcohol known to mankind. You had no business drinking one of those—I should have known better—but *I* was too drunk to pay attention." He rubbed his face, another sign of his bad mood.

"That was after the Zombies Taye ordered earlier, and the champagne—shit, Rhees, after last night, your liver's as pickled as mine." He frowned, pursing his lips a few times.

"It must have tasted good if I drank it."

"We both drank everything regardless of the taste. By the time we got to that point, taste didn't matter anymore." He leaned his head back and he stared at the ceiling. "Aw Rhees . . . I messed up. I *really* messed up."

She crawled over to the tub and put her hand on his shoulder. "What's wrong? What happened?"

His head fell forward again and he covered his eyes with his hands, trying to rub the whole incident away.

"Oh, Dani Girl . . . I'm sorry, I'm so sorry." He shook his head slowly, over and over.

"Paul. Tell me what's wrong. It's killing me to see you like this. I want to kiss you and make it all better, but I have puke-breath."

He huffed a humorless laugh. "I don't want you to kiss me."

"I understand. In spite of how much I love your mouth on mine, I wouldn't kiss you if *you* had puke-breath either."

"Did you seriously just say you loved my mouth on yours?" He looked up at her, incredulous. He hissed and then hung his head again, defeated.

She watched him make angry faces and she listened to his labored breathing as he struggled with whatever he struggled with.

"Are you going to keep doing that or do you think you'll get around to telling me what's wrong?" she asked. He reluctantly rolled his head so his eyes met hers.

"I'm no good for you. I wish you'd never walked into my life."

She pulled her hand from him as though she'd been bitten. She'd seen this mood before, but after the zip line, she thought she wasn't supposed to see it again. Instead, he'd become a roller coaster, up and down, back and forth. She backed away and pulled her knees to her chest, curling into a ball. She wouldn't look at him.

"Look at how much I've already changed you. I don't want you to change, but I'm slowly dragging you down to my level. That's the last thing I want. You're perfect. You're so lovely and innocent, and I don't want to change you, but it's inevitable if you're going to be around me."

"You're breaking up with me," she rasped. It was her turn to shake her head slowly, over and over.

Hearing her put it that way shocked him. He struggled to breathe; she did too.

"No," he finally choked out. He closed his eyes again. *I should, if only I could.* He knew it would be best for her. Being with him put her in constant danger, but still, he'd never bring himself to do the right thing. "But we need new rules."

The despondency evaporated, and she willingly looked at him again.

"New rules? Okay." She seemed to perk up.

"From now on, we can't . . . we can never, both, get drunk, at the same time again. Understand?"

She nodded enthusiastically. Apparently she thought

that an easy enough rule, but then she looked disappointed when he continued. She thought he'd finished, but he was just getting started.

"No more kissing in bed, in the bedroom, period." He said each item as it came to him, not really thinking it through, but he desperately brainstormed, trying to convince himself it could work.

"Or when we lay down . . . anywhere. We have to stand up if we're going to kiss." He reconsidered. "Hell, even standing isn't safe with me." He stared at her, warily, and for too long before he continued. "No kissing when we're alone, got that? Only PDA from now on. No more private intimacy." He stared at the ceiling, thinking. "We start using two sheets. We'll each have our own, like the bundling bag in that movie. No more skin touching skin in bed."

"But, snuggling . . . the nightmares. You know it's . . ."

He sighed. "All right, snuggling is all right—but *only* when you have nightmares. That's where double sheets come in, to keep us from having too much skin contact. You should get some pajamas, real ones—flannel."

She laughed, interrupting his rant. "I am *nawt* wearing flannel in the Caribbean."

He shot her an icy glare, thinking her disagreeable when he was only trying to protect her.

"I'm from Utah. I've survived twenty-four winters in the Rocky Mountains. You, on the other hand, have lived your whole life in the heat and humidity. *You* can wear flannel jammies, not me." She glared at him, holding her ground.

"Okay, no flannel, but . . ." A trace of desperation appeared in his tone. He seemed a little stumped.

"Geeminy, Paul. You're all over the place this morning. Are you planning to tell me what's wrong?"

"You think *I'm* all over the place," he shouted. "Last night, I was all over *you*. I still am!"

She didn't like how brusque he sounded, though she

had no idea what he meant.

He rubbed his face again and she could see his distress. "Look at your panties."

It took her a second but she turned her back to him and checked. She could see it, feel it, but still didn't know what it meant.

"That's me. That's my dried cum, all over you." He watched her warily, waiting for her reaction.

She humphed, thinking it through, and not giving anything away as to how she felt about it. "So why are you in the tub? If it's that bad, if we already—what good did you think sleeping in the tub was going to do?"

"I don't know." He seemed to realize she was right, but only just at that moment. "I honestly don't remember. I can't remember a fucking thing."

She tried hard not to let on how satisfied, relieved, she felt. Somehow, she knew it wouldn't go over very well with him to admit how grateful she'd feel to have it over with. And if it happened when she'd been too drunk to cringe, flinch, wither away from him, or scream for him to stop— she hoped she hadn't—all the better.

She really couldn't remember. She looked at him again, sure he would have stopped if she had. She'd heard the Coitus Club gossip about some of his drunken induced, not-so-flattering behaviors, but none of the other girls ever made it sound like a bad thing. They definitely weren't afraid of him because of it. On the beach the night before last, he'd personally admitted he could be forceful at times, and it worried him, for her sake.

She pinched her lips into a tight line to keep from appearing too content.

"I came too fucking close!" His swearing steadily increased—a sign of his frustration. He'd tamed his language so much since they'd been together, but sometimes, when things slipped beyond his control, he reverted back.

"I don't even know how close I came. Fuck! I can't remember. I was too fucking drunk! Shit, Rhees. This is serious. I'm all over your panties, all over you. It's too close to—I didn't plan to let myself get anywhere near you, like that." Paul's intensity had increased to yelling by the time he finished.

They both startled when they heard a loud bang on the wall. Someone in the room next door yelled for them to shut up. Paul rubbed his temples and sighed, but it made him calm down.

"I don't think I did," he said quietly before he launched into another one of his fast thinking, hard-to-follow rants. "I hope to God I didn't. I don't believe I did. You still had your panties on, but I can get around those without taking them off, so that's no assurance, and I found semen on both sides of your panties, inside and out, but the fabric is sheer, maybe it just seeped through."

Dizzy from the roller coaster ride that was Paul when he was disappointed in himself, she looked off at a spot in the corner, waiting for him to ride it out until she had a thought.

"Could I be—" She paused and glanced down at her panties again. "Could I get pregnant?"

His body went slack and the color drained from his face. He hadn't thought of that. He'd stopped carrying condoms months ago as a deterrent to keep him off of—out of her. Of course he hadn't worn one.

"I don't know." He was fraught with disdain for his own behavior. "It depends on what I did—"

"It depends on what *we* did. We, Paul, we," she scolded. "There's semen all over my panties, inside and out. That means it could have gotten inside me, right? Even if we didn't actually do it? My mom said that could happen when she gave me her own version of Sex Ed since I didn't participate at school."

"Technically, yes, in theory." His own mom had warned him of the possibility, but curious, he'd looked it up as a teen. That scenario didn't rank high on his list of concerns. "It's not impossible, but people all over the world are messing around every day. There'd be a lot more virgin mothers running around. I've never met one, have you? We'd hear about it, besides in just the bible."

She nodded but sat quietly. She still didn't look up.

"But if I penetrated you—that's just it—I don't know. I don't know what the fuck I—*we* did." He carefully corrected himself after her little objection. "I don't *think* I did." His eyes darted to her and he corrected himself again. "*We* did. I didn't see any blood."

He let out a shaky breath. He slowly and hesitantly turned his gaze from her. It wasn't enough. He had to close his eyes to ask the hard question.

"You *are* a virgin, right? If I had—" He cleared his throat. "Penetrated you, there'd be blood."

Rhees didn't answer. It was as though someone had sucked all the air out of the bathroom and he had to look. She appeared sick. She *was* sick, she drank too much the night before, but she looked a different kind of sick as she sat stoically on the floor, trembling.

"Rhees?" Based on what he'd witnessed since he'd known her, Paul knew he'd pushed her farther than she could handle. He sighed and then retreated, hoping to bring the focus back to himself—bring her back. "There wasn't any blood. I didn't deflower you. Rhees? I think we're okay."

She finally nodded and he watched as she slowly came back from the dark room she'd locked herself in for those few seconds. They sat silently for a while until his disgust with himself got the better of him again.

"This is entirely my fault, not yours, but no matter what I did, exactly—it was too much. It should never have happened."

"I wouldn't have cared," she said in a soft voice.

"Oh my God." He snapped back to frantic. "God damn it, Rhees."

It didn't matter anymore what he might really be saying or trying to make her understand. She'd tried to tell him she could be okay with more physical intimacy but he'd made it clear. The idea repulsed him. She only heard rejection and she knew why he'd want to reject her. She stood and hesitated, unable to decide what to do, yell at him or run away. She did both.

"I'm not a fucking idiot! I understand plenty! I understand you hate the idea of being with me, and I don't blame you. Actually, I am an idiot. I get it, okay? I just thought things might finally be different, but nothing's dif—I—I'm still dirty." Her shoulders went limp and she stopped herself. She'd never come so close to spilling her personal feelings aloud, she never allowed herself to even think them. She looked around the room a few times, as if lost, as if she'd lost her bearings in the small room.

She ran out of the bathroom, but it wasn't far enough. She needed to get away, but she couldn't think straight. She ran out the door and headed down the long hallway of the hotel.

Paul heard the door slam.

"Aw shit!" He jumped out of the tub and ran out the door after her.

He didn't catch her until she'd made it to the elevator and stepped inside. He grabbed hold of her and dragged her back out before the doors closed again. She fought, but he ignored her attempts to get away, holding her to him until she finally gave in and hugged him back. She buried her face in his chest and cried.

"It's going to be all right. I promise." He let her cry it out, but winced at his own words. He'd just made a promise he wasn't sure he could keep. No, actually, he'd made one before. He'd promised she'd leave their island the same way she'd come, and though he hadn't broken that one exactly, he'd come too close. The more he thought about it, the more he realized how much he had changed her.

She would never be the same again and it wrenched his conscience, unable to decide if it was a good thing or not. She once couldn't bear him touching her. He knew that wasn't good. How seriously messed up does a person have to be, to hate being touched as much as she once did?

She didn't mind *his* touch anymore and he thought that was good, but only for a second. Now she didn't mind *too* much. Maybe he hadn't done her any favors after all. He believed himself to be the last man she should get so comfortable with. The fact that she still freaked out when anyone else touched her only added to his concern.

He'd come too close. Yeah, he felt sick inside and needed to get his mind off this line of thought. He winced again because he couldn't help himself. He squeezed her to him even tighter. He knew she'd be better off without him, but he never wanted to let her go.

"You are aware we just locked ourselves out of our room?"

Rhees shook her head as best as she could without having to break contact with him. His chin rested on the top of her head and after quietly holding her for several minutes, he spoke calmly, soothingly, and began rubbing his hands up and down her back. It felt good and she started to feel better.

"The key is in my jacket, on the counter, in the room, behind the door that is now shut . . . and locked. My phone is in there too. We're standing at the elevators on the top floor of a five star hotel. We slept in our clothes. Neither of us is wearing shoes." His chest vibrated with a quiet chuckle. "My mom would die. She'd say something like, 'People will think we're a bunch of hillbillies or trailer trash'.

"My dad always responded to her social concerns by saying, 'Dude . . .'." Paul laughed again at his dad calling his mom, of all people, dude. "'You can take the trash out of the trailer, but you can't take the trailer out of the trash'. I never really understood what that meant when I was a kid." Paul's chest shook with another chuckle. "You know? I haven't had a fond memory of my parents in a very long time. My very prim and proper mother and my dad who grew up poor, but clawed his way to the top, how they ever wound up together will forever be a mystery. "

"Opposites attract," she mumbled into his shirt.

"Falling in love is a curse enough. Falling in love with your opposite, someone you have nothing in common with, makes it even worse."

She looked up to see his face, hurting and hating how he'd just reconfirmed he could never fall in love. Not with her, or anyone else. She rested her cheek against his chest again and breathed him in as deeply as possible, wishing he hadn't been so damaged as a young boy. She understood why she would never deserve his heart, but sadly for him, she believed his brother and the girl who stole Paul's innocence were the real curse. She didn't want to cry again.

"At least we both have our clothes on," she said. "That's pretty lucky considering you just got out of the tub."

Chapter 21

*T*he gang had brunch, the last thing they would do together for another year. They all had flights to catch and would be heading their separate ways until the next Testosterfest. The men, nearly inseparable through junior high and high school, realized as they got older, their friendship would eventually take a backseat to real life. They'd come up with the idea to take one week a year to revisit their wild, carefree days. Taylor and Bryce still lived in Miami and got together occasionally, but David had taken a job in Washington D.C.

Paul had missed a couple of years when he *got lost*. His friends were happy and relieved to finally find him again, via his father's team of private investigators, but Paul refused to return to Miami for any reason. Every now and then, the three men made their way to the island for a one-on-one visit with him, but as predicted, Testosterfest had become the only opportunity they had to all get together at the same time.

The girls on the other hand, would probably never see each other again. They just didn't know that yet. Of the three, Ashley, at the beginning of the week, may have had the best chance of returning, but David had finally decided to take Paul's advice. He'd confided in Paul how meeting Rhees, and seeing the two of them together, made him realize there really were more important things to look for in a woman. He mentioned he was toying with the idea of taking a ski trip to Utah that winter and asked the guys if they wanted to join him.

The mood among the group seemed more subdued than it'd been all week. Everyone was tired, a little sad about parting, and hungover, but no one missed how much quieter Paul and Rhees seemed to be, toward each other. He'd pulled his chair closer to hers and sat, leaning toward her with his arm over the back of her chair, marking his territory as usual, but he never touched her and they never made eye contact.

"Rhees, are you all right?" Liz asked. "I hope you won't let the way that jerk had his hands all over you ruin your impression of the whole vacation. I know, after the way you reacted to Taylor's hug, it must have really upset you, having that complete stranger getting so personal."

The look on Paul's face made Liz's voice falter. The color drained from his face. Rhees watched Liz expectantly.

"When did that happen?" Taylor shook his head. "I don't remember anything after I drank the wine at dinner," he said to get a laugh. David and Bryce laughed too, nodding and comparing their own memories, or lack of them.

"Liz?" Paul asked, anxiously. She gave her eyewitness account of the incident, including the fact that Paul had been ready to slug it out with Taylor at the moment it happened. Jeannie filled in a few holes from her own point of view and everyone glanced around at each other in uncomfortable silence. They'd all witnessed Rhees' reaction to someone she knew, Taylor's hug, and were sure she'd have a problem with the new revelation.

"I don't remember a thing." Rhees laughed and leaned back in her seat. "Wow!" she said thoughtfully. "Alcohol is useful for so many things. The list just keeps growing. I wish I would have known, years ago." She refused to look at Paul.

Everyone laughed, except Paul. The new information only made him feel sick inside, more than he already did.

oOo

Paul and Rhees sat in their first-class seats, headed home. They'd been in a quiet mood the whole flight, not angry, just quiet as they reflected on the circumstances.

"I'm sorry I overreacted this morning. I just *really* didn't want anything like that to happen. I'm so sorry that it did. I shouldn't have."

"Paul, I don't believe for a second that you forced me to do anything, so stop beating yourself up. I'm just as much to blame." She looked out the window of the plane when she whispered the next words. "And I said I didn't care."

Paul thought about her comment at brunch. She seemed a little too relieved she'd been too drunk to remember the new creepazoid. It probably was a stroke of luck, for her sake, though he had to wonder if her disappointment about not getting it 'over with', hit her for the same reason—she wouldn't have to remember that, either.

He let out a frustrated sigh. He didn't want to argue again. "Okay, but let's make sure it doesn't happen again, all right?"

She shrugged indifferently, and he sighed again.

A few minutes later, still at a loss for words, but hating the silent treatment, he playfully bumped her shoulder with his own. She looked over at him, finally, and he gave her a cheesy grin, trying to cheer her up. She gave him a faint smile and he took her hand in his, brought it to his lips and kissed her knuckles. She rested her head on his right shoulder and snuggled up to him while he caressed the hand he still held. They sat quietly for a while, but they both felt a little better.

"Rhees?" Paul sounded somber. "Why did your brother run away from home?"

She hadn't thought about her brother since the night she'd mentioned him to Paul. She moved one shoulder up and then down.

"I don't know. I was only ten. My parents never really let me in on it. He was seven years older than me. He was born, and then my mom couldn't get pregnant again. When she finally decided she'd never be able to have another baby, voila, she got pregnant with me."

Paul reached for her hand and held it.

"I remember a lot of yelling. My parents would send me outside, or to my room when they started up. I could hear the yelling, but not what they were saying. And then one day, they were all screaming at each other, and Perry just walked out and never came back. I cried myself to sleep for weeks. My mom worried about me. She always worried about me, but she had to sleep with me for a while, because I guess I had nightmares then too." She had to stop long enough to keep her composure, realizing how much she'd come to depend on Paul the way she'd always depended on her mom.

She didn't like the realization that Paul had taken, not only her dad's place, but her mom's too. She suddenly wondered how she'd manage if he left her too—when. It was only a matter of time.

"Hey." Paul kissed her forehead. "There's nothing wrong with wishing painful things could have been different, that I know from experience."

"Why do you have to be so wonderful?"

"Wonderful?" He humphed, showing his doubt about her description.

"Man. I really am such a baby." She leaned into his lips and he kissed her again. "Perry and I were never that close because of our age difference, but we were family. It really scared me that he could just leave us like that. He just walked away and never came back, never said good-bye, never gave us a second thought or second chance." She'd always believed he left because of her.

"Rhees," Paul said a while later. He was nervous, hesitant. "I—I'll tell you why I ran away from home if—" Her eyes shot to his. That topic had always been unquestionably off limits. "If you'll tell me . . . why you don't like to be touched."

"No," she said definitively, without having to think

about it. She seemed to have thought better of it, as though she didn't want to give him more reason to be curious. "I know how hard it is for you to even think about that part of your life. I don't want to know."

She'd outmaneuvered him by making it sound like he'd be the one who would have trouble keeping his end of the deal. He glanced down, sad and even more worried.

"I could do it. It wouldn't be hard, now, not anymore, not with you."

"No," she snapped again, but then quickly forced a smile. "I don't know why. There *is* no reason—it's just one of my crazy OCD issues. It's not a big deal." She tried to laugh, but didn't sound convincing. "I don't react that way anymore—not with you."

He nodded his agreement and decided to let it rest, but the nervous tick in his mouth became very active the rest of the flight as he realized he would need to do a little research when they got home. He didn't really want to, but he couldn't make the nagging go away. He needed to learn more about victims of child abuse.

Chapter 22

"*Y*ou decent?" Paul stood outside her bedroom door. He'd left the room so she could get ready for work.

"Come on in."

He opened the door and walked in. She stepped out of the bathroom and leaned against the wall while she brushed her teeth.

"Aw . . . sorry." Paul turned, embarrassed, and headed out of the room. "I thought you said to come in."

"I did."

"Rhees, is this a joke?" He didn't turn around, his back to her still.

She realized what freaked him out. "Paul, it's a bikini. I'm not flashing you in my undies."

"Bikini!" He still didn't turn around, sounding a little befuddled. "What happened to your tankinis? I thought you preferred tankinis."

"One bit the dust before Costa Rica. The other two are going to die any day, and I don't want to be too close when it happens. I bought two new swimming suits on my shopping spree." She grew confused about why he seemed upset. "You made me promise to buy stuff. I did. I actually needed new suits."

"Yeah, but—" he sounded a little breathless. "I thought you didn't like bikinis. Why didn't you get new tankinis?"

"I tried. I couldn't find even one."

"In the whole mall?" His voice registered a few octaves

higher.

"No."

"One piece?"

"Do you realize, in a one piece, you have to strip down, almost naked, every time you have to use the bathroom? No way."

"But—"

"Turn around. You didn't even get a good look."

"I did."

"You don't like it? I bought this brown one and a coral one." She couldn't help the disappointment in her voice that he didn't approve of her choice.

"I have a dick, Rhees! Of course I like it. That's the problem."

She finally understood, dashed to the twin bed, and pulled on a camisole, knowing why he'd been acting so weird. The camisole's wide straps over her shoulders were brown like her suit while the body was a soft, lightweight chiffon with colored frilly layers, each layer was a different tone of off-white to tan, but complimentary with the brown of the bikini.

"I couldn't find any tankinis, but I found two bikinis and two camis to match. The camis make the suits look like tankinis, don't you think? They cover me so I don't have to feel so self-conscious being half naked all day. I figure the only time I'll actually only be in just the bikini is when I have to take off my cami to put on my dive skin. It was the best compromise I could come up with. Do you think it'll work?"

He finally dared to look and breathed a sigh of relief. He stared at her in wonder.

"Paul. I asked, do you think it'll work?"

"Yeah. That's good. You look nice, *very* nice."

She smiled. "Good. I'm glad you like it. For a minute there, I thought you hated it and were going to rip it off me like you said you would." She giggled.

An eyebrow cocked up and he stared at her. He'd

wanted to do just that.

"I said I like it. You always dress so well. I like it best with the cami, though." He exhaled. "But *He* liked it better without."

She looked down like he'd embarrassed her, but then her eyes slowly rose to meet his. "Really?" She bit her lower lip to suppress a smile he didn't understand. She looked almost beguiling, but Rhees didn't do beguiling, he had to be wrong.

"Let's go." He suddenly felt anxious to get somewhere public.

oOo

"I want to go home early," Rhees said to Paul. He checked his watch and couldn't believe the hands already read three o'clock. He still had a long list of things to do since they'd been gone a week. He was about to step onto the Porgy, but stopped to talk to her. "The apartment hasn't had a thorough cleaning since I left. I'm not going to be able to relax if I don't scrub it down."

"I can't leave just yet."

"Paul, I can walk home by myself."

"See if Tracy or Regina will go with you."

She rolled her eyes. "I already asked. They're going straight to Lorencio's place from here."

Lorencio had shown up as a new student while Paul and Rhees were in Costa Rica. Very charismatic and carrying himself in a way that made people feel like he genuinely cared about them, he'd already made quite an impression. Everyone at the shop had already accepted him into their inner circle.

Rhees looked Lorencio's way when she mentioned his name. "He's so pretty, don't you think?"

"Pretty?" Paul shot her a cold glance. He looked over at Lorencio standing with a group of the shop people and a couple of friends from the island gathered around him, listening to stories about his visit to Cuba. Paul's mouth twitched. "I thought *I* was pretty, though I hate being called that."

Rhees giggled. "I know and I don't call you pretty . . . anymore. You *are* beautiful, however, and you know it," she patronized, and pretended to punch his arm. "Lorencio doesn't." She sucked in her cheeks, trying to hide the huge smile that threatened to break on her face.

"Hey, watch it," he said.

"You have nothing to worry about. You're still number three on my short list of the *best looking men in the world.*" She fought her smile again. "But Lorencio may be number four." She gave Paul a devious wink and smirked before looking back at Lorencio.

"Did you know he's Rastafarian? I never would have imagined I could think dreads were attractive, but they're perfect on him, don't you think? He's so tall and slender, but muscular, like you. His skin is such a pretty color." She had a faraway look in her eyes as she stared at the new man.

"Hey! Earth to Rhees." Paul waved his hand in front of her face, and she turned to see what he wanted, blinking out of a daze.

"Have you noticed how pretty his eyes are?" she asked, looking into Paul's eyes as if comparing the two. "So green—I've never seen that color of green before. It's like they're transparent, but intense at the same time, almost ethereal."

"I thought you liked blue—*mine.*" He leaned down, giving her a closer look at his own, trying to use his powers on her, but he was flustered and not in the right frame of mind. He gave up.

"He's a pud," he said, as if Lorencio disgusted him.

"I *said* I think *you* are better looking than he is. I don't even know him. He's just really . . . *pretty.* I like looking at him, but only in the way that I like to look at pretty flowers or a sunset, that's all."

Paul rattled his head as he turned his attention back to

the Porgy. He needed to replace one of the tank clips that had broken while he was away.

"Okay, I'm going home to clean, all right?"

"I said I didn't want you to go alone."

"For crying out loud," she said, a little too forcefully. She folded her arms and looked off, like she was angry.

Paul suddenly grew nervous and agitated. He stepped back out of the Porgy in a hurry. He put his hands on his hips and stared at her while he seemed to be considering something.

"On a scale of one to ten, how important is this to you?" he asked.

She stared at him, blankly.

"You said you wanted to go home, *alone*, I said I don't want you to go home, *alone*. I need to know how important this is to you before I put my foot in my mouth . . . by putting it down."

She stared at him incredulously. "This is your solution to the zip line crisis? Then ten!" she blared defiantly.

He sighed loudly. He looked away and back again.

"Okay." Luckily she'd reconsidered. "Seven."

He sighed again.

"You know how important a clean house is to me."

"Okay," he conceded, reluctantly. "But go straight home. Don't stop to get groceries, don't stop to talk to anyone, don't dawdle, lock the door when you get home, and take your *freaking* phone with you! Keep it where you can hear it." He gave her a knowing look before he gave in to his grin. "Just because I'm grinning like an idiot doesn't mean I'm not serious. I'm only grinning because you're so dang cute."

"Well, even your *idiotic* grin is gorgeous. It's reaching award-winning proportions at this moment." She smiled back.

"I'll text you when I finally get out of here and am on my way home," he said.

She'd thought he would give up on the whole phone

thing since she refused to use it, but he didn't. He continued to throw his money away, as she described it, on the unnecessary item. He'd waited her out and won. He always won, even when he let her think she did.

"Okay." She tried, unsuccessfully, to be annoyed with him, and looked down to hide her grin. "You know you're a control freak, right? You just put every form of control possible on every aspect of my win, but thank you for agreeing to let me go—without a fight." She wanted to kiss him good-bye, but didn't dare after the way he'd been acting since his big freak out in Costa Rica. She stood there a few seconds, summoning the courage, but changed her mind and turned to leave.

"Hey! Aren't you forgetting something?" He'd moved in close. His thumb brushed softly across her cheek as he slowly wrapped his fingers into the hair at the nape of her neck and pulled her to him for the kiss she'd wanted, the first real kiss he'd given her since that night.

"Mm!" she grunted.

oOo

"Rhees, I'm home. You decent?" Paul called from the porch, through her bedroom window.

"Almost," she yelled back. "I made you a quesadilla to hold you till dinner. It's in the microwave." She reached around the doorjambs to pull the lock off the screen door so he could come in.

He waited a second for her to close her bedroom door so she could finish getting ready in private. Paul walked into the kitchen and opened the microwave he'd bought for her. She insisted on cooking for him once in a while in exchange for all the nights he took her out for dinner and never let her pay.

He snarfed down two-thirds of his quesadilla immediately, but set the last piece on the counter to grab a beer from the fridge. Rhees walked into the kitchen as he picked up the remaining quesadilla and took another bite.

"I can't believe you ate that after setting it on the counter. Do you have no fear of germs, whatsoever?"

He smirked, his tongue in his cheek. "When was the last time you disinfected the counters?"

"About two hours ago. I used a whole bottle of disinfectant on this apartment. I am pleased to announce that the kitchen and bathrooms are clean enough for even me. No one is going to call me a dirty girl."

Paul swallowed wrong and coughed, knowing she didn't realize what she'd just said. "Dani Girl, you are without a doubt, not a dirty girl. *And,* with you around, I'm more afraid of the chemicals on the counter because of your immaculate cleaning habits than I am of any little ole germs." He stuffed the last bite into his mouth with a snap of his teeth.

"Oh, great!" she exclaimed. "Not only do I have to worry about germs. Now I have to worry about chemicals too."

"Oh, no! Chemicals are our friends." He realized what he'd done. "They keep us safe from all the bad—" He couldn't bring himself to say it. He laughed, flashing one of his best smiles, and shook his head at her with a sigh. He tolerated her obsessive-compulsive behaviors, but he couldn't bring himself to tell her that her fears were normal.

"I'm sorry, Baby, but I've been a slob my whole life, and I haven't died yet."

"You're not a slob," she said. "You're quite good at picking up after yourself and keeping things in their place—as long as you know where that place is."

"Once you organized the office, the media room, the room that has no purpose, our gear closet, the equipment room . . . and my apartment, yeah, I've managed to *keep* things organized." He finally had to smirk. "I wouldn't dare disrupt your tidy little world. I'm still working on keeping my clothing piles to manageable proportions, though. I'm sorry I don't take care of it right away."

"You don't have piles." She smiled at his description. "You leave the clothes you wear in the evenings on the twin bed, but you put them back on in the morning before you run to your apartment to change into your swimming shorts."

"But *you* don't leave your clothes on the twin."

"It doesn't bother me. It's not really the clutter or dirt, just the germs."

"Clutter and dirt don't bother you? That's why you scamper around cleaning and organizing everything."

"That's only because I like to keep busy. Yes, I like to organize, but it doesn't bother me when Claire undoes it almost as fast as I get it done." She giggled. "And you should talk. You don't like dirt any more than I do. You just pay people to clean up after you, while I prefer to do it myself."

Paul's eyes widened and then narrowed as he thought about it. Before Rhees, a few of his Coitus Club groupies took turns cleaning his apartment, but he'd had to "fire" them. They refused to believe a romp on cleaning day was no longer part of the job description. He'd found an older, married woman he could pay to do it.

"Germs aren't a problem for me. If I can't see 'em, 'live and let live', I say." He licked her face from bottom to top to make his point. Rhees surprised him by returning the gesture from his collarbone to his Adam's apple.

"Mmm . . . Where was I?" It took a minute to get his brain to work again. "I . . . uh—I just—I like the way *clean*, high quality sheets feel, but I hate changing them." They used to need changing regularly. Nowadays his apartment was nothing more than a place to shower and change his clothes. "But now that I don't sleep there anymore, I'm pretty much paying Edna to keep my surfboard dusted off."

oOo

"Does anyone know why Lorencio decided to leave?" Mitch asked. "He flew out on the first plane this morning."

Paul and Rhees sat in the gazebo and had just shared lunch. They sat close, looking through one of the books on the sea life in the area, trying to identify a creature they'd seen on their morning dive. Rhees glanced over at Mitch and Christian.

"No. It's so weird. He told me just yesterday he planned to stay a while, but all of a sudden, he up and leaves us for the Phoenix Islands," Christian answered.

"Did you know he left?" Rhees asked Paul.

Paul pretended to be engrossed in the sea life book. He shook his head slightly.

"How do you not know why one of your students walked away? He didn't ask for a refund?"

"Nope." He still didn't look up at her.

"That is so weird. He must be a flake, fickle . . . and obviously rich enough to keep up with his high-speed whims." Paul finally glanced at her out of the corner of his eye.

"We can't expect everyone to love it here as much as you and I."

"I know, but I thought he did. It's just weird."

"Yeah. Weird, and I'm sorry." He felt a twinge of remorse, and wanted to kiss her to remind himself why he'd done what he'd done. He leaned in for one but missed when she excitedly pointed to a picture in the book.

"That's it!" She smiled proudly about finding the nudibranch they'd been searching for.

"You're right. A Red Tipped Sea Goddess." Paul read the name under the picture. "I've never seen one of those. Good spot." He put his arm around her and leaned over again, successfully planting a heartfelt kiss on her cheek.

He thought he might tell her how he'd talked to Lorencio the night before, after she went home to clean. Paul had gone on and on about his diving experiences around the world and convinced Lorencio the diving on the island was mediocre at best. If Lorencio really wanted to experience good diving, he had to try the Phoenix Islands. He'd even loaned him four thousand dollars to do it.

"You'll pay me back, someday. No hurry." Paul thought he might tell Rhees—he would, just as soon as Lorencio paid him back.

Chapter 23

Rees stood on the boat, staring at her gear, but not setting it up.

"Come on, Pokey," Paul said quietly in her ear as an excuse to get close. He gave her earlobe a quick nip with his teeth. "We're diving today, not memorizing the way our gear looks."

"I think I need to call this dive. I'm not feeling so well."

"What's wrong?" Paul didn't attempt to hide his worry.

"I'm nauseous."

"You'll feel better once you're in the water. I didn't know you get seasick."

"I don't. The diesel fumes really got to me on the way here. I'm hoping it'll pass, but right now, I don't think I should dive."

"Dive with me, please, please, please?" he whined, putting his arms around her, acting all clingy and needy. "You can throw up through your reg. Just hold it in your mouth to make sure it stays in place while you blow the vomit through. It happens all the time."

She gave him a look of disgust and he laughed.

"Okay, okay." He started massaging her neck and shoulders while nuzzling his nose into her hair. "Does this help?"

"Mmm . . ." She nodded and took a deep breath. "It does. Thanks."

"We diving then?" He looked hopeful.

She nodded again.

The nausea came and went throughout the day, but she braved through it until the next morning. The boat fumes made it impossible to hide how ill she really felt. She actually did throw up over the side of the boat and Paul refused to let her get in the water.

"I feel better now. What happened to, 'Throw up in your reg'?" she'd complained.

She told Claire, later that day that she'd suddenly developed an allergic reaction to diesel fumes or something.

"I've always hated the smell. Maybe I've just finally reached my tolerance level."

The next day, Rhees walked into the office feeling sick again.

"I'm calling your dive again today," Paul said. "I'm starting to worry about you, Baby."

"Don't. It's just food poisoning. I must've eaten something bad."

"That's it!" he said indignantly. "You've got to stop killing every germ that comes within a mile of you. It's messing with your body's ability to resist normal, everyday bacteria."

"You'd both have dippy tummies if she had food poisoning," Claire said. "You two eat the same thing every meal. You guys share food like real lovers, it's gross, and I'm not the germ-o-phobe. Food poisoning acts faster and more furious than this unless it's the really bad stuff like E. coli. You didn't drink any contaminated water, did you? It could be Giardia. Did you get mosquito bites in Costa Rica? They have Dengue fever."

"Shit," Paul said under his breath, suddenly very worried by the things Claire tossed out. "Rhees, if you're still sick in a couple of days, we're flying back to the States to get you checked out."

"No way! I'll just go to the clinic, *if* I need to."

"No. You won't."

"No sense arguing with him, Rhees. I've heard him say, several times, he'd charter a jet back to the States rather than let the local doctors touch him. He hates the health care system in this country," Claire said. "He's never going to let them get anywhere near *you*."

"It's good enough for the locals. The population wouldn't be booming in this country if the doctors were killing everyone off." Rhees reached up on her toes and kissed Paul's chin. "It's pointless to even discuss this. It's nothing. I'll be better in no time."

"I'll call my dives too so I can stick around." He put his arms around her. "I'll do some research on your symptoms. I'll figure it out."

"Don't call your dives because of me. Go."

"Oh, *pleease*. I'm not leaving you here to be miserable without me. You know how much I like to be around for that."

He insisted she get some rest and walked out with her as she made her way to her favorite spot on the edge of the deck. Paul grabbed their mat, and rolled it out for her.

"I'm serious. We're flying back to the States if you're not better soon."

She rolled her eyes.

oOo

Rhees slipped into the office the next morning and plopped down in the chair.

"Still sick?" Claire asked.

Rhees nodded. "Please don't say anything to Paul. He's driving me crazy with concern. I think if it were something serious, it would get steadily worse, not come and go like it does."

Rhees used every bit of reserve she had to make it through her dives, in spite of how close she felt to throwing up most of the time. The dives were okay. It got her mind off of her misery, but the boat fumes about did her in on the way to the dive site. The ride back was more than she could handle.

The boat docked and Rhees jumped off before the usual chaos commenced, leaving her gear. She ran to the end of the deck and threw up over the edge.

Tracy, the first one to notice, shrieked, "Ew! There she blows!"

Everyone heard and either gawked or moved as far away as possible and tried not to look at all. Claire came out of the office to see, and both she and Paul raced to grab Rhees, who looked like she struggled to keep her balance as she heaved.

Paul's expression was an equal mix of concern and annoyance. He worried about her, but after their discussion the day before, he didn't know what to do. He wasn't up for another argument. He held her, and Claire kept the hair from Rhees' face until she finally made it past the worst.

"If I didn't know better, if this wasn't Rhees we're talking about, I'd have to ask if she was pregnant." Claire laughed riotously at her own joke and missed how the color completely drained from Paul's face. Rhees choked and Claire reflexively started patting her back.

Paul staggered to the edge of the deck a few feet away. He looked back to meet the lost and disbelieving expression on Rhees' face, his own expression stoic, no expression at all, just dazed. He looked out over the water and then he leaned over the edge of the deck and vomited too.

"Yep. You two must have caught something in Costa Rica. Paul's constitution just took longer to give in to it," Claire said, without thinking a thing.

oOo

"You left me! You left me on my own to absorb all this," Rhees sobbed. The two of them sat on their mat on the deck. Dinnertime had come and gone, but they were both too stunned to be hungry.

As soon as Paul had stopped heaving into the ocean, he'd turned in circles several times, like he thought he was supposed to be someplace, but couldn't remember where. He finally stalked off, jumped onto one of the jet skis, and sped away. He didn't come back until past the time to put the schedule on the board and shoo everyone away for the night.

"Maybe I thought you needed time to think."

"Oh, you were thinking of *me*? You thought I needed time to think?" She sounded sarcastic and very annoyed.

"No," he confessed, shamefacedly. "But I did—I didn't— *couldn't* process—I'm sorry, I didn't think about anything but myself."

She cried some more and he felt terrible, but he didn't know what to do. He sat on the other end of the mat, not daring to touch her, though he wanted to . . . or not.

"I should take a pregnancy test, right? Do they have those on the island?"

"Yes, Rhees," he huffed. "People on the island get pregnant." She gave him a dirty look, and he regretted his own sarcasm. "They have quite a teenage pregnancy problem here."

"I'm going to go get one then." She started to get up. He sighed, took her hand, and gently pulled her back down, closer to him this time.

"It's only been five days. It's too soon. Most tests won't give you a reliable reading until you've missed a period." He started calculating in his head. "Your last period was the fifth. That means—jeez, your cycle is so fucked up, I don't know."

"How do you know all that?"

He almost went cross-eyed before he rattled his head, feeling overwhelmed and weary. "First of all, my mom's an Ob-Gyn. She sat her sons down and explained the birds and the bees—and a hell of a lot of other stuff, many times, even though she knows I don't forget. I'm sure Mary got her own version of the hellish lecture too, because heaven forbid, her children might do something to embarrass her or make her look like anything less than the most perfect parent on the fu—on the planet."

He noticed the troubled look on Rhees' face and regretted letting all that slip out. He glanced down, embarrassed, licked his lips a few times, and continued on, back to where he'd meant to go before his tirade.

"The girls, here at the shop, tell me they can't dive certain days. I don't need to ask them why, it's the way they ask, all uneasy and embarrassed, but I remember. The next month, I schedule them accordingly. I get it right eighty percent of the time. It's just easier. I figure I'm saving us all a little awkwardness." He sighed.

"Damn it, Rhees. Most of the girls are pretty regular—most of them are on the pill."

"I've never had a reason to be on the pill," she snapped.

He looked at her, realizing how she'd misunderstood him. "The pill lets you choose when, or even if, you want your period. Most of the girls at the shop take a week off. It's pretty easy to figure it out, but you—you go anywhere from eighteen to thirty-three days between periods. I've never seen anything like it. If I was on speaking terms with my mother, I'd call and ask her about it. I've thought about looking it up on the Internet, but it seemed so personal. And since I never planned to have a *reason* to know—" He put the palms of his hands on his forehead in exasperation.

"You know more about my cycle than I do. This is my fault then." Tears fell again, but without the sobbing.

"Gaaaw!" Paul couldn't even finish taking the name in vain, he was so overcome with a truckload of emotions.

"Okay, Mr. *Menstrual-Cycle-Savant*, when do I take a test? How long before I know for sure?"

"*We!*" He pulled his hands down his face from top to bottom, stretching his skin and muscles along the way. "Aw, Baby . . . Aw *shi-it!*" He'd upset himself again. "*Nawt* a good time to call you Bab—*that!*" He couldn't even say it. He groaned and then alternated between random intakes of breath and loud, frustrated exhales. "I know I should never be allowed to touch you again, but I *really* need to just hold you in my arms right now. Is that all right?"

She sat, quiet for a minute, but about the time he felt terrible that she didn't want him touching her, she suddenly dived at him and hunkered down into his lap.

"Yes, please."

They sat, holding each other, for a very long time without talking. Paul broke the silence first.

"Look, I'm all into denial. I say we just pretend like nothing's wrong and see what happens—until we absolutely have no other choice."

She nodded in agreement, but then broke into uncontrollable laughter.

"What?" He grinned, but carefully.

"We're pathetic," she yelled and continued to laugh.

It took him a few seconds but he finally laughed too, not as hard as she laughed, but somehow it made him feel better, hearing her.

"Maybe one of these days, we should try doing something for reals—you know?" she choked out between her fits of laughter. "Maybe we could try something that doesn't require any pretending."

"Yeah, maybe." He forced a smile. "Someday." He seemed thoughtful for a second. "You've been throwing up a lot. We should go find you something to eat."

"I'm really, *so* not hungry." She stressed the word, so.

"Let's *pretend* like you are."

oOo

Over the next two days, Rhees got worse, not better, and she refused to let him take her back to the States. Paul tried very hard to be attentive, but he was scared out of his mind. He couldn't think clearly and people noticed how addled he acted. Luckily, no one suspected the reason. Logically, he kept to his hypothesis about virgin pregnancy rates, but for the life of him, he didn't know what he'd done that night. Sometimes he even allowed himself a little pity over the loss. Whatever happened in that hotel room—he'd kill to have the memory back.

She would have preferred to stay home, but everyone knew she normally showed up with Paul every day. They didn't want to give anyone reason to wonder, just in case.

The dive school world was a very transient environment.

People moved on and others moved in to take their place. They'd lost Shelli, then Ulla soon after. Peder, Assif, and thankfully, Sarah, trickled away when they'd finished their courses. Eventually, Eddie and Brita moved on too.

Six new students had taken their places, which gave Rhees a believable reason not to be on the boat. She waved it off each day with a forced smile and then ran to Paul's apartment to lie on his couch. Paul said his couch was bad enough, but he'd asked her to promise she'd stay off of his bed—as if she'd be tempted to climb up and down the ladder every five minutes. She lay on the couch and worked to convince herself she didn't need to throw up. She hated throwing up. The constant need to use the bathroom was bad enough.

Paul stocked every fridge in their world with yogurt. He told her to eat at least a spoonful every half hour to keep her blood sugar even. It actually helped—Rhees that is. It made him worry even more, remembering his mom's random babbling at the dinner table about the way her patients chose to suffer with morning sickness when, if they'd just listen to her . . . it did nothing to help his own increasingly sickened anxiety.

oOo

Paul woke three days later to find Rhees curled up in a ball, whimpering quietly. "Hey." He leaned into her from behind and placed his cheek against hers. "Still not better? I'm so worried about you."

"I started my period this morning. I have cramps," she whimpered. "Isn't it bad enough I've been so sick? Do I really need cramps on top of it all?"

"You don't get cramps." Her announcement had left him feeling too relieved, but he'd never known her to get cramps. Guilt swept over him—the same guilt he'd felt since Claire and her stupid joke about Rhees being pregnant.

"I do, sometimes, but not like this. I usually just work through them. This virus must be in cahoots with Tom. It really hurts this time."

"Tom?" Paul leaned over her to see her face. "Who's *Tom*?"

"Time of month."

"Oh." He felt stupid. He'd heard it called many things, but never that. He relaxed, no longer feeling a neanderthalic desire to kick some pud's ass, but then his guilt doubled as his thoughts reverted back to the problem at hand. He sensed something deeper in her mood than just illness and hormones. It scared him. "Please. Let me take you to a doctor."

"Why?" Once again, her tone suggested she thought he'd come up with the stupidest idea ever. "It's a period. And you've been on your computer researching what's wrong with me. You said it was probably Gastroenteritis, a virus. They can't do anything for it except tell me to stay hydrated and wait it out. You're always pushing water on me." She cast an annoyed look his way. "It's not possible to get dehydrated with you around."

Again, the way she ground out the words—he sighed. His insides churned with turmoil.

"I know, but I'm not a doctor and the Internet's not a doctor either. If you're still sick on the tenth day, I'm throwing you over my shoulder and taking you to Texas. You *will* see a real doctor—I promise you that."

"I was starting to feel better—until Tom showed up for a visit."

He held her, the only thing he could think to do. The relief he felt about her period vanished with the nagging thought it could have been more than just a virus—might be more than just cramps and a period. He didn't want to think of the possible ramifications. If he did, he'd feel even worse. Damn that night. Damn getting that drunk with Rhees around, and damn letting Rhees get that drunk—with *him* around.

He caressed her arm and kissed her cheek a few times. He thought of a few things he could say to make her feel better, but he couldn't bring himself to say any of them.

I'm sorry—I promise we'll never let anything like this happen again—we will *let this happen again, someday.* It all caught in his throat, like a knot making him feel like he would choke.

The words, *I love you,* came to mind. He couldn't breathe. Did he? The idea had been stalking him since Taylor had made that redonkulous comment about him being in love with Rhees. Panic threatened to strangle him as his chest constricted, brutally and relentlessly. While part of him wanted to run, all he could manage was to close the small gap between them, kissing her on the cheek, over and over. It didn't make sense.

"Paul?" she asked. "What about your rules? You're a stickler for your rules, but you're being pretty snuggly right now."

"Nightmare snuggles are permitted, remember?"

"But I didn't have a nightmare."

"I did."

"Don't." She laughed a quick laugh. She reached back and caressed the side of his face and he leaned into her touch. "I know you're internalizing a whole lot of guilt right now. Please don't."

He shook his head. He couldn't speak. He buried his face in her hair, burrowing through it to kiss her behind the ear.

"It was too much pressure anyway."

He pulled back with concern, wondering what she meant.

"I mean, I know you're always telling me I'm a good person and all, but the strain of being a virgin mother . . . I don't think I could have lived up to that." She laughed, a little too forced, confirming his suspicions—*God! She wants a baby.*

He squeezed his eyes shut, dumbfounded and scared to death, but once again, despite her misery and the ache of her letdown, she still tried to help *him* feel better.

oOo

Paul wished he could have convinced her to stay in bed, but she wouldn't have it. They stepped onto the porch, ready to head to the shop. Paul watched as Rhees walked slowly toward the stairs, rubbing her stomach in a soothing motion.

"Hey, come here," he called.

She turned back a few steps to see what he wanted, and he surprised her by lifting her into his arms. She wrapped her legs around him. He gazed longingly into her eyes, but still had no words, so he just kissed her, very tenderly.

"What's that about?"

"We're not in the bedroom anymore." He shrugged.

"But we're not exactly in public either."

"Close enough." He carried her down to the street where he'd arranged for Ignacio to be waiting for them.

oOo

Rhees slept on Paul's couch, but woke when he tapped on the door and walked in.

"You didn't lock the door," he scolded.

She rolled her eyes. "I'm here on your couch because I'm sick. You come and check on me every thirty minutes. If I have to get up to unlock the door every time you show up, I'll never get any rest."

He looked down, embarrassed she was right. He pulled the hand he held behind his back, around to the front. He had flowers, not roses of any color to imply any kind of meaning, just very cheerfully pretty purple and orange flowers in a lime green vase, her three favorite colors. He set the vase on the coffee table and glanced between her and his gift, waiting. He'd been acting so nervous all day. She smiled her approval and watched the tension drain from his shoulders.

"Beautiful," she whispered, gazing at him. "The flowers are beautiful too."

He actually almost blushed. He went to the kitchen and busied himself with something, moving and banging things around, more than it seemed necessary to Rhees, but she smiled, wondering what he was up to.

It only took him a few minutes, but she thought it the most time he'd ever spent in a kitchen without her. He finally walked back to the living room with a small bowl and held it over her.

"Just what the doctor ordered. A Rhees' peanut butter cup." They both smirked at his play on words.

She sat up and took the cup, curiously. It held a large dollop of peanut butter with chunks of dark Italian chocolate protruding from the creaminess of her coveted nectar, all in a small cup.

"I read once that chocolate is proven to alleviate women's menstrual-related symptoms."

She smiled at his awkward attempt of an explanation for the sweet gesture. He sat next to her and waited for her to try it.

"Share with me," she said.

"Nope. The doctor prescribed that. You're not supposed to share prescriptive medications."

She giggled. "If I'd known I'd get this kind of treatment, I wouldn't have tried so hard to hide my cramps all this time."

"Yeah! You don't need to be so freaking tough all the time. You can lean on your friends."

"I've never had friends to lean on."

"Maybe if you'd lean once in a while, you'd find that you do. You have to give people a chance to step up."

"Thank you for stepping up, Paul," she whispered, suddenly overcome with gratitude.

He looked off with a frown on his face. He rolled his gaze back to her and tried to smile. "I just opened the last jar of the peanut butter we imported from Utah. We're going to have to tap in to some smuggling network somewhere if we want more."

"Do it then!" She feigned a gasp of horror. "I could sell my body if we need more cash—wait! You're prettier than I am. You'll have to be the one to sacrifice yourself." She giggled again.

"You did nawt just call me pretty." He cocked his head and cautioned her with his eyes.

"Only in the name of peanut butter." She did all she could, but lost the battle to maintain a serious face.

"I hate being called pretty, but I'll let it slide, this time, and only for you—not the peanut butter."

He took a piece of the chocolate, swirled it around the cup to make sure it scooped up as much peanut butter as possible, and held it to her mouth. She opened up with a waiting tongue, watching his eyes. He swooped in and flicked her tongue with his a couple of times and finished with a soft, but passionate, kiss.

"Sorry. That's not what you expected, is it?" He bit his lower lip and scrunched his nose to accentuate his apology. He looked so cute.

"Even better," she said and opened her mouth again. He placed the chocolate drenched with peanut butter on her tongue. She closed her eyes and moaned with pleasure.

"Shhiiit."

Chapter 24

By the eighth day, Rhees had recovered enough for their routines to get back to normal, but with a little awkwardness. The couple acted cool with each other at times, warmer than usual at other times. They were each insecure about their feelings for one another, but neither of them was brave enough to broach the subject.

"What's going on with you two?" Claire and Rhees were in the office. "Is everything all right?"

"Yep." Rhees fidgeted and seemed to be trying to look absorbed in her work on the computer. She finally sighed. "I don't know where we stand anymore. It's like we've hit a brick wall. When the river stops running, the water grows stagnant." She started to blubber. "I'm worried we're not running anymore."

"Oh, Rhees." Claire put her arm around her. It embarrassed Claire to ask. "Are you two sleeping together yet? I mean, you're so . . . lovey-dovey. I haven't been able to help but speculate."

"No." Rhees wiped her eyes and grabbed a tissue. "But . . ." She hesitated to admit it. "Please don't tell him, but—"

"I won't. You know I like you so much better than I like him." Claire smiled.

Rhees laughed. "Claire, I want to."

Claire's eyes grew bigger. "Well, why aren't you then?"

Rhees gave her a bug-eyed look. "He won't!"

Claire tossed her head back and laughed, a little too

emphatically.

"It's true," Rhees sobbed. "I've been trying to tell him I want to move forward since my birthday, but he refuses."

"No bloody way! Paul would—that doesn't sound like the Paul I know. Are you sure you've made your intentions clear? I mean, look who we're talking about here. All you have to do is have a vagina."

Rhees' eyes filled again. "I don't know. I don't know what the heck I'm doing wrong. I've never done this before. I've told him I want to do the things he suggested we do, back when he actually *did* want me."

"Oh, he still wants you—he actually says, no?" Claire sounded stunned. Rhees just nodded.

"There was one time, in Costa Rica, we both were *very* drunk and apparently *things* happened—not the real thing—we *think*. We can't even remember what we did or how far it went. But since then, he hardly touches me when we're alone, and then he goes *crazy* on me when we're not alone. I'm so confused. He gets me all—oh, my gosh! Claire! I've never had these feelings before, or these *thoughts*."

Claire laughed again. "It is so strange to finally see you acting *human* in that regard, but—" Claire stifled another laugh. "It's not funny. I know it's not funny. Have you talked about this with him? Surely you're not making yourself clear."

"I don't know—obviously *not*. Paul and his stupid promises," Rhees mumbled, and then she rolled her eyes at Claire. "They're not stupid, they're wonderful, and he's wonderful, but in this case—every time I try to bring it up, he says, 'No', like, end of discussion."

"Maybe you should just get him pissed, or, as you Americans say, drunk. Get him piss-drunk again." Claire raised her eyebrows with a devious smile.

"Not going to happen. Since Costa Rica, he won't drink more than a glass of wine or one or two beers."

"Hmm." Claire looked really shocked. "Maybe you need to be cheekier."

Rhees didn't understand.

"Bolder. Brazen."

"How do I do that?"

Claire shrugged. "Remember how you said it happened the night Dobbs socked him?" Claire grinned. "Something about, 'Even Christian wouldn't have been able to resist'."

"That's easier said than done. I'm afraid I was all talk, no knowledge, or experience—or *confidence,* to back it up."

"Believe me. It's not that hard to seduce a man, any man, let alone Paul . . . until you've been married a while." Claire scowled, but then snapped out of her funk. "We need a plan. Paul won't know what hit him."

"I don't want to hit him. I just want to show him how I feel about him."

oOo

The boat was well on its way toward the intended dive site, and Paul carefully observed as Regina and Tracy analyzed their tanks for their first dives on nitrox. He'd gone over it with them before, when they'd finished the bookwork for the course, but he wanted to see them use the analyzer one more time before they dived with enriched air. While air is usually twenty-one percent oxygen, nitrox tanks are mixed differently, more oxygen and less nitrogen, allowing longer bottom times with less risk of decompression sickness, otherwise called the bends.

Paul hadn't noticed the boat swing wide, close to Duna Caye, and his heart thumped hard against his chest when he heard the scream.

"Mon overboard!" Randy called.

Paul panicked even more when he realized he'd recognized the scream. Rhees had fallen off the boat and he scrambled, yelling orders, and preparing himself for a rescue as he scanned the water, looking for her. It only took him a second to spot her, and he relaxed. She watched him, a big smile on her face, while casually making her way toward the small island, wearing her mask, snorkel, and fins.

He realized she had something in mind, and now he understood why she'd asked him to schedule an afternoon dive to the northeast end of the island that day. She so rarely asked him to do her any favors—he didn't know why—he didn't think he could refuse her anything she really wanted.

He dived, like a hero, into the water without hesitation or taking the time to put on any gear. He swam toward her, effortlessly, and she, when she saw him coming, pretended to be unconscious, but with her snorkel in her mouth. Such a pathetic swimmer, she couldn't hold her breath for more than thirty seconds.

She's so dang cute. A silly grin masked his face as he made his way to her.

Paul pulled her to shore, a little more like a man swimming with his girlfriend than rescuing a drowning victim. He lifted Rhees' listless body from the water and carried her to the waiting blanket he noticed as soon as they hit the beach.

He grinned, wondering how she'd managed to pull this off without his knowledge. The boat headed off toward the intended dive site, leaving them alone. Apparently, one or more people at the shop were confused as to where their loyalty should be, but he didn't mind, and he didn't blame anyone. People who knew Rhees well enough simply seemed to slip naturally into nurturing or protective roles.

He watched for a second, wondering how far she expected him to take it since it wasn't really a training exercise. He pretended to check her breathing, and she held her breath.

"Oh no, the victim's not breathing. I'd better try mouth-to-mouth." He grinned and leaned over her. "Wake up, Sleeping Beauty." He grazed her mouth softly with his teeth.

Her arms snaked around his neck, and she pulled him to her, kissing him back. He slipped a hand around her waist, the other into her hair and he kissed her hard, with more enthusiasm than usual.

"Mm . . ." Paul said—if you could call that saying something—it spoke plenty to Rhees, and she gasped, afraid the fear her nerves imposed could derail her desires. She had plenty of concerns, but she really wanted this. She concentrated on the way she loved how he touched her, the way he tasted, how he made her feel, in her heart—and her *body*. She'd never thought about a man, any man, the way she'd been thinking of Paul. She wanted this. She wanted him.

He paused for a half a second, looking uncertain, but she pulled him back to her lips, persuading his mouth with her tongue. She didn't want to delicately tease him the way he'd been kissing her since she'd complained about being assaulted with his tongue. She wanted to be assaulted.

She wore her new coral bikini, no camisole, and the skin-to-skin, belly-to-belly, contact lured Paul, beckoning him to that sweet paradise that had always swept him away. He returned her signal by tackling her mouth with a vengeance. She boldly countered with her hips, twisting them to meet him square on, a move that made him forget who he was with and yet remember all too well—the pent up energy, emotion, and desire since the zip line, the night in the hotel room, five months of abstinence in spite of sleeping next to the most beautiful woman he'd ever known. He shifted, and she landed on top of him in one quick move. He held her to him as close as he could get her.

She didn't let up, taking as much as he wanted to give as his hands made their way down. He squeezed her butt with both hands, drawing her apart at the seam. He growled, imagining what he could do with that. His finger skimmed along the gap, over her swimsuit, and he hissed through clenched teeth.

His fingers effortlessly found their way inside her suit, *sliding* along—

Rhees wouldn't have thought it humanly possible for him to be under her, in her arms one second, doing unspeakable things to her, and a split second later, be twenty feet away, pacing and cursing aloud, throwing an ugly tantrum. It was all a blur—and a stab to her heart.

"I. Am. So. Sorry!" He finally stopped long enough to speak to her instead of swearing at the sand beneath his feet. He looked down again and scrubbed the back of his neck with his hand.

"Paul," she called, but he didn't listen, too distraught and busy cursing himself.

"I can't remember what we did that night, but *He* does and now he wants more. I promise, I haven't been drinking, but—*He's* out of control. I'm sorry, I don't know what's happening to me."

"Paul, listen." Rhees sat up on her knees. "Will you please stop freaking out and listen to me?" She scolded him to snap him out of his own world of misery. It got his attention. "Sit! We need to talk." She patted the blanket next to her.

"I can't."

"Get over here!"

He made the distance back to her and sat, unenthusiastically, a few feet away so they wouldn't be touching. She rolled her eyes.

"Why do you think we're here?" She swept her hand, gesturing that she meant the caye. "All alone?"

He shook his head, watching her.

"Instead of trying to pretend like there is no elephant in the room, how about we just invite it to stay? I've been thinking, a lot, about that night and . . . Paul, I don't think it was just '*He*'."

"He?"

She blushed. "You always call your penis, *He*."

"Oh." Paul looked down, embarrassed. "Yeah."

"Maybe it's time—maybe we're just ready. Maybe the other night was simply a natural progression, and there's nothing wrong with that. I think we should go with it and see what happens."

"I can't believe you just said that." Paul tried not to laugh, but it wasn't easy. "Do you know how badly I've wanted to hear you say it? But now that you have, it doesn't feel right. Dani Girl . . . I appreciate the gesture, but it's not right."

"I think it is. That morning—when you said we didn't. I felt so disappointed. I wished we had."

"Because you would have been happy to have it 'over with' while you were too drunk to care." He sighed loudly and fell on his back.

She followed his example. After a minute, he rolled onto his side and rested his head on his outstretched arm, watching her. Again, she did what he did, and they faced each other. He smiled warmly as he watched her for another minute.

"We still have your second twenty-ninth birthday, remember?" He forced a smile, wanting to lighten the mood. "You said once that your favorite thing about Christmas was the anticipation, that you didn't understand why some people sneak around, secretly opening their presents. You think the waiting is what makes it special. Let's just enjoy the anticipation."

She thought it sweet he remembered a conversation they'd had so long ago. "This isn't the same. *I* like the anticipation. You, on the other hand, said it drove you crazy. You were one of those people. You were the one who sneaked around, secretly opening your presents because you couldn't wait."

He looked guilty.

"I want to be the present. I'm offering myself, telling you it's okay to open me early." He burst out laughing, so she did too.

"Wow." He laughed a few more seconds but slowly shifted to a more serious mood. "Aw, Dani Girl." He scrunched up his beautiful face and closed his eyes. He worked his mouth a little. "You're not ready."

She didn't want to be offended, but she couldn't help it. She couldn't bring herself to look at him. "Unless you're psychic or something, you can't possibly know that."

He stroked the side of her face, trying to bring her back. It didn't work, so he leaned over her, trying to make her look at him, the concern unmistakable in his expression.

"Not too long ago, you completely lost it, just because Taylor wanted to give you a hug."

"I'm not trying to convince *Taylor* to make love to me!" She tried to laugh to hide the sting of what felt like rejection. "I haven't *lost it* on you for months."

The truth of it made him look worried and he rolled onto his back to look up at the sky.

"Geeminy! You really aren't interested, are you?" She sat up and scooted away so her back was to him, purposely putting a little space between them.

Paul raised the fingers he'd had on her to his nose and breathed it in, savoring the lingering scent.

"You're closer than you were last time." He shook his head to clear his wayward thoughts. "*Gawd*, girl! I *know* you're closer than you were that night on the deck—but I can't. I *could*, easily. I just don't want to—no. I *wawnt* to, I just . . . *Gawd*, I don't know what the hell I'm trying to say."

He'd thought about having her, dreamed of it, almost obsessively at times. But the stronger his feelings for her grew, the more he didn't really want her to lower her standards for him. The thought of her being with him didn't sound right, sounded dirty, dirtier than the way he'd ever thought of sex before.

He wasn't worthy of her. She was so pure—he was anything but. And then there were the fantasies that stopped cold with the thought of her being repulsed, pushing him away, screaming for him to stop. He didn't know if he could handle that. Being rejected by her would . . . *hurt*. More than he cared to admit.

Finally, he feared losing control. He thought himself

an animal. She'd said she wanted him before but changed her mind. Luckily, he'd gone into it expecting to stop, but he couldn't guarantee he could do that every time—*again*. Not now, not with the way he felt for her. If he reached the point of no return, but she wanted to return.

"It's better to wait."

"I'm done waiting!" She exhaled a loud, angry breath.

"You made yourself a promise to wait. I made myself a promise to get you off this island—" He made a face. "—the same way you came." If he really meant it, she'd be gone already, but instead, he'd kept her there at every turn, and she'd already changed because of him. She shouldn't be asking this of him. She would never ask if not for his bad influence.

"Yeeaah. I made that promise before I knew you were going to come along and turn my world upside down. If I'd known, I would have marked this day on my calendar."

She made him smile. He liked the sound of it, but he didn't think he should.

"I wasn't ready last time. You were right, *then*, but it's different now. I haven't freaked out on you for quite a while. I absolutely, positively, do not freak out when you touch me, *now*." She turned her body to face him. "I'm ready. I'm really ready. I want this. Paul, I *wawnt* you!"

"Please, don't say that." He rolled onto his back again. "Rhees. This is hard for me, but the truth is, I don't want you to give up . . . not for me. You've been waiting for Mr. Right—I'm everything wrong."

She looked like a rock, no, a boulder, just dropped into the pit of her stomach. Or was it her heart? This conversation continued to get worse and worse, and he felt terrible.

"I like how innocent you are. I could never forgive myself if I selfishly robbed you of one of the things that make you so special."

She turned away again, huffing and puffing out little humorless laughs. "At home, all the boys joke about girls who are *special*. It means they think a girl's nice but *no one* really wants to . . ." She didn't finish.

"Part of me still holds out on the hope that you'll go back to Utah and meet a nice boy—someone more like you, someone good and innocent, someone who *deserves* you. That someone isn't me. I'm too selfish and self-centered. It would be greed and lust, and I want more for you. I want you to have your happily ever after, the way you've always hoped it would be."

Saying the words was hard, believing them another thing entirely. The thought of her with anyone else drove him insane.

"You, apparently, know nothing about what I want. I've told you how I feel about Utah. There's nothing there for me, and those *nice* boys don't want me. They never have, never will. I never want to go back!"

"You'll come to your senses and realize I'm right."

"Paul!" She crawled back to be close again and snuggled up to him, wrapping an arm and leg around him, desperately claiming him, and he responded by resting his arms lightly around her waist. She looked into his eyes, pleading.

"Don't say things like that, please." She fought back tears. She didn't want to cry. "I don't expect you to feel the same way, and I can live with that, but I thought you wanted me. I'll take whatever you can give. You give me more than you realize. I want to be with you, be close to you. I want to be intimate with you. Paul . . . I *love* you!"

"Jesus!" Again, Paul jumped up and away from her so fast it left her dazed. He stood staring at her in utter shock. "What the hell is wrong with you?"

"Nothing is wrong with me. I didn't mean to feel this way, it just happened. I can't help it. I love you."

"No!" He cursed and started knocking his forehead against the palms of his hands. "No! No, you don't—you can't!"

"I do." She choked back tears. His reaction hurt. "I love you." She sat up straighter. "It isn't enough for me to say it.

I want to show you. That makes you the perfect man—you said yourself you were the perfect man for the job. I want you."

"I didn't give a fuck about you then," he growled. "All I wanted was to get inside your panties."

"I don't believe that."

"You'd better believe that," he snorted incredulously. "That is exactly the kind of man I was."

"Was!" she yelled back, jumping up. She tried to get close to him. She wanted to calm him, convince him, but he kept moving away from her. She finally stopped chasing him and folded her arms, something she did when she began to feel the need to get away.

"*Was*, is the word of the day. I don't believe you are as bad as you always think you are." She spoke calmly and more quietly than before.

"Oh my God!" He ran both hands through his hair and then threw them in the air, glaring at her accusingly. His tone escalated. "You are so gullible! Just what do you think that was . . . the night at the hotel?"

"Us! Having feelings for each other." She moved back to the blanket and sat down. She pulled her legs to her chest. Phase two of her retreat.

"Look how well that turned out!" he said recklessly.

"You said you'd stopped pretending. You said you love me."

"I never said that!" He staggered, taken aback, but the look on his face showed he wasn't completely convinced he hadn't.

"It was right after you said you weren't pretending anymore. Before I got in the van to go shopping, you said, 'Love you', as though you said it every day of the week." She watched him squirm, fidgeting as though he wanted to crawl out of his skin.

He pinched the bridge of his nose and made a few agonized faces.

"I thought we'd moved forward." She closed her eyes. "You don't want me either. I get it. I don't know why I'm surprised."

Paul knew Rhees well enough to recognize the signs, but he desperately needed to think of a way to turn things back, to save her from him. He couldn't do that *and* take away the pain he'd caused her, continued to cause her.

"You can't love me. Rhees. Don't waste yourself on me, I'm not worth it—I'm not worthy of you."

"Stop it. Just stop it!" she screamed. "You're only saying that because it's easier than admitting what the fuck is really going on here." She closed her eyes and puckered her mouth. Her lips trembled. She'd reached her limit, and she attacked. It didn't happen often, but he'd learned that when she did—she let loose and inserted more swear words than even Paul could have.

"Apparently, you'll sleep with anything that has a God-damned vagina . . . except me. Shit! Maybe I *should* go find Taylor."

"Rhees, don't."

"He's not as picky as you are. He said if I really wanted you, I should fuck him first. He said you *like* it that way—I think he's wrong. You still wouldn't want me, but shit! Actually—" She laughed eerily and acted like she'd just come up with a brilliant idea. "Mario wanted to fuck me too. Maybe he still does! Do you think the prison has a conjugal visiting program?"

"Just stop it! You're being . . . *redonkulous.*"

"Pfft! The pot calling the kettle black," she yelled. She finally looked out over the water, trying to catch her breath.

He took a deep breath and let it out, wretchedly. He hung his head and both stood quietly for a minute.

"Rhees . . . look at me." He sounded hoarse and cleared his throat.

"Why, so you can glamour me?" She laughed jadedly, and looked everywhere except at him. "So you can use your magical eyes to make all this go away—make me forget how I feel about you so that I'll stop complicating—fucking up your life?"

She finally mustered the courage to look at him straight on. His eyes shined, but not with their usual sparkle. Sadness.

"Do it! Glamour me—I want to forget."

"Rhees . . . I told you I have a dark past." He glanced down at the ground. "You deserve so much better."

She folded her arms again and braced herself for the bad news she knew was coming. He finally looked back up at her.

"I do love you." The desolate look in his red-rimmed eyes deepened as the words spewed out like a death sentence. "I love you. I shouldn't—I've been denying it because it's so wrong, but—" His eyes were wet, the tears pooled, ready to overflow, but they didn't. "I love you too much to defile you."

She gasped for air as she staggered away from him. She stopped at the edge of the water and looked out across the channel. He watched the strain on her face grow heavier and heavier as she tried too hard not to cry. She zoned out and didn't hear anything he said after that, until she reached down for her gear and headed back toward the water. She waded in until the water lapped at her waist. She put her mask on and slipped into her fins.

"Rhees," he called, wading in after her. He gently caressed her arm. "What are you doing? Remember what I said about the current?"

"I need time to think," she snapped, yanking her arm away from him. She put her face in the water and started kicking. She headed south, sticking to the shoreline as he watched her, warily.

"Please don't run from me. You always run," he called after her. She didn't stop. He threw his hands up behind his head and paced a little, disgusted with himself, worried about her. He realized how much better off she'd be if she would've run from him long ago, but he'd let his selfishness get in the way. He always did.

His jaw set tight and his mouth twitched, frantic to

think of something to say to make her come back—make it all better. She swam farther and farther away from him, but she hugged the shoreline, so he sat down and let her have the time she'd asked for.

He leaned back on his hands and let the sun absorb into his soul while he waited for her to come back, trying to figure out what he could say to her when she did. When he finally opened his eyes again, he looked to check on her. She wasn't near where she'd been the last time he saw her.

"Rhees!" he shouted. He jumped to his feet and looked around. It took him a second, but he shifted into full panic mode.

He finally spotted her halfway across the channel. It looked like she'd swam south for some distance and now cut across at an angle toward the island, trying to counteract the current, but the flow was too much for her. He tried to calculate the distance she had left and the rate at which she swam. She would miss the island and was in danger of being carried out to sea, but she didn't stop.

"Oh God, no," he prayed. Without hesitation, he started out into the water after her. He swam for his life, but he didn't have fins. When he reached the current, it pulled him north faster than it took Rhees. He'd never reach her. He turned back and swam until the worst of the current released him. He treaded water, waiting.

He'd become painfully aware he couldn't save her. She would miss the island, of that he was sure. She was already too far across for him to get to her, so he calculated again and waited for her to drift into a better position. He'd try again when the current took her a little farther north. He couldn't save her, but he would at least be able to keep her company until search and rescue found them—or they drowned. But they would be together.

He watched, without realizing how he held his breath. He let out a loud sob, a sign of his relief, when he watched her miraculously reach the large rock outcrop fifteen meters off the tip of the main island. Her hands frantically grasped for a hold as the current carried her by. Her fingers took hold and she hung on for dear life, catching her breath. Paul turned and made his way back to Duna.

"She made it!" he choked out. He collapsed on his knees within a few feet of the beach and dragged himself up out of the water. He stood as soon as he found the strength to haul himself onto his feet and look back. "She made it." He laughed giddily with relief. "She's tired. That's good."

Paul knew, even though it was only a short distance, the current flowed strong between the rock and the north shore of the island. He assured himself she was too tired and too scared to attempt to swim the rest of the way.

"Hang on Baby. Wait for the boat. We'll get you," he said, willing her to listen to him even though she'd never hear him across the distance.

His hope dashed to pieces when he noticed her pulling herself around, hand over hand, to the other side of the rock. He couldn't see her anymore, but he said another prayer, understanding she had no intention of staying on the rock.

"Damn it, Baby! Just stay put!" Too late. He saw her seconds later, making a swim for the island. He bent forward, resting his hands on his knees, concentrating on his breathing. He paced, clasping his hands behind his head, shifting from cursing to praying back to cursing again. It felt like a lifetime, but she finally dragged herself out of the water and collapsed on the sand. She'd made it.

Paul fell to his knees, exhausted from his attempt to swim, and even more weary from the weight of fear. He watched her remove her fins and pull herself up to stand. She turned to look at him, too far away for him to see her expression. He longed—needed—to see her expression. The image of her standing there, holding her fins, staring at him across the channel, haunted him. He had the feeling she'd just taken her one last look before she walked into the jungle and disappeared. He withered.

He dashed away the tears that fell down his cheeks. Was he crying? He couldn't believe he was crying. The dreadful fear, watching her try to kill herself, and the knowledge he'd been helpless to do anything about it had just about done him in. Love sucked—big time—just like he'd always believed it would. So why couldn't he turn it off? He wished he could, but—impossible. He needed to concentrate on a different emotion.

Now that he knew she was safe, he allowed his concern for her to be replaced with anger. Anger was easier. He planned every word of the scolding he planned to give Rhees while he waited for Randy.

oOo

Paul swam out to meet the boat and didn't wait for anyone to let the ladder down. He grabbed the rail and pulled himself in, yelling, "Get me to the other side."

"Where's Rhees?" several people asked.

"She swam the channel," he muttered, and climbed out to the bow. He stood, watching the tree line as they crossed the channel, looking for any sign of her.

Randy beached the boat on the sand and Paul called for her. He jumped off and pushed the boat back into the water before he jogged south along the shore, looking into the trees, calling out to her. Randy followed along the edge of the island while everyone on board speculated about what was happening.

It took some time, more time than the people on the boat had patience for. They were anxious to get back to the shop, but no one dared say anything. Paul reached the small development of beach homes on the otherwise deserted end of the island. He spoke for a few minutes to the only man he could find, and Paul finally motioned for Randy to pull the boat up to the small pier. He hopped onto the bow.

"Let's go. She hitched a ride on Carl's water taxi." A stoic Paul slapped the roof of the boat a couple of times, anxious to get under way.

Randy backed the boat out away from the pier, but when he pushed the throttle forward, the boat's motor died. Paul didn't mean to give Randy the killer glare as he tried to start the engine again and again, and Randy seemed to know Paul's glare was meant for the boat, not him.

The Tow'd had done it again. They were dead in the water.

Chapter 25

Claire stood in the doorway of the office and watched Paul jump ship. He swam the last two hundred feet to the shop, making it faster than the tow boat could get *The Tow'd* to dock. She stepped inside, anticipating his arrival. He ran into the office, dripping wet.

"Where is she?" he huffed, still breathing hard.

Claire had been waiting for him, crying. She turned on him.

"You bloody wanker! What did you do to her?"

"Where is she?" he yelled this time.

Claire backed away a step, recognizing his anger. "I don't know where she is *now*. She's leaving. I don't know if she made the last plane or not." Claire watched the blood drain from his face.

"She's leaving?" He ran his hand through his hair, looking unsure all of a sudden. Claire remembered the day he'd called her from Costa Rica. This time, she witnessed him falling apart in person. She put her hand on his arm.

"Paul. What happened?" she whispered.

"She's leaving?" he said again, in a daze. He slumped against the wall and put his hands to his face.

"*Why* is she leaving? Paul?" He didn't answer. "Paul! Damn it. Why is she leaving?" Claire used her stern, motherly tone.

Paul finally moved his hands and looked down at her like he'd only just noticed her there. He puckered his mouth. "She wanted me to have her."

"And . . .?"

"I said no. I couldn't do that to her—she doesn't really want me to do that. She wants to wait for the man who'll marry her. I made a promise." He scrubbed his hand over his face and then rubbed the back of his neck. "She said she loves me," he said dismissively, believing it couldn't possibly be true.

"Of course she does. And you love her."

He stared at Claire, blankly.

"It's not a secret." She snorted, amused at how she seemed to be the only person who knew. "You've been in love with her since the day she came rolling her gigantic duffle bag down the Plank. I still remember the look on your face as you stood right there." Claire pointed to the spot in front of the window. "You were in awe, and you told me, 'We have a visitor from the royal family'. I'd never seen you look at anyone like that before."

He looked lost, confused.

"Paul. You love her. She loves you."

"Love." Paul closed his eyes and let his mouth twitch.

"Yesss," Claire said slowly. "Keep up Paul. She wants a grown-up relationship. Give her one."

"I can't do that," he barked as his eyes popped open. He took a second to calm himself and his voice turned accepting. "I don't deserve her."

"Of course you don't." He shot her a confused but acknowledging glance. "But she doesn't agree. She loves you—the barmy lass actually loves you, and I don't get to tell her heart what to feel—neither do you."

"Pfft."

"You'd rather watch her walk away?"

His eyes grew wide, and then narrowed just as fast. "I can't let her compromise herself for me."

"Good." Claire almost smiled. "She'll be just fine without you."

The look on his face . . .

"She collects nurturers. It's a talent. She's got me—*me*, the anti-nurture woman—looking after her like she's my own kid—I hate kids. I hate needy people. And yet, she's got me *so* looking out for her. She'll be fine. She'll leave here, with a broken heart, but she'll find someone else to look after her—of course, *you* can take care of her better than anyone else—"

He met her eyes, challenging her statement.

"Oh, come on. You know what I'm talking about. You have the means, the whole alpha male thing going for you—the killer instinct. And you love her enough to use it all if she needs it, no holds barred." Claire checked the effect she had on him. "She'd be better off with *you*, but she'll be fine—eventually."

"She will, won't she," he said.

"She'll be married in less than two years."

"Jesus!" He leaned over, rested his elbows on his own knees, overwhelmed. He wondered if he'd cry, again. He hadn't cried since preschool, but this would be twice in one day. "I don't know how I'll breathe without her."

"Are you afraid you're going to stop loving her—is that it?"

He glared at her like she was crazy. "Stop loving her." He humphed and shook his head. "My God, I can't imagine not loving her—ever." He took a second to backtrack. "But she needs someone who can marry her. It's that simple."

"Hmm," Claire said. "You love her, but you want her to find someone who'll marry her, even though you know you'll love her forever and you don't want to live without her. She's always been in love with the idea of marriage, but now she loves *you* even more. She wants to be with you for as long as you'll have her."

It took him a minute, but— "*Aww . . . shit.*"

They both froze, staring at each other as they heard the drone of the afternoon plane take off from the middle of the island.

"Rhees!" they both said at the same time.

Paul jerked up straight and ran out the door, but his hand grabbed hold of the jamb at the last second. He used the leverage to pull himself back into the office where he proceeded to give Claire a long, grateful kiss on the cheek.

"Thank you. I love you! You know that, right?"

Dobbs came through the tunnel at that moment. "What the . . . get your hands . . . and your *mouth* off my wife!"

Paul let go of Claire and pointed his fingers at Dobbs with both hands, animated with anticipation. "I freakin' love your wife, man!" And he was gone.

oOo

Paul ran next door to Randy's and didn't stop to knock. "Randy, I need your bike." He ran straight through the house and out the back door as Randy and his wife sat on the couch, shaking their heads.

Paul pushed the motorcycle to the street, started the motor, and was on his way toward Rhees' place, full throttle. When he reached Oceanside, he killed the motor, jumped off at a run and leaned the bike against the fence before it stopped sputtering. He ran around the yard and up the stairs three at a time, yelling Rhees' name.

Rhees lay folded into a ball on her bed, weeping. Her windows were open, so she was careful not to cry so loud the other tenants would hear. She managed to keep the sound down, but she couldn't control the convulsions as the tears flowed freely.

She'd made it home, and it was all she could do to get packed before she buckled onto her bed, sobbing into Paul's pillow, hugging it and breathing in his scent, knowing it would be the last time.

"Rhees!"

"Oh no! Paul." She couldn't believe it. She looked at the clock and noticed more time had passed than she'd realized. Panic set in. She should have known, but she wasn't ready. She'd wanted to make a clean get-away. No more confrontations, no more talking. She wanted to walk away and get started on the miserable rest of her life. She should have known Paul wasn't the type of man to let her do this her way.

"Crap!"

She jumped up and scurried around the room in a panic. She double-checked. The padlock hung on her bedroom door, not locked, but it hung, holding the lock hinge in place. She thought about hiding behind the door, but Paul would know she had to be home by the fact the lock was on the inside. It would be stupid to pretend she wasn't home.

"Rhees!" he called, sounding closer than before. She heard him on the stairs. He was coming. She did the only thing she could think of. She bolted for the bathroom and threw the shower on. She waited, huddled in the bathroom. Her heart pounded. She thought she'd be sick.

"Rhees!" he called, from just outside her window.

She held her breath, as if he'd be able to hear it if she didn't.

"Rhees, open the door. We need to talk."

She ignored him and planned to wait him out.

"Come on, Rhees." His voice grew louder. "I'm coming in."

"Crap!" She panicked again. Two doors with locks stood between them. She took comfort. He couldn't get in. She relaxed a little, feeling safe, until she heard a loud crack. "Shit!" she mouthed. He'd just forced his way through the screen door. *He's coming.*

She tore her swimming suit off, tossed it onto her bed and jumped into the shower just as she felt the building shake and she heard a thunderous boom. She turned her back to the bathroom door, giving herself a fantasy impression that if she couldn't see him, he wouldn't see her. She slipped her head back into the water.

"Arrgh!" The sound slipped out as the cold water hit her back, stunning her the way it always did. She thought she heard Paul chuckle, but couldn't be completely sure it wasn't just her heart trying to beat its way out of her chest.

oOo

The screen door didn't give Paul much of a fight. He'd always suspected it wouldn't do much to keep a determined intruder out. Rhees' door was another story. He knocked to give her a chance to open it. He thought he heard the shower.

"Rhees, open the door. I swear I'll break it down." He waited three more seconds. "If you're there, please move, I'm coming in and I don't want you to get hurt."

He took a second to study the door, calculating where the weakest point would be. He exhaled a deeply rooted growl and drove his foot near the hinge of the lock. Hyped up on nerves and adrenaline, he intended to talk to her and wasn't about to let an insignificant slab of wood stand in his way. The door swung open wildly, taking a big chunk of the doorjamb with it, slamming with a thud on the wall behind it. He stood looking for her, but found only an empty room as splinters fell around him.

He heard water running, and then he heard her gasp the way she always did when she stepped into the cold shower. It made him chuckle, in spite of his ever building exasperation.

He looked around on his way to the bathroom. She'd stripped the room of all her personal possessions. Her suitcase and backpack sat on the twin bed, packed and ready to go. He winced and reminded himself to feel lucky she'd missed the three o'clock plane.

A few T-shirts, two e-readers, and an assortment of things, *his* things, lay neatly piled on the desk. The velvet jewelry box with the necklace he'd given her sat on top of the pile, next to a folded piece of paper bearing his name. He opened it up and read.

As much as I love the necklace
(DO NOT TRY TO TELL ME I DON'T!!!)
Wearing it will only make me think of you.
I know how much you hate when women cry,
so keep it.

He sighed, letting his shoulders drop as he looked up at the ceiling, thinking of what a mess the whole thing had become. He looked around the room again, wondering how he was going to smooth this over. He noticed the other bed, their bed. She'd been lying on it, he could tell by the indent in the sheets, and then he saw the wet spot. She'd been crying, crying on *his* pillow. He touched it and frowned.

It stabbed at his heart to know he'd caused her so much pain. It devastated him to know he was the reason she'd cried, the reason she'd risked her life—He deadpanned as the memory of her stupid stunt hit him in the face. Every swear word he could think of coursed through his mind.

How the hell could she do that to him? She wasn't the only one aching from the crushing emotions their conversation had triggered. She'd admitted she loved him. Some love—if she really believed she could just walk away. He looked at the tear stain again. He knew it was selfish to feel a little satisfaction at seeing it, but it meant she didn't want to leave any more than he wanted her to, at least, he clung to that hope, but he wasn't letting her off the hook so easily.

He turned and looked into the bathroom. He slowly reached and moved the shower curtain, just far enough to see her inside. She stood very still, her back turned to him, shampoo rolling out of her hair and down her back. She didn't give any indication she knew he was there.

He closed his eyes, and using every bit of self-control he barely had left, he stepped away. Seeing her like that tempted him to watch and wait for her to turn around. He wanted to see her face, her eyes, her reaction when she saw him, but he decided against it. He was angry, and she was beautiful, and naked, and he wasn't sure at the moment that he could keep himself from joining her and giving her what she'd asked for.

That's when it hit him just how much he *really* did love her, no more reluctance, wavering, or confusion. Instead of fostering the anger, the way he usually did about everything, he'd already started making excuses for her. Her dreams now felt like his, and he planned to do everything in his power to make them all come true.

oOo

Rhees trembled, half expecting Paul to drag her out of the shower any second. If he was angry, he wouldn't care about discretion. She knew he'd forced his way into her apartment. He was there, somewhere. She kept her back turned to the opening between the bedroom and bathroom, pretending as though, as long as she didn't turn to look, nothing could happen. She hated not knowing what to expect.

She imagined him ripping the shower curtain open, leaving her standing naked and exposed—vulnerable— while he gaped at her, demanding an explanation of her stupid stunt. She still couldn't believe she hadn't killed herself earlier by swimming the channel. When she'd first set out to do it, part of her believed she would die.

Miraculously, she didn't. No, she'd lived and now she'd missed the last plane of the day. After all her effort, her attempts to get away, she'd still have to deal with Paul. How did she end up naked in the shower while her, what she'd always considered her very own time bomb, lurked right outside? She loved that about him, his ability to do whatever it took, no matter the situation. But she didn't like it right now. That quality about him that had always made her feel safe had now become her worst nightmare.

That's what she got for being a coward. If she hadn't panicked, if she'd just had the courage to face him, she wouldn't be in this predicament. She wished she could turn the clock back. She should have just met him at the screen door and stood her ground.

Nothing happened. No yelling, no ripping the shower curtain open. She couldn't believe it. It wasn't like him to show so much patience in such charged circumstances. He was a doer. Why didn't he do something? The thought occurred to her—he didn't care enough about her to do anything. She stifled the sob trying to squeeze its way out.

She didn't want him to hear it. Maybe he'd given up and left.

The shampoo she'd thrown in her hair, to put on a convincing show in case he looked, had rinsed clean. She slowly turned around and tried to see through the slit between the curtain and the wall—nothing. She hesitated before turning off the water. She still wasn't ready for another dreadful confrontation, *if* he hadn't left. If he had, it hurt to think he wouldn't fight for her, but either way, she couldn't stand the blasted cold water another second.

"Aw, shit!" She stood in the shower, remembering she'd packed her towel, and then she thought about how much Paul had forever impacted her life as it hit her what she'd just said. "Aw shit?" she whispered to herself.

She threw her head back in dismay. The towel was a stupid oversight. She stepped out, dripping wet, and squeezed the water out of her hair over the sink. She stared at herself in the mirror, not liking the stupid girl staring back. She'd been a fool to think a man like Paul could ever love her. It made her angry with herself, but the anger bolstered her courage.

She steeled herself and with her head held high, she stepped into her bedroom, naked. Her false courage deflated instantly the second she saw the shattered door. She stood, wavering, trying to make her feet work, to run back into the bathroom, but then her eyes landed on Paul. He lay diagonal across the twin bed, leaning his shoulder and head against the wall. He looked so casual, as if he broke doors down every day of the week.

She saw his eyes widen at the sight of her standing before him, nude and wet, but the shock faded fast and he switched to pretending not to notice. She squared her shoulders, too late to hide, he'd seen her.

"You broke my door." Her voice sounded flat and cold.

"You didn't open it." He met her cool reserve with his own, but his facial tick gave him away. He was as nervous and as scared as she. "I'll fix it," he said in the same flat tone she'd used.

He tried so hard, *too* hard, not to look at her. He'd seen thousands of naked women so she didn't understand why seeing her made him so uncomfortable. Still holding her head up with feigned confidence, she moved toward her suitcase, sitting right next to him. She unzipped it and started rummaging through her things, looking for her towel. She needed to get dry and dressed.

"You'll *have* to fix it. I won't be here," she said, still trying to find her towel. Under normal circumstances, it wouldn't have been so hard to dig it out of the bag, but she was nervous, and scared too, trying to act as though standing naked in front of a man was normal for her.

"Running away?" he asked. "Typical," he said under his breath. "That's a surprise—back to Utah?"

"No."

He cocked his head to one side, suddenly confused, and she braced herself for his reaction to her answer.

"California," she said, as cool and collected as she could.

He sat up, the, *who can keep their cool the longest,* act, apparently over. "California!" he exploded. "The hell you are!"

She refused to look at him. Her trembling grew worse. "My decision seems to disagree with you."

"You know it does. How could you even think about going to California? That's crazy—you need to go home."

"I have no home!" That did it. Tears flooded her eyes. She pursed her lips and glared at him until she resumed her focus on the task at hand. She finally found the towel buried at the bottom of her bag and tugged, but it hung up on the tank clip of her BC. She cursed her decision to drag her gear all the way back to her apartment after all. She'd considered leaving it, not wanting the reminder of her time on the island—it would be a constant reminder of him. Apparently she liked torturing herself.

Paul watched her struggle with it long enough. He let out a frustrated breath and stood to help. She moved out of his way, giving him the room to grab hold and pull it out. He draped it around her shoulders, finally giving her some cover.

"Were you doing that on purpose?" he asked, his voice hoarse and quiet.

"Yes, I'm going to California on purpose. How many times do I have to fucking tell you? There's nothing for me in Utah."

"That's not what I meant." His lips twitched. "You were jiggling your boobs in my face. Were you doing it on purpose?" He frowned.

She flushed pale. "I didn't expect you to come busting in here like a mad man. I just got out of the shower. I didn't realize I'd already packed my towel, and . . . I'm happy to see *you're* just fine with the state of things, but *I'm* feeling a little out of sorts. You're not supposed to be here!"

He hung his head.

"No!" she whispered. "I had no idea my boobs were *jiggling* in your face!" She ran into the bathroom.

He closed his eyes. This wasn't going well, and he continued to make her miserable. He thought it selfish of him to hope to do that to her for the rest of her life. He stood, stumped, waiting for her to return, but she never did.

"Rhees, you okay?" he asked humbly.

She didn't answer. He looked around, unsure what to do. He noticed her orange blouse in the suitcase, the one she'd worn the day she first stepped into his life. He ran his fingers over the fabric, put it to his face and stroked his cheek with it a few times, smelled it.

He realized why she hadn't come out of the bathroom and rummaged through her bag until he found a pair of white shorts to go with the shirt. After a second of hesitation, he grabbed a pair of panties and a bra from the bag as well, and walked to the bathroom door.

"Here." He held the clothing out for her to take, trying not to look at her more than necessary.

She leaned against the wall next to the sink, her

head down. She'd wrapped the towel around her, but she looked lost, like she didn't know what to do. She didn't acknowledge him.

"Come on, Baby." He tried to sound reassuring as he stood, offering the clothes, but she didn't move. He finally set them down on the bed and reached for her hand, gently urging her into the bedroom. He put his arms around her shoulders and held her for a minute, with no reaction from her. "I'm sorry."

She stood, almost catatonic, and mindlessly let him take her towel. He focused his attention on his actions, and not on her body, as he took the bra and slipped her arms through the straps. He reached behind her to fasten the clasps.

He picked her panties up from the bed and closed his eyes as he bent over to guide her feet, one by one, and pulled them up into place. He repeated the process with her shorts.

"Raise your arms," he said softly, and steered the sleeves of her shirt over her hands and pulled it down. He took care adjusting it, and she was dressed.

"I love this shirt," he murmured, rubbing the fabric tenderly between his fingers. "You never wear it anymore."

"It's starting to look worn," her voice rasped. "I've been saving it for special occasions."

He stood so close, breathing in the smell of her freshly washed hair. His hands caressed up and down her arms. He rested his forehead against hers.

"I love you," he finally said, watching her face.

She looked down, away.

He repeated it.

"So you get to feel that way, but I don't."

He lowered his eyes, looking like a lost little boy.

"You'd be better off if you didn't, but I won't tell you not to say it again." He closed his eyes. "It sounds too good—frightening as hell—but so, so good. I love you," he said again.

She looked up and groaned. "I know—too much to *defile*

me. I remember! You won't make love to me because then I'll be damaged goods. Is that why you need a different woman every night? You don't like to touch what you've touched before?" She shook her head at him. "Pfft! And I thought I was the one with germ issues."

Paul didn't mean to, but he laughed at how she'd misinterpreted what he'd said.

"That's not what I—"

"Oh, and I guess I wouldn't be the life of the party anymore, the court jester. If I'm no longer ignorant on the subject, I won't be able to keep you so amused with all my stupid naïve antics. 'Why do you have to be so damned cute'?" she mocked. She tried to get by him, going for her suitcase. "I have a ferry to catch."

He rolled his eyes and threw out his arm, catching her around the shoulders. He pulled her into him, standing behind her.

"Don't," she huffed and turned her head, trying to get away, but he took advantage of her exposed neck and kissed it from the base of her neck, up to her chin.

"I meant what I said in the context of me being the defiler, not you being anything but better off if you'd never crossed my path."

"Are you trying to make me feel better?" She turned her head to look at him with angry eyes.

"I love you," he said, trying to stay on track in spite of her ability to turn everything upside down. "I've never said that to anyone before."

"Are you looking for a trophy? Or were you expecting me to organize a banquet in honor of your accomplishment?"

He snorted another non-humorous laugh. "You're *nawt* making this easy. I never meant that it—that you— would be dirty if we . . . I'm the one—I'm dirty, Rhees. I've participated in just about every depraved, self-destructive act imaginable. Well, there're one or two things I didn't quite get to. I had to draw the line somewhere."

He grew frustrated trying to convey his thoughts. "I've managed to sully myself with more stains than the average degenerate can chalk up in a lifetime, so yes, I believe that doing what you wanted today would have been a mistake—can we please just slow this down a bit and really talk?" He planted his lips on her cheek and left them there while he spoke into her skin. "I have something important to ask."

"No." She tried to get away from him again.

He didn't let go. "It'll only take a minute. *Pleease?*"

"Fine!" She turned in his arms and he loosed his grip on her. Things looked a little more hopeful than before. Rhees grabbed his wrist, removed his watch, and sat on the edge of the bed. She held it in her hand, staring at it for a minute.

"When I say go, you have *exactly* one minute. After that, I'm on my way to the ferry. If you try to stop me again, I get violent, understand? You're bigger and stronger than I am, so you'll probably win, as usual, but I promise, if you try to stop me again, you, or I, or both of us, will wind up hurt—" She paused. ". . . *Physically* hurt anyway—the emotional damage is already done."

He felt terrible about the pain he'd caused her.

She locked onto his watch again. "Go."

"I'm sorry," he whispered, standing in front of her at a loss.

"Fifty-five seconds."

"What?"

"Fifty."

He laughed briefly. "I should have thought this through. Give me a minute."

Her eyes shot up from the watch to meet his with an icy glare. "Forty-five."

"Shit," he said. "You're serious!"

"Forty." She looked back at the watch.

"Damn it! I don't have this planned out . . . I've never thought about how I'd do this." He watched her, looking for something, anything.

"Thirty."

"God damn it! Stop counting down."

She gave him a look to suggest his time was running

out—because he'd said to stop counting down.

He panicked. He knelt down in front of her on one knee. "Fuck! I don't know how to do this."

She shook her head, impatiently watching his watch.

"Dani Girl, I love you!"

"Ten," she whispered, faintly.

He stared at her with befuddled eyes. She'd confused him. He panicked and just blurted it out.

"Marry me!"

The watch wasn't working, or Rhees didn't notice it anymore, even though she stared at it. It took forever for her brain to resume working again. She blinked slowly.

"No."

Paul glanced down, stunned, confused.

"That's the wrong answer." He looked back up at her, but she still hadn't taken her eyes off the watch. "Look at me."

"No."

"Why?"

She took a minute to answer. "Because you'll just hypnotize me with your beautiful, sparkly, magical eyes, and then I'll say yes, and then we'll get married, and then you'll hate me for making you think that you had to marry me, when you've always said you never wanted to get married, and then we'll both be miserable, and then you'll leave me, and then you'll be happy, but then I'll be miserable, and—"

He pushed his way between her legs and kissed her to shut her up. She did shut up, but she looked down.

"Look at me. Come on, Dani Girl, look at me," he breathed softly next to her ear and then peppered her cheek with tender kisses all the way back to her lips. "We both know you want to."

She bit back a smile, but turned her head, still refusing to meet his gaze. He leaned up even closer. He pulled her chin around with his finger, but she closed her eyes. He slowly began grazing her jaw with soft, caressing kisses.

"I could never hate you." He kissed the other side of her face the same way. "Look at me," he cooed.

She shook her head, her eyes still closed, but she leaned into his mouth, savoring the way his lips warmed her skin, the way his breath tingled.

"You don't believe in love," she whispered. "You don't want to get married."

"Yeeaah." He took her face between his hands and brushed her lips with his, repeating her own words quietly between kisses. "I decided that before I knew you were going to come along and turn my world upside down. If I'd known, I would have marked this day on my calendar."

"You can't use the same argument you rejected only a few hours ago."

"Yes, I can."

"No, Paul. You can't."

"I can."

"No, you—"

"Just did."

She finally looked at him with narrowed eyes. "You big baby, you don't fight fair."

"Hmm . . . I usually fight to win, but I hope this time . . . we're both winners." He finally had her eyes and he knew he had her. She put her hands behind his neck, he moved his around her waist as they stared into each other's eyes. They both looked frightened and uncertain.

"You'll get tired of being stuck with the same woman for the rest of your life. You're going to get tired of me."

He pondered what she said for a second, but suddenly, he climbed onto the bed. She moved back, away from his advance, but he followed and landed on top of her, pinning her beneath him. He kissed her once.

"Never." He enveloped her in his arms and leaned in. "You are my nectarine."

Wet Part 3 Preview

Chapter 4

"We're here, Baby." Paul softly kissed each of Rhees' closed eyelids. "I can't believe you can sleep right now. You've slept almost the whole way."

He'd waited until the last minute to wake her, after spending the last two hours and forty minutes furiously bouncing his leg and tapping his thigh with his fingers. The anticipation of their destination, his plans, *their* plans, made him wish he could get in a good session of hard, physical exertion to work off his nervous tension.

The bus he'd chartered to get everyone from the capital pulled through the gate of the Historical Park. The ruins where they planned to have the wedding loomed ahead.

"Hmm?" Rhees stirred, raising her arms up in a long stretch before she smirked. "I didn't sleep well last night. My snuggle buddy wouldn't snuggle with me, and to top it off, he shook his leg all night, vibrating the bed—kind of like he's doing now." She opened one eye, her gaze going directly to his bouncing leg.

"Sorry, I couldn't sleep, and I couldn't chance touching you."

"Hmm?"

"Snuggling—I couldn't chance it. I've been a little wound up, but now I'm just so relieved I didn't screw it up."

The bus came to a stop and the driver opened the door. The people in the seats ahead of them, all friends from the island, and a few from the States, made their way off the bus.

"Mmm . . . it's close." She looked up at him and smiled adoringly. He kissed her cheek.

"Yeah, I know." His lips made their way to hers and he kissed her passionately.

"Wow. That's some kiss," she said breathlessly when he finally pulled away.

"I've been holding that in for a while, my promise always in the back of my mind. But I figure I can't get too carried away—well, I fully intend to get too carried away later tonight, *after* I make you a new promise—my vows."

He kissed her again and they both moaned deliciously, pawing at each other as much as possible with a bus seat armrest between them. She finally sighed uneasily, and Paul pulled back to check on her.

"You're scared."

"No." She dropped her gaze. "I'm not freaking out, I promise, but maybe—*maybe,* I am a little nervous."

"I know, and that's okay." He put his hand around the back of her neck and pulled her forehead to his lips. "We'll take it slow. We'll go at a pace you'll be comfortable with." He took her hand in his and brought it to his lips. "It'll be my first time, too."

Her confused eyes darted up to meet his. "Liar." She smiled like she thought he'd only said it to tease her.

"Serious. One hundred percent." He gave her a little more time to be confused, taking a second to enjoy watching her try to figure it out before sharing his recent thoughts.

"As in, your first time in months?" she attempted to clarify.

He shook his head, still with a look on his face to suggest

he had a secret.

"What is on that brilliant mind of yours?"

"Okay." He grinned. "I've had a lot of sex with a lot of women. You know that."

"I don't care about that. You know I don't."

He nodded in agreement.

"I've had *sex*. That's all it's ever been. But tonight will be the first time—" He pressed his lips to her forehead again. "With you—I plan to *make love* to you. It won't be just sex." He paused to clear his throat, and then panted out a laugh, surprised at himself for getting emotional.

"I can't wait to have you, take my time with you, *for* you. I plan to make adoring, tender, glorious love to you, as my wife, my partner for the rest of my life, the most exquisite woman I've ever known, the only woman I've *ever* loved. So yes, my beautiful Danarya, it will be *my* first time, too."

She blinked a few times, never taking her eyes off him. She took a breath, and opened her mouth as if she wanted to say something, but she didn't. Her eyes welled up instead, as she nodded in understanding, before she buried her face into his neck, and they embraced.

"I didn't mean to make you cry."

She shook her head against his shoulder, trying to get a hold of herself. "You're so perfect," she choked out.

"I'm far from perfect." He glanced down, uncomfortable with the description. "I got that out of a fortune cookie."

She let out a half laugh, half sob and they gazed at each other for a second, smiling giddily like two kids overcome with puppy love.

"Not perfect, but I'm better than I was. You've made me a better man than I've ever been."

She reached for his cheek when Taylor's voice broke the spell. They hadn't noticed he'd boarded the bus again and stood, looming over them.

"Glad you two are blissfully in love, but that selfish sentiment has made you oblivious to the rest of us." Taylor and Paul locked eyes as Paul tried to decipher how much his friend had heard. Taylor gave nothing away, but the somber look in his eyes didn't match his words. "We have needs, too. We'd just like to get this mushy stuff over with so we can get drunk and work on finding our *own* destinies. I've seen at least four of the local girls out there, waiting for me to declare my undying love for them . . . behind the storage shed." Taylor laughed.

Rhees made a disgusted noise and Paul rolled his eyes.

"I'll go take care of the last minute details." Paul leaned over to give Rhees a quick peck on the lips. He looked her over, as if taking her in for the last time, but then smiled so big, he worried he'd pull a muscle in his cheek—but he couldn't stop. "This is it."

"Yeah," she said back with her own excited smile.

"I'll tell the girls to come and help you get dressed," Paul said as he ushered Taylor off the bus.

S. Jackson Rivera

Wet

Made in the USA
Middletown, DE
25 July 2022